CITY OF DEATH

City of Death

MISTY THOMAS

Contents

Dedication

For those of us who have taken our sharp edges and reshaped reality.

Author's Note

In this thrilling conclusion to the Blood and Silk Trilogy, there are a few content warnings to be aware of. Please take note of the list below for a full list of potentially triggering content.

References to:

pregnancy and miscarriage, abuse (sexual, physical, and psychological), torture, death, murder, gore

On the page:

swearing, torture, blood, violence, death, light bondage, and semi-explicit spice

Chapter 1

Elora

"So, do you kill him or do I? Because that piece of shit isn't staying alive much longer." Damien's voice filled the silence in the car, and she glanced at her uncle sitting beside her. Silas was providing her with an escort to the Tower. Establishing herself there was the first step in what was proving to be a long process. The next stop would be the Ravenwell headquarters. She had only wanted Darian dead along with protection from those who were hunting her. Technically, she had accomplished both, but it had come at a steep price. Elora could still feel Darian's heart in her palm, still feel the scrapes that came from the broken fragments of ribs that scratched her hand as she thrust it into his chest. Dealing with Viktor wasn't high on her list of priorities.

"He could prove useful in stopping Elizabeth. Not to mention the information he has on the Resistance," she responded after a moment, not bothering to meet his eyes in the visor mirror. There was no question about what she would see. Simmering rage that wouldn't be held at bay too much longer. Self-control could only do so much when your best friend's murderer was at your mercy. There was a reason why Viktor had been sedated and tied up before being put in the car that had left before them. Elora had taken the collar from his neck after the drug had hit his system, ignoring the pleading expression in his impossibly

1

light brown eyes. They were the same ones she had stared into when she needed to be grounded in reality after a therapy session or when her memories were triggered.

Now, they brought only pain and confusion.

Damien couldn't be near Viktor, and she didn't have the time to dedicate to keeping them apart. She could see his hands clenching and unclenching, could see the way his shoulders tensed like he was preparing for a fight. He wanted Viktor's blood, and she understood. Every time his name was even mentioned, every time she caught the scent of citrus, the image of Lukas on his knees flashed in her mind. She could see the resignation and acceptance etched across his beautifully warm features. The agony she felt when that vision assaulted her made her want to curl up and hug her knees to her chest. Without a second thought, she would have traded places with him. His life hadn't been worth less than hers, no matter what he had believed.

"We're letting him live." The venom in his words settled in the car, permeating the leather seats and her skin. She scratched at her forearm absentmindedly and glanced at Silas, who maintained a passive expression. This was her call.

"Yes, we are. Until I have what I need from him." Her tone made it clear that the conversation was over, that she had made her decision. Elora didn't want to remind him of the fact Viktor had been a gift to *her* from her foster sister, an offering that *she* had accepted. And Damien may not be hers to command in any official capacity, but Viktor was. They hadn't discussed whether Damien would join her or if he would stay with Silas as part of the Corvin family.

Why couldn't they just go back to the hotel room before Elizabeth showed up with a small army and Viktor on a leash?

"And what would you need from him?" There was suspicion lining each word and she shifted slightly in her seat, tugging at her sleeves in a way that felt so reminiscent of her years at the psychiatric hospital. Silas reached over and laid his hand on hers before squeezing softly. She straightened and met Damien's accusing glare in the mirror.

"Information. Locations. Names. In case you forgot, there's a group who is growing by the day and will quickly overrun this city." Her voice rose slightly, and she scolded herself before continuing.

"We also have the issue of the Resistance who are still looking for me. And Viktor was a part of their group. Important enough to send after me and to trust with Elizabeth. Think this through, Damien. I'll let you have him, but not yet." The heat in Damien's glare eased slightly, but the suspicion remained. Did he think she was letting Viktor live because of their history? Did Damien believe this was all because she still cared for Viktor enough to protect him? It would be lying to say there wasn't something uncomfortable in her gut whenever she thought of Viktor, some mingling of who he had been to her and who he was now.

"Either way, he's been put in a cell on the third floor where Killian kept his blood donors and sources," Silas explained and Elora nodded, forcing herself to look away from Damien. The expression on his face was too close to betrayal for her to stand.

"Are we expecting any problems, Silas?" Elora didn't bother looking at the two vampires in the car with her any longer as Damien's question turned the conversation in a different direction. She heard her uncle sigh softly while she watched the buildings pass by. The Tower wasn't that far from The Rose Hotel, where her ill-fated wedding had almost taken place. There were very few people on the street at this time. Some were heading to work, she assumed, while others seemed to be opening their businesses. The scent of coffee filtered into the car, and she almost demanded they stop to buy some. It wouldn't solve any of the problems staring her in the face, but it would potentially make the process a bit more manageable.

"None that I have heard about," Silas explained. "From what I understand, most expected either Elora or you to take over. It wasn't a surprise that she would be in charge." Someone made a slight noise as if in agreement. Damien, she assumed.

"The problem," Silas continued, "will more than likely be the Ravenwell family."

"What have you heard?" Damien's voice had taken on that hard tone again. It was the one he used when he had spoken to Killian, had reported Elora's behavior to her father.

"Nothing official. Just rumors and whispers about not wanting to be combined with another family and that they don't want someone like Elora in charge of them." Her head snapped to her uncle instantly. She could almost hear the names they had called her at the banquet and wedding. They were etched into her skin just as much as her scars were.

"What do you mean someone like me?" Silas shifted as her eyes bore into him, waiting for him to say the words she knew were coming. Somewhere in her mind she knew that it was cruel to make him voice them.

"Blood whore, primarily. Others are more concerned about how you killed Darian. They call it underhanded and claim that it shouldn't count." She snorted at the familiar name. For the vampires who knew about her, she had never been Killian's daughter. They only saw the scars and assumed how she received them. She would have to give her speech again and again, reveal her darkest secrets for their consumption so they would accept her. And if they didn't recognize her as their head, they were welcome to leave. Then again, violence was always an option.

"You would think they would come up with better names. That one is getting a little old." She chuckled darkly as Silas gave her a sad smile. It seemed to bother her uncle much more than it did her.

"Anyone who uses that name will be dealt with." Damien's promise warmed her heart, made her recall the way he had given her the necklace that was currently lying against her chest. A black pearl surrounded by white crescent moons made from Jonas's canines. They may not agree on the best way to deal with Viktor, but that changed nothing between them at its core. He would still strive to protect her even if she didn't always need it. Not a single part of her feared the vampires who were waiting for her to officially declare her position to them. She could imagine them in the Tower as they prepared for her arrival, for her to summon them to demand their loyalty. How many would decline? How many would leave?

"It isn't your concern, Damien." His focus shifted at the sound of her comment, brows furrowed as he seemed to struggle to understand what she was referring to. "You're a Corvin, not an Ashcroft or Ravenwell." Finally, his eyes widened in understanding.

"I think it's clear that I'm no longer part of the Corvin family. Where you go, I follow." She felt her face heat slightly at his declaration and her eyes went to her uncle, who only nodded in agreement. Either the two of them were in perfect sync, or they had discussed this already. Both were equally possible. All that mattered was that Damien would remain at her side and that he wouldn't be going back to Corvin manor as she had feared. It had been a nagging thought in the back of her head. She had pictured it, watched it play out before her. Alone she would face Killian's office. Alone she would face the vampires in the Tower and attempt to force them into submission. Alone she would enter the bedrooms where her light had been dimmed so many times. Hearing Damien claim her as his was something she could easily become addicted to.

The Tower quickly came into view as they turned to drive down into the garage. Her body constricted tightly at the familiar sight. Somehow, she thought it would look different, like what occurred within its walls should be displayed on the outside in some way. Lukas's death in that very spot should have left some type of scar that would act as a reminder of the life that was lost. Her eyes searched through the garage, lingering on the cars that lined the back wall. Killian's collection, or she supposed it was now hers. Did she gain everything he owned now that she had taken his place?

The SUV came to a stop in front of the elevator. One door opened and then another as she felt Damien and Silas exit. Yet her hand wouldn't move. To open the door and leave the car would be to step into a memory that was still too painful. A part of her had died the moment Viktor revealed his intentions, when Lukas had sacrificed himself and she saw that Denise was already dead. Her former psychiatrist was the only person capable of answering her questions, of explaining why there had been so much lying. It was like a tumor that had never been removed, slowly poisoning the healthy parts left behind. Not that she thought there were many. Killian and his favorites had taken so much from her that the pieces that remained were very few.

Her eyes roamed over the ground to the spot where she knew Lukas had knelt, searching for any hints of blood. But there was nothing. As if all traces of his sacrifice were gone, erased from existence. It destroyed something inside her to witness it.

The door opened before her, and she stared up into dark brown eyes with flecks of gold as they watched her with a wary expression. Damien extended his hand, and she took it, forcing herself to absorb the strength and comfort he was offering. She hadn't considered what coming back here would mean, what it would drag forward kicking and screaming from the place she had forced it into.

Memories.

Emotions.

Sensations of phantom fingers and teeth.

Elora drew a deep breath and held it for a moment before exhaling as she exited the car. Her grip on his hand was crushing and she knew it hurt from the way he winced slightly. Was he remembering the same thing, seeing the same image over and over again? His jaw ticked and he stared at the entrance as he seemed to refuse to even glance in the direction where Lukas's body had laid.

Damien didn't release her hand as they entered the elevator and pushed the button for the floor that contained Killian's office. Silas stood on one side of her while Damien stood on the other like twin pillars of strength. For now, she could allow them to hold her up because very soon she would need to not only stand alone but also command hundreds of vampires and bring them under her control.

Chapter 2

Elora

The door to Killian's office looked exactly the same and she froze in front of it. Within a single heartbeat, Silas and Damien disappeared as she heard her father's voice whispering promises of both love and pain, assuring her that he would be gentle.

"Elora." The voice that said her name was so far away it as if it was coming from down the hallway and she couldn't decide if it was real or something from her memories. She could almost hear that nickname that had haunted her nightmares and poisoned her days. It would always reach her without warning as if the wind had brought it to her.

"Come back." The voice again. It was so familiar, so reassuring and warm. She felt a hand on her shoulder and a slight squeeze before she shook her head and glanced towards the body that it belonged to. She met the eyes that she had so often lost herself in, the eyes that she wanted to swim or drown in. Either way, it would be perfection. Damien's expression was laced with concern. He knew where she had gone, where she had been dragged. Only he knew how to bring her back from the brink.

"Thank you," she whispered and turned back to the door, grasping the cold metal before turning it and thrusting it open. The space was exactly how it had been the night she fled, carried out the Tower in Damien's arms after she killed her father.

Her eyes darted around as if his ghost was waiting for her, like it would jump out from the corner or from behind his desk. Both Silas and Damien stood behind her, waiting for her to make the first move, to take the first step. A deep breath. In and then out before she took another.

Her movements were more assertive than she thought possible at the moment. One and then another until she stood in the center of the room. The air was heavy and she could have sworn there was the scent of Killian's blood. It felt like someone had wrapped a rope around her, tightening it until she couldn't move or breathe or think. Damien began to move around the room, no doubt taking stock of what was there. Her own focus shifted instantly to the spot on the floor where the tarp had laid, where she had left the knife.

"It doesn't look like anything was taken." Damien's voice reached her, and she jumped slightly before finding him as he pulled out the desk drawers. She could hear the contents shift as he opened and closed them, muttering slightly about it still being a mess

"Darian probably didn't see the need to take anything from here," Silas responded, and she felt him step so close she could feel his body heat. He reached out his hand and took her own, squeezing softly in a way that she hadn't been able to become accustomed to. She returned the gesture before letting go and moving towards the bookshelves, reading the titles printed along the spines before finding the leather-bound books towards the end. Elora had a feeling she knew what these were and as she turned to the first page, her suspicions were confirmed. Slowly, her eyes ran over the handwriting that felt familiar though she wasn't sure why. She had only seen Killian's handwriting once in a note he sent her and had never seen these journals before. But it felt like him in a way that didn't make sense, like something was tugging at her mind and creating an itch that needed to be scratched.

Slowly she sank into one of the chairs and continued reading, noting how this entry seemed to detail when he met her mother. A party of some sort, from what Killian had written. He had sensed her before anything else, could smell her blood as one of the few humans in attendance to what was meant to be vampire only.

The Corvin heir is beautiful, but her smell is more intriguing than her appearance. She commanded the attention of everyone in the room. Everyone watched her like something to be taken into their possession. Iris is her name. Even if she wasn't named for the flower, she is a credit to her namesake. Just as beautiful as the flower itself.

Elora let out a harsh exhale and closed the journal, unsure that she could continue reading. She could hear his voice in her head. The tone and deep sound of his words as they always seemed to rumble in his chest. The rhythm of his speech and the slow drawl that always meant he was irritated but desperately trying to hide it. For a moment, he was in the room with them, kneeling beside her as he spoke directly into her ear, crowding out any and all sounds that may exist at the same time and in the same space.

"Files. On you." She turned her attention to Damien, where he stood at the desk with a stack of papers in his hand. They were closed but he met her eyes as if he were waiting to see something there. Elora stood and approached him while she felt Silas fall into step beside her. Without a word, Damien extended the files to her. Her hand shook as she took them and rounded the desk, sinking into Killian's chair. The leather was cold and she felt it through the thin fabric of the dress she wore. It had been one of the few options left in her hotel luggage and she threw it on as they left. It didn't matter what she wore. Nothing would protect her from what this place would end up doing to her.

With a harsh exhale, she laid the files on the desk and began to flip through them, noting the way Damien and her uncle remained before her with a desk acting as a barrier. She could almost feel their desire to read the files along with her, to learn exactly what she was and what it meant. The first page was a picture of her as a child, maybe five or six. To the right of the image was a list of basic information about her. Parents. Birthday and birth location. Lineage. Blood type. Below that was a list of the contents of the dossier. Lab results. Experiment protocols and results.

The majority of the text on the following pages were basically another language. Scientific terms and jargon. Mentions of experimentation and tests, genes to isolate and enhance. None of it made sense to her. But one refrain was present on almost every document where the scientists summarized their findings: The extent of the changes are unknown.

Elora had known she was unique, carefully crafted by a vampire who wanted to create a perfect blood source that would render humans obsolete. For Killian, it was the solution to the human problem, as he had referred to it numerous times. No one knew what he was ultimately giving life to. Not even the very scientists who did the majority of the labor.

"What does it say?" Silas rounded the desk and stood at her side, peering over her shoulder at the document beneath her shaking hands. She dragged them into her lap to hide exactly how much being in this room was breaking her connection to reality. Her uncle reached out and dragged his finger down the page as he seemed to skim the document. Little sounds escaped his mouth, some of surprise, others of confusion or anger. It seemed that he understood more of this than she did and Elora envied him that.

"Honestly, I have no idea other than not even the scientists knew what Killian was doing and what the long-term consequences would be. Nothing I didn't already know." There was a bitterness to her words and she knew that Silas heard them from the way his hand went to her shoulder. The room itself seemed to grow colder the longer she stared at the papers, flipping through them despite the fact the words had lost their meaning and had started merging together to create a single label, a single title. It was the one Chloe had flung at her during the meeting in The Rose Hotel—Abomination. And at this point, Elora wasn't sure she would argue against the vampire's conclusion.

"I would like your permission to make copies of these and read through them. I'll leave the originals with you. However, I think that you should try and talk to some of the people who worked on this project. They may be useful if you want to pursue this." Elora only nodded before letting her eyes trace over the room again and tried to ignore the instant revulsion she felt in the very core of her being. This room was not an option. She had been a fool to think she could return and stay here like it didn't hold the very worst of her memories. And where would she even sleep? She would never enter her old room again. If she could, Elora would burn it to the ground. Was the only other option Killian's old rooms?

With a sigh, she pushed herself up from the desk and met Damien's eyes. That concern had returned, contorting his features into something soft and gentle. His hand twitched as if he wanted to reach out for her but didn't.

"How would I go about getting this office remodeled? Or any other room, for that matter?" Her question was directed at Silas, but her eyes never left Damien.

"I would assume you need to officially take your place before you could order any changes made." Her heart stopped beating for just a moment at Silas's explanation before she straightened her spine and lifted her chin. The ghost of her father's presence would not stop her from achieving what needed to be done. He would never stop her again. Or prevent her from sleeping. Her eyes closed as she considered her options, but the thought of silk sheets under her body made her shudder as her arms wrapped around her torso.

"You can stay in my old room, if you like. I can sleep in another one. There should be a free one somewhere." Damien's voice was gentle yet held no room for discussion. She nodded her thanks, unable to form words or even thoughts. He knew exactly where her mind had gone, knew exactly what she needed. And once more she wondered if it was a consequence of whatever Killian had done. Damien had told her that he had been drawn to her even before her blood, but maybe that was part of it. Maybe Killian had done something to her that caused her to draw in those around her in order to ensnare them. Considering what Killian had wanted her to ultimately achieve, it would make perfect sense. He may have been a monster, but he had also been intelligent in a way that was terrifying.

"We need to deal with Viktor." Damien broke through her spiraling thoughts, and she searched his face. There was a promise of violence, and she wasn't sure Damien would be able to handle seeing the human currently held in their cells.

"I talk. I ask the questions." Her tone was cold, and she could have sworn she saw him flinch slightly as if her orders hurt him. Damien nodded and held up his hands in a placating gesture, but she saw the cold heat in his eyes, the severe lines of his face that only ever happened when he was holding himself back.

Elora let out a sigh before heading towards the doorway and away from everything that still somehow smelled like her father. Viktor had some questions to answer if he wanted to prolong his life in even the smallest amount. Damien wouldn't be held off for long.

Chapter 3

Viktor

He wasn't in the same cell as last time. For some reason, when he woke up surrounded once more by black and crimson, he had expected to be. Then again, he was surprised he had woken up at all. He had expected Damien to kill him at the first possible chance. When Elora had ordered him drugged, a small seed of hope had taken root. Not enough to make him think he would survive this, but enough to not fear falling unconscious.

"Viktor." His head shot up at the sound of her voice. He had been staring at the floor, the black rug that covered the tiles as he considered exactly how long he would be left alive. From the look on Damien's face from where he stood behind her, it wasn't very long.

"Was my old room taken?" Viktor watched her expression as he spoke, as his comment reached her. Damien wasn't worth his focus. His reactions would be one of two options. The first would be the blank and emotionless face that Damien had worn during the few times Viktor saw him in the Tower. The other would be pure rage and hatred. Only Elora was holding him at bay. If it wasn't for her presence, Viktor knew he would be dead.

But Elora's expression was much more interesting, more informative. He noted the slight wince at his attempt at a joke. The rush of anger followed by something that looked like guilt.

But was it for his current situation or for the fact he was alive? Either way, her struggle was written in the twitch of her lip, the scrunching of her nose, the way her eyes widened then narrowed slightly. He realized then exactly how well he knew her. Exactly how easily he could read her. Could Damien claim the same? And why did the thought of him being able to do irritate him so much? This wasn't the first time he had tried to decipher his feelings for her. And it wasn't the first time he had come away empty-handed.

"I could have you moved there, if you like. It's open from what I understand." Her response was robotic but held a slight tinge of humor. It was the sarcasm he had come to know in the hospital when he had to make sure she took her medication or asked her how therapy had gone.

"This one seems just fine. It isn't like there's a whole lot of difference between them." Damien shifted at his response and Viktor finally turned his attention to the vampire standing at her side. Hands clasped behind his back as if to keep himself from breaking Viktor's jaw.

"Oh, Viktor. There is indeed a difference. Trust me when I say that I can and will put you somewhere worse. It all depends on your level of cooperation." Her voice was close to a purr and he had never heard her use anything like it. It was jarring and there wasn't a single part of him that didn't believe her. He leaned back against the wall after twisting his head one way then the other. The collar may have been removed but he could feel its weight, the soreness of his muscles, the bruises that seemed to reach his bones.

"I say we move him either way." Damien's suggestion came as no surprise, but the harsh glare Elora gave him did. Obviously, he didn't agree with her decision to keep him there. After a brief moment, she turned back to him with her face the empty mask he had seen before. He wanted desperately to know what was hidden under there and whether it would spell his death or not.

"Comfort is a luxury. A privilege that I'm more than willing to rip away if you don't answer my questions." There was a promise there and Viktor's body tensed, increasing the growing ache in his shoulders.

"And now we get to it." Viktor's words were met with silence as if they expected him to continue without prompting. But what information did they deem more important? And how important was it?

"I'm going to need something to go on here, El. A question. A hint." He saw her flinch at the sound of her nickname, at the familiarity.

"Let's start with how you managed to scheme while in here. How you managed to plan my friend's death?" Damien again and once more Elora shot him a glare. Apparently, the vampire was going off script and Viktor had to suppress the urge to throw him a smirk.

"Not all humans here only worked for Killian. But you already know this, so the question is pointless."

"I want names." Viktor considered Damien's demand. He honestly didn't know. This was the very reason names weren't exchanged.

"I couldn't even if I wanted to. We don't give names. You can understand why." Elora crossed her arms over her chest and watched, her expression growing more irritated by the minute.

"Then we can go for a little walk, and you can point out every single one." Viktor chuckled and watched as Damien's gaze darkened. He was walking on thin ice and knew it. But a part of him wanted to see if Elora would step in if it went too far, wanted to see if she would let it get that far.

"My guess is they were pulled out as soon as that mission failed, and Killian was dead. But I'm always happy to go for a walk." And then there it was. The reaction Viktor had been try-ing to goad from him. Damien stomped forward, his movements so quick Viktor was barely able to exhale before he was at the plexiglass, hands balled into fists and murder carved into his al-ready sharp features.

"Damien." A single word from Elora. Her tone was cold and commanding. Every bit of strength he had known she possessed was on display. Damien froze as his body went unnaturally still. He didn't turn to look at her but kept his focus on Viktor, who refused to break away first.

"I'll finish this. Go start gathering those left in the Tower in the ballroom. I'll be there in twenty minutes." Her tone left no room to argue, and he saw the struggle on Damien's face, the warring emotions and desires that were displayed there. Finally, after a few long moments, Damien turned from him and stalked past Elora, not once even glancing in her direction.

They both listened as the elevator chimed and closed behind Damien and Elora seemed to relax a bit. Her shoulders lowered just a fraction, her features seemed to soften slightly. It was closer to the woman he knew before.

"You two got close since I left," Viktor remarked and she rolled her eyes before settling against the wall, watching him with a calculated expression.

"He wants you dead." A slight chuckle escaped his mouth at her statement of pure fact. She had said it like he didn't know, like he couldn't read it in Damien's face the moment they both had approached his cell.

"Only him?" Something shifted across her face before she schooled it back into cold indifference.

"How about we talk about my sister? What do you know about what she's doing?" Viktor attempted to run his hand through his hair, but his fingers became tangled in the knots and dried blood. He grunted slightly before dropping his hand to his lap once more. His clothes were filthy and he hadn't been given a shower before he was deposited in his cell.

"Give me a shower and haircut and I'll tell you what I know about her." He almost added that he didn't know much, that Elizabeth had kept her ideas and plans to herself. Elora shifted slightly as she moved closer to the glass, letting her gaze travel over him.

"It's adorable that you think you have any bargaining power here." She gave him a cruel grin that revealed her teeth. No fangs. Not even slightly sharpened canines. Yet he knew what she was even without the usual proof. His mind traveled back to Elizabeth as he tried to remember if she had them or if hers were hidden as well. All he could recall was the strange glow that seemed to radiate from her eyes. The same one Elora's had now.

"I think you want information and that I want to wash off all of this. We can both benefit."

"Or I bring Damien back in and let him convince you to talk." She shrugged as if it didn't matter, but he saw her hand grip the folds of her dress. The fabric hung low on her chest, falling to just above her breasts and revealing the scars there. But the sleeves were long, ending at her wrists. So much about her had changed and yet stayed the same.

"We both know he would kill me before you got anything useful." He was right and she knew it. The way her face contracted and rearranged itself was evidence enough of that. He could almost hear her thoughts, could read her body language.

"Tell me and I'll let you wash. I'll even let you cut your hair. I can't have you polluting the rest of the food, can I?" Viktor let out a breath as he rubbed at the thick layer of dirt on his wrist.

"What do you want to know?"

"You took her as a consolation prize when you didn't get me." He nodded at her statement as he waited for her to ask him something. She gave him an exasperated sigh and a gesture for him to continue from there. He jumped into an explanation of how he brought her to the Resistance with the promise of having her help them find Elora. He told her how they took her blood to experiment with and that he had brought her with him that night on the Resistances orders. He outlined how Elora's blood could be used as a cure for vampirism and that Elizabeth's was being used until they got their hands on their true target. She listened closely the entire time, not once moving or even twitching. No reaction to a single word he said.

"And after that night? Obviously, you found her again."

"It honestly wasn't that hard now that I think about it. A visit to Connie's apartment—"

"What did you find?" Elora's interruption came instantly. The concern and utter fear in her face was enough to make him suck in a breath. He never expected her to care that much about the old woman. Never expected Elora to care about what happened to her. Though he supposed he had been somewhat stupid to doubt it. Elora never cared about people with anything less than complete devotion. It could be all consuming if someone wasn't careful. Someone like Denise. Someone like him. Maybe he was the one who had been chasing a connection, had been racing towards it and she had offered it willingly and without question. After shoving a steak knife into Jaime's neck, he hadn't bothered to get close to anyone. Until she came along.

"Nothing but some bloody scrubs and signs of a struggle. But she left that apartment alive." He found no purpose in lying to her or trying to sugar coat the truth. Elora's eyes closed and her fingers went to her neck, tracing one of the scars there. He could practically see the guilt settling around her along with the darkness she fell into. It was as if the sky had fallen and landed on her shoulders, diminishing her before his eyes.

"Thank you. For telling me the truth." Her words were almost whispers as if she thought Damien was standing beside her. Viktor nodded before reclining against the wall.

"I ran into an old man on my way out who said the three of them mentioned heading to a warehouse. A few questions around the Industrial district and I had the name of one that had strange visitors. When I went in, I found more scrubs along with cots and signs of other people. Clothes. Wallets." He considered adding the bit about the child's dress but worried she would fully collapse. The knowledge a child was turned would be the thing that ultimately destroyed her.

"Then a visit to a nurse I had been friendly with followed by the hospital where I was captured." She didn't need to ask him to clarify which hospital. He watched as she seemed to fall into her memories. Was she remembering the conversations where he comforted her? Made her laugh? Changed the bandages on her neck after Elizabeth attacked her in an ill-fated therapy session? He knew all of them were racing through his mind as well and their gazes locked in mutual understanding.

"And during your stay? What did she say?" He shrugged at her question.

"Honestly not much more than you heard outside that hotel. You're a deity to them. There were so many of them, El. She's turning them for you. She thinks it's what you want. A city of your children." He saw the horror of this reality settle and his heart squeezed in his chest as a sense of hope rushed through him. Even after everything, Viktor had known she wasn't involved, that she didn't support whatever Elizabeth was doing. They lapsed into silence as she stared at something far beyond him. He only studied her, taking in each and every feature as he searched for signs of exactly how different she was now.

"Elora. It's time." Damien's voice filtered in, breaking the moment between them, the shared memories they had fallen into.

Elora's focus shifted as her eyes snapped towards Damien and she nodded.

"Don't get comfortable," she threw over her shoulder as she approached her fellow vampire and went to address her new underlings to embrace the role she was never meant for.

Chapter 4

Damien

The expression on Viktor's face when Damien approached them made him want to do something horrifically violent to the human. It was one he had seen before at the hospital and in the Tower when he had brought her down to visit him. It was a mixture of affection and what could only be described as love. But there was no heat to it. No desire. Had he misread Viktor's feelings for her?

It didn't matter. The human wouldn't live long enough for anything to come from whatever he felt for her.

Elora was silent as they rode the elevator. The only sound was the annoying music that had almost always played. His eyes moved over her, searching for any sign about what had been said. She was tense, like she was a thread pulled too tight. One more issue and she would snap. Silas should have warned her what it would mean to be in charge of not one, but two vampire families. At least until she officially combined them. But that would take time and could produce numerous issues. Already Silas had heard whisperings of the Ravenwell family planning to deny her despite their long-standing tradition.

She wasn't one of them, they whispered in the dark corners of Ravenwell manor.

How can we trust someone so underhanded to run our family?

Darian's death had come as a shock to everyone but Elora and her uncle. They had plotted and schemed, both of them placing each and every person in place. He still wasn't entirely sure how he felt about it despite what he had told her that night. A part of him knew he couldn't be angry with her, couldn't resent her for not telling him her plan. After all, he had done the same thing the night he goaded her into a rage to make sure all the necessary players ended up in Killian's office.

The elevator chimed and they both stepped off. For a moment, she seemed to hesitate just outside the door. From either memories or nerves, her hands moved to her wrists before she began pulling at the skin around her nail. Instantly, he slid around and faced her, pulling her hands into his to stop the self-destructive nervous tick. If it wasn't for the fact she healed quickly, her fingers would closely resemble Jonas's after Damien had been done with him.

"What's the plan?" His voice was steadier than he truly felt. All he wanted was to demand what Viktor had said, ask if she had found out enough that the human could be handed over to him. But this was a crucial moment for her. It would either solidify her place or result in a mass exodus at best and an uprising at worst. She shrugged before glancing around him to where a ballroom full of vampires waited. Their chatter filtered down the hallway to them, but nothing was clear enough to understand. Just snippets of words—Killian's daughter. New head of the family. Killed him. Proof.

And that was why Silas had helped set up a projection screen. She was going to show them exactly why she was in charge now. That scared him more than anything. He had no idea how she would react when they played the scene before her on a massive screen. She wouldn't be able to hide away from what was there or react. Not if she wanted to keep her place.

"I don't have one," she muttered, and he raised his hand to her cheek, smiled softly when she leaned into it and closed her eyes.

"Just go in there and announce who you are. Claim your title and deal with those who deny you however you see fit." Elora nodded slightly and he watched as she changed from the vampire he knew her to be into the one she needed to be in this moment. All he could do was savor the fact that he was one of the few who ever saw who she was when the masks and personas were stripped away. Only he and Silas could make that claim.

And Viktor, a harsh voice interjected from the very back of his mind as if it were dragging itself forward with fingernails that dug into every bit of trust he had.

Her spine straightened as she pushed back her shoulders and lifted her chin becoming the very image of a leader. No one could look at her and deny the strength that seemed to radiate from her very being. Another nod. This one was curt and cold. Her eyes took on that dark sheen that promised only violence yet always made him consider other unspeakable things. He mirrored her nod and stepped aside so she could enter first with him behind her.

The mutterings and conversations halted the very moment she seemed to glide into the room, her steps the definition of power and confidence. She didn't fear a single vampire in that room and he felt the air grow tense as they all waited for her to take her place on the small stage that had been erected for this reason. The vampires parted down the middle and watched her with fascination and suspicion as she made her way to the front and up the stairs. Damien followed suit, standing just a few paces to her right. He clasped his hands behind his back and squared his shoulders, planting his feet against the wooden stage as he prepared for her to begin. From the expressions he saw as he scanned the crowd, this could easily go horribly wrong.

"Most, if not all of you, know exactly who I am. And if you don't, then allow me to introduce myself. I'm Elora Ashcroft, the daughter of your previous family head." She paused as she allowed her announcement to settle among them. There would be no confusion. No repeating herself.

"I'm also your new vampire head." Murmuring broke out instantly. Vampires in the audience turned to one another, sharing their anger or confusion or disgust.

"I'm aware that being his daughter is not enough to earn me this place. I know how the succession works, and I promise you I fulfilled everything necessary. And I'm more than willing to offer you proof."

A cascade of shouts filled the space as they demanded exactly what she offered. Damien wished he could see her face as she nodded and turned to the screen behind her just as the scene began to play. A quick peek at the video being played revealed that the angle of the camera that recorded the event was perfect. It had been placed to record all of Killian's meetings, focusing on the space in front of his desk. He didn't turn his attention to the screen, but kept his focus on the crowd, noting that each and every pair of eyes were locked on the scene displayed before them.

Damien heard his voice offering her Killian's life and heard her take it. The video had started right after she had come to realize it wasn't a trick, that Damien hadn't worked with her father to fool her into submission. It started after she declared to everyone in that office she didn't plan on walking out alive.

A collected gasp pierced through the sounds of the video as it reached its climax. Damien could hear the blade entering Killian's flesh and her own screams of rage. And then silence as the scene ended with Killian's blood covered body on the floor of his office. The crowd seemed to shift slightly as they absorbed what they had seen. He wanted to glance at her, to meet her gaze and offer her some semblance of strength. She hadn't seen the video before this moment and he could only imagine what it brought forward.

"I will never accept a blood whore as my leader." Damien's hands twitched as he forced himself not to react but to search the crowd for the source. It was silent for only a moment before a cold chuckle erupted from the stage. It was a terrifying sound and there was only one vampire something that dark could come from. He let himself glance at her, noting the way she shook her head before lifting her chin.

"Blood whore. I've heard you all call me that before. At the banquet that most of you were at. It's a poorly kept secret what you all believed me to be. So, let me tell you the truth." She pulled her hair away from her neck, letting it fall down her back.

"This is what you have seen that results in your label for me. But what you did not see were the chains on the bedposts. Or the drugs that were forced into my system since I was a child. Calling me a blood whore implies I allowed him to feed on me. That I offered myself to him and obliged. Let me be clear. There was no consent, no offering. There was only taking and every vampire who did so is now dead." Once more the silence stretched as she took a moment. No more cries of dissent rang out. Instead, the very atmosphere in the room seemed to change.

"If my being the head vampire is so repulsive to you, then leave. I won't stop you. Join another family if you're able. The Ashcrofts and the Ravenwells are both under my control. You'll need to pick one of the other options left." Elora seemed to wait as if giving them a chance to leave, but not a single vampire moved.

Not even a twitch and Damien felt an overwhelming rush of pride and relief. She was everything and more. The universe couldn't contain her strength and the power she exuded simply by being in a room. And they all felt it now. Not just him.

Elora seemed to wait for questions and demands as if she didn't trust their silence or stillness. They stared at her, watching her with wary eyes before a familiar sight took place within the confines of the room where they had once repeated horrific gossip, had sneered and looked upon her with nothing less than disgust. One by one, each vampire standing before her placed their fist over their hearts and knelt, heads bowed. He heard her sharp intake of breath at the gesture and they both watched the crowd as they fell to their knees in a wave until there was no one left standing but her and Damien.

She turned to him with the slightest look, but he saw the strange hesitation there. Slowly, he took a step forward, footsteps heavy on the wooden platform until he was directly by her side. He gave her a small smile, just the slightest tilt of his lips before he followed the movement of the crowd now behind him. His fist pounded on his chest as he sank to his knees, head bowed before he snuck a quick glance at her. Elora's cheeks were flushed with a slight pink as if she was also remembering the last time he was in this position. There was a heat there in her gaze, a promise of something that made him want to throw her over his shoulder and dart from the room, leaving every single vampire behind.

"Stand." At the command in her voice, he was instantly on his feet with his hands clasped behind his back, shoulders straight as he awaited her orders. But she turned from him and faced the crowd once more.

"You are all aware of Damien and the role he has fulfilled here. It's now that I ask him to become my second-in-command and continue that role." The crowd stayed silent, but he could hear them shifting behind him, standing up now that the moment of submission had passed. His heart stopped in his chest as she turned to him and waited. It wasn't a command, but a request. Did she realize what she was asking him? What part he would perform once more? The silence stretched on as she waited for his answer. With each torturous second, her eyes revealed the fear lingering below those luminous green pools. Yet her face remained impassive—a cold and cruel mask that hid the concern and terror that was clear to him.

"I accept. My loyalty is to you." His words were loud and seemed to echo throughout the room. There was no applause or cheering, only the sound of fists on chests once more as the vampire family welcomed him back into his role as enforcer and punisher. Just as he was for Killian, Damien would be for her.

Elora didn't nod or say anything to the silent crowd, only turned and descended the few stairs before marching out of the banquet hall. He instantly fell into step beside her as he forced aside the warring thoughts and emotions from his mind. There could be no hint of dissent on his part, no sign of anything but pure loyalty. And he would give her anything she needed from him.

Chapter 5

Thorne

It was still jarring to see the vampire spread out on the gray leather sofa in the middle of the room. Thorne didn't know this one despite her extensive experience with them in her previous life. The vampire's whiskey brown hair was pulled into a high ponytail, and the green shirt and jeans made her seem almost human. But the wide smile on her face revealed the sharp canines of who and what she was. The vampire was beautiful and young in a way that Thorne would have been if she had turned like Killian had wanted. Silas had wanted that as well, but for different reasons. For Silas, it had been about companionship—someone to share the burden of running an entire vampire family, the very position they had both been groomed for since their adoption. It had taken a long time for her to understand that it had been about control for Killian, not love, as she had desperately believed.

"She has officially taken power over the Ashcrofts. They bowed to her from what I saw." Thorne listened to the vampire's report even as she tried to remember her name. Chloe had told Thorne that the vampire would be the middle person between them to keep anyone from discovering they were working together. But it wasn't helpful if Thorne didn't remember who this person was.

"As expected," Thorne responded before reclining in the chair across from the vampire. There was a strange malice to her eyes that Thorne knew wasn't hunger but a type of hatred that came from jealousy. She had seen it enough when she was with Killian to recognize it now. If only the vampire knew that Killian had been no prize to gain, no prince who would lavish her with love and affection, treat her like she was the only thing in the world. Killian had only seen those around him as pieces to be played, as commodities to be used and traded at his command. Or maybe this vampire knew that already.

"She will probably make her move on the Ravenwell family next. But there's gossip that she won't be accepted." There was a glee to the vampire's words, like she was anxiously awaiting the moment Killian's daughter would be brought low and removed from the overall equation. Thorne's thoughts froze as she remembered that she was not simply Killian's daughter. She was also hers. A rush of memories that Thorne had fought so hard to keep locked away hit her like a punch to the stomach.

Holding Elora in her arms after hours of labor.

Watching her face light up when she laughed.

The first time she took her to meet Silas.

No, she wasn't "Elora." She was something else. Someone else. If Thorne was going to kill her, then that vampire couldn't have a name and couldn't be Elora. She was the target. It was better that way. An entire race of people depended on Thorne's ability to rip those memories and feelings out by the roots and scorch the ground so they couldn't sprout back up.

"Any word on what her plan is?" Burgundy lips stretched into a smile at Thorne's question.

"Not yet, but I have one. Or a suggestion for one." A single nod from Thorne, and she continued. "I want to try and gain her trust. Work with her. Offer her my loyalty and help."

"What about the other one? Damien, or whatever his name is." Thorne watched the vampire visibly flinch, which was a tiny piece of information that she would tuck away to be used if needed. There was history between them, which Chloe had failed to mention. History had a nasty habit of causing problems in the present.

"He won't be a problem. But there's a chance he could be useful." There was something strangely dark and heated in the vampire's eyes as she spoke of using him. If the target truly felt something for him, then Damien could indeed be useful.

"They also have your human." Thorne's eyes snapped to the vampire, whose name appeared suddenly as if it were written in the air above her head. Korina. That was what Chloe had said. The fact that Viktor was still alive was not necessarily a shock, but it was a bit of a surprise. Thorne had known he had been given as a gift to the target but hadn't known he had survived after that. The conflicted emotions on Viktor's face when he talked about the target appeared before her as if he were standing there in the room.

"And?" The coldness in Thorne's voice must have shocked the vampire because she straightened slightly and seemed to study Thorne with renewed interest. But Korina said nothing more about Viktor, only shrewdly watched Thorne for a few moments longer.

"I know who you are. I know what she is to you." Thorne wasn't surprised. Chloe was sure to have told her little spy any information that could be used if needed. The fact that Thorne was not truly Thorne, but Iris was something Chloe believed would be useful.

"I'm glad to see the intelligence of vampires has increased since I left." Korina's lips curled slightly at the edges even as a hardness settled onto her face, sharpening her features like a weapon. Thorne wondered exactly how many had been cut by her. The answer was probably dozens, if not hundreds. This was a vampire who enjoyed what they did, who fed not for substance but for enjoyment.

"Killian never got over you." And there was the jealousy Thorne had detected from the moment Korina's eyes had locked onto hers.

"Of course he did. It's easy to get over someone you believed you killed. If you believe Killian was capable of anything even close to love or true affection, then I take back my previous statement." Korina shook her head in an attempt to hide the flash of pain along with the evidence that Killian must have used her at one point. Thorne wondered briefly how long it had lasted and if he had hurt her as well. If he had tossed her aside like he had so many others. He hadn't been truly faithful while they were together, and she had always turned a blind eye since he always tired of them after a few weeks. Thorne was certain that was the case with Korina, and she felt a stab of pity at the thought.

Killian had been so incredibly charming. He could coax a smile from a marble statue. In a single night, he had promised her the world, and she had taken the bait without a second thought. Her only companion for so long had been Silas, the brother who had quickly become enamored with his future role. He had been such a studious pupil to their parents and the tutor they employed. Each lesson was quickly etched into his mind while her own had wandered back to the human world she had only briefly known. Silas never understood why she sought others or why she was so lonely in that giant manor filled with vampires who saw her as nothing more than their future leader. They had respected her and shown her deference at every moment. But never friendship, and as she grew older and desired more than companionship, her loneliness had grown.

Killian had seen that in her instantly and had taken advantage of it even as their budding relationship increasingly grew to be a problem. It had caused a rift between her and Silas as their fights over it became more intense. When she had left to join Killian in the Tower, Thorne had never looked back. At least, not at first.

"You two are so similar." Thorne raised a brow at the statement. Was she referring to Killian or the target? She decided not to ask for clarification. The answer wasn't one she wanted.

"Let's get back to the important things, shall we? A walk down memory lane was not the point of this meeting." Korina gave her a small, lopsided smile before shifting slightly, resting one leg on the other.

"Fine," she drawled as if her favorite toy had been taken away. "There's no sign of Elizabeth. But there are more than enough rumors about people going missing. Entire families. We sent someone to the warehouse that human of yours found and searched it. She seems to be turning anyone and everyone. Even children."

There was a layer of disgust in Korina's words as she finished her report. It was a small bit of relief to know that even this vampire found turning a child repulsive. Was this only Elizabeth's doing? Or did the target have a role in it?

"It's insane that this vampire is able to completely disappear without a trace, especially if they are turning people at this rate. I give it two months before there isn't a single human left in the city." Thorne caught the expression on Korina's face at her explanation and tsked her tongue lightly before continuing. It was complete indifference, a lack of concern or empathy for the plight that they both would share in time.

"After humans are gone, who will they go after next? If we have two months, you have maybe three. Four at the most. Honestly, my earlier statement is proving more and more incorrect."

Thorne savored the way Korina almost leapt to her feet, almost rushing her. She could see the way the vampire's muscles tightened and her limbs twitched from the suppression of her movements. There was a flash of something harsh on her face, as if not acting was physically painful. And Thorne hoped with everything in her that it was.

"I'll send out some of my people. We found her last time by simply canvassing the streets. And humans will be better at that than your people." Korina didn't bother trying to disagree with what they both knew to be a fact. Humans knew instinctively when they were in the presence of a predator and knew when they were the prey. Though Thorne supposed that with Elizabeth and her kind rapidly taking over the city, vampires would be the prey very soon.

With a curt nod of her head, Thorne watched Korina stand and stretch before sauntering out the front door, leaving behind the sickening scent of blood.

As the door closed, Thorne shut her eyes and reclined back in the chair she had stayed in during the meeting. Her muscles relaxed slowly as the threat melted away and the reminder of her past disappeared. Already she knew that Korina would be a problem no matter how much confidence Chloe had in the vampire. Her emotions were too near the surface, her face a canvas that displayed every thought and flash of irritation and jealousy. Korina's desire for Damien would be the largest hurdle. It was clear that no matter what the overall goal was, Korina was playing her own game, and he was in the middle of it all. Thorne had no doubt that the vampire would be willing to do anything if it meant getting what she seemed to so desperately want.

After only a brief moment of silence in which Thorne pushed back every memory and hint of emotion left over for who had once been her daughter, she prepared to issue the commands that would hopefully result in finding Elizabeth.

Chapter 6

Damien

Flora had gone directly to Killian's office, gathered the leather journals on the shelves along with the one she had left on the side table, and tossed her duffle bag over her shoulder. Her features were tight as she marched back out without a word. It took him a moment to understand where she was going, but when she pushed down on the elevator, he knew.

"Wait. We don't know if my room was taken over or if someone else is in there." He watched her shoulders tense as she gripped the journals tighter. There were three in her arms, but he knew there were more along the shelves. If Damien were to hazard a guess, he would say there had to be at least fifteen. He had seen them over the years, watching as their numbers grew and they took up more and more shelf space. Trinkets and trophies that Damien had brought back were shifted and taken down, moved to another spot in the office.

"Then they will leave," she responded. Her words were like ice, and they sent a shiver down his back. He felt it in every part of him as she barreled her way out of the elevator and to the first door on the right. She didn't knock or hesitate. It was like she thought if she didn't force her way in now, then she would lose the nerve.

His hand contracted slightly as he remembered the last time they were both in this room, when he had learned exactly what he had done. It had been the final crack that had shattered his reality into a million pieces, and there had been no hope of putting it back together in the same way. Washing the blood from her body, from her hair. Bandaging her wounds and helping her dress before she slid into his bed had only been a precursor to learning he had been a vital part of Killian's plan. Damien had always wondered why Killian had sent him with the laced blood—a nightcap he had called it. It wasn't because Elora had trusted him or because they had grown close. Was it meant to add even more insult to what would happen?

He shook his head as he followed her in, exhaling when he saw that no one had moved in during his absence. Drawers were open, as was the closet, but both were empty. It was probably the aftermath of Korina gathering his things after they fled. The bed was still made as if he had woken up there this morning and fixed it before he left. Elora wandered over to the bathroom and glanced inside before turning back towards the room. Only then did she seem to relax as she set the journals on the table and sank into one of the chairs, dropping the duffle bag to the floor with a loud thud that seemed to ricochet through the room. Damien wished he could do the same, but all he could see was her body on the carpet, curled up in his bed with her damp crimson hair spread out on his pillows.

"I'll get fresh bedding," he muttered as she pulled one of the journals into her lap and started reading. She may have made a noise in acknowledgement, but the words on those pages were all she saw. Nothing else existed anymore for her as he left and wandered down the hall to where a closet full of blankets, sheets, and pillowcases was housed. He sifted through them, searching for the normal linen he preferred. Silk was obviously not an option, and he grew more and more frustrated until a small triumphant noise sounded in the empty hallway.

When he returned with a pile of bedding in his arms, the first thing he saw was that Elora hadn't moved. Her focus was narrowed on whatever she was reading as her fingers reached towards her neck, tracing the scars. It was a strangely vulnerable gesture, and he watched her for a moment before changing the sheets and pillowcases. He could have sworn there was the faintest trace of perfume on the comforter as he tossed it into a corner and laid out the fresh one. Only then did he enter the bathroom and search for any leftover products.

"There are things in my bag," Elora called out from where she sat, brows knitted together as she chewed on her cuticle. Whatever she was reading in those journals was destroying her, flaying the flesh from her body with each page she read. She stopped her assault on her fingers long enough to gesture towards the duffle bag at her feet. He didn't bother answering before he finished setting everything up for her. Shampoo, conditioner, and body wash sat on the small table near the bathtub. A brush and other toiletries lined the counter in front of the mirror. He gave himself a moment to collect his thoughts and to steady his breathing before he headed back into the bedroom. When he took the other chair by the table, she didn't look up or flinch.

"We should talk." Damien waited for her to close the journal and set it aside, giving their conversation her full attention.

"About?" She chewed at the skin around her fingers as she turned the page and continued reading.

"Viktor, for one. Unless you don't plan on sharing what he said after you sent me away." He tried to keep the irritation and impatience from his voice but failed based on the way she slammed the journal shut and met his gaze.

"If you had just behaved, you would have been able to stay."

"I didn't think you liked it when I behaved." She rolled her eyes even as his smirk grew wider.

"He didn't say anything we didn't already know. He took Elizabeth from the hospital after he failed to get me. He explained how he managed to find her after the apartment. She's turning anyone and everyone for me. To worship me. She thinks I want this. That I want a city of vampire abominations that I control." A flicker of disgust and horror raced across her face before she covered it with the flat expression that hid every thought and emotion. His mind raced through the information and the implications of what Elizabeth was attempting to achieve. Or was successfully achieving.

"Do you?" She leveled him with a glare that would have killed him if it had been a physical thing. It was cold fury that radiated from her, as if it were an insult that he would ask. He didn't believe that she wanted whatever Elizabeth was planning, but he had needed to hear her say it. An army that answered only to her would be quite the weapon against her other enemies, against the Resistance.

"I'm not answering that. If you think that I would want that, then I have made a horrible mistake once again." He flinched from the vitriol in her tone. Each word was a slap to the face, a punch to the gut. After a moment, Damien cleared his voice and moved on.

"And the human from the apartment? Wyatt." He wasn't sure why he was asking about him, but that seemed to be a theme for him tonight. Asking stupid questions that would only hurt her or him.

"Turned. Devoted to me, just as Elizabeth is. Another one of my victims. You saw him at the hotel." The defeat and self-hatred in her tone, in the way her body slumped forward, was torture. He reached for her hand, but she drew it away, hiding it away in her sleeves like she did when she started to retreat from the light.

"Not your victims, love. Hers. Elizabeth's. You tried to save him from that fate. And he willingly followed her and believed her story. None of that is on you." She nodded her head as if she believed him, as if she had absorbed his words. But he noted the way she continued to curve inward.

"You once told me that I had bodies piled at my feet. I didn't believe you then. But I do now," she whispered into her hands. "There is no end to them."

Damien slid from the chair and onto the floor, kneeling before her so he could see her face. There were tears along her lash line waiting to be let free.

"I also told you that I was a prick. Those bodies aren't at your feet. They are at Killian's or Elizabeth's. I understand blaming yourself. I can see the thread of logic you're following to come to that conclusion, but it's ignoring the fact that Killian was the creator of this. It's ignoring that Elizabeth has free will. You may be tied together in some strange way, but that doesn't influence her actions. You didn't tell her to do this." Her eyes closed, hiding the bright green he had found he couldn't live without. This was a weight he couldn't carry for her, no matter how desperately he wanted to. All he could do was support her while she worked through it and be there each time she fell under its weight.

Elora saw all of this as her fault, a product of a single mistake she had made when she was nineteen and left with no one to support her. The one person who had been tasked with guiding her through the healing process had used Elora's guilt as a control tactic. Denise had reinforced it, building it into a veil that Elora now saw the world through. In her version of reality, every death and tragedy traced directly back to her. The threads wrapped themselves around her limbs, coiled themselves around her neck, and squeezed until she couldn't breathe or even think clearly. Assuring her that it wasn't her fault seemed to do nothing, but maybe hearing it enough times would start to fray the threads until she was able to break them.

And she could. He knew she could.

Damien stood and glanced around the room even as he heard her pick the journal back up and flip open to whatever page she had been reading.

"We also need to decide what we're doing going forward. You took control here, but you still need to officially claim the Ravenwell group. And then there's the matter of combining them under one name." He ran his fingers through his hair, ignoring the guilt slicing through his chest at laying it all at her feet once more. It was a list that seemed to have no end. "Plus, there is the issue of Elizabeth and the Resistance."

Once more, only a noise sounded from her, even as he waited for a response.

"Elora?" She sighed heavily and used her finger as a bookmark before closing the book.

"My intentions right now are to go to Ravenwell Manor in two days and do the same thing as today. I'll make the announcement and then give them the opportunity to leave if they want. But I'll remind them that only Corvin and Radcliff are options. Then, I'll tell them that I'll be officially combining the two groups in two months. As for Elizabeth and the Resistance, I have no plan yet. I barely have this plan for the vampire groups." He nodded along as she spoke, watching the plan materialize with each word. It was simple and effective. No need for anything complicated.

"I'm glad that you finally decided your second-in-command should know what you were planning." Damien hadn't meant it to come out sounding so bitter. He hadn't realized how much that position bothered him. It was the same one he had held under Killian, the same one that resulted in her being dragged back to being under the previous vampire's control. It may have ended with Killian dead by her hand, but it didn't change what she had gone through to get to that point.

"Did you want a different title?" Elora's brows raised as she asked the question, and she finally set the journal on the table, pages down to save her place. He wasn't sure that he wanted a different title.

"I just—" He hesitated, not sure how to explain or if it would make sense. He took a deep breath and chewed his cheek for a moment before continuing. "It was the title I held under Killian. It feels wrong to hold the same one under your leadership as well, considering everything."

Elora nodded as her features seemed to soften and understanding filled her eyes.

"I'm sorry. I didn't consider that." She stood and made her way over to him, stopping directly in front of him before touching his cheek. "I'll give you any title you want. Anything you would feel more comfortable with."

He grinned as he leaned into her touch. It was a strange feeling having the vampire head, or anyone, apologize to him. Killian never had. Not once in his entire time working under him. Not when he had beaten Damien for some failure or when he had been injured during a mission. Killian had always been better than that, always been better than him.

"I'll think about it. I'm sure I can come up with some ideas." She smirked and removed her hand, stretching slightly before eyeing the bed behind him. He noted the movement and stepped aside.

"Go to sleep, love. I'll find somewhere to go." The look she gave him was all at once one of hurt and confusion.

"Why? You'll sleep with me in here." He shook his head even as he fought back a smile.

"A second-in-command doesn't sleep in the same bed as their vampire head. It would be seen as favoritism, and that could cause problems." She waved her hand dismissively before stepping around him, towards the bathroom.

"Maybe under Killian that was true. But I'm in charge now, and your new head orders you to not leave this room." And he saw it once more in her face. Despite the steel in her command that made him wonder what else she could order him to do, there was a vulnerability. It was a fear he would leave her there, that he would laugh and be gone once she returned to the bedroom. The wolfish grin on his lips brought the loveliest of pinks to her cheeks as he bowed dramatically. Only then did she disappear into the bathroom. She needed to understand that he would follow any command she gave him, follow any request no matter how mild or insignificant.

The door clicked, and he heard the water turn on as the image of her removing her clothing piece by piece forced itself into his head, followed by memories of her failed wedding night. What could have easily been a honeymoon filled with agony at Darian's hand had quickly turned into the two of them and a hotel room. Almost without thought, he picked up the journal that had demanded so much of her attention, that had held her so tightly in its claws. He recognized Killian's handwriting instantly. The penmanship was harsh, none of the looping cursive that Denise's had been. These were the pen strokes of someone on the edge, someone so tightly wound they were sure to snap at any moment.

Damien felt his face contort as he read, as the reminder that he had fed from her pushed itself forward from where he had hidden it in the darkest recesses of his mind. It had taken him time to understand that the act of drinking her blood had done nothing to him, hadn't made him obsessed or addicted to it like it had for Killian and his two favorites.

Yet, the lines written on this page had his heart frozen in his chest as his blood seemed to stop circulating. Line after line of

Elora's name, lamenting prose about missing the taste of her. Bile rose in his throat as he tossed the journal down, debating ripping the pages out and burning them to ash.

Chapter 7

Viktor

It was only Damien who got out of the elevator this time. His arms were crossed over his chest and there was a scowl on his face that seemed to only go away when he looked at Elora. It was only then that his features softened and something akin to adoration made an appearance. Viktor wanted to believe it was love. Elora deserved for someone to love her unconditionally and without question, without any limitations or expectations. But the more he thought about her, about how those who met her seemed inexplicably drawn to her, he wondered if that was even possible. If the emotions that those around her felt were somehow created, did that count? It would be exactly as she deserved. Unconditional and all consuming, but there would be no choice in it for them. And for Elora, choice was everything. It was what she had always sought, what she had killed for.

"Just you today. Is she finally ready to let you kill me?" Damien's jaw ticked as his mouth straightened into a line. Viktor could see why Elora was drawn to him. He had a beauty to him that was enviable. But that had never been Viktor's type. With men, he had always preferred softer features, gentle eyes, and a face that revealed every thought and emotion. Damien's was the opposite. He could hide everything behind a facade of indifference or simple boredom unless pushed too far. Then, it was only violence that was revealed.

Jaime had been Damien's exact opposite. All smiles and warmth. He had been handsome in a way that felt welcoming. His smile ushered someone in until they were happily stuck in his orbit. And Viktor had revolved around Jaime without even considering something or someone different. When the center of that orbit had ceased to exist, Viktor had been left floating in an endless wasteland, desperate to grab hold of anything that would root him back in the ground.

"I have a few questions. Want your insight." The words were forced out as if someone were dragging them from his mouth, ripping them out of his throat as they tried to claw into his tongue.

"And she can't be here for this?" Viktor savored the way Damien's brows furrowed. Maybe he would be easier to read now that Elora had broken down whatever barriers had been in place. "I bet she doesn't even know you're here." Damien's tightened fist gave away the answer to that.

"What exactly does the Resistance want with her? We know they want her blood, but why?"

"I already answered this question." The surprise on Damien's face was instant. Had Elora not told him what they had discussed?

"Answer it again." The command was low and cold. Viktor only nodded as Damien rested on his shoulder as he leaned against the plexiglass.

"Her blood could create a cure, from what I understand. Or potentially a weapon. Maybe both. But they never specified what that would look like. At least not to me, and I wasn't exactly in high favor with them, thanks to Elora and her sister."

"Her blood is the key to a cure for vampirism." Damien seemed to mull over the words, ignoring Viktor's comment about his place in the hierarchy.

"That seems to be the plan. But I never saw anything concrete. I know they were using Elizabeth's blood while we had her captured, but it wasn't yielding any results."

"Then how do they know Elora's will?" Viktor considered the question that he had never asked or considered. Thorne never said exactly how they knew this. She had said that Elora's blood was the key.

"Above my pay grade, I guess," he responded and shrugged, but a dark churning had settled in Viktor's chest. How did they know so much if they had never gotten their hands on Elora? Had it been part of Denise's research while treating Elora? Now that there was a distance between him and the movement, there were too many unexplained elements. He had always thought Thorne's knowledge was vast even for the head of the Resistance but had never questioned it. It was annoying how many parallels there were between him and the vampire on the other side of the glass.

"All I do know is that they would need her blood and a lot of it. Denise always said it would require her death eventually. That they would start by draining her and then feed her until she healed. But the demand would grow, and they would get too greedy. Too ambitious, and Elora would be the one to pay the price." It had always been distasteful to him, and he had hoped it wouldn't come to that. In Viktor's mind, he would be able to protect her from that fate despite being the one to drag her to it, offering her up like the sacrifice she was meant to be. He had been naive, and the realization made him feel like a fool, just as Elora had accused him of being not too long ago.

Damien made a small grunting noise as he seemed to stare at something down the hallway. They lapsed into a tense silence. He had already told Elora all of this, which meant either she was keeping secrets from Damien or she simply hadn't gotten a chance to tell him. He knew which option he would bet on. She had always held information close if she thought it would cause problems or pain for those around her. Viktor assumed this was a similar situation and could only imagine Damien's wrath as he killed his way through each and every member who had planned to hurt her.

"I want addresses. Names of those in power." There was an underlying promise to Damien's demand. He wasn't gathering this information for Elora or for them to use in the ongoing fight between vampires and humans. Viktor's assumption had been correct. The information was so he could remove the threat and protect her. And once more Viktor marveled at how this vampire, who seemed to hold such hatred for her not too long ago, had grown so dedicated to her. He could recall every sneer Damien had shot in her direction, every comment. Damien's obvious obsession with her in the hospital had never felt like anything but dislike or pure revulsion. It had been clear in how he spoke about her, goading her into attacking him in the day room. Though Viktor doubted Damien had truly understood what he was attempting to unleash that day. But he had quickly found out.

"Answer my own question, and I'll tell you what I can. I'm curious about something." Damien's brow rose as if surprised by either the negotiation or by his willingness to offer intel. He nodded and then waited, eyes locked on Viktor as he considered how best to word this, to explain the growing theory in his mind.

"What do you think the extent of Elora's effect is? We know her bite is incredibly potent and that she can compel anyone. Vampire or human. We know she's stronger than other vampires. She's the first of her kind, and if the Resistance's scientists are right, she remains the only one. Elizabeth's transformation made her a pale imitation of the original, not a perfect copy," Viktor explained slowly, both to himself and to Damien, who only gave him a deadpan look as if to say he already knew all of this.

"But I've been wondering about her influence. About whether or not she draws people to her. If she naturally makes people want to be around her, then that would be quite the skill to have. Whether she knows it or not."

"Are you trying to find an excuse for coming to care for her? Pathetic, Viktor. She isn't to blame for whatever you do or do not feel." Viktor shook his head at the accusation. It was a fair one. Maybe he was searching for a reason why so many seemed to want to protect her—a reason for why he was willing to risk his place in the Resistance for her.

"I've made it clear I don't feel anything for her." But the words rang hollow, and Damien knew it. The smirk on his face said as much, and they stared at one another for another heartbeat.

"You were drawn to her fairly quickly." Viktor's assessment broke the silence, and Damien chuckled.

"I went into that hospital already looking for her. To figure out if she was who I needed her to be. I wasn't drawn." Damien seemed to be sorting through memories as he spoke, as if he were trying to pinpoint exactly when his feelings and intentions had begun to change. It was obvious they had, but the question was when.

"But you were at some point, or we wouldn't be here. She would still be under Killian's thumb, and you would still be play-ing the role of a guard." Viktor paused before continued. "Or she would be dead either by Killian's hand or the Resistance."

"What about you? When did it change?" Viktor considered the question, trying to figure out exactly when that had hap-pened.

"I was in the same situation. I was sent there to monitor her. But after her first breakdown and helping her work through the aftermath, that was it. My reports became useless because they felt like a betrayal. She changed everything."

"That doesn't seem manufactured." Damien's jaw worked before he spoke again. "It sounds like she became more than a mission. That she became a person and not an object to observe."

Viktor wondered if Damien recognized the tie they seemed to share—a strange thread that connected them. It was more than their histories with Elora. Instead, it was the way they both had sought to use her to complete a mission given to them by people who only wanted to possess her. And how they both couldn't do it after meeting her. Was that manufactured? Or simply a natural progression of events? Viktor had been so sure that there was an external reason for whatever he felt for her, that it would explain away how he couldn't identify what emotions washed over him at the mere mention of her name. All he knew was it wasn't love. Not in the way Damien seemed to feel. It was an urge to protect, to be in her world no matter what form it took. Or how many lives it required to build it.

Viktor shook his head, regretting instantly even starting this conversation at all. He had hoped for a resolution, but it had only left more questions.

"When did you fall for her?" Damien twitched slightly as his brows furrowed at Viktor's question. Viktor had been curious about it since their escape from the Tower, since he had seen Damien hold her in his arms and kiss the top of her head like she was his entire world. She hadn't been a job at that point, and somewhere between the hospital and their escape, everything had shifted.

"Upset that I may have taken your place in her heart?" Viktor huffed a laugh at the question. Despite how close they had been, he wasn't sure it was ever like what he saw between the two of them.

"I've never had that kind of place with her." Damien's face contorted into something that made Viktor involuntarily scoot away from the glass just a bit.

"She fucking loved you. Maybe she still does, and that's why you're still alive." Damien froze before seeming to collect himself. "But you never loved her, and she knows it now."

Viktor only nodded along, recalling the warmth in her eyes when she looked at him. Her blushing cheeks and the way she had always leaned into his touch, how she had always sought his company. A part of him had known and had played on it. Disgust and guilt coiled in his gut until it was all he could feel. Not fear of what would eventually happen to him, but the type of self-hatred that came with seeing exactly who you were as if a mirror had been held up.

Damien sighed deeply before glancing at the ceiling as if he were choosing his words carefully or drawing forth memories.

"It had been happening gradually, I think. But it had been the night of the banquet that everything changed irrevocably for me." Viktor straightened slightly, moving closer to the glass. She had only alluded to what had happened when she came the next morning dressed in clothing he was certain didn't belong to her.

"She never really told me what happened. Only said they had hurt her again." Damien dragged his hand down his face, and as it fell back to his side, Viktor saw a guilt that matched his own.

"I won't tell you what happened to her. As you once told me, it isn't my story to tell. But she came to my room after. Collapsed on the floor in a bloody heap. Killian had given her drugged blood." Damien paused as if preparing himself for what was coming next. "I was the one to give it to her. I didn't know it had been laced with a sedative until she told me the next morning."

And there it was. The core of guilt and shame Viktor had recognized so clearly in Damien. It was in the way he seemed to diminish with each word he spoke, with the confession that had passed his lips.

Once more, there were no words to say as they both sat with their choices and the consequences of them. The silence stretched until a familiar voice rang out from down the hall.

"Sharing stories?" There she stood, her red hair pulled back into a messy bun that was so at odds with who she was meant to be now and the role she was meant to fill. Damien instantly stood straighter at the dark expression on her face and the way her arms were crossed over her chest. The short sleeves of her shirt and low neckline revealed everything Viktor knew she had always kept hidden. For some reason, it filled him with pride to see her no longer hiding, no longer ashamed of the scars that lined her skin.

"We're going to be late." Her eyes moved between Viktor and Damien once more before she turned and entered the elevator with Damien darting forward to follow her. As the doors closed and he was left in silence once again, he realized he had gotten no answers to his questions. Instead, he and Damien may have found common ground, and if that was the case, maybe it would be the thing to save his life at the end of this.

The question was if he still wanted to.

Chapter 8

Elora

As far as Elora could remember, she had never been to the Ravenwell headquarters. Moving down the long driveway that had only stones and hedges along the concrete brought back no memories, no hints that disappeared before she could grab them. At some point since seeing the childhood photos that lined her uncle's shelves, Elora had come to accept that not everything would return. She had understood that the fact some memories were gone was one of the few things Denise had been right about. It felt like there were levels of severity as it pertained to her memory loss. Some were pictures, steady scenes that she saw as if through fog or an opaque window. Others were flashes, mere hints of colors or smells. And then there were the burned-out portions—the cigarette burns in the tapestry.

Some things that were lost could never be regained. And it had taken her years to come to terms with what that absence meant.

A hand reached for her as she watched the house draw closer. Damien's fingers wrapped around hers as he pulled them to him, letting them rest on his thigh. Comfort, pure and complete, that could only exist in the confines of this car seeped from him to her. Once they stepped out, he would take his place beside her, fulfilling the role she had outlined for him. It wasn't the role she had wanted him to take, but so much had happened quickly, so many decisions had been made without even a single second to discuss them. In that moment, as she stood before hundreds of vampires who had answered to the one she had killed, Elora had wanted him near her. Taking on that role would allow that to happen.

His fingers squeezed around her hand, and she tore her eyes from the windshield to give him a small smile, just the slightest curl of her lips. Reading the journals and consuming each word and page had kept her from sleeping. How could she when so many answers waited between the covers of Killian's journals? So far she had read about Killian meeting her mother and the scheme that had formed when he recognized how lonely she was with only Silas at her side. She had seen the outlined plan he had made for what he imagined his creation being. Most of it had come to fruition. The question was exactly how much of it had, and Elora wasn't sure she wanted the answer. At least not yet. Not until this was over.

The manor in front of her was smaller than her uncle's, but she imagined the location had a lot to do with that. While Silas's was located about an hour outside the city, the Ravenwell manor was right outside the city limits. They had driven through a small suburb before approaching the driveway. There were no sprawling gardens or extensive grounds that someone could get lost in. The house itself looked very similar to Silas's—red brick and vines. The car circled around the fountain in front of the house and came to a stop just before the entryway. She didn't move at first, staring at the building that was now hers. Each word of her upcoming announcement and speech had been carefully planned, but the response that awaited her forced her heart to race and her body to warm in anticipation.

Each potential scenario filled her mind, displaying themselves one after another. The best option was for them to simply accept her and make this easy on them all. Another possibility was that there was a mass exodus of vampires who would seek to join the Corvin and Radcliff families in an effort to not be under her rule. And the worst option her mind could conjure were mirror images of Killian's and Darian's deaths. She would be left on the floor in a sea of blood.

She listened as the driver exited the car and began his trek to her door. Damien released her hand as they both prepared for the roles they now needed to play. Elora felt herself slip into the version of her that was violence and darkness. The side of her that could rip a heart from a chest without batting an eye or experiencing even the slightest hint of guilt. Feature by feature, she schooled her face into one of ice and stone as the door opened and a hand reached out. With one last deep breath, she took it, left the confines of the car, and stepped out. The dress she had changed into in the car fell in a wave of fabric to the dirt, and she could feel the cold air on her exposed skin—another carefully curated costume for this role. Part of her choice came from her desire for each vampire in that manor to see the evidence carved into her skin, each scar that stood for every reason both Killian and Darian had found their ends at her hand.

Not long ago, Elora would have felt her skin crawl at having them on display. She would have felt the overwhelming panic that came with being perceived in such a way. It was akin to standing on a pedestal in the middle of the busiest part of the city completely nude. There had always been the staring, the gossip, the theories that were shared in loud whispers that were meant for her to hear. Yet now, she heard the seamstress's words from the days leading up to the banquet, finally believing them.

Wear them like armor. They are proof you survived. Don't let them diminish you.

And she would. As she squared her shoulders and felt Damien step into his position at her side, Elora savored the rush of strength that they granted her in that moment.

Car doors shut, and she sauntered forward with confident steps. The knife Damien had given her was strapped to her leg, while another smaller one was nestled between her breasts. If the vampires waiting for her attacked, she would be ready.

She didn't knock once she reached the door. Instead, she gripped the cold metal of the handle and pushed it open before entering as if she owned the space she walked into. And she did. Elora owned each wall and floor. Each light fixture and room. Each piece of art and furniture. A human stood to the right of the entrance, eyes traveling over her form as she raised a brow and he inclined his head in deference.

"This way." His voice was gravelly, as if he had spent his life smoking. Once more, he bowed slightly before turning away from her and began walking down the hallway before her. Elora supposed, no matter how ill it made her feel, she owned the human now as well, just as Killian had owned each and every person in his feeding rooms. That would be one of the first changes to make. If the Resistance would simply speak with her, they would understand she didn't want the conscription of the most vulnerable. She didn't approve of forced feedings and attacks from vampires on humans. Her goal was to dismantle it all. To tear it down in a crushing wave that left nothing in its wake. There would be no gentle easing into the changes. No hand holding as she slowly ushered in the change she sought.

It would be swift and instant. They could either fall in line or meet the same fate as the others who took and stole just as Killian and his minions had.

The design and decor of the manor were softer and more delicate than she had imagined. In her mind, she had expected something like Killian's aesthetic with the Tower—dark and cliche with black, crimson, and gold. This was the opposite with its whites and creams. The only similarity was the gold accents, but with the color scheme, it didn't seem as tacky and garish. Her heels echoed down the hallway as she followed the human until she heard the sound of voices filtering through the closed doors in front of her.

"In here, madam. They are gathered and waiting for you, as requested." Once more, he bowed slightly, and she briefly wondered if that was something Darian had required of the humans under his control. An act of subservience and submission would be in line with who he was and the unearned ego that was displayed at every possible moment.

Elora inhaled a deep breath and held it for a moment, counting silently as she did.

One.

Two.

Three.

Four.

Five.

The air slowly seeped between her lips as she exhaled and nodded at Damien, who only returned the gesture. Just as she had done, he squared his shoulders and arranged his features into the coldness she had seen when they had both been under Killian's control. Both of them, now perfectly shifted into this version of themselves, began the performance that would determine what would need to happen next.

He pushed open both doors in a somewhat dramatic move that drew the attention of each vampire waiting there. The conversations ceased instantly as each pair of eyes moved to her and others shifted in an effort to see the vampire who now ruled their family. Damien once more took his place, falling in line only a few steps behind her as she began her trek to the small stage awaiting her. Had this been set up specifically for her? She hadn't ordered any preparations be made for her announcement and hadn't necessarily wanted to stand above them as if she were better than them. Or had this already been here, a remnant of Darian's days as head of the family?

It didn't matter either way as the crowd parted and she confidently strolled down the path made for her. On all sides, she could feel their eyes. Their judgements and hostility, and she absorbed it, let it feed the rage that always simmered right below her surface. Her shoes clicked on the marble, echoing until she came to a stop and Damien held out a hand to assist her. It took everything she had to not clutch it tightly and draw him to her. Instead, she opted to incline her head and step onto the stage. Only then did she stare out at the sea of faces watching her with open distrust and anger. She let her lip curl slightly at the edges as she met each pair of eyes, letting the silence hang in the room before settling among them, filling the gaps between each body.

"You know who I am and why I'm here. I can see it on each face staring at me. But in case you don't, and you find yourself in the minority, I'm Elora Ashcroft and your new vampire head." She paused, tracking the slight shift in the crowd as they seemed to push forward and closer to the stage. To her left, she felt Damien tense as if he noticed the change as well.

"I've already heard what you all have to say about this change in leadership. Some of you disapprove of how I disposed of Darian. Some of you see me as beneath you because of your assumptions about me. And some of you, I'm sure, simply do not want to be under the leadership of a woman, vampire or not." Heads nodded as she listed off the rumors and gossip Silas had made her aware of before he retreated to a home he had in the city. He had explained he wanted to be close by as they uncovered more and more of what Killian had done along with overseeing the renovations made to the office and bedrooms. Elora had only wrapped her arms around him in gratitude, whispering her thanks into his perfectly pressed shirt.

For the role he played in her plan to eliminate Darian from the equation, she would never be able to thank him properly. Even now that all was said and done and she was in her place of power, Silas still seemed aged from the first time she had seen him in front of his own manor. It left a perpetual pit of guilt in her stomach that threatened to make her ill anytime she took in the new wrinkles, the harsh lines on his once youthful face.

"I can regale you with the same story I told in place of my wedding vows. The same history I repeated when I addressed the Ashcroft family. But if you know how Darian died, then you already know the story, and repeating it serves no purpose other than feeding a morbid and perverted curiosity. All you need to know is I killed him. Held his heart in the palm of my hand after I ripped it from his chest."

Again, the crowd shifted closer, and Damien took a step forward as if to dare them to even hint at violence aimed at her. She noted a few fearful and uncertain glances at Damien before they moved back to her. Elora had known Damien could be the piece that kept chaos from erupting, the piece that kept everything in place. There were too many who saw her as a weak woman, someone unfit to be in charge of them despite adhering to their rules and traditions. It was insulting. Infuriating, and she considered briefly showing each one exactly how powerful she was and what her rage could do when unleashed.

"Blood whore." She rolled her eyes as the chant filled the room. At one point, the label had made her cringe and retreat into herself. But she had also blamed herself then for everything that had happened. Her shame and guilt had been her most constant companions. And they still appeared from time to time from the place she had banished them. That word held no meaning now. Not to her.

"Boring, really. And insulting that I'm not worth a better name." The crowd quieted at the sound of the laughter that erupted from her and drowned out their chant.

"Call me whatever you want. It changes nothing. If you hoped to send me running after stepping down from the position I killed for, you misjudged me. Either way, I'll still be merging the Ashcrofts and Ravenwells into a single family. You're welcome to leave and join one of the other two options. I won't force you to stay. With me, you have a choice, which is something I was never afforded."

At her declaration, two things happened at once. The first was the tension that poured from each vampire settled around them like a mist. They seemed unsure about their next move, as if they hadn't expected to be given the option to stay or leave.

The second was that two vampires rushed the stage at the same time, pushing at bodies and snarling as they began their assassination attempt. She smirked down at them as she pulled the knife from its holster on her thigh. The dress had been crafted specifically to allow for easy access since this had been exactly how she saw this playing out.

Silver sliced through the space between them that was rapidly disappearing. She didn't even glance at the vampire, who now collapsed to the ground in a mess of blood and wheezing breaths. His throat was slashed, severing the vocal cords that had been used to repeat the label she had lived with for years.

A choked sound erupted as she thrust the blade forward, striking the second attacker who had sought to capitalize on the distraction. Her fingers dug themselves into his shirt as she yanked him forward, forcing the knife further and further into his chest. The fear in his eyes was bright, and she smiled at him—cold and cruel and feral until defeat filled each feature and sank into the wrinkles around his eyes and lips. Only then did she rip the knife from him and leave him sinking to the floor with a gaping hole in his chest.

"As I said, you're welcome to leave. I won't force you to stay. But I also will not be attacked unless you would like to share their fate." Without waiting to see if there would be a response, she stepped off the stage and over the two bodies lying in pools of their own blood as their flesh began to knit itself back together. As she left the room, heels once more clicking on the marble with Damien at her side, Elora felt the respect that now seeped from them.

There would be no deserters.

Chapter 9

Elora

S he recognized the vampire standing in front of her instantly. More specifically, she recognized the hungry expression on her face when she glanced at Damien when she first walked in. The way her lips curled into a seductive smile. A lesser woman, or vampire, may have been filled with jealousy, but Elora only smirked. Damien stood at her side and slept in her bed. No one else's.

"Elora, I'm—" She held her hand up, silencing Korina, who almost let a flash of anger show. Almost. Elora had to guess that the vampire hadn't survived this long under Killian's control by displaying her emotions so openly. There was something cunning about Korina, something that Elora would have sought and brought to her side if circumstances were different.

"I know who you are." Elora snuck a glance at Damien, who nodded as if they were sharing an unspoken conversation. She felt it as Korina seemed to shift from foot to foot in either impatience or irritation. When Elora turned her attention back to the vampire, her eyes were roaming over the office, taking in the changes that had occurred in less than a day, thanks to her uncle. Silas had done more than put on a new coat of paint and change the flooring. The entire room was transformed from top to bottom—from the new desk, which was a smaller version of Killian's, to the seating that stood behind Korina.

The office had been severe in its aesthetic, no doubt to elicit fear from those who stepped inside. She didn't want to make people scared but uneasy, as if there was a hint of violence even if they couldn't fully recognize it. If she learned one lesson under Killian's control, it had been that people were more afraid of the possibility of violence. When it was promised, as it had been with her father, it lost its power. Vampires had come into this room knowing they would be hurt or killed. They had been able to prepare for it. In her presence, there would always be a tiny voice in their mind warning them without any real rationale for it.

That was power, and Killian had accidentally taught her that each time she flinched at the sound of a knock on the door or recoiled from the blood delivered to her room.

"Quite different from your father," Korina commented before turning her attention back to Elora. After she had received the request for the meeting, Damien had outlined Korina's history with both him and Killian. He had explained how Killian had promised to draw her up through the hierarchy but had tossed her from this very office when he grew tired of her. Korina had been there when Damien was first turned. It had been her and Lukas who had helped him through the transition and the bloodlust that Elora couldn't fully understand. She had never undergone the change; she never felt her mind and body shift into its new form.

Not a single detail had been kept from her.

"He was always dramatic. A walking cliche." The fact that Elora wouldn't be was left unsaid, and she had proven that already. Killian had worked in the shadows, preferring to keep his hands clean. It was why so many bodies were laid at Damien's feet. Darian's heart in her hand and the bodies left on the marble floor at the Ravenwell manor were proof she was not her father's daughter. She was something much worse.

Korina lifted a single brow in response as they waited each other out. A stalemate to see who would break first. Elora smirked as the vampire seemed to grow more and more irritated until her cheeks appeared to redden.

"I asked for this audience to offer you my loyalty as the new head of both Ashcroft and Ravenwell." Elora heard Damien hold back a slight chuckle that warmed her heart slightly. Slowly, she nodded as if considering Korina's declaration.

"You aren't going to ask what I'm willing to give you? I heard your loyalty is usually bought. How would I ensure someone wouldn't be able to take it away for the right price?" At the sound of the question, Korina's face darkened into a glare that wasn't directed at Elora, but at Damien. Apparently, she hadn't expected him to tell Elora anything and give her such insight into who Korina was and how she operated.

"Maybe I'm just happy to follow a woman. A female vampire as the head of a family."

"Follow Chloe, then." Another flash of anger, and Elora caught the way her hand flexed slightly.

"You have more power. More control than Chloe. And as Damien obviously told you, I follow power." There was something honest in her explanation. Yet the best lies were always hidden in the truth. It was impressive in how well she played the game.

"You want my power and influence. Probably hope to use it to your benefit, and I can respect that considering how Killian treated you." Elora leaned back in her chair and studied the vampire, noting each detail. The suit fitted her form perfectly. The curls in her hair and purple lipstick only enhanced her beauty. As a human, she would have been gorgeous, and as a vampire, she was painfully exquisite.

"But you haven't explained what you offer me. What do I gain?" Elora repeated with an air of disinterest. Korina's eyes darkened as she seemed to consider the question while guilt swirled in Elora's gut. At their core, they were the same, even if Elora didn't necessarily want to admit it when so much hung in the balance. Ignoring the threat that Korina could pose would be dangerous now that everything was settling into place.

Both of them had been used and tossed aside until they were wanted again. In their own ways, they had seen exactly how much control men sought over the women around them. It was never about anything more than that. Yes, Killian and Darian had sought her blood, but it had also been about her submission. About allowing them to feed from her without question. Even without Damien telling her, Elora would have recognized the intelligence and strength that lay behind Korina's eyes, the rage that quietly fueled each choice and action. It was the same for her.

"Information. Connections. Support." Elora stood and came around the desk, leaning against it as she considered the options. Sending Korina away would be a mistake. And yet keeping her here could also prove to be a problem. Damien shifted and came beside her, only a few steps away as if prepared to intervene if Korina decided to try and take over the vampire family herself. But that didn't seem to be the vampire's style based on limited experience with her. Korina worked behind the scenes, shifting people into place before striking.

"Such as? Offer me something now. Give me a piece of information that I could use." The blouse Korina wore under the blazer didn't even wrinkle as she shifted from one foot to the other while she seemed to pick her piece of intel in order to answer the question. Elora could practically see the thoughts moving behind her eyes, tracking the way she was probably carefully isolating something that would be useful but wouldn't render her redundant. It needed to prove her worth, but not so much that it made her seem dangerous. At least, that was what Elora would do if their positions were reversed and she had a feeling they were similar enough.

"Chloe is actively working against you. She was pissed after Darian and feels like you tricked her. I heard she's trying to contact the Resistance to have them help." Korina paused slightly and darted a glance at Damien before returning her attention to Elora. "The enemy of my enemy and all that."

The intel wasn't necessarily surprising considering the expression on Chloe's face when Elora had explained exactly how everything had been maneuvered for her to take over two vampire families. But potentially working with the Resistance was intriguing. It was something she had considered herself when she had discussed what to do about Elizabeth with Silas and Damien. If Chloe had beaten her to this, then that could be a problem.

"How close were you with Darian?" Korina jerked slightly at Elora's question as if trying to keep up with the topic change.

"Close enough to take me to the meeting." Her eyes drifted over to Damien and seemed to drink him in. Elora nodded slowly, pretending that she didn't notice the subtle power play occurring under her nose. She had already been told that Korina had been offered as a consolation prize for Damien to claim once Elora was ripped from his grasp.

"That doesn't mean too much. He also took Jonas, after all." She let the insult linger between them in an attempt to goad her into some type of reaction. Something beyond a flinch or flash of anger in her eyes. Elora wanted to see something authentic, something not carefully crafted for consumption.

"I actually served a purpose, as Damien can tell you." There was a flash of rage on Korina's face, a tightening of her lips and a clenching of her jaw. Elora's smile stretched across her face in a way that was almost painful. She had seen it. Only a glimpse, but it was there.

"And yet you never fulfilled that purpose," Elora observed and shook her head before facing Korina once more. The brief view of who the vampire was had disappeared once more. "But I think you are better suited to jobs that don't require that type of distraction. Men tend to be so narrow minded when giving us tasks. The lack of creativity is always disappointing."

A true and genuine smile curled at the edges of Korina's lips and she huffed a laugh before seeming to visibly relax. Elora straightened and made her way back around the desk, easing once more into the leather chair.

"I want you to go to Ravenwell manor. They know you there, I assume." Elora paused as Korina nodded her head in confirmation. "Listen. Talk to others. Report back."

"That's it?" From the tone of Korina's voice, Elora couldn't decide if the vampire was insulted or surprised. Perhaps it was a mixture of both. Maybe she had expected something danger-ous as a way to remove her from the equation. Or maybe she had expected to remain nearby at Elora's side. Either way, she would have been wrong. Elora didn't want her as an enemy and could recognize that there was a game being played here even if she couldn't identify the rules or players outside of herself and Damien.

"Yes. That's it. You just need to spend your time there. Re-port back once a week if all is well. More if there are problems. Let me know if there are rumors or plots against me. I would hope my demonstration would be enough to keep any issues at bay for a while, but that isn't a guarantee. And unfortunately, I cannot be in two places at once." Silence stretched out between the three of them as Korina no doubt considered the offer, prob-ably trying to fit it into whatever original plan she had devel-oped prior to walking into the room.

A curt nod from Korina caused her hair to fall in pieces around her face.

"I'll leave right away."

"Don't make me regret this, Korina. I have no problem adding to my current body count." The threat wrapped itself around Korina like a scarf as she nodded and turned on her heel. A groan fell from Elora's lips as the door clicked shut. The pain radiating from her stomach had returned with such intensity, she would have collapsed if she hadn't already been sitting.

"I'll have something brought up." Damien didn't wait for a response before he sent a message on his phone and reclined against the desk, facing her. She could feel him studying her face, probably noting the strain currently etched into her features as the hunger pangs washed through her again. The frequency with which she needed to feed was an issue and if Elizabeth was the same way, then the problem was far worse than Elora had originally thought.

Elora closed her eyes as she took a deep breath—inhaling and holding it for a moment before releasing it. The pain eased slightly into a dull ache and she lifted her gaze to Damien's concerned expression.

"Is that look on your face about the hunger or about Korina's task?" He smirked slightly at her question before pushing back a strand of her hair that had fallen into her face.

"We need to have a better system to make sure you don't get this bad."

"It comes out of nowhere." Her protest was met with a shake of his head, and she sighed. "But yes, we do."

"Did you just say that I was right?"

She gave him a heatless glare, a smile playing on her lips.

"Don't expect it to happen again."

The laugh that left him warmed her entire being, easing the tension that Korina's visit had left in its wake. Damien lifted her chin with the tip of his finger and leaned down, pressing his lips to hers in a way that was gentle. Every move he made with her was soft and light, as if he thought she may break under his touch. As if he feared it would bring forward those memories that still resurfaced in her dreams, leaving her trembling and struggling to regain her grip on reality. He would reach for her, pulling her close so that she was nestled in his arms, head resting on his chest. No words were ever spoken. No questions were ever asked.

Elora stood, pressing herself further into his kiss as his arms wrapped around her waist and pulled her close. Her lips parted slightly, granting him access, and he took it without a single moment of hesitation as the kiss grew into something hungry and demanding. His hand slipped under her blouse before his fingers pressed into her skin, as he could somehow bring her even closer. The heat of his touch forced a soft moan from her, and she could feel the curl of his lips in response.

Her hand traced their way around his neck and into his hair before gripping a handful tightly. He groaned as she pulled his head to the side, instantly missing the feeling of his lips on hers even as she lowered her head to his neck, trailing small nips along the flesh there. Goosebumps erupted as she lingered at his collarbone before languidly moving back up until she reached the sharp line of his jaw.

As she adjusted, maneuvering his head to allow her access to the other side, his hands tightened around her hips, lifting and spinning her around in a single fluid motion. A squeal of surprise erupted from her, and then there was that sound again. His laugh—deep and warm and she wanted to lose herself in it and him. The cold wood of the desk radiated through her pants, providing a brief reprieve for her flushed skin as her lips met Damien's once more. Time stood still as they became a blurred mass of teeth and tongue.

Each movement was pure desperation as she sank her hands under his shirt to feel the hard planes of his chest, the scars along his ribs and stomach from years of doing Killian's dirty work. Like the night of her failed wedding to Darian, reality melted away in this moment, leaving them in a confined void that she never wanted to emerge from.

Fingers deftly shifted to the buttons along the front of her blouse, undoing them one by one before sliding the garment from her shoulders. His smile grew when he spotted the pendant nestled between her breasts. Her souvenir from the punishment Damien had gifted the vampire after her attack.

Her back arched, and she pressed herself forward, pleading for more. Begging for him to not handle her as if she were fragile and ready to break if his touch was too harsh or his movements too firm. It was maddening even as his lips began to mirror her own ministrations for him and trailed tiny nips and kisses down her neck and onto her chest. Searing touches trailed along the crest of each breast, biting at the skin until her breathing hitched and became desperate pants. Her hands curled into his hair, holding so tightly she vaguely wondered if it was painful.

The knock on the door broke them apart and a curse all but erupted from Damien's mouth as they froze, both trapped in their positions as if it would force whoever was there to turn and leave.

"It's for you, love." She left out a whimper as he backed away, straightening before pulling the blouse back up over her shoulders.

"Impeccable timing," she groaned and he only nodded, fastening the buttons of her shirt one by one. For a moment, neither of them moved as he lowered his face to hers until their foreheads met and she could feel his breath on her face. A heartbeat—only a single heartbeat later he once more leaned back and pressed a kiss to her cheek before stepping away. He extended his hand and she took it, gripping it like it was a life raft as she pushed herself off the desk and sank into the leather chair. One final adjustment of her shirt and she nodded before calling out for the vampire with her meal to enter.

They entered quickly with a bottle and two glasses on a tray. It was a sight that made her hands clench into fists. She forced her breathing to remain neutral as they set the items on the desk before her and turned, nearly darting for the door. Her stomach contracted again now that the distraction of Damien's affections had been removed. It was as if her body knew what laid before it and was demanding its consumption. And yet, for an agonizingly long second, her hands refused to move, to reach out and pour the liquid into the glass.

She huffed slightly as she finally willed her limbs to listen to her, yet her fingers trembled as they opened the bottle. The aroma filled the room in an instant and her eyes closed of their own accord. The scent caused a shiver to race down her spine as her mind screamed at her to move faster, demanded that she simply drink it from the bottle in an effort to speed up the process. Restraint was nearly impossible as she poured it into the glass and brought it to her lips, taking the smallest of sips to prolong the ecstasy she felt and the shame that accompanied it.

"You can't trust Korina, love." She let the blood sit on her tongue before swallowing and nodding her head.

"I'm not stupid enough to think that I can." Another sip and then another before the ache began to subside. "She's ambitious, as you told me. And she can be useful. She's smart. Willing to be violent, which is something I happen to find useful."

"If you can keep her loyalty. She defected to Darian instantly and offered me her support if I wanted to take over the family. That intelligence can prove to be a problem."

"I know, Damien. I didn't say I trusted her. I gave her a job that I can easily keep track of while also keeping her away from here. It isn't like she will be the only vampire I plant over there for intel." Damien's hand reached out and his thumb traveled along the edge of her bottom lip, coming away with a spot of red. Even as a shadow crossed his face, Damien nodded, and Elora had to wonder if he actually trusted her to do this job and take her father's place. Or if he was waiting for her to fall apart a moment's notice.

Chapter 10

Viktor

No one had come to collect his blood despite the others around him being escorted from their cells, only to return weakened and pale hours later. They would meet his eyes with something that could be anger or jealousy if they had the strength to do more than be carried by the vampires in charge of them. Viktor spent his time watching as they came and went without any type of schedule that he could discern. All he had were his thoughts to obsess over, trying without any real luck to understand Elora's hold over him and how it had all fallen apart so quickly.

The conversation with Damien had yielded nothing and everything all at once, leaving behind more questions that he had wanted to ask before the vampire had stepped off the elevator. Viktor had expected Elora, had expected to see her with her shortened hair that suited her better than the long locks he had grown used to seeing. When he heard the chime go off and the doors slide open, he had prepared himself for another interrogation, where he would witness the battle that seemed to be waging between her head and her heart.

Viktor had seen it the night Elizabeth handed him over. While Damien had exuded the hatred he had expected, Elora's face had revealed something more complex. He had seen it the day at the apartment when he had foolishly looked back at the

73

window where he found her watching him leave. There had been glimpses of it the night Viktor had brought Elizabeth in a failed attempt to force Elora to leave with him

And he saw it now on Elora's face as he glanced up at her from his cot that was too small for him to lie on comfortably. Her hands laid at her sides, but he could see the redness around her nails where she had picked at the cuticles. Those eyes that were unnaturally bright stared at him as if he were a puzzle she was trying to figure out. A riddle she was attempting to solve. Behind the glass that separated them, he was a specimen that she was studying and it was agony. His fingers went to the scars along his cheek and neck, remnants of Lukas and Elizabeth. Both fights had left their marks on him, constant reminders of the man he had become.

"They aren't taking my blood," he stated as a way to break the silence that seemed to stretch on and she smirked at him, the light in her eyes glowing bright somehow.

"I don't need you broken before I rip out every drop of information from you." Viktor shrugged. Despite the harshness of the words themselves, there was no vitriol in them. No hatred or even anger. Instead, he swore he heard the tiniest hint of the dry sarcasm he had sought out while they were a nurse and a patient at the hospital.

"And what information do you want this time?" He leaned forward towards the glass, arms resting on his thighs as he waited for her to begin. She seemed to study him for a moment, eyes wandering over his newly washed hair to the scars before her focus darted to something behind him.

"Since we already covered my sister, I suppose we move on to your friends. The Resistance." He opened his mouth to start forming an excuse, but she lifted her finger to her lips.

"I'll tell you when it's time to talk." Elora paused and raised a single brow as if daring him to speak. When he didn't even blink in response, she smiled slightly.

"I already know the basics. Denise gave me a little synopsis before you had her killed. My blood as a weapon or cure. They would need to take more and more until there was nothing left of me." Viktor listened as she rattled off these facts as if she were naming her favorite shows. There was a boredom to her tone and her hands moved slightly as she spoke, gesturing one way and then the other. He inclined his head, considering exactly how much Denise would have been able to tell her. And then there was the question of how she had done it. He wanted to protest Elora's summary of events, her accusation that Viktor had Denise shot that night.

"I didn't know she was going to be there." Her eyes snapped to him, heated with fury and he reined in the urge to back away.

"The goal is eradicating the vampires and I'm assuming Elizabeth, along with those she has turned, is included in that." Another silent nod from him. "My question then is about specifics. Names. Addresses. I want to know who and where they are."

"You're going to attack them." A flash of hurt raced across her face before she schooled it once more into stone. He didn't want to believe that she would go after them, but every edge of hers had been sharpened into a weapon that he knew she would use to remove any threat that surrounded her. From what he had heard from the gossiping vampires, Elora's enemies were falling one by one, which only made him question why he was still there.

"I'm going to protect myself if I need to. Nothing more. Nothing less. They started this, Viktor. Not me." His mouth opened and closed as he tried desperately to contradict her, but every reason he could conjure fell short. The Resistance had gone after her first, had drawn her into a game she never knew was be-ing played.

"I want to be left alone. I want to exist. Not as a source. Not as the first of my kind and some type of abomination, but as me. And I will destroy everything in order to get that." He turned towards her, noting the vulnerability in her confession. But was that even possible for her? Even after murdering Killian and Darian, she was still a prize to be caught, a tool to be used. For each enemy torn down, there seemed to be two more.

"Everything? Everyone?" The question seemed to draw her out of some daydream that had ripped her out of reality, and she blinked as if registering his questions.

"Yes." The answer was so simple and said with such malice and promise that fear replaced any other thought or emotion in him.

"That isn't the woman I knew." Her eyes darkened to the point that the light in them seemed to vanish, leaving behind two dark pools of ink.

"The woman you knew was shattered. Body and mind. Now that I am piecing myself back together, I refuse to let anyone stop that. And I have the means to do that now."

"I heard about that. Two bodies on the floor of Ravenwell manor is quite the way to demand loyalty. Is the plan to kill any-one who doesn't recognize you as head? What about choice?"

"I gave them a fucking choice!" Her voice echoed down the hallway before her eyes closed and she took a deep breath, as if centering herself. "They could stay or leave. They picked a third option and paid the price."

"And what about humans, Elora? Are you just going to leave them to their fate as food? Kill off everyone who worked for Thorne? Even the people who only cooked meals?" Viktor stood from the cot and approached the glass until his face was mere inches from it. Without it in place, he could reach out and touch her cheek as he had so many times before. The desire was almost overwhelming, and he felt his fingers twitch slightly.

"Are you planning on letting them remain a source for your kind? Keep them ignorant until something happens and the person they love is killed? Or worse, turned?" It was pain and interest in her eyes as she listened to each question he posed.

"Is that what happened to you? I always wondered how you ended up with them." Elora seemed to be attempting a nonchalant tone but failed. Underneath the boredom she tried to project was genuine curiosity. He studied his hands for a moment, studying the nails that had grown long and the calluses that had developed over the years. What would it matter if he told her? If he laid his soul bare for her to see? It felt like a fair trade in a way. After all, he had seen the darkest parts of her, had borne witness to the nightmares and memories that came back in flashes.

"His name was Jaime. We started dating in high school and stayed together in college, living in a dirty apartment. I was taking my nursing classes and he wanted to study viruses and such." He let out a breath as she reclined against the wall and waited, allowing him to progress through this at his own pace.

"The school raised tuition, and Jaime was struggling to afford it. I offered to help, but he wanted to pay his own way. A pride thing, I guess. I knew he picked up a second job, but he said he was working in a lab. I didn't ask questions. Then, he suggested we turn."

"Neither one of us were sheltered from knowing vampires existed. There are large pockets of the city that know. Especially those with money. It's how they protect themselves and offer those without money as food." She made a sound of disgust at his explanation. Viktor hadn't expected any other reaction from her. He had tried to make Thorne see that Elora was someone they could work with, not simply use up and toss aside.

Maybe if Thorne had listened, he wouldn't be in a cell and Elora wouldn't be fighting a battle on all sides.

"I said no," Viktor continued after a heartbeat. "Jaime was being paid to be a source and had grown close to one of the vampires who fed from him. They convinced Jaime that turning was wonderful and he got this romantic notion in his head that if we turned, we could live together forever. We fought, and he turned anyway. The first few weeks or months are the hardest if the vampire doesn't have help. And he didn't. The bastard left him in an alleyway and Jaime made his way home to me with a trail of Resistance members following him."

"I killed him. It was self-defense and I know that. But it doesn't stop the guilt. They helped me clean it up and I joined that night. No questions asked." Viktor didn't even glance at Elora as he finished his story. Instead, his focus was back on the hands that had held the knife that stabbed Jaime in a dozen different places, that had held him as he bled out and was unable to heal from the sheer amount of blood lost. It was quiet for a long moment. Or maybe only a few seconds. He wasn't sure until he heard her shift and let out a breath.

"I don't have a kind, Viktor. You know that. Even Elizabeth isn't a perfect replica of me. Not the way vampires become replicas of the one who turned them. And no, I don't plan on that at all." No comment on the tale. No cruel statement about how he had a habit of killing vampires. No joke about hurting those he claimed to love. Instead, there was only acceptance, as if she had absorbed his story and filed it away with everything else she held on to. If she wasn't going to force him to add to his confession, then he wouldn't offer anything else.

"Then what is your plan?" Elora grinned and shook her head. For a moment, he wasn't sure she was going to answer the question.

"Burn it down. Dismantle everything. Tell humans everything. If your leader had just spoken to me, I would have worked with them. Made a deal of some sort. Even if everything in the hospital was a lie, you should know that." The last part of her statement was spat out with such venom, Viktor was almost sure it would infect him if possible. He nodded slowly, staring at his bare feet as the guilt ate at him.

"I'm sorry for that. I need you to know that." She let out a harsh breath that may have been a laugh and he pressed his fingers to the glass, suddenly desperate to explain himself. Every time they had met since that parking garage where his involvement with the Resistance had been revealed, it had been as two opposing sides. There had been no time to explain when the only thought in his mind was finally proving himself to Thorne.

"I stopped giving them information after that breakdown you had. It had been a really bad session with Denise. One of the early ones where she tried hypnosis. Remember?" She nodded as a distant look crossed her face. "You had broken down in the day room and used something to hurt yourself, screaming they couldn't take you back."

"You held my arms down, but didn't sedate me. Told me a story while I cried in your arms." A soft smile spread across his lips at the memory. The other patients had been dragged back to their own rooms in order to let the nurses deal with her. Even then, she had gained a reputation for her violence and what she could accomplish when she lashed out. No one had known she had somehow gained a paperclip from the nurses' station and held onto it. Viktor had frozen for only a moment before he wrapped his arms around her and pulled her close, whispering a story about a girl who fell into a storybook. With each word he had said, she had softened, and the tears had ceased, leaving only her limp form behind.

"I bandaged the wounds, and you told me about your nightmares. About how you always dreamed about someone taking you away to hurt you. From then on, we talked every day during my shift. And my reports back to them became less detailed."

"So, you grew a conscious? Came to realize that what you were doing was wrong?"

"I think I came to see what Denise saw. A woman who only wanted to heal. Who wanted peace and friendship. You weren't a potential weapon or cure anymore. You were Elora." He shrugged and heard her sharp intake of breath.

"I loved you." Her whisper was barely audible despite the silence in the hallway.

"I know," he replied, preparing himself for one more confession. "And I loved you. Just not in the same way, which makes what I did even worse."

Viktor almost admitted that what he did feel even now was difficult to deal with. But he at least understood it. It wasn't the love that he had felt for Jaime, but the type one felt for a sibling. The kind that made someone want to do nothing more than protect them, and the breakdown had been the catalyst for that.

"I want names, Viktor. I want addresses." He shook his head, realizing that this may well be the moment he signed his own death warrant. Slowly, he sank back down onto the cot and accepted whatever would come now.

"I can't. It would mean their deaths, and you know it."

"Did you not listen to a single word I said? I don't want to kill anyone. I don't want to go in there and murder each human I find."

"Maybe not you, but those you send. You can't promise their safety from other vampires. Not even you have that type of power."

"Then you're no longer useful to me, and that was the only thing protecting you."

"You can't scare or threaten me into talking." He knew his statement sounded more confident than he truly felt and the unease rushing through his veins only grew more intense as she stepped forward until her nose almost touched the glass. Her breath fogged the barrier between them as she stared at him for a long moment. His heart raced in his chest, pounding against his ribs, becoming more and more painful by the second.

"I could make you, Viktor. I could command you to tell me every secret you've ever had. Tell me every dark thought, every hidden shame. And then, I could force you to slam your head against this glass over and over until you either fell unconscious or dead." Underneath the harshness of her words and the darkness of the threat, there was an undercurrent of pain that unraveled every part of the picture she painted for him. He closed his eyes and shook his head before meeting her gaze once more, refusing to look away even though he knew exactly what she was promising him.

"Humans have never had a choice. This would be no different. I just never thought you would be the one to take it away." Her hand reflexively reached for her collarbones, for the scars that lined her skin there. The words had been perfectly crafted, aimed at the weak spot he knew existed inside her healing psyche. And there was still something he wanted to test, something that had bothered him since Damien's visit.

"It seems humans don't have much choice when it comes to you." His heart sank to his feet as her face instantly paled and her eyes became saucers. Her mouth hung open for only a moment as panic seemed to flood her system, spilling out until it threatened to drown them both. Without a word to contradict him, Elora turned and fled, leaving only his confirmation behind.

Chapter 11

Thorne

Thorne had all the workers leave the house before Korina pulled up and parked in the driveway. There was a tightness to the vampire's movements as she came up the walkway to the front door. Not a hint of the confidence or ease that Korina had exhibited during the last meeting was there. Each step was heavy while her shoulders slumped in, making her body appear concave, as if it were folding in on itself. At the sight, Thorne took a deep breath and centered herself as the doorbell rang through the house.

In the brief moment it took to open the door, Korina had transformed from the broken vampire that had walked up to the house to the confident and threatening woman Thorne had originally met.

"You have an update?"

"Isn't that what the message said?" Thorne smirked at the ire in Korina's voice. Whatever had happened to warrant this meeting must have rattled the vampire beyond simple irritation. After Thorne shifted slightly to the side, Korina marched in and stood in the center of the room, limbs rigid and stiff as if she were turning to stone. And for reasons Thorne didn't quite understand, her heart went out to her. At her core, she recognized the ghost that seemed to haunt her, the undeniable desire to be not only loved, but respected. That wasn't something Korina had received from Killian. Thorne knew that more than anyone else. Underneath the promises and declarations and poetry, she had been a means to an end. The combination of two desires merged into one package. An insult to the Corvin family and the means to create what would grant him more power. It had taken so long for her to understand that, and by the time she did, Elora had been born. Only then did she find out what Killian had done to their daughter at a genetic level, and it was too late to do anything about it.

"She gave me a job," Korina began, not bothering to hide the ire in her tone. "I'm to stay at the Ravenwell Manor and report back any rumors or gossip."

"An informant. Decent job to have." Thorne's response was met with a derisive chuckle and a shake of Korina's head.

"It isn't what Chloe was hoping for. She wanted something that would keep me at Elora's side, but I guess he talked to her before I managed to meet with her. Fucked the whole thing up." The vampire collapsed onto the couch and leaned forward, head hanging down towards her knees where her arms rested. Thorne said nothing in response as she pulled a chair from the dining table and positioned herself across the room, reclining against the back. It was nearly impossible to keep her mouth shut, to not let the question lingering behind her teeth out. In the end, Thorne failed.

"And what could he have said that messed it all up that badly?" Korina didn't move or react to the question, as if she had expected it to come.

"All compliments, I'm sure," she responded sarcastically, before taking a deep breath. Korina's gaze traveled across the room, probably noting the blank walls. The thumbtacks were left behind after they took down the maps and notes that listed their research and locations. Addresses and phone numbers. They may be working together, but there were limits to the shared information. Especially where humans who had killed vampires were concerned.

"Any word on the sister?" Korina finally broke her silence after a long moment. It was clear whatever Damien had done bothered the vampire immensely. Hurt her, even.

"Only more missing person reports. Rumors of families going missing. There doesn't seem to be any rhyme or reason to who gets chosen or turned. We even tried to see if there were any clusters or common areas, but there's nothing." Thorne leaned forward as frustration flushed her system, forcing her to jump to her feet and start walking towards the wall where the map had been.

"Either the sister is incredibly smart or there just isn't anything to find in her chaos."

"You're telling me your people haven't been able to find anything? Not even hints or rumors? I thought you said canvasing the streets would work." Thorne bristled at the accusation, at the insinuation that her team wasn't doing their job correctly. The problem was Elizabeth's plan was exceedingly simple—turn humans and set them loose.

"I have people trying to capture someone turned by Elizabeth's group. We can question them, and they can lead us to them," she explained, desperate to keep the annoyance from her voice.

"And if that doesn't work?" Korina's question brought to mind a few options, each more unsavory than the last. This very question had kept her awake most nights, ever since it became clear that it wasn't going to be simple to find and capture Elizabeth. Thorne had underestimated her, had discounted her as insane and incapable of anything like this. Viktor had paid the price along with every human who had come in contact with her growing cult. The best alternative plan she had developed involved once more using the tie that connected Elora to her sister, even if it had gone disastrously wrong the first time it was attempted.

"I did have an idea. Well, a vague plan," she reluctantly admitted and Korina adjusted, suddenly interested in everything Thorne had to say.

"We use her." There was no question who Thorne was referring to based on the vampire's reaction. It was pure excitement, an almost frantic energy to enact whatever this scheme would include.

"I don't know how much Chloe told you, but there is a tie between her and every vampire turned by her. And by extension, Elizabeth. It's how we found her the first time. We could use that tie to draw Elizabeth out." Korina jumped to her feet, pacing back and forth over the worn carpet as Thorne spoke.

"The question," Thorne continued, watching the vampire with some hesitation, "is how we get her." Instantly, Korina stopped as if the threads of the carpet had grown and latched onto her feet, rooting her in place before she turned towards Thorne. Her eyes were bright as she began speaking, hesitantly at first, before the words began rushing out in a never-ending stream.

"Damien. We take Damien. She'll come for him. But we'll need to be prepared for her." Word of her violence had reached everyone, it seemed. After the display at Ravenwell, Elora had become feared and begrudgingly respected by most. In their community, strength was prized above all else and she had that in abundance. It wasn't just physical. The strength it took to rip a heart from a chest or to slice open two vampires until they bled out on the floor was impressive, but it was more than that. Thorne had heard about the speech at the wedding and about the gown itself. There had been pictures delivered shortly after her meeting with Chloe that had provided crucial context. She should have felt repulsion. Anger. Disgust. Instead, it was pride and that was an emotion that had to be shoved down so deep inside her that it would never surface.

"You think she will come for him? That she will come herself?" The plan had merit if Elora was as attached as Korina seemed to believe she was.

"Yes." The response was firm and direct, leaving no room for disagreement or questions. Thorne wasn't stupid enough to not realize that Korina had her own stake in this beyond gaining control of Elora and finding Elizabeth. Damien seemed to be almost an obsession for Korina, leaving her willing to do anything to steal him away. But did she truly believe he would come crawling to her when she helped kidnap him?

Thorne wanted to shake Korina by the shoulders and slap her across the face until she gained some semblance of rationality. No man or vampire was worth any of this. Thorne knew intimately how all-consuming seeking their validation and affection could become. It is what Killian had preyed on, granting her small smiles and gifts and promises until she was putty in the palm of his hand. Maybe if she had been stronger, they wouldn't be here planning the abduction of one vampire in order to capture her only child. Thorne shook her head slightly. Guilt had no place here and she would not take the blame for Killian's greed and ambition, nor his sick fantasies. There was only one thing in her life she felt regret for and it wasn't that.

"Do you have any idea how to accomplish this? I doubt we can just take him from the Tower." Thorne watched as the vampire began to pace once more, hands twitching at her sides as her eyes darted around the room. She wasn't seeing anything. Thorne knew that much. Thoughts and plans were connecting in that mind of hers until Korina stopped.

"I am supposed to tell her if there are any rumors or threats being made at the Ravenwell manor. I could tell her that there have been a few. Vampires who are angry about her being in charge and wanting to try to take over by killing her."

Thorne nodded, a small smile on her lips as she listened to Korina explain the plan. It was detailed to the point that Thorne wasn't sure if the vampire was making it up in the moment or had considered this before.

"Do you need Chloe's approval for this? For your part in it?" Thorne asked as she mulled over the details that had been outlined. Korina nodded and pulled out her phone, eyes dazed a bit as if she was coming out of a dream. A one-sided conversation filled the room as Thorne retreated to the kitchen to make herself some tea. Chamomile, this time. It would ease the rising anxiety that was filling her body, threatening to cause her hands to shake. She had planned and executed dozens of missions that resulted in deaths—both vampires and humans. Over and over she had sent her people to die in raids on vampire compounds or steal stores of blood to hurt the overall supply. It had always been justifiable to her. They were hurting the group that kept them under their thumbs and controlled every aspect of their lives. It had been the part that led to her refusing to turn. Having a pinnacle role in that system was too much.

The fact that Thorne knew Killian was raging with every successful mission she ordered had also helped her sleep better at night. Hushed words filtered in as she put the kettle on the stove and grabbed a mug from the cabinet. Each dish in the kitchen had been donated or bought from a thrift store, leaving them the strangest collection of styles and humor. This one said, "you're tea-riffic." A terrible pun that always brought a small grin to her face.

Despite the deep breaths, Throne's hands still shook slightly as she finished preparing her drink and took a sip, hoping it would finally do its job. It wasn't the plan itself, which she knew. There was little chance of loss of life, even if it was a failure.

And any risks could potentially be dealt with beforehand. Was it the possibility of coming face-to-face with her? Would she recognize Thorne? Would Thorne know her daughter? And what if she was forced to attack her? Kill her?

"Chloe approves. But she wants access to Damien once we have him." Thorne raised a brow before taking another drink. She had considered interrogating their captive while they had him. Damien had been Killian's right-hand enforcer, which meant he would have information that could prove useful. Not just locations or hierarchies, but technology. He could give them access to the scientific reports Killian had hidden away. Even before everything had begun, he had been secretive about Elora. No one was allowed to know what exactly was done or what the results had been.

For what?" Korina shrugged at the question. Either she hadn't asked or that information was being withheld. For a moment, Thorne debated demanding that Korina tell her what Chloe was planning by appealing to their shared interests in protecting the city.

"She can have him once I'm done." Thorne laid the tea bag in the sink and watched the vampire for a reaction. Nothing. Her eyes had a distant sheen to them as if she were lost in her thoughts. Korina was going to end up being a problem and Chloe had to know that. It was obvious in every word that Korina said about Damien and Elora and their relationship that she could not be fully trusted here.

"Korina. Did you hear me?" Korina jumped slightly as if pulled from a daze and stared at Thorne like she was trying to reconnect to reality. Maybe that was what was wrong here. A fractured reality. A poisoned sense of self. It was common enough from what Thorne remembered of her time with Killian. Humans turned into vampires in the hope it would fix something deep inside them. In their minds, becoming a vampire was the cure for every disease that ravaged their bodies and minds, the banishment of every ghost that haunted them. They didn't realize until it was too late that turning only dragged the demons along with them, rendering them inescapable forever. What had Korina's life been before she turned? What curses had she dragged along with her?

"Yes. Chloe has access to him once you are done. I'm assuming you plan on questioning him." Thorne nodded as Korina seemed to regain a sense of self and adjusted her disguise once more. Cocky and exuding a sense of danger as she studied Thorne and the almost empty cup in her hand.

"I do. If I have someone as knowledgeable as Damien in my grasp, it would be foolish to not take advantage of the opportunity."

"And if he refuses to answer your questions?" There it was. The hesitation that Thorne knew would eventually make its appearance. This was the undercurrent of every decision Korina had made to this point. Damien. He was her obsession, and Thorne's heart broke just a bit for her.

"You know the answer to that." A tiny, choked sound fell from her lips before she turned away, no doubt developing a contingency plan that could undermine this entire operation.

"He won't give you answers. He's stronger than that. He's overcome more than you can imagine." Thorne nodded, not doubting the truth in her words. But it meant nothing. She had made dozens of men break, dozens of vampires. He would be no different.

Chapter 12

Damien

This was the only floor in the Tower he had never visited. The labs where Killian had both humans and vampires working on various research projects hadn't intersected with his own missions. Instead, he had accepted that an entire laboratory existed within the confines of the Tower and didn't ask questions about why they would need one. Or about what type of research would be conducted.

Now that he was in there, it was strangely both exactly what he had expected and the opposite. Everything was gleaming and pristine, with each piece of furniture in shades of white or pale gray. Simply stepping off the elevator had been a shock to his system which had come to expect black and red from Killian's decor choices. Though he supposed Elora was steadily working to undermine that. The office had been the first to fall and be stripped of anything that resembled the previous vampire head. Then it had been Killian's personal rooms. Damien didn't say a word as specific pieces of art were removed from the walls and found themselves stacked in the sitting room with a large cloth draped over the various canvases and frames. If he pulled back the covering and glanced into the bottom corner, he knew he would see two initials—I.A.

Iris Ashcroft.

It was embarrassing how long it had taken him to figure out who they belonged to. He had walked past those paintings every day, had watched Killian move them if there was a possibility that they would be damaged during an interrogation. Again, he had never questioned it and now questions were all he had. Why would Killian keep the paintings Iris created if he had used her? Were they there as a reminder of the human he loved and lost? Or a reminder to never allow someone to betray him?

The answers were in the journals that Elora had been poring over during every spare second of the day, reading late into the night. More than once, he had pulled her into his arms when she had begun to weep over what she had learned. Her body had shaken with her sobs as she seemed to absorb Killian's innermost thoughts. There was a unique cruelty to the process, as if Killian was torturing her from beyond the grave. A final joke.

"The lead scientist on the project is in that office there." Silas's voice dragged him back to the uncomfortably bright room filled with long tables and machines that Damien knew had cost a fortune. Bodies in lab coats either stood at the various stations with goggles and gloved hands or walked around the space as if their trio was not standing there watching it all.

Elora moved first, stepping towards the young woman who had pointed them in the right direction. No other thought was spared as Damien and Silas fell in line behind Elora, who marched into the office full of filing cabinets and shelves lined with books. Damien's focus moved over the space, noting the lack of windows and personal knickknacks. No photos of family members or drawings done by children. Not even a personalized name plate. The office was as nondescript as the person currently occupying the space behind the desk. An older female vampire with severe features. In a way, she was almost a perfect twin for Denise and from the slight intake of breath he heard come from Elora, he knew she had seen exactly what he had.

Her silver hair was pulled back into a low bun and pale blue eyes lined with crow's feet stared out at the three of them with something akin to curiosity and resignation.

"Please, sit. I have a feeling this will take a bit of time." Her voice was deep and raspy as she extended a slightly gnarled hand towards the chair in front of her. There were only two, and Damien took a step aside to allow Silas to take the second one. Elora sank into the thinly padded seat and crossed her legs before resting her hands in her lap. Slowly, she seemed to bury her fingers into the folds of her blouse, gripping the fabric and Damien clasped his hands behind his back to prevent him from reaching out for her. Their relationship hadn't been made public yet and a show of comfort wouldn't exactly fit into the roles they were portraying.

That was a different conversation to have, even if it kept being postponed. He hadn't decided what he wanted to be known as in relation to her. There had never been two vampire heads who ruled side-by-side in the Ashcrofts or the Ravenwells. Instead, there was always the ruler and then the consort, if they engaged in a long-term relationship. Iris had been Killian's consort and Darian had one before she died years ago. In his wildest and most pleasant of dreams, the two of them lived somewhere where they could exist. Not as a vampire head. Not as second-in-command or consort. As simply Elora and Damien—two parts to a whole.

"Dr. Hartley, I assume?" The woman nodded at Elora's question and folded her fingers together in a move that was so reminiscent of Denise that it was almost like they were back in her office.

"It's Anne. And you're Elora. The product of one of my most ambitious research projects."

"I hope I'm not a disappointment then." Anne raised a brow at the comment before grinning softly.

"If the rumors about what is happening in the city is any indication, disappointment isn't the right word to use." Damien noted the way Elora's hand spasmed slightly, clutching the fabric a bit tighter before relaxing. Not for the first time, he found himself wishing he could solve this problem for her. But it was more complicated than taking care of Jonas. More complicated than setting the stage for her to kill her father. Elizabeth was her foster sister and Elora loved her. That much had been clear when they left the hotel and faced her on the sidewalk.

"What did Killian ask you to do?" Elora's question was curt and sharp. This was the vampire head who would demand answers and punish those who didn't give them. If Anne was smart, she would lay out all the research for Elora to consume.

The vampire across the desk sighed heavily and leaned back in her chair, eyes darting around the room as if trying to decide where to start.

"He came to me decades ago. This was before he ever met Iris, or even considered how his idea would work. It was a fever dream born out of frustration and ambition." Anne's words were slow and precise in a way that put Damien on edge. It was the cadence of someone trying to hide information, of trying to avoid lying by offering tidbits of the truth. Or perhaps easing into what would prove to be painful for those listening.

"He wanted to make a bid for being head vampire over all the families. He wanted to be a king, basically. Saw himself as a vampire emperor." A nod from Anne verified Elora's addition to the story and Damien wondered if this insight came from her knowledge of Killian or from the journals.

"Exactly. His idea was an alternative blood source. At first he didn't have any ideas on what form it would take. Instead, we experimented with human blood. We tried additives to the blood itself and then tried adding it to the water system when the first plan failed. Then, he had a dream of a physical blood source. A vampire who would act as a catalyst to an entire controlled group that would provide an improved blood alternative." Damien desperately wanted to see Elora's face while this was explained, try to see if she had known of this before now.

A slight incline of Elora's head and Anne continued after a moment, leaning forward to rest her hands on the desk.

"Even before Iris was chosen, he had made a list of what traits he wanted the source to have. What he wanted them to accomplish. At first, we didn't have the technology for it, but Killian's money knew no boundaries and he sank all of it into the program. Slowly, but surely, we designed the genetic modifications that would take place. The only hurdle then was to find a human who would have desirable traits and genes to carry the child and give birth."

"Bastard," she whispered softly and Silas scooted forward towards the desk. His folded hands hung between his knees as he seemed to study Anne, seeking any sign that a detail was missing.

"Chosen?" The word was sharp, almost begging the vampire to lie to him so he could expel some of the rage building with each detail of the story. Anne shrugged as if this was nothing more than a tale of romance and courtship, not manipulation and deceit.

"He didn't set out to use her, if that's what you're thinking. An opportunity presented itself. An insult to another family combined with a beautiful human who coincidentally fit the parameters perfectly. It helped that she was gorgeous. Killian truly was attracted to her." Silas huffed and leaned back, but Damien noted the way he had grown more tense. Muscles constricting under his perfectly tailored suit in a way that had to be painful. To think that Iris was picked simply for her beauty and ties to the Corvin family had to be agony.

"What was on the list?" Elora steered the conversation away from Iris and Damien shifted closer towards her, ignoring the way Anne's focus moved to him for just a moment. For the first time, the scientist looked uncomfortable. Perhaps even afraid, and his palms began to sweat in anticipation. Before this, Anne had been nonchalant, regaling them with Elora's creation story with the same ease one told a fairy tale to a child.

The chair squeaked slightly as Anne adjusted her position, resting back against the leather as if attempting to create distance between them.

"The list was long in the beginning, but we narrowed it down to two key traits. The first and most important was the potency of the blood itself. If it was meant to replace humans and become desirable, then it needed to be better than what was currently available. The second was—" Anne froze as her eyes darted between the three of them like she was trying to assess who would be the one to attack her once she spoke.

"The second." The cold tone that commanded obedience and promised only violence was back as Elora demanded the scientist continue. He glanced at her hands, noting the way her fingernails dug into her palms, and for a moment he could have sworn he could smell her blood. His own hand twitched slightly before he let it rest on the back of her chair, hoping she could sense it there and take some type of comfort from it.

"That the source be a beacon for humans. Irresistible no matter who they were nor their preference in partners. Neither would matter since they would draw them in without them even realizing it. It would make it easier to turn humans into a collection of sources that Killian could sell and gift to various vampires while keeping the original for himself."

A choked sound fled from Elora's mouth as the explanation hit her like a brick. Damien's mind raced back to the conversation with Viktor, the very pointed questions the human had asked about the effect Elora seemed to have on those around her. At the time, Damien had brushed it off as Viktor crafting an excuse for why he seemed to develop feelings for her. Yet, it seemed there was some merit to it.

"However, I told him that there could and probably would be unintended consequences. Playing with genetics can yield results that were not planned. Unfortunately, he never let me study you as you grew up. To try and find out if there were any unforeseen changes." Anne's brow rose as she stared at Elora, a professional curiosity lacing her features.

"We're getting tired of prompting information out of you," Silas drawled. Anne adjusted once more before she met Silas's gaze and prepared to respond to his comment.

"We don't know for sure. There were theories, but obviously nothing was substantiated considering I was denied access to her," she explained before turning to Elora, a calculating expression on her face. "I would like to remedy that now, if I can. Is there anything that's different?"

Damien wasn't sure Elora should answer as he searched for any hint that Anne could be working with someone else, gathering intel to pass on in hopes of removing Elora from her position.

"I'm afraid I don't trust you enough for that." He could imagine the grin she was displaying for the scientist. Feral and welcoming, like a predator attempting to draw in prey. A quick hint of fear flooded Anne's eyes before dissipating and she shrugged.

"My question is about undoing it." Three sets of eyes locked onto Elora once the question left her mouth. While Silas's expression was one of anxiety, Anne's own held a strange gleam as if she had been given a precious gift.

"Now, that is something Killian never pursued or even mentioned for obvious reasons. But it is intriguing. I'll need blood from you to test with. We can't change the genetic make-up completely, but we may be able to alter it." A curt nod from Elora had Anne letting out an audible exhale, as if she had been holding her breath in anticipation. Word had spread about Darian and the two Ravenwell vampires who had attacked her. The scientist obviously thought she might be next on the list, the latest body added to the growing pile.

"Go ahead. I expect an update by the end of the week." Dr. Hartley opened her mouth no doubt to protest as Elora stood, but snapped it closed at whatever was displayed on the head vampire's face.

"Of course," Anne responded smoothly before following Elora's lead and standing, gesturing towards the office door. "We can draw your blood in this room over here. Please be sure to feed once we are done. It may leave you feeling weak."

"I am familiar with the feeling." Silas flinched as if he were to blame, as if he was the one who exposed her to that sensation. The guilt her uncle still felt was almost carved into his skin, always on display for anyone who looked close enough. It was in the way he took over the remodeling of Killian's rooms, the way he stayed in the city instead of retreating to his manor in the countryside. Damien knew intimately what Silas felt. A similar guilt churned in his gut and despite Elora's reassurances that it wasn't his to bear, it never ceased its torture. He doubted it ever would, and he knew it would be the same for Silas.

And as they stood on either side of her while someone in a lab coat siphoned off her blood, Damien could only prepare for the nightmares that were sure to come for her that night.

Chapter 13

Damien

It was her sobs that woke him. Damien's arm reached out towards the other side of the bed, clutching at the empty space. In his hand were only the sheets, long since gone cold. He jerked up instantly, brushing his hair from his face. The soft light of a lamp illuminated the corner of the room where Elora was curled up in a chair, a throw blanket covering her legs while she stared at the wall before her. He couldn't see her face but noted the way her shoulders shook slightly. The journal was laid out, pages down, over her knees.

The bed didn't make a sound as he tossed the blankets aside and stood, shivering slightly at the coldness of the room. Every movement was soft as he made his way over. He followed her gaze to the painting on the wall—a garden with hedges and a collection of flowers he didn't know the name of. In the center was a rose bush with white and yellow and pink blossoms. It was the same as the one Elora wanted ripped out at Silas's gardens when she disappeared after her uncle had answered her questions. In the bottom right corner, the initials were different this time—I.H.

"Roses were my mother's favorite. He said that's why he started calling me his little rose. A term of endearment based on my mother's love of them." Damien watched her hand go to her cheek and wipe away the tears there. The blankness was back in her voice, as if her every word was devoid of any emotion or inflection. Sterile in a way that quickened his movements until he was kneeling in front of her.

Elora didn't meet his eyes but kept her focus on the painting behind him like there was something hidden in the brush strokes that would reveal everything she had forgotten. He didn't say anything as he took her hand in his own. Slowly, Damien kissed the top before moving to each fingertip and pressing his lips to the center of her palm. She shuddered slightly as her eyes fluttered shut at the sensation.

"I need you to call Silas. He needs to come now. Please." Damien's brows furrowed at the change in her demeanor. Despair had been replaced with determination even as her voice wavered slightly.

"Now?" The question tore her attention from the painting and to him, giving him a glimpse of the deep pools of green that seemed to hold every drop of pain and guilt and shame she felt. If he could, he would take it away. Remove each place where it had infected her like a surgeon removing a tumor. She deserved peace and he saw every moment of each day just how fiercely she was fighting for it. Tooth and nail, she was clawing out a space where she could simply exist.

He stood and found his phone on the nightstand. His fingers were a blur as he dialed Silas's number and waited for the vampire to answer. It only took a few rings before the call was answered.

"What's wrong?" The fear that erupted in Silas's voice was immediate, filling each syllable until there was no space for anything else.

"I don't know. She just asked me to get you here now." Damien paused and glanced back at her. She hadn't moved an inch, eyes still trained on the painting as her fingers played with the edges of the book in her lap.

"I think it's something she read. In Killian's journals. She's been obsessed with them," Damien explained in a voice so low it was almost a whisper. He wasn't sure if it was because he didn't want to disturb her or if he didn't want Elora to overhear him categorizing her as obsessed. But it was the truth. Every spare moment that wasn't dedicated to figuring out the Resistance and putting out fires because of the merging of the two families was spent on one of two things: the journals or the lab where they drew her blood. There had been no updates as far as he knew. He always came at the end of the session, scooped her up in his arms like he had the day he brought her here the first time, and took her back to her room. Elora would sleep and he would have blood ready for her, which she drank before returning to meetings and the journals.

"Give me ten minutes. I'm not far." A click as Silas hung up and Damien tossed the phone on the bed before running a hand through his hair and pulling on a t-shirt. He didn't need to be half-naked when her uncle showed up. For a moment, Damien stood frozen in place, like the floor was holding him hostage. He wanted to burn the journals, light a pyre, and throw each one in to watch them turn to ash. There was nothing in there for her but pain.

And answers. The small voice echoed in his mind as he shook his head. Yes, there were potentially answers to every question she had about herself. About her childhood. About Killian's motivations and goals along with what he wanted her to be. But they could hand those pages over to the scientists. There was no reason she needed to absorb Killian's innermost thoughts, read what he wrote after he hurt her.

He grabbed the phone once more and sent a text to the number associated with the blood storage to bring up a bottle. She hadn't noticed that he had been tracking how often she fed and how quickly she seemed to get hungry. His findings were concerning, to say the least. Once a day was the bare minimum, but twice seemed to be the optimal amount. With only one bottle, she grew irritated, lashed out more easily. If Elizabeth and the vampires who gathered outside the hotel that night were the same, then they were potentially fucked.

"Is he coming?" Her voice drew him to her like a siren's call and in a heartbeat, he was back, kneeling in front of her. Some color had returned to her cheeks, but her eyes were still rimmed with red. He slid the journal from her legs, fully expecting her to protest or grip it tighter. Instead, her hand laid on top of the blanket as she allowed him to take it and set it on the table next to her.

"Yes. He said ten minutes."

"I—" She swallowed and watched as she started to pick at the skin around her nail. Whatever she had found out, whatever she needed to tell Silas in the middle of the night, was destroying her. It was eating away at her core and he grabbed her hands to prevent any more damage to the already red and bleeding cuticles. It would heal quickly, but the damage was constant. Newly remade every day when she thought no one was watching.

Damien pulled her up, letting the blanket fall to the floor between them as she stood. He didn't say anything as she fell into his embrace, resting her forehead on his shoulder with her arms limp at her sides. His own wrapped around her waist, bringing her closer until their bodies were flush. Her movements were almost hesitant as she adjusted, moving her hands so they rested on his chest.

"Do you think—" she paused again and turned her face so her cheek was against his shirt. He was sure she could feel every beat of his heart as he waited for her to finish her question, to tell him what had caused this.

"Do you think they were successful in making me—" Again, a pause as if the words were getting caught in her throat and refusing to be voiced because it would mean her question would need an answer. He knew what she was asking without her finishing the thought. The sound that had escaped her in the lab had been enough of a clue. His mind had gone to the same people he knew that hers had—Wyatt and Viktor. Both had their own ramifications, and he could only imagine the tangled logic her own thoughts had weaved together to reinforce what she already thought of herself.

"No, I don't. I don't think they were drawn to you because of something Killian did. That doctor said not everything Killian wanted had worked."

"Then why?" His heart skipped a beat before he felt it being ripped from his chest. Slowly, he reached out and lifted her face to his, only to have his breath catch in his throat. The raw pain etched into her face felt unfathomable, like she was already drowning.

"Because you're beautiful. Fierce. Kind. Fuck, even that's an understatement, love. Viktor cared for you on his own. Wyatt saw the woman you are and fell head over heels, even if I want to punch him for it. No genetics required." Damien took a deep breath to steady his own rapid thoughts, slow the words that wanted to pour from his mouth as he explained each and every way she was perfection. She nodded slightly, but her eyes gave away how little his declaration had impacted her. It had left a mere dent in the prison Killian had built for her with every moment of abuse, every statement about her usefulness. And if it took every minute of the rest of his life, he would tear it down until she saw what he did.

"We should go to the other room. Silas will be here soon." She tiptoed and pressed a kiss to his cheek, giving him a soft smile that didn't reach the rest of her. His fingers wrapped themselves in the red coils of her hair and gently pulled her head back. Just as he had expected, her expression shifted and her eyes darkened instantly. There was something feral in her that only came out when doors were closed or blood needed to be spilled. Damien hadn't pushed it out of fear that he would be pressuring her into something she wasn't ready for. Let her lead. It was the constant refrain in his head when she pressed against him in bed or crawled into his lap in her office.

She huffed softly and moved away, letting his fingers fall to her shoulder and then skim down her ribs before lingering on her waist. His entire being emptied as she turned and grabbed the journal, gripping it tightly in her hand before going through the bedroom door to the sitting room beyond. Their timing was perfect as a knock sounded before the door opened, revealing a very flustered and anxious Silas. Damien was instantly ignored as he darted to his niece, stopping short just in front of her.

"What is it? What happened?" Silas's hand reached out and wrapped around her biceps before she handed over the journal. The fear in her expression was terrifyingly similar to what had been on her face before she revealed that she had given him her blood. A revelation was coming and it was about to upturn their world, shift their reality until it was no longer recognizable. The only sound was their breathing as Silas took the journal and opened it to the page Elora had marked. Her arms wrapped around her body as she turned away, moving towards the shelves where a line of photos stood.

Every trinket Killian had gathered had been removed, had been thrown in a room somewhere in the Tower and forgotten. In their place was a small collection of frames containing pictures. Each one had come from Silas's home, gifted to Elora along with the remodel of Killian's rooms. Some were of her—all wide smiles and eyes filled with mischief. Others had Silas and Elora side by side or candid shots of them together reading or gardening, which was not a pastime Damien had expected the vampire to take part in. Only a few held photos of Iris, smiling and somewhat sad as she seemed to stare directly at the camera. There was only one that had both Elora and her mother.

"This can't be true, Elora. He has to be lying."

"Why would he lie in his own journal? For what reason?" Her voice was small as she stared at a photo of Iris, and Damien itched to go to her. But his focus was on Silas, who looked like every truth he had ever known was a lie.

"He's lying!" Silas had never raised his voice that Damien had heard and the reaction was instant. Elora flinched and recoiled slightly from the sound while Damien stepped forward, preparing to intervene and force Silas to apologize to his niece. But there were tears in his eyes as he dropped to his knees on the carpet, the journal lying open before him. Elora was instantly at her uncle's side, kneeling on the ground and wrapping him in her arms. His head lay on her shoulder as he seemed to melt into her, both of them weeping for whatever they had learned.

Damien adverted his gaze from the scene and picked up the journal, opening to the page she had marked for Silas. Slowly, with their sobs as background noise, Damien read each line. He could hear Killian's voice in his ear as he read, like he was in the room, standing behind him speaking into his ear.

The bitch got away. Her body was gone when they went to collect it. I'm impressed as much as I'm angry. I had beaten her within an inch of her life. Stabbed her multiple times and left her barely breathing on the carpet, which will need to be replaced.

We had wanted to keep her body, collect as many usable parts of her as possible for future experiments. Considering we lost my rose and everything she had to offer, I needed Iris's body. But she's gone, either taken by someone else or by crawling out. I don't know. But I intend to find out.

His breathing had grown quicker the longer he read, as he absorbed the reality of Killian's explanation. She wasn't dead. Silas's sister. Elora's mother. Somewhere out there in the city or the world, Iris was possibly living and breathing within a new existence. A new name. New family and reality.

Damien let the journal hang from his hand before he tossed it on the chair, focusing now on the uncle and niece who had indeed learned that every truth they had thought they knew was a lie.

Somewhere out there, Iris was alive.

Chapter 14

Damien

The knock on the office door was far from welcomed and Damien considered ignoring it. After all, he had Elora laid out on the desk making the most delicious sounds. He had been leisurely making his way down her body, kissing and nipping every exposed bit of skin. But that had come to an end in a flurry of adjusting clothing and smoothing out her hair before Elora assumed her position behind the desk, waiting for him to let whoever was there in.

It also happened to be the last person he wanted to see at any given time. Korina's nose crinkled slightly as she took in his appearance and he smirked before moving aside, allowing her to move into the room with that easy grace she always had. This time, Korina's eyes didn't seem to travel over the walls or furniture, judging the choices made in the remodel. There was something firmer about her demeanor, like she was on a mission that needed to be completed. She stopped a couple feet before the desk, staring at Elora as Damien returned to her side.

"You said to report if I heard anything." Elora nodded before interlacing her fingers and setting them on the desk. "There have been threats made. A plan to remove you from power and take your place."

Damien shifted slightly as his hands clenched. He had expected this to happen but had hoped it wouldn't. Elora's display at Ravenwell should have been enough to stave off any ambitious vampires. If it had been Killian or Darian, it would have been. But her reputation had been built before she even took power. They had all made up their minds about her once she stepped into the banquet in the Tower.

"Is that all the details you have?"

"It's two vampires who are friends with one of the ones who attacked during your appearance at the manor. I think it would be smart to capture these two and gather more information. There may be more involved."

"All you have is a report of vague rumors about someone wanting to hurt me? That's fairly standard, so I'm not seeing how this is a risk." Damien stared at her, shocked at the nonchalance of her tone and the fact she wasn't taking this seriously. Once more, there was that lack of self-preservation he had seen so many times before. It led to problems and it would this time as well if they weren't careful. They needed to look into this. It didn't matter if they discovered nothing. It wasn't worth the risk.

"I disagree. Respectfully, of course," Korina amended quickly. "If rumors and threats are left uninvestigated, it would show weakness. Whether they're actual threats isn't the point. It's about appearances and shows of force." Damien agreed with every word out of Korina's mouth, no matter how difficult it was to admit.

"Let me discuss it with Damien. I'll call you when you're needed. Don't go far." Korina inclined her head before spinning on her heel and leaving the room. There was a moment of silence as they both seemed to think through the report.

"What do you think?" Elora's question lingered for a moment as Damien rounded the desk and leaned forward, palms flat on the wood.

"I think it would be smart to look into it. As much as I hate saying it, Korina has a point."

"It could also be nothing. It could also be a lie. You said she couldn't be trusted."

"You're right. I did say that. But it doesn't change the fact that I think we should check on this. This is a matter of you trusting my judgement." Elora nodded, but Damien didn't miss the brief flash of hurt in her eyes. He took a deep breath and returned to her side, staring down at her as he brushed a knuckle across her cheek. Her eyes fluttered shut at the contact, just as they did every time he touched her.

"I trust your judgement," she whispered and opened her eyes once more, revealing the fear lingering behind the disguise she wore. It didn't matter to Elora that her life may be in danger or that there were threats out there. That was simply a fact of her existence. Her fear was for him, that she would lose him, and he understood that because it was the same for him. It was why he needed to investigate this to at least try to make the world a bit safer for her.

"We'll go over there now. I'll find them and extract any information they have. If it's a true threat, I'll dispose of them." Damien knelt in front of her so he could see every detail of her face. "And I'll report to you regularly." She leaned into him and pressed a kiss to his lips, lingering for a moment as if savoring the feeling.

"Fine. Bring her back in. I want this over with. I wasn't done with you." He gave her a wicked smile before standing and doing as she commanded.

His desperation matched hers.

Damien hadn't been done with her either.

* * *

If Korina's report was true, then it meant that the growing pains he had expected were in full force. Since Elora couldn't kill everyone who opposed her, it was his job to stave off any signs of aggression. Concrete and potentially credible threats couldn't be dismissed. And despite his instinct to distrust anything that came out of Korina's mouth, Elora deserved for him to check this. Just because she couldn't remove every potential threat didn't mean he couldn't.

"Who made these threats?" Damien switched off the music that had been playing and twisted in the passenger seat to study Korina. Her focus was on the road, hands gripping the steering wheel tightly while her perfectly arched eyebrows were threaded together.

"Like I said, they're friends or something of the ones she stabbed. Bryan was one of them. And that other one who never leaves his side. Jake? No, Jacob." She seemed to be working through the information she had overheard, as if the details were hazy.

"And you think they're an actual concern?" Damien wasn't sure they were, but that didn't mean he wouldn't deal with them. At the very least, it sent a message that threats wouldn't be tolerated. It was a show of force that regrettably Killian would have approved of, but he wasn't about to tell Elora that. She already feared that she was her father's daughter. He could see it in the subtle doubt that flashed behind each action, underlined each statement or order. Maybe that was always the plight of children with terrible parents. A curse that followed them through their life. A parasite that fed off the insecurity and terror that one day they would make the same mistakes and hurt the same people, morph into the monster they had fought so hard to escape.

Korina shrugged slightly as she turned down the road that would take them directly to Ravenwell. Large houses lined the street, each surrounded by iron fences and hedges. Some had trees in the front yard, blocking the view of the front, but they all looked the same as if they had been traced from the same outline. Copied and pasted like some type of unhinged utopian fantasy.

"I think you should talk to them. You were always talented at getting information, weren't you?" Damien felt the corner of his lip curl slightly at her comment. Coaxing intel from Killian's enemies or prisoners had been a skill he had developed over the years, starting a few months after he had been turned. Murdering his father had placed Damien high on the vampire's list of those he saw as useful. With each body, human and vampire, that had been dragged into Killian's office for Damien to play with, his skill had improved and the victim lived longer until it was practically an art form.

"How do you know they'll be here?" Korina took a long moment before answering his question as he waited. Unease swirled in his gut while a plan formulated in his mind. If the two vampires were there, it would be easy to isolate them and demand answers. Darian would have rooms for interrogation and other activities, if the rumors were to be believed. His hands clenched as they did whenever that piece of shit ventured into his thoughts. If those rooms did exist, Damien had no doubt that Elora would have found herself in one of them if her plan had failed.

"I honestly don't, Damien. But they always return to the manor. Even if they aren't there right now, they will be." The manor came into view, along with a line of cars parked over to the side. His focus went to each one, counting them and noting the make and models. Nothing seemed out of the ordinary. Nothing was different from his previous visit with Elora. Korina parked them in the same area as the others before getting out and waiting for him to follow. There was none of her easy confidence or allure present, but there hadn't been since the night Darian died. If Damien didn't know better, he would have thought there was something between her and him that had left Korina a partial shell. But he wasn't sure if she could even feel love like that, only obsession and ambition and rage.

Damien adjusted his shirt as he followed her towards the manor and searched along the windows for any signs that there was a threat waiting for him. He didn't imagine that solving this problem and dealing with traitors would be welcomed. If Elora was unpopular, then he would be guilty by association. Not that it was a problem, but it did put a target on his back and he needed to be prepared for it. He would willingly take any hit necessary if it kept her safe.

"I'm actually surprised you told her about it. I thought for sure you were going to be creating problems, not trying to fix them." Korina hesitated as she reached for the handle and opened it. He could almost see her collecting her thoughts, pulling her emotions under control, and it put him on edge.

The manor was silent as they stepped inside. Not a single vampire wandered up or down one of the hallways. No voices trailed out from the multiple rooms on the ground floor. It felt deserted, and he wondered if the vampires had taken Elora at her word, leaving to join Radcliff or Corvin.

"I know your opinion of me has decreased lately, but that's quite rude."

"In what way? You called her an abomination." He felt the irritation return as he outlined the reason for his opinion of her. She scoffed and pushed her hair off her shoulder before jerking her head towards the hallway to their left.

"It seemed like the best option for me at the time."

"She isn't an option for you to pick up and then toss aside when something else comes along."

"The two of you are absolutely disgusting. Did you know that? It's sickening to see how soft she's made you." He bristled at her accusation. Only part of him had eased, melted under her touch, cracked under her smile and laughter. That part of him belonged only to her and the rest of him remained as dark and violent as it had been before he dragged her into his life.

"There's nothing soft about what she does to me." Korina gave him a repulsed expression before nodding towards a door a few feet away from them.

"I doubt that child knows much of anything," she spat, and he pushed past her. He didn't believe that it was love that made Korina behave this way. It was an obsession, a desire to own him in every conceivable way. In the alley, she had said that he was the only one who had been kind to her. She wanted to possess that, use it every time she found herself retreating.

"She could teach you a thing or two." Damien inched open the door, eyes peering into every corner of the room as he searched for the vampires he was meant to deal with. He felt her behind him, hovering in the doorway.

"Is she frigid, Damien? I imagine that after everything, she doesn't enjoy being touched. Or maybe she enjoyed it and is only playing the victim now." He spun towards her, hands clenched into fists as he met her expression. Elora wouldn't mind too much if he dealt with Korina at the same time.

"She's everything you aren't, Korina. And you better remember that. Insult her again, and I'll kill you."

"Which is why I don't regret this." Damien felt the bodies filling the room behind him and before he could turn to fight, a syringe plunged into his neck and he fell to the ground.

Korina's grinning face was the last thing he saw.

Chapter 15

Elora

Killian's words on the journal page in her hand were gibberish as she attempted to decipher her own annotations in the margins. It was a strange process to write comments and questions alongside her father's innermost thoughts. It was a conversation that would never happen. There would be no answers to the questions she posed, no rebuke for the curses she lobbied at him. Her obsession with reading each word and page had only grown after the visit with the scientists. Only now, Elora was attempting to focus on entries about either her mother or what Killian had attempted to do. The lab report and notes were useless even when they were explained in simple terms. Even the vaguest of references had led to another tiny sticky note to mark the page. Red for mentions of her mother. Purple for anything to do with genetics and experimentation.

Yet now, the words had ceased to have meaning, simply became a collection of letters that made no sense when combined together into words and sentences. Damien leaving with Korina had left her body tightly wound, leaving her desperate to escape her skin. Every instinct had screamed at her to tell him they should wait before doing anything. They should investigate the claims instead of taking Korina's report at face value. Or Elora could deal with the problem herself. What type of leader did she look like when she sent others to deal with threats made against her? Weak. She appeared weak and maybe that had been Korina's goal.

And it had been hours since they left. Hours since there had been any update or message. It felt wrong even as someone knocked on the door to the sitting room.

"Come in." There was only one person it could be with Damien gone and even though she knew it wasn't him, Elora still hoped it would be him who came in the door. And her heart sank when it was Silas.

"You needed me?" he asked as he stood before her where she sat on the couch in her sitting room. A sense of foolishness rushed through her as she gestured towards the chair beside her and prepared to explain why she forced him to come to the Tower so late. It had to be past midnight and there was always the chance she was overreacting to the lead pit in her gut that screamed something was wrong. Korina wasn't trustworthy in the slightest amount but Elora had wanted to give her a chance. Being used and underestimated was an experience they shared, but Elora had been naive to believe that it meant anything to the other vampire.

"Have you heard any rumors of a plan to attack me? From the Ravenwell vampires?" Since the two of them read the pages in Killian's journals that said there was a chance Iris was alive, Silas had been haunted. Shadows under his eyes and tiny lines around his lips was the only hint that something was eating him alive. Otherwise, he was still a perfect example of a vampire in power— flawlessly trimmed hair that was combed back away from his face and perfectly fitted clothing, even the more casual outfit he wore now.

Silas's brows furrowed as he seemed to try to recall any gossip or hints of violence. After a moment, he shook his head.

"No, nothing. I've heard things about vampires being somewhat apprehensive about you in charge, but that comes with any change in command. I dealt with it when I took over. It smooths over quickly enough." The pit in her stomach grew, widening into a void she was sure she would collapse into. Something was horribly wrong. Elora pushed herself to her feet, chewing on the skin around her thumb as she began pacing the room. One deep breath and then another, repeating the mantra in her head that he was fine, that she was overreacting.

"Why do you ask?" Silas's question rooted her in place.

"Korina came by earlier and said there were rumors of a plan to get rid of me. There were a couple of vampires over at the Ravenwell manor who were upset about my display during my announcement and wanted revenge." Silas shook his head before staring at the carpet in front of him, eyes moving from side to side as if attempting to tie threads together, as if seeing the entire map before him and tracing each line.

"It could just be too soon for me to have heard about it. Maybe it hasn't reached any of my sources yet. Not even I can know everything the moment it happens, though I do try very hard." Elora knew her uncle was trying to alleviate her fears, but they both knew that there was something wrong.

"He hasn't checked in. Not once. Doesn't that seem odd to you?"

"Have you tried calling him?" She shook her head before starting to bite at her cuticle once more. The taste of blood hit her tongue, causing her stomach to clench and constrict as if screaming at her. She hadn't fed since before Damien left with Korina, whose smirk was the last thing Elora had seen before the door closed.

"No. I didn't want to bother him or sound crazy if I called and nothing was wrong." A harsh chuckle fell from her lips as she picked up the phone and sent a quick message for blood to be brought up. "Not exactly the confident behavior of a vampire who is in charge of two families."

"Call him, Elora. I can promise you he won't think you're crazy for checking in. And that's exactly what a good vampire head would do. Check in when something doesn't feel right. Trust your instinct." She nodded as a knock sounded and Silas opened it, grabbing the tray from whoever was on the other side. Her focus moved warily from the phone in her hand to the collection bottle and glass. Usually she had it tasted, either by whoever brought it or Damien, who took that job upon himself. Until her position was more firmly established, it was simply a fact that she was potentially at risk, that there was a target on her back.

The scent of blood filled the room as Silas poured the blood into the two glasses and she dialed Damien's number. Her heart hammered against his chest as she began to pace, eyes focused on the rug beneath her feet. One ring became two and then three. Four. Five. Movement in the corner of her eyes drew her attention to Silas, who held out a glass now filled to the brim. Her hand clenched and released as Damien's voice erupted from the phone, a curt statement about leaving a message. Words formed in her mind, but were caught in her throat as she struggled to say anything in case he listened later.

"No answer?" Elora tossed the phone on the table, letting a growl of frustration race forward as she took the glass from Silas.

"It isn't dosed." Silas took a deep drink before she followed suit, draining the glass before thrusting it back at her uncle.

"He isn't answering. Why wouldn't he answer?" The rug under her bare feet was agony as she paced across the room, trying desperately to lose herself in the sensation of blood flowing through her system. Any distraction was welcomed at this point as possibility after possibility rushed through her head, with betrayal being the common thread. If Korina was as ambitious as

Damien said she was, then she was more than willing to turn him over to the highest bidder.

"There are multiple reasons that aren't necessarily bad. He could be questioning the vampires who made the threat. He could be searching through the manor or lost cell reception." She huffed at his attempt to comfort her, to ease the scenarios racing through her mind. Of him bound or unconscious or bleeding out once more from laced bullets.

Her lungs ached as she sucked in a deep breath, filling them beyond capacity and held it, counting down from five before exhaling.

"I know, Silas. I do. But—" Her thoughts were interrupted by her phone ringing, the sound causing her to jump as she darted forward to cradle it in her hands. Damien's name stretched across the screen as she let out a harsh breath, pressing the button and holding it to her ear.

"What happened to checking in?" She chuckled softly as she scolded him, prepared for him to tease her about being worried about him. He didn't seem to realize there was never a moment when she wasn't scared for him or terrified of losing him.

"Checking in will be somewhat difficult right now. Being unconscious in a trunk tends to cause that." Every part of her body seized at the sound of Korina's voice on the other line, each limb rigid as her blood turned to sludge in her veins. Time seemed to stop and reality disintegrated as Elora's hand gripped the phone tighter. She met Silas's eyes as he stepped up beside her and mouthed a single word: speaker. Within moments, Korina's taunting voice filled the room,

"I guess he was right when he said you were a traitor," Elora responded, imagining the pinched expression on Korina's face that always appeared when Damien was mentioned.

"Harsh. I'm not sure I agree with the label, but I'm not about to argue with you. All you need to know is he isn't coming back in the near future." Behind her voice, Elora could make out car horns and other sounds of traffic. They were in the city, but that told her absolutely nothing.

"Where are you taking him?"

"Don't worry. It's not really him they want. It's you." That had been her fear since Damien's call hadn't come hours ago. He was an obvious choice if someone wanted to force her hand. They hadn't flaunted their relationship, but it wasn't a secret either. The rumors already reported that Damien had killed Jonas for her and that he had protected her from Killian before that. Her fingers reached for the pendant that never left her body. Did they understand exactly what they had unleashed by taking him?

"In that case, tell me where to go. I'm more than happy to accept an invitation." Silas vigorously shook his head, practically begging her to not be so impulsive, to think this through before charging into a trap.

"Talk to your little friend in the cells. He should be able to help you. Until then, I'll be sure to keep Damien entertained. We did have fun once upon a time." The other end disconnected with a click before the phone in Elora's hand exploded against the wall. All she could do was stare at the spot where they had collided, breaths slowing as something calm flooded through her. It wasn't the type of calm that came with contentment or peace. It was the type that came before a storm, when the air pressure grew until it was a force that pressed down until you couldn't breathe or think or move. And when the storm brewing in her did break, it would be blood and chaos.

Silas backed away slowly as if giving her space, but she noted the unease in his face. It wasn't fear, but it was close as he only clasped his hands together in front of him as if awaiting her commands.

"Time to visit Viktor."

Chapter 16

Thorne

Thorne could see why Korina was obsessed with the vampire tied to the chair before her. He had classic features with sharp angles and soft lips. Dark hair and darker eyes that watched her with curiosity and arrogance. Not an ounce of fear was there as he rolled his head from side to side, causing his hair to shift around his face. She leaned against the table that held all the items that would eventually be needed based on the expression on his face. Viktor had told her everything he knew about Damien and his role in the target's initial kidnapping. But she had heard his name before, had heard reports of what he had done for Killian. She had lost so many lives because of him and now Thorne had him under her control, drugged and bound. She could ask him about anything, force out information about the most vital and hidden inner workings of the vampires and the Ashcrofts, or whatever the name was now. Yet the only questions that came to mind were about the one vampire she needed to know nothing about.

"Can we hurry this up? Staring at one another is getting old." She chuckled at his bored tone, as if this was an inconvenience. Every muscle in his body was relaxed as he reclined in the chair and stared at her.

"This doesn't have to be unpleasant, you know. It can simply be conversation. No need for blood or violence." Even as she said them, Thorne wondered how many times Damien had said his own version of these words to both vampires and humans alike.

"Would it be a conversation about your brother? About your ex-husband? Or about your daughter, Iris?" She fought and failed to keep the shock from her face, the pain that came with the mention of her old life and name. He only smirked, lips twisting as an amused gleam made the gold flecks in his eyes brighter.

"How did you know?" She almost followed the question with another about if Killian had known, but stopped herself. Damien studied her for a moment, his knowing gaze seeming to move her face as if noting all the similarities.

"Your daughter once taught me a game. A question for a question. I'll answer yours if you answer one of mine." She barely held back a flinch at the mention of her, of Elora. But she wasn't Thorne's daughter. She was Iris's. She nodded and waved her hand in a gesture for him to continue.

"Two ways. The first is a portrait your brother has on his wall. You're obviously younger in it, but the resemblance is there." He paused as if letting that bit of information sink in. And it did, plunging into the pit of her stomach like an anchor, dragging her back to the day it was painted. Iris and Silas had stood side by side as the artist sketched and finally put brush to canvas. She had fidgeted the entire time, shifting and adjusting her posture and position while Silas remained perfectly still, hissing at her to follow directions. There was never a time that their differences were clearer than in that moment.

"The other is Killian's journals. Do you know how many vampires and humans he killed when he found your body gone?" She didn't need Damien to tell her the number. It was permanently etched into her mind, a constant refrain when her guilt broke free from where she kept it caged.

"What else is in them?" Damien clicked his tongue and shook his head in faux disappointment. She forced down the rising irritation, setting the question aside for later. Thorne wasn't sure how much time she would have with him before they were interrupted.

"Fine. And what's your question?" He grinned as something dark flashed across his face, something violently unhinged.

"How does it feel to know you turned your daughter into the very monster you're so afraid of?"

"She's not my daughter!" Thorne's shout filled every conceivable space in the room, pushing out the oxygen and settling onto their skin. Her eyes closed as she forced her racing pulse to slow, her mind to stop. But all she saw behind her eyelids was a child with bright red hair, paint splattered on her nose and cheeks as she stared up with nothing but adoration and trust. Damien's chuckle drew Thorne back to reality and she felt the hatred pouring off of him. Korina's report about his attachment to Elora had been vastly underestimated as hope and desperation caused her to latch onto the delusion Damien wanted anyone else. His hatred for Thorne wasn't from orchestrating his abduction or the lives that had been lost on her orders, but on behalf of Elora.

"You won't survive her, Iris. Taking me was a fatal mistake and I give it three days before she's here to rip you apart along with everyone who helped." There was no heat to his declaration. No anger or even hatred. Instead, it was stated almost carelessly, as if it was nothing more than small talk. Only his dark eyes revealed any hint of what was going on in his head, and it wasn't what Thorne expected. It was pure adoration, reverence for the vampire he loved as if even now their darknesses reached out to one another. She felt a sliver of ice down her spine as she attempted to block out the truth of his words. It's why the entire headquarters had been emptied beyond a small collection of armed guards.

Thorne gave him a grin and moved forward until she was inches from him. Slowly, she knelt to meet his eyes. He didn't glance away or even twitch as her expression hardened.

"I think we should get started then. I wouldn't want to waste time." He shrugged as Thorne stood and strolled over to the chair waiting at the table. She let her gaze travel over the instruments there— knives, a hammer, and others that she never used when taking part in interrogations. Instead, she reached for her favorite knife—a tiny, thin blade that was more like a straight razor, but had a better handle to improve her grip. One hand wrapped around the tool while the other gripped the back of the chair, dragging it behind her as she approached him once more.

Damien's focus darted to the blade in her hand and the corner of his lips twitched slightly, like he was suppressing a grin. No fear, which could potentially make this more difficult.

"I'm sure you know how this works. You did plenty of this for Killian, so I won't insult your intelligence by going into a long explanation about how I ask a question and you either answer or get hurt until I get what I want." Another grin as he raised his brows at her opening lines. It was like they were on equal footing despite the fact he was restrained.

She sank into the chair and crossed her legs, letting the blade hang from her hand as she rested her arm on her knee. He didn't even glance at it, but kept his eyes on her.

"Let's start easy. Is Elora working with Elizabeth?"

"No." The answer was instant, no hesitation. As soon as the question left her lips, Damien had answered.

"Really? Those two are sisters. Do you expect me to believe that they aren't working together?" Damien chuckled and shook his head, as if she were stupid, and she bristled slightly.

"Answer me," she demanded when he didn't respond, only laughing softly.

"Do you regret that you don't know your daughter at all? If you did, you would know the answer to that question." Thorne's hand struck out before she realized what she was doing, the sound of the strike echoing in the empty room that contained only a table with tools and two chairs on top of a floor covered in plastic tarps.

His head snapped to the side as the smell of blood filled the air. Another laugh, dark and deep from somewhere in his chest. Thorne's pulse raced as Damien turned back to face her, the split in his lip bleeding freely. She forced her breathing to calm as she pointed the blade at his face.

"I'll only ask one more time. Are they working together?" He spat at the floor, the bloody saliva landing just beside her shoe.

"No. They aren't." A part of Thorne had known that, but needed it voiced and verified. The woman Denise had described in the journals and her reports back to the council before her loyalty shifted was empathetic, kind to a fault at times. Or at least, she had been.

"Good boy," she drawled and leaned back. "How does she plan on dealing with her sister?"

The blood continued to seep from the cut on his lip, dripping onto his t-shirt. With the dose of medication they had given him, the skin wasn't able to piece itself back together and heal. But it seemed to not bother him as his tongue licked at his lips and he nodded knowingly.

"The same medication Elora took. Interesting. And smart."

"Are we going to do this every time I ask a question?"

"Aren't you enjoying our time together?" Thorne shook her head before leaning towards him and placed the edge of the knife against his bare chest, digging the tip of the blade into his skin until it drew blood. Nothing. No reaction as he smirked.

"Maybe you could ask more personal questions? Try to understand her or at least know who she is." Slowly, Thorne dragged the knife across his right pectoral just above the round scar as he hissed in pain and twitched slightly.

"That—" He sucked in a deep breath and released it slowly as Thorne removed the blade, leaning back once more in the chair. "That scar is from your daughter, you know. Stabbed me with the stem of a wine glass when she found out she had been drinking Viktor's blood." He glanced down at the blood running down his chest with an odd detachment before glancing back up at her.

"And this scar on my neck? The three puncture marks? She did that when I told her Viktor was in one of the feeding cells and available for those interested. A fork was her weapon of choice that time."

"Is there a point to your adorable love story?" Thorne ignored the wave of guilt over Viktor and what she had tasked him with.

"Just trying to give you an idea of who your daughter is and what she will do for those she cares about. Those she loves. And make no mistake, she did love Viktor before she found out the truth." Another peek down at the still bleeding cut across his chest as Thorne took in the warning he had given her. If she had done all of that for Viktor, what would she be willing to do for Damien?

"What is her plan for Elizabeth? Or does Elora plan on letting her infect the entire city?"

"She wants to stop her. That's all I can say." Thorne clicked her tongue before pressing the blade into the left side of his chest, sliding it through flesh and muscle until he finally made a noise. Not a cry or a shout, but she savored the victory.

"Fuck." Each breath seemed difficult as they turned into shallow pants and Damien threw his head back, jaw clenched. "Didn't like the answer?"

"It wasn't much of an answer. And I find it hard to believe she wants to stop her sister. But we can move on for now." The door behind her opened and the room filled with the sound of boots. Thorne grinned as she stood and stared down at Damien, now covered in his own blood pouring from wounds that weren't going to heal any time soon. He had roughly twenty-four hours before he would need another dose, but for now he was completely human.

"These gentlemen are going to loosen you up a little bit. Maybe it will make you a bit more cooperative and less mouthy." She turned to the three men lined up behind her, nodding to each of them.

"Make sure he's still able to talk when you're done with him." A chuckle filled the room, but it didn't come from the men in front of her. Instead, each set of eyes snapped to the body tied to the chair.

"You're more like Killian than I expected." Thorne used every bit of restraint she had to calmly walk out of the room and let the door click close, muffling the sound of fists striking skin.

Chapter 17

Viktor

"How would you like to be useful?" Viktor glanced up towards the voice he knew all well as his own. From beneath tangled hair, twin blazing green eyes stared at him with a violence that made him want to disappear from his spot on the bed. Her entire body was tense, as if each muscle had constricted until she was nothing but a solid mass of stone. Something had happened and it did not bode well for whoever caused it.

"Depends on what I get for being useful." Despite the ease of his words, Viktor's focus was on her every twitch or movement. Her hands clenching and unclenching. Her feet moving slightly in place as if preparing to leap at some unknown enemy. Or maybe he was the target and, if so, the fate he knew he had earned was only minutes away. Somehow, it no longer brought him the same level of fear. There was an acceptance of his fate somewhere deep in his bones. Was this how she felt when she walked into Killian's office, fully prepared to die after accepting what she had seen as inevitable? No. For him it was different. It wasn't darkness or desperation that drove him to accept it. Instead, it was guilt. A desire to atone.

"What do you want?" His brows raised at the undercurrent of fear in her voice. Beneath the wrath, was a terror and he knew instantly who this was in regards to.

"To be let go, Elora. But if that isn't possible, an easy death. I don't want to be tortured." She stilled. The perpetual twitching that had propelled her movements so far ceased in a single moment.

"How about you do it to simply make amends? You can't bring Lukas back, but you can help me get Damien." Viktor flinched, and the garage flashed before his eyes.

"I didn't want to kill him. I just needed you to come with me."

"Don't fucking blame me for being a murderous prick. You made your choices."

" I wasn't trying to—" He took a breath to steady his racing pulse. "I wasn't blaming you. And I wasn't excusing it. I was—" Viktor stopped and stared at the hands that had held the gun that killed Lukas, that had held the knife that had entered Jaime's neck and chest.

"Help me, Viktor. Or I turn you. And that would be worse than what Damien has planned for you. I would turn you and then let you wallow in bloodlust. Do not test me." She knew that was his deepest fear, understood what it would mean for him to be turned now after he killed Jaime to prevent that very fate. But underneath the harshness of her features, the determined set of her lips, was hesitation.

"You won't. We both know that. Don't waste both our time with empty threats."

"You don't know what I would or wouldn't do." He chuckled harshly at her assertion about his knowledge of her, at her assumption that he hadn't learned anything about her during the four years he had spent with her. Viktor had spent every moment of their time together watching every move she made, memorizing every word she said, absorbing the worst of her fears and darkest thoughts only to replay them in the privacy of his room later.

"I know that you want to believe that you're violent and can kill without remorse. But if that was the case, I wouldn't still be alive. You could have gained the information I gave you from anyone else. It's not secret or covert. You kept me alive because you aren't sure you want me to die." Her face tightened and the light in her eyes dimmed just a bit as her lips thinned into a line.

"Don't, Viktor. Will you help me?" He sighed deeply and laid his head against the wall, closing his eyes briefly. It was ridiculous, but he wanted to help her. His agreement was waiting behind his teeth as he finally met her expectant face.

"Help with what?"

"They took Damien. Your friends. They have him, and I'm getting him back. With or without your help." The desperation in her voice now made perfect sense, as did the attempt at threats they both knew she wouldn't follow through on.

"If you know who has him, it seems like you wouldn't need my help." He shrugged slightly before staring at the wall in front of him, counting the notches that had been made by someone before him. Was it one for each day they were here? If so, they didn't last very long.

"Locations, Viktor. Where would they most likely hold him?" She took a step forward, not bothering to hide the feverish gleam in her eyes as she waited for his response. They would have taken him to the main headquarters. It was the only place secluded and secure enough to house him and potentially torture him. Thorne would use the opportunity of having him in her clutches to draw out every possible piece of information.

"I can't condemn them to death, Elora. Not for him." The remorse he felt was stronger than he had anticipated as her expression slipped for just a moment. Devastation and fear and something more unhinged flashed.

"I won't kill anyone if they don't try to stop me. Killing humans has never been the goal." Viktor believed her without a shadow of a doubt. This is what he had tried to convince Thorne of, what he tried to explain before everything had escalated this far. Elora wasn't Elizabeth or Killian's daughter. Every action was fueled by her desire to be safe and have some semblance of peace in her life.

"I—" Viktor ran his hand down his face as the two parts of him battled viciously within him. He wanted to say yes, divulge the information she needed so she could retrieve Damien. Thorne had made a horrific mistake by taking him, and he was prepared to let her deal with the consequences. Another, albeit smaller part of him, screamed that the Resistance had saved him after he killed Jaime, that he owed them his silence no matter the cost. Even if Thorne had written him off as expendable, had ignored the very insight they sent him into the hospital to gain.

"I can take you. There is only one place they would have taken him." Her brow arched as if she never expected him to agree, or at least not this quickly. But Elora would find them eventually, even without his help. He had seen the lengths she would go to in order to protect those she loved because he had been among those privileged few not that long ago. At least this way, he could try to prevent the eradication of every human unlucky enough to be stationed at the headquarters when Elora arrived.

"Which is where?" Her palms were flat against the plexiglass wall between them, each line in her skin pressed as if she would merge with it. Now that he had agreed, there was something almost relaxed to her posture and face. No longer crushed under the weight of Damien's kidnapping, but set free by the vaguest outline of a plan.

"Outskirts of the city. Near the hospital. It's an old apartment building. They'll have him either in the basement or in the interrogation rooms on the second floor." She flinched at the reference to Damien being questioned as her hand fell to her side.

"Will they hurt him? Torture him?" Viktor almost couldn't handle the level of terror in her voice, the harsh whisper of her words as they filtered through the wall between them. When Elora loved, it was fierce and beyond anything that felt possible. He didn't realize that a single person could feel so strongly, so completely. She would give her entire being if they only asked. Remove a limb. Excise a piece of her soul. There were no limits.

"Yes," he whispered, not sure he wanted to see what her reaction would be to the truth. "If they want information, they'll do what is necessary to get it."

"Then they will die, Viktor. Anyone who hurts him. I'll do my best to prevent death, but do not expect me to spare them." He nodded.

"I won't ask you to."

"What do you want for this? What's your price?" That was a question he wasn't sure he had an answer to. He could ask to be let go and be allowed to return home. But he doubted the Resistance would welcome him back. Already they were suspicious of him and his perceived fractured loyalty. If they did allow him back, it would be with precautions that meant living with their distrust for the rest of his life, and Viktor wasn't sure he wanted that type of existence. He could request to not be killed, either by her hand or Damien's. It still left the question of what he would do with that life. He could try to leave the city, start a new life somewhere else in hopes no one would try to find him.

A weariness settled into his bones as he considered and traced each potential option.

"Have Damien make it quick. That's it." Her brows furrowed, but he couldn't hold her gaze. He couldn't let her see the defeat and acceptance he knew was painted across it. If anyone would recognize that expression, it would be her. After all, he had seen it on her face so many times.

"You don't want to be let go? I could give you money. Let you leave the city. You could ask me for anything and you know I would give it to you if it meant I got him back." His harsh laugh filtered out into the cell.

"No. I just want to be done, El. I know you understand that."

Nothing. No response. Only unbearable silence as he struggled to read her face, to understand the expression that seemed unable to settle into place. The only truth he could see was that she couldn't decide if she wanted him dead or not.

"We can talk specifics after Damien is back," Elora finally responded before taking a step back. "I need to gather up reinforcements. I'll have someone come get you washed and ready for this."

She stared at him, eyes moving across his face as if searching for something. Damien's voice rang in his head, repeating over and over that she had loved him. Viktor was willing to bet that some part of her still did, that killing him wasn't as simple as Killian or Darian. There had been no tender moments between them. Only pain and torture and cruelty—nothing to make her feel even the smallest shred of remorse or make her hesitate.

As if she had heard his thoughts, Elora approached the glass and whispered softly, "I should want you dead." It was a confession that she refused to look at him while making. "It's an insult to Lukas and Denise to let you live."

He couldn't think of a single word to say. Nothing to discount her statement. Nothing to argue against it.

"I know." His words were equally low and he wasn't sure she heard him as she spun on her heel, marching towards the elevator to put in motion the plan to get her love back.

Chapter 18

Elora

The ballroom on the top floor of the Tower was filled to capacity. Each corner held a body and anyone else who showed up would need to stand in the hallway. Elora hadn't been confident that the vampires she now led would answer her summons. In her mind, when she imagined this exchange, she had stood on a stage begging an empty room for a group to accompany her to retrieve Damien. Yet, here they all stood, their chatter rising up to meet her as her focus moved over them, searching for any hints that this was an ambush. But there was nothing, not even weapons strapped to their hips or whispers of their previous name for her. Either she had won them over, or the mention of Damien's name in the announcement brought them forward.

"I need ten vampires to assist me tonight. One of our own has been taken by the Resistance after being betrayed by a fellow Ashcroft member," Elora began, moving smoothly into the speech she had practiced in her office only minutes ago. As she had anticipated, anger moved through the crowd like a wave. Even from where she stood, Elora could see the shift in their demeanor—the stiffness of their bodies, the violence displayed on their faces, the fury radiating from them. Her heart swelled as she witnessed their loyalty to one another. She may not fully have it, but they were all fiercely dedicated to one another and insults such as these would not be tolerated.

"Damien left yesterday afternoon to investigate a claim that our safety was at risk. Korina, a high-ranking vampire, was the one to bring this threat to our attention. As you all can guess it was a ploy to get Damien out of the safety of the Tower and abduct him."

She paused, letting their anger grow until it was a thread that bound them all together in solidarity. Damien was well-re-spected within the family. It was part of why Darian had wanted him on his side. The idea that anyone would attack him was grounds for war.

"She handed him over to the Resistance like the traitor she is. I know where he's being held and I'll be leaving in thirty minutes to retrieve him by any means necessary. I'm asking for those with training to accompany me. But even if none do, I'll still be going." The response was immediate and overwhelming as she tried desperately to keep the relief from her face. Elora pointed to ten of them before gesturing for them to come forward and stand before the stage.

"Meet me in my office in fifteen minutes," she announced before glancing at the crowd, all staring at her expectantly, wait-ing patiently for her orders or final words. But now that she had those who would be coming with her, every nerve ending was on fire and invisible strings were pulling and yanking her from the room, dragging her to Damien. Nothing else mattered as she pictured the state she would find him in.

"We'll bring him back and remove any obstacle in our way." Her declaration rang out and was followed by a mixture of shouts of support or applause, creating something so loud it could bring the Tower down. In the midst of it, Elora stepped down from the stage and marched down the aisle the crowd created for her. The applause and cheers only ended when the elevator doors closed and took her down to her office where Silas was waiting. Elora froze in the doorway as she studied him, eyes moving over his determined expression to his outfit. She had never seen him in anything but slacks and perfectly pressed button ups. It was a shock to see him now in jeans and a leather jacket with a t-shirt underneath it.

"Don't try to order me to stay."

"I wouldn't dream of it, uncle," she responded, setting her hand on his shoulder as she went around to her desk and began pulling out the few knives in one of the drawers. Weapons were not her strength beyond simple slashing and stabbing, which was why she needed others to accompany her on the mission.

"How are we approaching this?"

"We use the intel and layout Viktor gave us to infiltrate. We retaliate against anyone who attacks us, but we won't be feeding. It's a distraction that we don't need while we're there. We find him and bring him back, by any means necessary." There was a cold and calculating tone to her explanation, and her uncle raised a brow, staring at her like she was a new creature he was trying to understand. This was the side that had been born the night she killed her father. A vampire who had no issue with death, either seeing it or granting it. It was the side of her that had evolved when she orchestrated the plan that led to Darian's heart in her hand. This was the monster they had all created, and she wouldn't apologize for it or banish it into the darkest pits of her soul. She would harness and unleash it, let them bear the consequences of every action.

"If Viktor is lying? If he's leading you into a trap?" She hummed softly at the valid questions. She had considered them after leaving Viktor to wash and prepare to walk into the Resistance headquarters side by side like old friends.

"I don't think he is, but if he did lie, then my plan is compulsion. I don't need to touch or even make eye contact, Silas. But I would rather not resort to that."

"Why is that? It seems like it would make the mission smoother." She leveled him with a glare so heated he flinched and looked away. There was no need to explain further.

Silas opened his mouth to say something else only to be interrupted by a series of loud knocks on the door.

"Come in." Her voice rang out as she sat to pull on her boots, listening as three sets of footprints entered, followed by an overwhelming human scent. Viktor. She would know his scent anywhere after drinking his blood and breathing it in for so long.

"Set it up on the table there. Thank you," Silas's orders filled the room as Elora glanced up, taking in Viktor who was dressed in jeans and a long-sleeve shirt, a canvas jacket hanging from his arm. His hair fell down around his face, hanging around his chin.

"You look better." Viktor huffed a laugh at her observation before his focus locked onto the collection of bottles and glasses on the table.

"I'm having them feed before we leave for this," she explained briefly. "I promised you their safety as long as they don't fight. I'm trying to make sure that happens."

"Silas," her uncle announced, approaching Viktor with a hand outstretched and Viktor took it willingly. "Elora's uncle. You killed Denise and Lukas." Elora froze as Silas's words filled the room and a tension settled among them. She had known Silas had contact with Lukas, but didn't know about Denise.

"I did kill Lukas," Viktor responded, voice tight as he seemed to take a step back. "But I didn't kill Denise. I didn't know she would be there. I didn't give the order for her to be shot."

"And yet it was your plan and your soldiers who executed her and left her in a parking garage." Elora bristled at the harsh tone as Silas took another step towards Viktor. She leaned against the arm of the chair and watched, studying the interaction. To Viktor's credit, he didn't seem afraid, only cautious. But Silas was doing a horrific job of hiding the anger in his voice and expression.

"How do you know Denise? Why would you care if I killed another human? We're disposable to your kind." They were excellent questions and mirrored the ones currently echoing around in Elora's mind. She raised a brow at Silas when he met her eye and he sighed softly before shoving his hands in his pockets.

"I had known her for years. From before I turned. We had problems after that and stopped talking, but once Elora was taken she contacted me. We worked together after that." Viktor nodded and began moving through the room, eyes lingering on the books along the shelves while a small grin curled at the corner of his lips. It was so strange to see it once more after everything. She had sought it out every morning as she took her medication, looked for it as she moved through her day or watched TV in the dayroom. Now, it made something in her chest tighten and squeeze until it felt like her heart wasn't beating.

"Were you friends with her? Did she know my mother?" Elora asked, and Silas shrugged.

"I suppose you could call us that. When I turned and she joined the Resistance, we grew apart due to our conflicting interests, as you can imagine. But she never met your mother as far as I know." She had no response or follow up question. It was strange enough to consider exactly how interconnected her life was, how all the branches intertwined. They were planets that had all gotten sucked into her orbit, forced to rotate around her until she managed to escape or eliminate those who wanted to own her.

"I like what you did with the place." Viktor's observation tore her from her thoughts and made her chuckle as he turned back to her, that small grin fully displayed on his face. She couldn't help but return it, to disappear into the familiar feeling of the two of them against everyone else.

"I don't share Killian's love of cliche decor," she responded, and Viktor made a small noise in response that may have been a laugh.

"You haven't changed the cells." Her eyes hardened slightly as Viktor watched her closely.

"It's a work in progress. I've been busy dealing with some issues," she bit out after a moment as a loud knock broke apart the growing tension. In the blink of an eye, the ease between her and Viktor dissipated, leaving behind only the lingering tension that connected them like a chain that wrapped around them both, keeping them together despite the complexity of their dynamic and history.

"Come in." Her voice rang out once more and body after body entered the room, arranging themselves in a straight line along the far wall. Each vampire stood in full tactical gear that Elora hadn't realized was available, hands clasped behind their backs and a gun strapped to their belts. She studied them each in turn, the determination and sharpness of their features, the darkness in their eyes as they stared directly ahead of them awaiting her command.

"We'll be entering the Resistance headquarters to get Damien back. However, there are rules and if you cannot follow them, you'll be staying behind." She paused for a second, collecting her thoughts. "We will not be killing every human we come across. Only those who attack us. We return fire only. Am I clear?"

"Yes, ma'am." Their voices joined together in a symphony and she nodded.

"We'll also not be feeding. It's a distraction that is not worth risking Damien's life for. We'll feed before we leave. Any vampire who disobeys me will be punished." Elora waited for the argument, for the questioning of her orders as her heart raced in her chest. This was the first true test of their respect, of whether they saw her as their vampire head.

"If you can abide by my rules for this mission, pour yourself a glass and finish preparing. We leave in fifteen and you will be informed of the building layout on the way."

Each of the vampires stepped forward without a single second of hesitation while Elora poured glass after glass of blood, handing it to them as they approached. Together as one, they swallowed the contents and set the glasses down as her focus moved to her uncle, who simply tipped his own cup and drank.

It was time to get Damien and destroy anyone who tried to stop her. It was time to become the villain they accused her of being.

Chapter 19

Damien

He heard screams first, followed by begging. Pleading before silence and a savage grin spread across his face, reopening the cut on his lip. Despite the chaos he could hear beyond the door behind him, Damien's body relaxed for the first time since he had woken up tied to a chair. His fists unclenched and hung limp from the handcuffs and even the bindings around his chest and legs felt loose. He stared at Korina who stood off to the side, near the table with the bottles of blood. She had been sipping it from a fairly garish crystal glass. It seemed like something Killian would use to make a statement, to play into the myths about vampires crafted by humans. It was with no small amount of satisfaction that Korina's expression grew tighter and paler the louder the screams became. Her hand twitched at her side as if to reach for a weapon that didn't seem to exist.

"Let me go. Maybe she'll let you live." Korina jumped at the sound of his voice, but her focus never left the door.

"She won't make it in here." He knew the words weren't for him, but instead a futile attempt at reassuring herself that she wasn't listening to the sounds of her own fate somewhere in the building. If a dozen or so humans along with a collection of vampires hadn't stopped Elora, then Korina had to know there was no hope for her. He chuckled cruelly when she flinched as a scream was cut short, followed by a brief moment of silence.

The number of cries and begging had decreased the longer they listened, bearing witness to a carnage they had welcomed to their doorstep. Damien didn't speak again, didn't try to convince Korina to try and ease whatever punishment was coming for her. It would be brutal if Elora had her way.

At this point, with the collection of footsteps gathering beyond the door, the best Korina could hope for was a quick death. Damien could hear the door behind him swing open and he inhaled deeply, savoring the scent of lavender and blood that filled the room. Most of it was human, but underneath it, calling to his rage, was Elora's. Not much, but even a drop was unforgivable.

A single set of footsteps entered first, stopping right behind him and he felt her. Without a single doubt in his mind, he knew it was Elora, could feel her in the very marrow of his bones, in every atom he was composed of. Her fingers brushed his neck, just the barest whisper of her touch, but it set him on fire.

"Release him. Now." There was something uniquely dangerous about her tone. It wasn't harsh or demanding. It wasn't angry or even cruel. It was pure violence. A promise of death and destruction. Just as he had warned Iris and the others, they had pushed her too far. Elora's hold on her sanity had been growing stronger, no longer falling into memories and nightmares on a daily basis, but this was an action that could threaten that. They saw her as a villain, a monster or rabid beast that needed to be put down before she killed everyone around her. Now, they had made her one and he refused to feel even an ounce of pity for them.

"I said release him, Korina. He only likes it when I tie him up." Damien heard someone shift as if uncomfortable, and he smirked. Silas must be in the room as well, or at least near enough to hear her comment. It wasn't technically true, but they would be finding out if it was once they got out of there.

Korina gripped the glass in her hand so tightly he was sure it would shatter. The calculating look he had seen so many times before settled onto her face as she studied whatever scene was behind him. He could sense multiple bodies, but the scents were too muddled to discern. There were both humans and vampires, but it was impossible to know who was dead and who was alive. Or who was on their side.

"Does he know you brought him with you?" Elora's hand settled onto his shoulder as he tensed. He? Who the fuck was Korina talking about?

"Not yet. But he will." Elora clucked her tongue in disappointment. "You're desperate, Korina. And it's somewhat sad. Pathetic, even."

Elora's words seemed to physically strike Korina as the glass in her hand shattered and the scent of blood filled the room.

"Pathetic? I'm pathetic? I've been fighting tooth and nail since before you were even a thought. And all you had to do was be born into the family. Killian plays with your genetics a little bit and now you're in charge of everything." Her voice became more shrill and frantic with each word she said. Damien felt Elora's hand leave his shoulder for just a moment before it returned, resting lightly as if she thought he was injured.

"This all sounds very cliche. I gave you a chance at respect and power. You threw it away. I would have built you up. Pulled you through the ranks without making you sleep with someone. And I think, even if you knew that, you couldn't stomach him with anyone else. We would have always ended up here." There was a mixed sense of pride and foreboding as he listened to Elora's explanation. She had met Korina with something like kindness. Empathy, even. And she had thrown it back in Elora's face.

Hands touched his wrists, and he felt deft fingers unlocking the handcuffs. The sound they made as they hit the floor seemed to echo. Korina hadn't responded after Elora stopped speaking and instead stared at her as if she had never seen her before. It was like Korina was emerging from a dark place where only the very worst of her thoughts had held sway. Damien could recognize it for what it was. After all, he had been the same. He had seen Elora through a very particular lens and hadn't searched any further than what was presented to him and the beliefs he had held onto so firmly before meeting her.

Damien rubbed at his wrists as his legs were unlocked and the rope started to fall away. As he stood, Damien stared down at the person who released him, expecting to find a vampire from the Tower or even Silas. But it wasn't even a vampire and he couldn't control the myriad of emotions that coursed through him—anger, betrayal, confusion. Above all of them, what Damien felt was shock. Viktor stood and took a few steps back until he stood next to Silas, who only shook his head at Damien as if to say this wasn't the time to ask questions. And he would be right. But later, when this was over and they were back in the Tower, he would be given answers to why this fucking human was there and what Elora had promised in return for his obvious cooperation.

Damien's eyes closed as he rolled his shoulders and moved beside Elora, staring at Korina whose face had gone pale. She couldn't have truly thought that this wouldn't happen, couldn't honestly think that Elora wouldn't come after him with everything at her disposal. Even Viktor, apparently.

"Where's Thorne? I would rather deal with the person in charge. Not an underling." Elora's words were almost bored, and Damien straightened at the flash of rage in Korina's eyes. Every part of him screamed to move in front of Elora, to shield her from what was coming, even if the consequences could be disastrous. If word spread that she didn't protect herself, but relied on him to do it, then the reputation she had gained would crack.

"I'm right here. No need to be rude to her." Damien's body reacted instantly to the voice as she entered, but it was Silas who drew every drop of attention. His gasp rang out as each person in the room turned to him. His eyes were wide, revealing a line of tears along his lash line, while his mouth was contorted in something that looked like pain except for the curls at the end. Silas took a step forward, hand outstretched before he stopped, staring at Thorne like she was a hallucination that they all just happened to share.

"Iris." The sound of that name had a ripple effect through the room. From the choked sobs from Silas as he stared at his sister to Elora, who went deathly still. Viktor's voice came from behind him, muttering something about how he should have known, should have seen it.

"Iris is dead." Thorne's words were frigid, even colder than when she had interrogated Damien. It was as if they had covered the room in a frost as they all stared at one another, not sure how to proceed with this revelation. Damien peeked at Elora as his hand twitched and he struggled to stop himself from reaching for her. There was an emptiness on her face that made him want to warn everyone to get out of the room, that what was coming would be brutal.

"And yet, I know she isn't," Elora began, words firm as she stared down at her mother while Thorne refused to meet her gaze. "Killian wrote about you extensively. Almost obsessively. I have his journals. I know he beat you and thought you were dead. Do you know how many vampires and humans died when he came back and your body was gone? Even more than when I disappeared."

Thorne betrayed nothing, but finally met her daughter's gaze. Elora took a step forward, then another even as her mother held her ground, not flinching or batting an eye at the approach.

"That girl is dead. That wife and mother is dead. Iris died."

"And now you spend your time hunting your only daughter so you can drain her dry and kill her." At that, Thorne flinched. Visibly and violently flinched. There was no emotion to Elora's accusation, but underneath she was a storm, the type that ripped trees from the ground and destroyed everything it touched.

"I spend my time trying to fix my mistake. I spend it trying to save humans from what your father created." The words barely left Thorne's lips before all hell broke loose.

Elora was a blur as she raced to Thorne and wrapped her hands around her mother's neck. The emptiness that had been in place during the conversation was gone, replaced with something Damien wasn't sure he could name. Pain. Rage. Betrayal. Violence. Each one radiated from Elora as she squeezed Thorne's neck and watched as her mother struggled to take in a breath. Behind him, Silas's breathing had turned to harsh pants and he kept shifting, adjusting his position as if he didn't know what to do, who to support. Sister or niece? Damien didn't envy him. For him, it wasn't a question. Elora was who he would defend with his life. He had done it before and was prepared to do it again and again until there were no more threats, no more enemies.

"Mistake," Elora spat. "A fucking mistake." Her hand squeezed more until Damien was sure Thorne's neck would break in her grip.

"Elora. Stop. She's—" Viktor stepped forward, dashing towards them as if to stop this.

"I didn't bring you here to interfere. Shut up." Elora's eyes never left her mother as she spoke and Thorne's desperate attempts to take a breath were the only other sound. Damien turned and his fist collided with the human's face, resulting in the most satisfying of sounds. It was everything he had thought it would be. Grunts and curses came from the crumbled figure on the floor and Damien glared down at him, begging him to stand up and try again.

"Your mistake was not asking for my help. Your mistake was coming after me. I'll deal with my sister after I'm done with you." There was surprise in Thorne's expression right before her finger twitched and Korina finally made her move. Throughout the exchange, she had been silent, not once moving or making a single sound. As if she had been waiting.

Korina darted forward, eyes blazing from the insults she had lobbied back and forth with Elora like bombs during a battle. Elora released her mother and straightened, preparing for the attack by widening her stance and gripping the knife that had been attached to her belt even as Damien moved to protect her. He shifted, ready to stand between her and Korina. Elora huffed slightly at the gesture, no doubt wondering if he still believed her to be weak. That was the last word Damien would ever use to describe her. She wasn't weak, but untrained and had never dealt with Korina, who fought like a rabid animal who wanted only to maim and destroy no matter how much damage the fight did to herself.

Damien waited, body tense and hands clenched into fists, playing through his potential moves in his mind like he was choreographing a dance. But Korina never came at him or Elora, but at *him*. A curse rang out and Damien followed the sound to find Korina fighting with Viktor, both of them struggling to gain control. Viktor was a large man with the type of build that would make most people second guess fighting him, but Korina was a vampire who had been trained to kill.

Viktor held out a split second longer than Damien thought he would before Korina gained the upper hand and forced Viktor around, blade to his neck. Where had that knife even come from? He hadn't seen any weapons on her and he doubted Elora had given Viktor any.

"Give yourself up. Send everyone here away and I'll let him go," Korina announced, eyes moving over the forms in the room. Behind her, Thorne only sat on the floor where Elora had left her, rubbing at her neck like one of her own wasn't being threatened. He had been right when he said she had more in common in Killian than he had originally thought. How many times had Damien been discarded and tossed aside, ignored while there was a gun pointed at his chest or a knife held to his throat? Killian had never cared about the vampires in his care, only about what their death brought him. Thorne, it seemed, was no different.

Damien scoffed. There was no way that Elora would hand herself over for Viktor. He waited patiently to hear her say those words, to hear her declare that Viktor's life meant nothing to her. Korina killing the human didn't change anything for him. As long as Viktor ended up dead, that was what mattered. It would have been more satisfying if it had been done by his hand, but he would settle for this.

Korina pressed the knife against Viktor's throat, drawing the smallest hint of blood and he felt Elora jerk forward. His arm snapped out, stopping her from whatever her plan had been. Not saving him. It couldn't be that she was trying to save the human who shot Lukas in the head, the one who was responsible for Wyatt being turned and had shot Damien with laced bullets. Sin after sin was placed at Viktor's feet, growing so tall it was a surprise that the human wasn't drowning in them.

Viktor stared at no one other than Elora. His eyes didn't even twitch or move away from her in the tiniest amounts as his hands hung limp at his sides. Elora struggled in Damien's hold, fingernails digging into the flesh of his arm until he felt his blood on his skin.

She was going to give herself up.

Betrayal sank like a lead weight in his gut, and he almost let her go, almost let her do this.

The wheels in Viktor's eyes were turning as he tried to figure out how to escape Korina's hold. He couldn't. Damien knew that. And he should be fine with that. After all, what did it matter? Viktor dies and Elora leaves with him and Silas, returning to the Tower so they could discuss whatever the fuck was happening right now between her and the human because something clearly was.

"Let me go," Elora ordered and Damien's grip tightened for a moment. "Now."

Damien did as she asked, half expecting her to dart forward into Korina's arms. Instead, she resumed her stance, forcing her shoulders back and her spine straight.

"Come on over here with me. I'll let him go," Korina explained lightly, almost like she was coaxing a scared child from a hiding place after a storm. Elora chuckled darkly and Damien braced himself just as Viktor gave the tiniest of nods. Permission. Something was instantly communicated between the two of them and that thorn of jealousy only dug itself deeper, festering and rotting the places around it.

"Is the idea that I save Viktor and give myself over to Thorne and you get Damien. That was the goal, right? For you, at least?" Elora asked sweetly, each word more condescending than the last. He saw exactly what she was talking about, exactly how Korina's mind would have warped this plan. Behind Korina, Thorne nodded softly as if in confirmation.

"Even with me gone, he won't take you back," Elora declared as Viktor threw his head back, hitting Korina in the face and shattering her nose. Her scream of agony filled the room as Viktor tried to dart forward, to use the opportunity to escape. Damien once more wrapped his arms around Elora's waist, pulling her flush with his body as she kept fighting—clawing and hitting with her fists and elbows before trying to hit his face with her head like Viktor had done.

Korina regained her composure almost instantly, the vampire part of her healing the injury and stopping the pain. She rushed forward, grabbing Viktor by his hair and kicking the back of his knees. He fell to the ground with a thud. Korina stepped up behind him, adjusting the grip on her knife handle before yanking his head back and moving to put the knife to his neck. But the human wasn't giving up and a part of Damien respected him for it. Viktor spun on his knees and propelled himself forward, taking Korina down with him. The two of them fell heavily to the floor with Viktor on top, pressing her body into the cheap linoleum.

Elora cried out, finally making contact as her head hit Damien's face and he loosened his grip in surprise. She rushed forward, kneeling beside their bodies before rolling Viktor over. For a brief moment she studied Viktor's body, the placement of the knife in his chest and the angle of it before turning to the other body on the floor. Korina jerked and tried to crawl away as Elora slowly followed her every movement, steps almost languid as she stalked her like prey. This was what Damien had warned her about. They had pushed Elora. Pushed and pushed until they had crafted the very creature they were trying to destroy. She had become the monster they all believed she was and it was fucking glorious.

Korina's back hit the corner of the wall and she stared defiantly at the vampire above her.

"I won't beg for my life."

"I didn't ask you to." Elora took Korina's knife off the ground where it had fallen in the struggle and straddled her, knees settling on either side of her and squeezing to keep her from moving.

Damien held his breath as Elora didn't give Korina a chance to say anything else, didn't give Thorne a chance to try and prevent this from happening. Thorne didn't really seem to care about what happened to her. In this moment, Korina was collateral damage, a rogue agent who had gone off script and this was simply the culmination of that. Elora thrust the knife up through Korina's jaw, angling it back towards her skull. Korina's eyes widened for only a moment before Elora yanked the blade out. Crimson splashed across her shirt as she dropped the knife and stood, staring with disgust at the vampire bleeding out on the floor. There was no coming back from that wound, not in the way Elora had done it. Korina would be dead in moments no matter how quickly she healed.

"El." Damien could only see a brief flash of her face as she spun away from Korina and towards the body still on the floor. The knife protruding from his chest was in a place Damien knew there was no fixing. Not unless she turned him. He shifted slightly, trying to force down whatever emotions were rising to the surface, as she fell to the ground and pulled Viktor into her lap, holding his head in her arms. It was too strangely familiar, too much like a full circle from when Viktor had held her in the hospital room.

And as Damien tried desperately to not feel betrayed, to not feel something that was very close to regret, he watched her weep over the human who had killed their friend.

Chapter 20

Elora

Viktor's blood poured from his body as Elora held him in her arms and the rest of the room disappeared. Her focus never shifted from the human in her arms, who was staring at her with nothing less than complete acceptance and submission. Each feature was soft, all the hard lines and deep grooves gone, leaving him looking so young. His bloodstained hand rose until his fingers touched her cheek, trembling slightly as he brushed away a tear. The offer to turn him waited on her tongue, fully formed and ready to be spoken. Yet, she knew what his answer would be.

Elora brushed away his hair as every memory of him played before her eyes. Both the good and the bad. The kindness and betrayals. The affection and the cruelty. The way he would leave chocolates in her room after a bad therapy session or how he made sure she had coffee every morning to make up for the horrible food. There were so many words to say, so many questions to ask, but none of them would come out. A small part of her could feel every pair of eyes that were glued to her and the dying human in her arms.

"I'm sorry. For everything." Viktor's words came out broken as he gripped her hand in his, fingers clenching tight until it hurt. She shook her head, unable to bear what she knew were his final words. Tears flowed freely down her cheeks as her shoulders shook from the silent sobs. There was such acceptance in his eyes. He had made peace with his death in his cell at the Tower when he had asked for Damien to make his end quick in return for his help. She would do that for him.

Viktor's hand shook as he dragged hers to the blade that was sunk deep in his chest and wrapped her fingers around the handle. Her heart pounded against her rib cage until it felt bruised, and she questioned whether she could do this. For so long, all she had imagined was a moment like this, where Viktor was at her mercy and she could make him beg. She had always thought it would bring her a sense of peace like it had when she killed Darian and her father. Now, it felt like she was removing a vital piece of her soul, tearing off a part of her heart as she gripped the blade tighter and leaned down towards it.

Her head jerked into a nod before she pressed her lips to his cheek, tasting the salt from his tears and sweat.

"I know. I forgive you." The words barely left her lips as she pulled the knife from his chest, flinching as the scent of his blood washed over her until she was nearly drowning beneath it. Red poured from the wound as the knife fell from her fingers and onto the floor where the blood had begun to pool. The room was silent other than Viktor's final rasping breaths, no one willing to break whatever this moment was. She stroked his cheek with her knuckle, silently saying her final goodbyes.

She felt Viktor's body go limp, the deadweight bearing into her thighs as her mind seemed to quiet, each thought receding into the fringes. Her eyes closed for a moment before she stood, allowing Viktor's body to slide to the floor. Blood dripped from her fingers before she faced her audience. Thorne first with a shocked expression on her face before moving to Silas, whose attention wasn't on Elora but on his sister.

Elora didn't meet Damien's eyes, couldn't force herself to see the hurt that was sure to be there. They hadn't fully discussed

Viktor, and she hadn't been willing to admit even to herself that she still harbored feelings for him. They were nothing compared to what she felt for Damien, but it was a type of love that was rooted in shared experiences. Her love for Damien was a wildfire, raging and all-consuming, and there was nothing she wanted more than to be engulfed in them. With Viktor, it was a whisper. The smoke after the fire burned out that was still clogging her lungs and settling into the fibers of her clothing. It would never wash out. Not completely.

"We'll be leaving now." Elora's announcement was met with silence, only the shuffling of feet as she felt Damien approach her, his hand wrapping around her waist. The heat from his touch thawed the ice that had enveloped her since the phone call, rendering each choice and thought methodical and cold.

"You can't," a voice forced out, and Elora followed it to its source to find Thorne staring at her with an empty expression.

"I think you'll find that I can and will. Come talk to me when you're ready to be smart about stopping Elizabeth. But don't try something like this again. Mother or not, I will kill you." Elora heard Silas's sharp intake of breath as if shocked by either her declaration or invitation or both. The space in her heart where she had held hope that her mother would welcome her back and kiss her cheeks as they wept for joy at being reunited had disappeared the moment Elora had realized who Thorne was, the role she had played. This was the woman who demanded her life be sacrificed, who sent Viktor after her time and time again. No, her mother had died that night on Killian's floor, and the woman standing before her was simply a potential enemy, someone to remove from the equation if she wanted any hope of living a normal life.

"Make sure you give him a proper burial, Thorne," Elora commanded as she turned towards the door. "I would say he earned it. Wouldn't you?"

The question was meant to be rhetorical. As far as she was concerned, Viktor had done everything Thorne and the Resistance had demanded of him. The least they could do was bury him. She froze, turning back slightly to look at Thorne over her shoulder.

"Next to Jaime, if possible. It's what he would have wanted." To her surprise, Thorne nodded before taking a step back, as if granting her permission to leave. Elora had no doubt that if it was possible, Viktor would be buried exactly where she had requested. It was the last act they could perform for him, the last gift and the sign that he had atoned for his sins.

Time seemed to stand still as Elora stared at her mother, their eyes locked as if they could communicate something this way. In the space between them, silent word after word spilled out onto the floor, merging with the blood until there was no way to understand them.

Elora turned towards the door. Silas stood to her right while Damien flanked her left, his hand still on her hip as if to assure himself that she wasn't going to vanish. Behind her, Elora could hear harsh breathing like someone had just run a marathon and was trying to recover. The sound seemed to grow louder with each passing second as the other vampires began to filter out of the room, one by one, leaving in a haze of blood-covered shirts and hands.

Elora froze as she approached the door, glancing back at Thorne, who was only watching them with something close to regret on her face. But whether it was for her daughter, brother, or Viktor was unclear. Perhaps none of them. Maybe it was for allowing Elora to leave without a fight.

"You can deal with her body," she called back, gesturing vaguely towards the dead vampire on the floor near Viktor. Thorne nodded before turning her attention to Silas for a moment, an entire lifetime of memories and emotions flickering across her face in a heartbeat.

Elora didn't think Silas believed that his sister was truly alive, no matter what Killian's journal had said. Or maybe he had been keeping his hopes contained, not allowing them to balloon to an unimaginable size. The potential for it to blow up in his face, leaving him grieving her a second time, was too great to even consider it. But now, they had seen her, heard her voice, and listened as she claimed that name and existence even if Thorne wanted nothing to do with them.

Step by step, Elora led Damien to the car waiting outside. Silas followed suit though he seemed to be dragging an invisible weight along with him, as if finding out his sister was alive was keeping him rooted in place. He wasn't able to see the two versions of Thorne as separate entities. For Elora, there was Iris and then there was Thorne. Iris was the mother who died to protect her, the one who had failed to do so. And Thorne, the woman in that room with two dead bodies and a failed mission, was her enemy who had hunted her like prey, who had planned on draining her dry and leaving her on the sacrificial altar.

If Thorne showed at the Tower and took the invitation, it would be a step in the right direction. But it wouldn't change anything at its core. It wouldn't change the fact Thorne had hurt Damien, had sought to use him to get to her.

It wouldn't change the fact that Thorne was incredibly lucky she still breathed.

Chapter 21

Damien

Elora's orders had rung out as soon as they parked in the Tower garage. Silas had gone ahead to check on the manor, leaving the two of them with the vampires who had accompanied her to his rescue.

"You—bring two bottles to my rooms. The rest of you, we will debrief in the morning. For now, celebrate. Feed, if necessary."

Each one of them nodded and muttered their acceptance of her orders, respect radiating as they inclined their heads. Damien watched as they left and the number on the elevator display steadily increased before finally stopping at the blood collection floor. His legs seemed to shake as he forced himself out of the SUV, cursing as he clutched the edge of the car door to keep from collapsing to the ground. The scene would be too similar to when Lukas died only steps away from where Damien was struggling to remain upright. Lukas's sad smile and expression of pure acceptance barged forward, appearing so clearly that he thought maybe he was reliving it. Maybe he had actually died, and witnessing Lukas's death again was a punishment Damien knew he had earned.

But Lukas's face melted away to have only Viktor, once more holding the gun he had used. Damien had vowed revenge and had fantasized about the exact method he would use. Every single detail had been planned out, down to the color of the tarp that would line the floor and the exact knife he would use to remove his eyes. But all that planning had vanished, dissipating like smoke as Viktor died in Elora's arms, bleeding out as she wept. On the car ride back to the Tower, Damien had pieced together a rough idea of what occurred. It wasn't difficult to figure out Elora had gone to Viktor when she found out who had taken him. She had demanded Viktor's help, who probably refused at first. Only after she promised him something did Viktor agree.

"Upstairs. Now." Elora's words were strained as she rounded the SUV and wrapped an arm around Damien's waist. His words of protest died on his tongue as he took in her expression. Determined, yet broken. Her mask was gone, letting Damien finally see exactly what his kidnapping had done to her. Everything she had done since they fled the safehouse had been to claim a position that would protect those she cared about as well as herself, because for Elora, they were one and the same.

Damien could practically hear her thoughts as he leaned into her, allowing her to partially carry him.

They only took him to get to me.

He was only hurt because of you.

Elora's mind, her very thoughts, would be attacking her from all sides, stabbing and cutting at her sanity in hopes of her unraveling. The elevator chimed as they stepped on, and Elora pushed the button with a single, trembling finger.

"I'm okay, love," he whispered and watched her empty eyes flicker slightly. But she said nothing as she adjusted her grip on him, pulling him closer. The heat from her body was an inferno as the two sides to him fought silently. One part wanted to show her exactly how 'okay' he was—for the rest of the night if she allowed it. But the other part was drowning in questions born from betrayal and something that felt strangely like jealousy.

The elevator opened, and she quickly maneuvered them into her rooms, kicking the door closed behind her before easing him onto the sofa. She turned away instantly, darting into the other room, and he could hear the sound of her searching for something. Supplies, more than likely. Gauze and tape. The wound wasn't healing as quickly as it should. The medication must last longer than he had expected. When Killian had first told him about the suppressant that had been used on Elora, Damien had shrugged it off. At the time, he hadn't thought it viable as a threat, but that had changed now that he had felt the effects. It wouldn't take much to dose a vampire and then kill them.

Damien could hear her cursing as she came back into the sitting room, tossing down a bundle of items on the couch next to him. She sank to her knees in front of him, gingerly touching the various wounds Thorne had left behind.

"They drugged you." The words were forced from her mouth, erupting between her clenched jaw as she grabbed the wet cloth off the cushion and began wiping away the dried blood.

"Who did these?" She gestured to the cuts along his collarbones and chest, now completely scabbed over.

"Thorne. I didn't cooperate with her questioning very well," he responded, chuckling in hope of diffusing some of the tension in her body. Every movement was jerky as she cleaned away the blood, gently touching his skin as she did so. Her eyes flashed at the sound of her mother's name before she forced whatever she was feeling to the side.

"Are you craving blood? How long ago was the last dose they gave you? Do you know how much they injected?" Her questions came out rushed, tripping over each other as she spoke and sat back on her heel with the cloth still in hand. Her eyes searched his face as she waited.

"I'm not. I was only given one dose when I first got there. They didn't give me a second. But I don't know how much they gave me. I was still unconscious when they did it." He answered each question systematically, hoping that when the time came for him to ask his own, she would do the same.

"It should be gone soon. Tomorrow at the latest, I think. I doubt they gave you very much. Probably what they gave Elizabeth. Just enough to make hurting you worth it." They fell into silence for a moment.

"What did she ask you?" Damien could almost hear the unspoken part of Elora's question, and it broke his heart because the answer he was about to give her wasn't what she wanted.

"She wanted to know if you were working with Elizabeth and what your plan was to deal with her." Elora nodded before continuing to clean off the blood, each movement distracted as she seemed to stare beyond him.

"Did she ask about—"

"Don't do this to yourself, love. Don't ask those questions." Damien grasped her hands in his, stopping her work, and brought them to his lips. He pressed a kiss to her knuckles before grimacing at the scent. Viktor. His blood still covered her hands, and Damien let his eyes move over her, taking in the shirt that was also covered.

"How did you find me?" Elora shrugged before pulling her hands from his and standing. The wet cloth fell to the table as she began to pace, arms wrapped around her stomach.

"I knew something was wrong, and I called Silas. He came over and tried to assure me that you were fine. But you hadn't checked in, and I knew something had happened. I tried calling you, and no one answered. I was trying so hard not to panic." He listened intently to each word as she paced from one side of the room to the other, eyes locked onto the floor.

"Then, Korina called me using your phone. Told me you wouldn't be coming back for a while and that they were only using you to get to me. I'm sorry, Damien. I should have seen this coming. I should have known they would do anything to get their hands on me." Tears appeared in her eyes and began rolling down her cheeks before she brushed them away.

"She told me to talk to Viktor. Said that he would know where to go. So, I did, and he agreed to help—"

"Why? Why would he do that?" His voice had an edge to it that he hadn't intended, but he couldn't make himself regret it even as she flinched. This was the part they both knew was coming eventually. They couldn't brush it under the rug and pretend it never happened. She stopped pacing and snuck a quick peek at him, as if she couldn't bear to meet his gaze directly. His hand clenched into a fist at his side as he waited for an answer, waited for something that would take away the sting of her weeping over his dead body, of her fighting his hold to get to him.

"First, he demanded to be let go with promises that we wouldn't go after him. I said no and told him that he should help to atone for what he had done. We went back and forth. Eventually, he agreed on two conditions. The first was that I would try to minimize the loss of human life when I went to get you. And the second—" Her voice cracked slightly, and irritation flooded his system, forcing him to stand and march towards her. She was crying over Viktor again. Again!

"The second?" Damien demanded, and she flinched before turning away, moving to the opposite side of the room as if trying to get away from him.

"The second," she swallowed and met his eyes, not bothering to hide the pain shining horrifically bright in them, "was that you would make his death quick. That you wouldn't draw it out and torture him." Damien's mouth opened and closed several times as he tried to understand what Elora had just explained. He had heard each word perfectly, but it was incomprehensible. Viktor's stipulation hadn't been to be allowed to live or be released but to make his death quick and painless.

"Why?" He didn't clarify what he was referring to.

"He said he was tired. That there was no life for him even if I did agree to let him live. He was done fighting." She shrugged slightly as her arms wrapped tighter around herself. "It was something I understood. He got what he wanted."

"You still love him," he bit out as his mind attempted to catch up, trying to absorb and comprehend what was being said. Damien thought she was going to deny his accusation, that she was going to promise and vow that love wasn't a factor in her decision.

"Yes," she whispered softly, as if afraid of the consequences of uttering that single word. Damien's heart seemed to stop beating at her answer. He had known it was coming, had prepared for it. But hearing it was something different. It was a slap across the face as she finally looked up at him and took a single step back.

"I know that you're angry and hurt. You have every right to be, and I'll deal with whatever the consequences are." She said each word methodically like a practiced script that she had memorized before this performance.

"How? How could you still love him after everything he did to you?" She closed her eyes as Damien asked his questions, his voice rising with each one.

"I don't know. I've tried and failed over and over again to understand. I hated him for what he did. I hated him for Lukas and Denise. But he was also all I had for four years in that hospital. He was the only one there who saw me as a person. I tried to purge all of those memories and attachments, but I couldn't."

"Seeing you cry over him was worse than any torture they put me through." He watched her flinch at his statement before turning away. Damien wanted to tell her that he understood her actions, understood how she could still have feelings for Viktor. But he couldn't. It wasn't simply that the words were stuck in his throat or that it would be too painful to say them. It was the fact he truly didn't understand how she had been able to look at Viktor and feel anything other than rage.

They lapsed into a silence, both standing in the center of the room as he watched her and Elora stared at the floor. Her hair hung around her face like a curtain, blocking any chance of seeing her expression. She was retreating. He could see it in how her shoulders hunched inwards, how she seemed to try and render herself compact. Every part of him hated to witness it, hated himself for being unable to move and go to her.

Elora's arms unwrapped from around her body as she approached him with hesitant steps, as if she was afraid of how her presence would be received. She stopped only inches away from him and stared up into his eyes as she chewed her cheek.

"I'm sorry. For what I did. For taking Viktor's death away from you. But I won't apologize for how I felt and still feel about him. I don't expect you to understand it or to forgive me." She brought her hand up and cupped his cheek, giving him a sad smile that said she believed this was the end for them. His heart fractured and broke as he realized she believed he was about to walk away from her because of this, that this would render her unlovable in his eyes and she would be left alone again.

"I don't need to understand it, love. Your feelings are your own, and I would never tell you how to feel." Damien leaned down, kissing her forehead even as he heard her release a shuddering breath. The lies he had just offered her were bitter on his tongue and he swallowed to try and get rid of the taste. He didn't want her to be in pain, even if it meant lying and pushing down his own feelings, which he was failing at. He wanted to believe he didn't need to understand why she had still held feelings for the human even after everything he had done to her. For years, Viktor was all she had, a single light in the darkness, and Damien had witnessed their connection firsthand. And it had seemed so genuine on both sides. Viktor had loved her as well, just not in the same way.

No, the only thing he understood was that he had lied to her, said the words that would hopefully give her an anchor to hold onto.

Elora nodded and laid her head on his chest, ignoring the remaining blood that had been forgotten during their conversation. He felt her arms wrap around his waist once more, pulling him against her as she seemed to breathe him in. Damien wanted the anger and betrayal currently poisoning his system to disappear, wanted to breathe them out, but they were stuck, ravaging his body like an inferno no matter what words he said to her.

"I love you, Damien. I need you to know that." His heart skipped a beat as the words hit him. She had never truly said them even if he knew she felt that way. It was there in every action, in the way she looked at him. At times, it seemed to practically radiate from her, washing over him like a warm wave. They stood there, arms wrapped around one another in silence as Damien's mouth dried and every word turned to ash on his tongue.

He couldn't say them back, not with her smelling of Viktor. He couldn't make himself say it when he was drowning in anger and hurt that was simmering just beneath the surface, threatening to boil over no matter how hard he tried to force it down.

Chapter 22

Elora

He didn't say a word after her confession, even though she was sure he could feel her heart pounding in her chest. Instead, his body seemed to stiffen, and for a moment, Elora thought he was going to move away from her. Her eyes closed as she prepared for the loss of his touch, of his presence. She had taken Viktor away from him, admitted that she still loved him on a certain level. Damien's lips pressed into the top of her head and she swore she heard him inhale before he took a step away, turning away from her.

In her chest, her heart twisted tightly, forming itself into a knot as she tried to ignore the pain of not hearing those words repeated back. Damien ran his hand through his hair before tilting his head towards the ceiling.

"I can't hold you when you smell like him." She marched past him, pulse racing as hunger pains ravaged her. Her plan had been to tend to his injuries, feed, and then bathe because the overwhelming scent of Viktor's blood was too much for her to handle. The door slammed behind her before she slid the lock into place. If he wanted her to wash off the blood, she would do so in private, where she could cry or rage or simply drown in memories if that was what she wanted. He had said enough, and she didn't want to hear another word out of his mouth at the moment.

Damien had every right to be angry, and she accepted that. This was a consequence she had foreseen even before walking into that room where Damien had been bound to a chair. But that didn't mean she would be a vessel for his disappointment and anger. It didn't mean she would stay in that room with him while he dealt with his feelings. She had apologized and tried to explain, but it hadn't been enough.

He hadn't said the words back to her and that was agony.

Slowly, she removed the shirt that was soaked with both hers and Viktor's blood. Elora threw it in the corner of the bedroom, planning to deal with it later. Burn it, more than likely. Her pants slid off her legs easily enough despite the stiffness from the dry gore, and she tossed it aside as well before staring blankly at the pile. That was what she had left of Viktor—bloody clothing. She felt the burning in her eyes once more, felt the tears begin to gather and pool as if waiting for permission to stream down her cheeks.

Her arms were shaking as she wrapped them around her stomach and entered the bathroom, turning on the shower. Hot water. No cold. Nothing to lessen the burning that would wash away the blood and her guilt.

She jumped, cursing loudly as someone pounded on the bedroom door. One. Two. Three times. Each time louder and harder than before, reverberating throughout the room.

"Elora!" Her name filtered through the door and into the bathroom, where she stood beside the shower. Damien pounded on the door once more, yelling her name.

"Open the door." She turned off the shower, grabbed the robe off the counter, and slipped it on, knotting the belt at her waist as she debated doing what he was demanding. Her heart raced in her chest as she listened to his heavy breathing on the other side. She wasn't afraid. He wouldn't hurt her and she knew that down to the very marrow of her bones. But he could leave, could tell her that he couldn't forgive her for what she did and then disappear from her life. And if he did, Elora wasn't sure she would be left in one piece. She had given so much of herself to him, removing them one by one for his consumption. There was no giving them back and putting them in their original positions.

Again, pounding on the door before the handle shook as he tried to force it open. Elora sighed deeply, preparing herself for whatever was going to happen. She marched to the door, unlocking it and yanking it open to see an expression that made her take a step back. Dark and angry, but something else as well.

"Shower. Now." She raised a brow as he pushed past her and into the bedroom.

"As soon as you leave," she snapped, staring at his back, his shoulders rising and falling with each harsh intake of breath. "Now, Damien."

He spun around and watched as she gestured towards the open door.

"No. I'm not leaving." Her heart skipped slightly at the words. It was as if he was vowing to stay, not just at that moment, but forever. Once again, he knew her darkest fears, knew where her mind had taken her in the wake of everything that had happened with Viktor.

"I don't want to argue, Damien. I can't. I have nothing left right now," she admitted before tossing the door closed and making her way back to the bathroom. Right now, all she wanted was scalding hot water on every part of her, washing away the evidence of what transpired. Of her mother being alive and the humans seeking her annihilation. Of Korina's betrayal. Of Viktor's death.

His hand wrapped around her wrist, and she stopped, letting her head hang as she waited.

"What did he say? As he was dying? He said something to you. I know it." Elora jerked her hand from his grasp and wrapped her arms around herself again.

"That he was sorry. That's all." She made to enter the bathroom once more, but he grabbed her again.

"Did you forgive him?" A sharp sigh fell from her lips as she closed her eyes.

"I don't want to do this right now," she muttered softly, unsure that he actually heard her.

"Did. You. Forgive him?" The repeated question came with an edge, a hint of the anger waiting beneath the calm exterior. Elora leveled him with a glare, yanking her arm away once more.

"Yes." Damien turned away from her, pacing through the bedroom, each step heavy as if he were made of lead. The silence between them stretched as Elora watched him. His eyes never left the carpet, as if the solution to this was hidden there.

"How? He killed Lukas." She shrugged slightly instead of answering because she didn't have an answer. Damien chuckled darkly at her reaction, and she sank into a chair, pulling her knees to her as if they could protect her.

"He had been through enough. With Killian and Elizabeth. Plus Jaime. I didn't have it in me to hate him after he helped me." She glared at him again. "Or did you forget that?"

"No, I didn't. But helping you doesn't absolve him of his crimes."

"It did for you," she snapped and he flinched before she stood, adjusting the robe. "I don't want to argue, Damien. I apologized and accepted that it probably isn't enough to fix it. I've tried to explain why I did it and have been honest even though I knew what would happen." Damien was silent as he seemed to watch her, and she shook her head slightly, unsure if there was anything else to say.

A soft cry escaped her lips as Damien charged forward and was inches from her before she could blink. She took a step back and then another as he matched her until her back hit the wall. Damien rested his hand on the wall beside her face, leaning in close. There was a darkness to his eyes, a hunger, and she fought down the small surge of panic.

"I don't forgive you," he muttered, his lips on the shell of her ear. Something warm twisted deep in her stomach at the feeling. "I don't know that I can."

Her heart dropped into her feet even as his mouth moved to her neck, his breath warm on her skin in a way that made her squeeze her thighs together. It was torture. Softly, his lips pressed along her neck, and her eyes closed, drowning in the overwhelming sensation. Somewhere a voice screamed to stop, trying to remind her that there had been a conversation happening.

Damien leaned back, and she whimpered slightly at the loss of his lips on her skin. He smirked at the reaction before his face grew serious, all the teasing and heat evaporating in an instant.

"But I'm willing to spend the rest of my life trying. I don't need to understand. I just need you with me. That's all. Nothing else matters." His lips crashed into hers as something feral took over the two of them, hands grasping and pulling. She felt his hands at the knot holding the robe closed as her mouth moved to his neck, licking up the long column where the moth tattoo was. A deep moan rumbled from him as he finally untied the knot and pushed the robe back, letting it drop to the floor so she was completely bare before him.

Her skin prickled against the cold air, her nipples growing taut as his hand roamed over her ribs until he reached her breasts. His touch was rough—eager and hungry as he pinched her nipple between his fingers, twisting slightly, and she moaned loudly against his skin. He chuckled lightly at the sound, and she couldn't find it in herself to feel any sense of shame at how desperate she was to feel every inch of him, to feel him press against her.

"Damien," she forced out, his name more of a plea than anything else.

"Yes, love?" He murmured against her skin as he pressed kisses along her neck, licking and sucking gently. Every word she knew disappeared, vanished from her mind as she lost herself in the sensation.

"Please." It was the only word that came to mind, the only word she was capable of saying.

"Please, what?" She growled in frustration as his hand moved to her neck, his thumb running along her jawline as he stared down at her. At the heat in his gaze, she swallowed before pushing gently at his chest, fingers splayed out over the muscle and scabs from where he had been hurt because of her. Step by step, she guided him backwards until he hit the bed, falling down onto the mattress. His brows knitted together as he watched her, eyes roaming up and down over her naked form. She fought the urge to cover up under the heat of his gaze, under his scrutiny.

Elora's heart raced in her chest, pounding frantically and seemingly without rhythm as she climbed on top of him, straddling him as his eyes widened in surprise. She could feel him straining against his jeans beneath her and she rocked her hip slightly, earning a deep groan that she felt beneath her hands resting on his chest.

Her hair fell around her face as she leaned down and pressed tiny bites and kisses to his neck and chest, smiling softly when she felt exactly how fast his pulse was pounding. His hands rose and held both sides of her face before bringing her down to him, pressing their lips together in a clash of teeth and tongue before his fingers began to roam over her. They seemed unable to decide where to linger as his hands moved from her breasts to her ribs before gripping her hips and pressing her down onto him so she could feel him.

Elora's body jerked as her fingers dug into his chest, trying to find traction as he seemed to consume her. Finally, she pulled back, panting slightly as he smirked up at her, mischief playing on his lips.

"Let's see if I actually like being tied up."

Her movements became jerky at his suggestion. It had been something she had said in the heat of the moment, a comment that she had said to mess with Korina. It had worked perfectly, throwing the vampire off balance as soon as she said it. Elora hadn't expected it to spark any interest on Damien's part.

"Hey," he whispered, sliding his arm around her waist, keeping her close as he sat up. She adjusted her legs so they wrapped around his waist and traced the cuts on his chest, letting her fingers run along each scab. Tomorrow. Everything would be healed by tomorrow, leaving only these lines behind. A testament to what they would do just to get to her.

"We don't have to do that, love," he said, pressing a kiss to her cheek. Her brows narrowed as she bit her bottom lip, sinking her teeth in to keep her thoughts in one piece. Elora met his gaze before snaking her arms around his neck, playing with the hair that had grown longer as they dealt with wave after wave of issues.

"I think—" She started, twirling Damien's hair around her index finger. "We should try."

"If at any point you're uncomfortable, we stop. Understand? I don't care how far we've gone or what's happening." She nodded and he brushed aside her hair.

"Go wash off that blood. I'll find something to use."

"Not chains. Not handcuffs." He let her go and she climbed off him, instantly making her way to the bathroom. Her movements were quick and efficient as she turned on the hot water and took in her appearance. Every bit of her skin was covered in blood, the scent of it overwhelming. A part of her screamed to somehow preserve it, to keep it as a token of who she had lost.

Tears once more. But they were softer. Almost gentle. Not the heaving sobs that had ripped from her earlier as she stepped into the scalding hot water and washed every last remnant of Viktor from her body and hair. She tried to tell herself that he would have died either way, either by hers or Damien's hand. But she had been prepared to give Viktor his only request if that was still what he wanted. An easy death. She could have ordered Damien to do exactly that.

Elora leaned her forehead against the shower wall, letting the water cascade over her as her stomach cramped once more, this time so tightly she almost cried out. She would need blood before this.

"Love." His voice permeated the bathroom and shower, drawing her from the growing pain in her body. Heat pooled in her core at the promise of what was to come. She wanted—no, needed—to do this. Killian wouldn't control her, would dictate her life or desires. This would be a transformation, a revisioning of her darkest fear, the nightmare that had plagued her sleeping and waking hours.

She turned off the water and stepped out, only to be met with a towel and cup of blood. Damien smirked down at her, wrapping the towel around her body.

"Drink up. I could hear your stomach from the bedroom," he laughed out, tilting the cup towards her lips. "Then, put that on. I'll be waiting."

Damien gestured towards a pile of lace on the counter and her brows narrowed before shooting him a confused expression.

"You'll see," Danien said in response to her unspoken question before spinning on his heels and dragging himself from the room. Elora finished the blood in her cup, giggling softly to herself as she always did with him. He could say the tiniest thing, say the most insignificant comment and butterflies would erupt, causing her cheeks to redden and the ground to dissolve beneath her feet. It made appearing like a fierce vampire head difficult.

Quickly, she dried off and rubbed her lavender lotion over her skin before picking up the lace Damien had left behind. A nightgown, she realized. Or lingerie, more specifically with the tag attached to the side. She wanted to kiss him for that as she removed it and held it up with her fingers. Lace straps that looked like they would tear at the slightest bit of force turned into a completely sheer nightgown that would fit her form, hugging all the right places. She slipped it over her head and adjusted it. It stopped just where her thighs were, barely making it to the point it would cover her if it wasn't lace.

Elora studied herself in the mirror for a moment before brushing out her wet hair, letting it hang loose down her back. A deep breath. First one and then another before she sauntered out of the bathroom and into the bedroom where he sat on the bed in nothing but his boxers with two lengths of silk dangling from his grasp.

His breathing hitched as he took her in, eyes moving languidly over her body in a way that felt like being consumed, absorbed into his very being. He was memorizing her, taking in every detail from the scars he knew so intimately to the dips of her waist and hips to the swell of her breasts and nipples as they pushed against the fabric.

"Fuck me." She giggled as he seemed surprised to have said it out loud.

"I thought that was the idea," she said, moving towards him, each step slow. As soon as she was close enough, his arm reached out and his hand wrapped around her wrist, dragging her between his legs.

"I can't decide if I want that to stay on or to tear it off of you with my teeth," he explained as he began pressing his lips to her stomach and ribs. His touch was like fire even through the lace and she let out a moan.

"It would be a waste of money to rip it to pieces," she breathed out, surprised she could form coherent thoughts or sentences.

"I'll replace it," he muttered in between nips, grabbing the lace between his teeth. She let out a harsh laugh as her skin erupted in goosebumps. He leaned back, holding up the silk he had gathered. Scarves, she thought.

"Do the honors?" She nodded, swallowing thickly as she took them. He scooted onto the bed, arranging himself against the headboard, arms held up to the two posts as he waited for her, giving her time to decide against this.

She knelt on the bed, crawling to him across the mattress as his eyes darkened, gaze becoming almost feverish as he watched every move she made. Elora gave him a self-satisfied smirk as she straddled him, settling on his lap before tying one wrist to the post and then the other. She felt his erection pressing against her and she rocked her hips, grinding down against him. He groaned, throwing his head back against the headboard.

"You're at my mercy," she purred into his ear and felt his body shiver.

"Always," he murmured back, nuzzling the crook of her neck before pressing soft kisses to her skin. "Are you going to make me beg, love?"

She didn't say anything, just ran her tongue over the column of his throat. She could feel his moan on her tongue, on her lips as she kissed his neck and then collarbones, taking her time as she continued to work her way down. With a slight grin, Elora bit his nipple before pressing a soft kiss to it, earning her the delicious groan that she felt through his chest.

Slowly, one press of her lips at a time, she made her way down his body, feeling him grow harder with each one. She hooked her fingers into the waistband of his boxers, pulling them down and off his body before she kneed his legs open, settling herself between them. She met his eyes for a moment, noting the undisputed lust radiating, the anticipation and hint of impatience.

Elora gripped him in her hand, giving him a small grin before running her tongue over his length and wrapping her lips around the head of his cock. His hips jerked forward at the sensation as she released him before sitting back on her heels.

"Behave. Or I'll leave you here." Determination settled onto his flawless features as he seemed to try and center himself. He nodded, licking his lips as he waited.

Elora leaned back down, taking him in her mouth until he hit the back of her throat and she swallowed, taking even more.

"Fuck," he whispered hoarsely and she hummed softly, letting the vibration radiate down him. Slowly, almost languidly, she worked him with her mouth and hand, hollowing out her cheeks as she wrung every moan and harsh curse she could.

"Love, please." The sound of him begging was everything perfect in the world, emboldening her as she released him and crawled back up his body.

"Please, what?" She asked, biting at his neck until he cursed again. "Do you want to fuck me? Do you want to be inside me?" His arms yanked at the restraints, pulling at the bedposts and she chuckled softly before straddling him and lining him up with her entrance.

"Elora, please."

"You're so cute when you beg." Before he could say anything, she slid down onto him, feeling him stretch her as he did. Her back arched at the sensation, at the fullness of him being so far inside. She would never get used to this feeling, never get used to the way he fit so flawlessly.

"Damn it, you're perfect. So fucking perfect," he forced out, jerking his hips as if to take control. She clicked her tongue in faux disappointment as she slid up and down his length, causing a growl to fill the room.

Elora kept her movements slow as she rode him, building the heat in her core as her muscles tightened, chasing her pleasure as she gave him his. His hands flexed, yanking slightly as if he wanted to be released. She leaned over, never stopping her rhythm and undid one of the ties, freeing his arm. There was no hesitation as he untied the other and his hand found her body, roaming over it like he was making up for lost time. He grabbed her breasts, tweaking her nipples before taking one into his mouth, biting at the tiny nub. They roamed as if they couldn't decide where to settle before wrapping around her waist and flipping them.

She let out a soft cry as her back hit the mattress and he continued thrusting into her. Her fingernails dug into his back. Fuck, she was close. So damn close.

"Come apart, love. Come for me." She cried out as she did, falling over the edge and into bliss so complete she only saw stars, losing connection with reality as wave after wave of pleasure hit her. She felt him pulsate inside her and his own moan matched hers as they collapsed together onto the bed.

His breathing was hard as he pulled her close and she let her head rest on his chest.

"So?" She asked between breathing, wishing desperately for more blood to drink. He ran his fingers over her arm, trailing them in lazy circles until they both fell asleep, sprawled out naked on the sheets. All Elora could think was this was perfection, this was the paradise they had earned with each moment of hatred, each moment of rage and violence.

This was the only place in the world she wanted to be.

This was where she was safe.

Chapter 23

Thorne

Both gravestones before her were nameless, but she knew who they belonged to. Viktor and Jaime, side by side, just as Elora had requested. Thorne told herself that it was for Viktor that she followed the request, that it wasn't because it was her daughter who had asked for this final act of kindness. Watching Elora weep so bitterly over his body in her arms, hearing him apologize for the actions Thorne had ordered, had shaken something in her. A crack in what she thought was an ironclad shield around herself, blocking out all memories and emotions from her previous life as a mother and consort. And Elora had done it, forgave him for everything he had done to her and Thorne had seen how Viktor's eyes had softened, the desperation evaporating instantly once her words reached him. He had been at peace when she ripped the knife from his chest.

"What did you do, Thorne?" The shouted question came from behind her, and she tilted her head back, breathing in the evening air. Somewhere nearby was lavender. There was a hint of it in the breeze. It had always been her favorite next to sunflowers and roses, but the latter had lost their appeal shortly after Elora had been born. Thorne took two more deep breaths, preparing herself for what was coming, while Chloe's steps seemed to echo as she came up the stone walkway. This corner of the cemetery was reserved for Resistance members or for bodies they needed to bury without attracting attention. Someone had to have told Chloe where she was, and Thorne could only hope whoever it was hadn't been hurt in the process.

"I have a feeling you already know and are asking unnecessary questions." Thorne's reply was curt, her annoyance shining through. She had wanted to spend time here grieving, wallowing in her regret and guilt before returning to the newest headquarters to decide what to do next. Elora had opened the door to collaboration, to working together to deal with Elizabeth. It was exactly as Viktor had said when he defended her. At the time, Thorne had thought that it was his emotions clouding his judgement, but it had been her who had been blind. She had wanted to see Elora as a threat, see her as a villain because it would make using her easier. That room had changed everything, but Chloe didn't need to know that.

"Korina is dead. You let Elora get away. What went wrong?" Chloe finally reached her, but Thorne didn't turn to her and even glance in her direction. Instead, her focus remained on the gravestone she knew belonged to Viktor.

"She came prepared."

"You were meant to be prepared as well, Thorne. Explain how you managed to get her there only to let her leave!" Chloe was almost frantic as Thorne turned to meet her heated glare, absorbing the rage that seemed to radiate from the vampire. It wasn't just rage. It was fear. Chloe was deathly afraid Elora would find out she was involved and come after her.

"You're right. We had her. And then Korina lost her shit and attacked. Viktor stopped her and died in the process." Chloe waved her hand dismissively.

"A human. No real loss." Thorne's hand reached out and struck the vampire before she realized what was happening. The sound of the hit echoed in the graveyard, disappearing and merging with the sound of bird calls as they both stood there. Chloe's head snapped to the side, staying there for a moment before turning slowly and meeting Thorne's gaze. Her fingers rose to her face, gently touching her cheek as Thorne's hand opened and closed in an effort to stave off the stinging pulsing in her palm.

"A human life is a loss, Chloe. Remember, you depend on us to stay alive. Viktor would still be alive if your vampire had been able to control her jealousy. That's what fucked the mission. After that, Korina was killed, and she left."

"I knew you wouldn't be able to turn on your daughter, Iris. I was a fool," Chloe spat, and the sound of Thorne's old name was like dirt being rubbed in an already festering wound. It had been years since she heard that name, had felt every emotion that came with it and now it was thrown at her at every turn. After escaping Killian, she had carefully crafted her identity before moving into a position of power. It had started as a desire for revenge against the vampire who used her, had abused her daughter, and had tried to kill her. Then, it became more. It was about human life, about giving them an informed choice.

"Those are bold words from someone who's clearly terrified of her and refused to be involved in any way. Don't fault my perceived failure because you're a coward. At least I faced her." Thorne smirked slightly and started walking back towards the house where the council was waiting for her to announce their next move.

"Don't walk away from me, Thorne."

"Our partnership is done, Chloe. You handle Elora in your way, and I'll do the same. I don't work with those who won't get their hands dirty." Thorne savored the way Chloe cursed, the way she screamed out threats of violence and retribution.

"By the way, I had Korina's body taken to your home. It should be waiting for you on the front step." It seemed like the correct thing to do. Thorne could have cremated the body or buried it in another unmarked grave, but that felt like a defiling of the ground where so many who fought against vampires were laid to rest. She could hear Chloe rant as she walked away, entering the new headquarters. It was previously a funeral home, and technically still was as a front for business. Over half of the building was remodeled into rooms that were similar to dormitories. Families were given their own rooms, but those who were single all stayed together.

It took everything she had to not let the door slam as she entered and locked it, just in case Chloe decided revenge was the best path forward. Thorne reclined against the counter that wrapped around the entire room, grey and white marble that was lined with files and loose papers. Every document they had was moved here once the decision was made to kidnap Damien in an effort to preserve it if Elora decided to simply burn the building to the ground. And from the expression Thorne had seen on her face, that had been a possibility.

Elora was fierce, an older and twisted version of how she had been as a child before Killian began his visits. Thorne's stomach churned as she tilted her head back and closed her eyes, unable to see anything other than Elora holding Viktor's body and then demanding for him to be buried next to Jaime. It was a kindness that Thorne didn't expect to see from her after everything Viktor had done to her, everything he had taken from her.

Silently, she planned her speech to the council, already preparing for their backlash. Thorne didn't foresee them agreeing to her suggestion, but she supposed that they could surprise her by seeing the logic in it. Thorne took a deep breath and exhaled slowly before heading into the back office where three other council members were waiting.

She was met with expressions depicting various degrees of anger and apprehension. Richard, an older man with salt and pepper hair and soft features marred by wrinkles, sat at the head of the table and stared at her with his eyes narrowed while Sarah's face held only rage along her sharp, bird-like face. Thorne's focus went to the final member, Daniel, who had been leading the Resistance as long as she had. He had started everything, began gathering humans who wanted to fight against vampires and their control over humans. Then, Thorne had entered the picture, taking the group from small time raids and acts of civil disobedience, to a full-scale resistance actively reducing the vampire population.

Thorne sank into a chair at the head of the table, folding her hands in front of her on the rough wood. A tense silence filled the space between them as they waited for someone to speak first.

"What's next, Thorne? Your little plan with the vampire head didn't exactly work, did it?" She bristled at Richard's tone, the almost sneering curl of his lips as he spoke. He had never been a fan of hers and had tried at every turn to undermine her, arguing that she didn't have the necessary experience to lead them. It was a laughable claim, considering he was only on the council because of his hefty donations. He had never gone on a mission, never fought or killed a single vampire. In a sense, he was very similar to Chloe—fully satisfied to sit back and let others get their hands dirty and risk their lives.

"Chloe underestimated the human aspect of the vampire she sent to work with us. It was an age-old problem that caused everything to fall apart." Thorne met each person's eyes, watching for their reactions to the explanation.

"Which was?" Daniel smirked slightly as he asked the question, as if he knew what role he was playing. She didn't expect him to disagree with her or to even speak up against her. He knew her story, knew the depth of her knowledge compared to everyone else and understood exactly what she had done for their movement.

"Jealousy. She let her emotions get the better of her and her actions caused the mission to fail. I've already cut ties with Chloe due to this."

"In that case, I'll repeat the original question. What's next?" Thorne smirked at Richard's attempts to make her seem weak, make her seem incompetent. The path forward was clear to her, and if they didn't agree, Thorne knew the only solution was to leave.

"I was given an invitation for potential collaboration with the very vampire we've been searching for." Each person at the table shifted slightly even as Richard let out a harsh breath like he was holding back a laugh. She knew what he was thinking and exactly what would come out of his mouth next.

"Are we joining forces with the vampires? In that case, why even have a resistance? Why not just lie down and let them drain us?"

"I assumed that would be your reaction, Richard, which is why I am happy to do this alone without the backing of the group. My only goal is to stop Elizabeth and her rapid turning of the population while there are still humans left. If that means walking into Ashcroft Tower, then I can do that. My pride isn't more important than human life." Thorne fought back a smile as Richard's soft features contorted into something like indignant rage, which warmed her heart to see.

"You're joking. You have to be. Working with one vampire failed and we're trying a different one? This isn't a shirt, Thorne. You can't just change when the first one doesn't fit." Thorne raised a brow at Richard's less than intelligent comparison, but said nothing. Instead, she looked at the two council members who hadn't said anything yet. Daniel seemed to bite his cheek as he met her eyes while Sarah shook her head at the exchange.

Thorne and Richard disagreeing was an expected part of any meeting, and they were waiting to get past it so decisions could actually be made.

"Why don't you explain what the invitation is and what it includes, Thorne? I feel like there's information missing that could be useful." Daniel's tone was even as he spoke, as if trying to keep the peace.

"She didn't say anything specific. When she left, she said to come to the Tower if I wanted to work together to deal with Elizabeth. An open invitation."

"And you plan on taking her up on that offer?" Finally, Sarah spoke, but she seemed intrigued and not repulsed by the idea. Working with Elora shouldn't matter as long as it saved human lives and if Thorne had simply done this from the beginning, perhaps more lives would have been saved.

"I do. Again, I'm willing to do this on my own without any ties to the Resistance. However, I believe that she wants to stop Elizabeth as much as we do. And, for my cooperation, I can negotiate. She's now the head of two vampire houses that she's combining together, and the presumptive head of a third once that leader decides to retire or dies. I could demand certain stipulations." Thorne could see everyone's mind working as she spoke, wheels turning as they began to see the vision she was presenting to them. Even Richard, for all his stupidity and arrogance, seemed intrigued by the idea.

Daniel leaned forward, glancing at both of the council members sitting beside him, and nodded. "What are we going to demand?"

Thorne grinned slightly before settling into her seat, prepared to finally put together a list of everything the Resistance had wanted over the years, everything they had fought for to create a better life for the humans living in their city.

Chapter 24

Elora

Hartley refused to explain any further after sending Elora a message stating there were updates in the research into exactly what Killian had done. As a result, Elora had called Silas to inform him that there was new information and to get over to the Tower if he wanted to be present when Hartley revealed it. He had shown up at Elora's office door within twenty minutes, hair perfectly in place and suit impeccably fitted and pressed. It was as if any piece of clothing he put on altered itself to match his expectations. Elora, on the other hand, was in jeans and one of Damien's t-shirts, hair slightly messy. But if she was about to potentially receive news that could rattle her existence, it didn't matter what she wore.

"As I said, we have updates." Dr. Hartley announced as Elora, Damien, and Silas stepped off the elevator and entered the lab. About half a dozen vampires and humans in lab coats worked diligently on their projects, which Elora realized with a hint of shame she knew nothing about. She had been so focused on Elizabeth that she hadn't thought to look into exactly what experiments the scientists were doing. In her mind, she added it to the ever-growing list of things she needed to learn and investigate. If she was going to be in charge of two vampire houses, then she needed information. Killian had believed brute force was power, that being able to scare or intimidate was the only path to total control. He had been wrong. It was knowledge and secrets, knowing weaknesses and exploiting them if necessary.

Elora dropped into a chair in Hartley's office and gestured impatiently. Everything was a show with this vampire. Every meeting was like she was giving a presentation to her investors while Elora just wanted the details.

"We're getting closer to creating something that could be called a cure or weapon," Hartley began as she folded her hands together and placed them on the desk.

"You called me here for that?" Elora's tone was harsh. If that was where the information began and ended, then this was a waste of time. To her credit, Hartley only gave her a lopsided grin before continuing.

"What we are currently working on would potentially reverse what Elizabeth has done."

"They would turn human?" The disbelief in Damien's words matched Elora's own reaction to the statement. Rendering them human again seemed too good to be true, seemed like a fairy tale ending and this was no fairy tale. Her brows raised as she watched Hartley shift uncomfortably in her massive leather chair.

"I didn't say that. And to be honest, right now I'm not sure. Our preliminary experiments with your blood have revealed a way to craft a cure. Or weapon, depending on how you look at it."

"What are your tests showing right now?" Silas leaned forward towards Hartley and seemed to study her, as if searching for signs that the scientist was untrustworthy or lying. She took a deep breath as her eyes darted between Elora and Silas.

"Death, as of the most recent test. Each experiment we have done has killed off the host cells. It's possible that there isn't necessarily a cure in the way that you are hoping for." Each word was hesitant as Hartley explained. "But this is only preliminary.

It does, however, require us to consider what happens if that is the only way to stop your sister."

Elora had no response to that and she hadn't allowed herself to even consider needing to kill her. A part of her wanted to believe that her sister was still somewhere in there, hiding underneath the frenzied fanaticism and unhinged madness.

"I would prefer to not have to kill an entire group of people because they fell victim to my sister. Do you have any idea how many she had turned? Hundreds. More every day. You're saying we may have to kill them all, including children." Damen shifted closer to her, placing his hand on the nape of her neck as Hartley held her hands up as if to placate her.

"I'm not saying that at all. It's only an update on what we have found so far. I understand the stakes here." Elora nodded at the scientist, easing back in the chair and savoring the warmth of Damien's touch. He squeezed gently before removing his hand and taking a step back.

"We'll continue working on it. I wanted you to know where we are, and it seemed better to deliver that type of news in person." Hartley gave Elora a calculating look, eyes roaming over her face as if searching for something. Her lips thinned into a line before she leaned towards Elora over the desk, hands once more folded.

"I would like to discuss something else, if you don't mind. And I think it's something we should discuss privately." Elora glared at the scientist before tracking the fear in her face, the way her eyes seemed to shift around the room. Then, Elora nodded before glancing at her uncle and Damien.

"I don't think this is a good idea," Silas began before Elora gestured for Damien and Silas to leave.

"Shut the door on your way out." Elora listened as both vampires huffed in irritation but did as she said. The door clicked closed as Elora crossed her legs, picking at a thread on her jeans.

"Okay, let's hear what's so personal that they couldn't be in here."

"Your father fed from you, correct?" She gestured to Elora's neck as if to point at the scars that lined her flesh. Elora shifted and raised her chin before meeting Hartley's eyes. Her hand twitched as if to pick at the skin around her nails as flashes of memories rushed back.

"I wouldn't call him a father, but yes. As well as others he deemed worthy." Elora spat the last word. "Does this question have a purpose?"

Hartley nodded and pulled out a file from her desk, opening it to a sheet of paper with a chart and table. Elora shrugged her shoulders and leaned back in her chair.

"You're going to need to explain that. I'm afraid that isn't where my talents lie." Hartley chuckled and closed the file, setting it off to the side.

"While we've been looking into stopping your sister, I have been pursuing a side project of sorts. Specifically, into how the modifications to your genetics have changed you and what Killian actually managed to create."

"I didn't ask you to do that." Elora snarled slightly and Hartley at least had the decency to look regretful at the intrusion.

"I understand that. But I feel it's necessary if we're going to try and deal with your sister along with those she created."

"Just tell me what you found out," Elora forced out, fighting off the feeling of Killian's teeth in her neck once more.

"Your—" Elora raised a brow at Hartley, who swallowed before continuing. "Killian was successful in some regards. Your blood is more potent, as I'm sure you know. However, that potency isn't as powerful as he wanted it to be. He imagined it as something a vampire couldn't live without. They would rush to his feet and offer anything they had for a taste." Hartley stood and came around the desk, leaning against it as she stared down at

Elora's face. There was a sense of sadness in her pale eyes that reminded Elora of Denise, of the expression she had every time a triggered memory was revealed.

"But that isn't what happened. The flavor of your blood is improved, and it can satiate hunger better and longer than human blood. I know that he acted as if your blood was addicting, like he couldn't live without it. And I can only imagine that has had some—" Hartley seemed to think through what she was about to say before continuing. "Consequences. That it has had some consequences for you."

Elora let out a choked sound and tried her best to retain her composure. Right outside the glass door, Silas and Damien were watching every move that she made, every twitch or wince. She swallowed and forced back the tears, not realizing just how desperately she had latched onto the idea that her blood was like a drug, rendering everyone who tasted it addicted. It wouldn't have forgiven them for anything they had done, but it would have provided some semblance of a rationale beyond the fact they were monsters.

"So, I don't need to worry about vampires feeding from me? If I were to allow it, that is." Hartley shook her head, graciously ignoring the way Elora's voice shook.

"No. Not at all. It would simply taste better and keep the vampire satiated longer. Think of it as a high-class meal compared to a fast-food restaurant." Elora nodded at the comparison before turning her head away from the office door slightly to wipe away a tear. She didn't need Damien bursting into the room to demand why she was crying.

Every moment she had spent scared of what her blood had done to Damien had been pointless. Until hearing those words, Elora had still been afraid that feeding from her had done damage in some way, that there had been consequences neither of them had noticed. In her core, she had been terrified that it meant he didn't truly love her, but craved her blood. She let out a harsh breath before sitting straighter.

"What else? You said he was successful in some regards. Where was he successful?" Silently, Elora prepared herself for what was coming.

"Killian wanted you to be a beacon to humans. He described it as a siren call, or a lamp that draws moths to it. It seems he was successful in that endeavor. Your blood emits a scent, like a pheromone, that draws humans in. At that point, all it takes is a touch and they will follow you anywhere. It would make it easier to turn them and keep them under control."

With those final words, reality began to fracture, a long crack beginning at the base of her sanity and moving through her psyche, undoing every bit of work she had done to even get to a place where healing was possible.

"It requires my blood for this to happen," She began, swallowing down tears as she thought through what Hartley had said. "While I was medicated, would it have still done that?"

Viktor's smiling face in the hospital rushed forward as she remembered the softness in his eyes and the way he sought to make her laugh when she was wading too far out into the darkness. Had that been a byproduct of what Killian had done?

"I don't know for sure. But if the medication suppressed everything else—the hunger, repulsion for human food, and the ability to compel others—then my answer would be no. The medication would have suppressed that as well. But once you stopped taking it, then you would have started drawing in humans again."

"And I would need to touch them? In order for it to fully work?" Hartley seemed to chew on her cheek as she considered the question.

"That's how it appears. Obviously, I haven't been able to do any concrete testing since I would need humans to do so. But from what I've seen so far, they are drawn in by your scent, no different than someone approaching someone because they find them attractive. At that point, they could still turn around and have no negative consequences."

"Once I touch them, though. That's when they become mine, so to say."

"Yes, tied to you."

"I am you, and you are me," Elora whispered softly, hearing Wyatt's words echo in her head. Guilt raced through her, causing her pulse to race and her heart to pound. Her eyes closed as she took in a deep breath, feeling her lungs expand as she tried without much success to calm herself.

"I'm sorry?" Hartley gave her a confused look as Elora stood, fingers gripping the edges of the long black T-shirt

"It's their motto. Their creed. My sister and those she recruited and turned." Elora stopped just as she turned. "I need you to study one more thing before we go after her. There's a tie that connects us. I can feel her when she gets near and it's the same for her. For everyone connected to me, I guess. If they die, what happens to me?" Hartley's eyes widened before her expression shifted to one of determination before nodding.

Chapter 25

Damien

She left that scientist's office without a word. The door slammed behind her and she darted to the elevator, leaving Silas and Damien to follow behind her. He looked her over, tracking the way she was picking at the skin around her fingernails, the glistening in her eyes that hinted at tears. She had retreated again and proved it when she darted into their bedroom, leaving Silas and Damien the sitting room. Both vampires listened as the bathroom door closed and locked before the water turned on.

"What the fuck did that woman say to her?" Damien asked before sinking onto the couch and staring where Elora was falling further into herself just a room away. He heard Silas exhale sharply and sit before his eyes went in the same direction.

"I don't know. But it did something to her. Have you seen her like this?" Silas asked and ran his hand through his hair, smoothing back the strands that had fallen down around his face. His eyes narrowed as he stared at the door, as if trying to hear Elora's thoughts. Damien sucked in a breath, trying to ignore the similarities to the night she killed her father before they walked into his office. It was the expression she wore when she pushed her pain down so far that it was unreachable, until she wouldn't have to feel it.

"In the days leading up to Killian's death. This is what Lukas must have described to you," Damien explained as he stood and started pacing slightly, eyes moving over the room before returning to the bedroom door.

"She can't shut us out, Damien. She can't shut you out."

"I don't know what to tell you. She can and she will. She is," Damien forced out as he continued to pace, trying desperately to contain everything in him that wanted to break down the door and get her to talk. Or fight with him. Scream and yell. Hell, he would even take her stabbing him again.

"You can reach her. You have before. After Jonas." They both fell silent. Damien wasn't sure Silas was right.

"That's different. She had been attacked and—" Silas held up a hand, silencing him instantly.

"No, it isn't. It was a moment when she needed you, but didn't know how to ask. Was afraid to ask for your help. I know you can understand that," Silas explained slowly, as if he thought Damien wasn't able to fully comprehend what he was saying. It was horrifying how much sense Silas's explanation made. He had seen it in the moments when she wouldn't tell him when things were wrong—when she was scared of feeding, when she was drowning after the banquet, when she was struggling with her feelings for Viktor. She didn't want to show weakness, and asking for his help was doing exactly that. Damien wasn't sure how to show her that it was strength to lean on him or Silas. He wanted her to understand that no matter what was put in their path, he would stand beside her, that she was never a burden or weak.

He never realized how desperately he wanted to hear her say that she needed him.

Damien nodded slightly at Silas and marched through the bedroom before listening at the bathroom door. He could only hear her sobs, quiet and muted as if she were crying into a towel.

Silas was fucking right. Of course he was. She didn't want them to hear her and when she eventually came out, Elora would be composed and artificial. Disguised. Hidden. And it drove him insane to think she still wanted to hide from him. Once then twice, he knocked lightly on the bathroom door, listening for her voice.

"Give me a minute. I'll be right out."

"No. Let me in. We are going to talk about this." He heard her scoff, muttering something that was probably very unkind before he heard the water start to drain. More movement reached him from the other side of the door until the lock clicked and she yanked it open, eyes red and empty.

"I'll talk to you and Silas both. I just need a minute."

"Why? So you can hide from us? From me?"

"You're being dramatic," she drawled slightly, but there was no inflection to it.

"And you're being impossible. Something upset you. That scientist said something that dragged you back to that dark place you fall into. And instead of talking to me or your uncle, you're hiding." Damien turned away from her and shut the bedroom door, sparing Silas a glance even as the vampire nodded. He sighed deeply before turning back to her, taking in the tears that seemed to have seeped through the shield she had put in place. Her arms were wrapped around her chest, holding the towel to her as her wet hair stuck to her neck and chest. Fuck, she was gorgeous even when she was on the edge of oblivion with no desire to draw herself back.

He approached her and ran his hands up and down her arms, wiping away the water droplets on her skin as he considered what he wanted to say. The scent of lavender reached him, and he inhaled deeply before he spoke.

"I want you as you are. I love you as you are. That means I love every bit of you. Your smiles and sarcasm. Your violence and your darkness. Give me your tears, love. Give me your pain and your nightmares and every single dark and broken part of you. It's not only yours to carry anymore." He brushed away the tears falling down her cheek before lifting her face so she was forced to look at him, forced to see the devotion that was carved into every part of him.

"It doesn't matter how desperately you try to hide from me, I will find you. I'll dig through every wall you put up. I'll crawl into every dark cave you try to hide in. There's no part of you that's unworthy or a burden. No part of you that I don't want to consume me. Do you understand?" She shook her head as if she were unable to absorb his words and her shoulders began to shake. A sharp cry tore from her lips as her sobs broke free and she collapsed to the floor, burying her face in her hands.

Damien only followed her, sitting on the carpet before gently dragging her between his legs and resting her head on his chest. His fingers trailed through her wet hair as she wept and he kissed the top of her head, unable to speak. If anyone was unworthy, it was him. He was the one who didn't deserve her.

"I'm never leaving you, love. You'll have to kill me," he chuckled and felt her laugh, the sound falling from her in between sobs. He grinned as pride rushed through him, as he savored the sound of her fighting through whatever this was.

"I love you. I'm sorry. For pushing you away. I don't know how to handle—" she hesitated. "Hartley has been studying me. My blood and what Killian did." Elora sniffled and sat back so she could see his face. Her hand rose and cupped his cheek as she stared at him like he was something precious. Damien knew she loved him but hearing her say the words again was like witnessing a miracle. It was a high that he never wanted to come down from because hearing her say it was the only sound worth hearing. Her eyes moved to the door as she bit her bottom lip slightly.

"He's out there, if that's what you're wondering," Damien explained, and she nodded before standing.

"Silas should hear this as well, and I don't want to say it a second time."

"I'll let you change." As he spoke, the towel dropped from her body and he groaned as he took in the sight of her curves. "That's cruel. And after I said such sweet things to you."

She giggled, and the sound was like the first drop of water for a dying man, like the first flower blooming in a scorched field. He shoved his hand in his pocket as he fought to turn away from her, leaving her to dress. He reunited with Silas who was perusing the books lining the walls. Her uncle raised a single brow and Damien only nodded before dropping onto the couch, trying desperately to ignore that she was completely naked just beyond that door.

"We need to talk." Her voice reached them before she walked out of the bedroom with her damp hair clinging to the long dress she wore. Those bright green eyes of hers went everywhere but Damien and her uncle as she planted her feet in front of them, preparing for whatever she was about to say.

"Hartley asked you two to leave because she wanted to give me privacy as she told me about her findings. She has been researching me as a side project and there are some discoveries, both good and not good." Elora stopped talking to finally look up at the two of them as she tried to hide the pain in her face.

"Let's hear the good first, love." She nodded at Damien's suggestion, swallowing roughly and he wondered when the last time she fed was.

"My blood is potent, like Killian wanted. But not addicting or anything like that. She compared it to an expensive meal versus something cheap." She flinched violently and he could see why she would say this is the good news. Hell, he knew it was one of the best things he had heard. In the back of his mind had always been the tiny fear that somehow everything he felt for her was a byproduct of her blood. This would finally put that voice to rest, bury it under concrete so he would never hear it again. They all waited in silence, none of them truly knowing what to say or how to respond.

"That is, indeed, wonderful news, my dear," Silas added, his words soft as if afraid of startling her. It was clear that she was already focusing on whatever was coming next.

"The not so good part is about what Killian was successful at. Hartley explained that my blood emits a pheromone that draws humans in." She shifted on her feet as she played with the sleeves of her dress and stared at something beyond either one of them. Damien felt his chest seize, felt his breathing stop. To his left, Silas stepped forward, hand resting on the back of the chair in front of him. His fingers dug into the fabric, the only sign that this was impacting him in any way.

"It makes me a beacon in a way. But that isn't enough. It's like an attraction, but once I touch them then they are tied to me, I guess. That part wasn't explained very well. But they're committed to me after that." Damien saw all the thoughts flash across her face at once and recognized each name that came to her mind. Viktor. Wyatt. Connie. Even Elizabeth. He knew whatever the news was would be devastating, but this was beyond anything he thought possible. This had the potential to destroy her.

No one spoke because what was there to say? They couldn't tell her it wasn't her fault even though it wasn't. Killian had built her piece by piece for exactly this purpose.

Silas marched to her, his movements harsher than Damien had ever seen, and wrapped his arms around his niece, crushing her body to his as he tried to hold her together. Silas kissed the top of her head as her shoulders shook and she pressed her face into his shirt. Damien could only look away, the moment too raw and vulnerable to be witnessed. Watching their relationship grow was a privilege, an honor as she reformed her ties to Silas. So much damage had been done and the relationship would never be the same. Elora wasn't the same person she was before Silas was forced to send her away or even before the abuse began. Neither was Silas the same, Damien imagined. The guilt had eaten away at him, leaving behind a vampire who would do anything for her.

Silas and Elora broke apart as a phone began to ring, the sound too loud for what was occurring in the room. Her hands shook slightly as she picked it up from the table and answered.

"Yes?" Damien could hear voices on the other side, muffled and incoherent. But it was her face that held his attention as her expression shifted from annoyance to something like fear mingling with pain.

"I'll send someone down." Elora hung up, her lip twitching in the corner like she couldn't decide if she was going to smile or not.

"She took me up on my offer," she said, looking at both of them. "Damien, escort her to my old room. We'll give her some time to think before we talk."

Chapter 26

Thorne

Damien smirked as he got off the elevator and sauntered towards her, hands shoved deep into his jeans as he seemed to size Thorne up. All eyes moved to the two of them, with some whispering to one another about the human standing in the middle of the Tower lobby. The receptionist behind the obscenely large marble desk made a show of not watching the interaction, but it was futile. Thorne didn't recognize any of the vampires currently glued to the floor, but that didn't mean anything. She had blocked out much of her time here. Fifteen years or so ago, this place had felt like home.

Despite the cold aesthetic of glass and marble and gold, there had been a warmth that wrapped itself around her. An illusion, as she quickly realized. Killian had hand crafted a reality for her within these walls and it had taken too long for her to see through it. Once she finally did, once the beauty and lies fractured and she could see through the cracks, it hadn't only been Thorne who was left damaged.

"That was quick. Less than forty-eight hours," Damien drawled as he grew closer, signaling to the vampires standing along the wall. Security, by the looks of them. Apparently, he anticipated her being a problem, or he was just enjoying the show of force.

"Which means my little gift to you has worn off. Tell me, how did it feel being mostly human again?" He shrugged at Thorne's question, his lips quirking in that condescending way of his. It had been his constant expression except for the moments he took to recover from a hit during her interrogation.

"It was nice being reminded of why I hated it so much. But I prefer myself this way. As does your daughter," he chuckled as one of the vampires, a giant of a man, gripped her biceps. "Speaking of which, she's prepared a room for you."

Damien jerked his head towards the elevator and Thorne followed him, not bothering to fight the vampire acting as her guard. She tried to take a breath and swallow, preparing herself to face Elora once more and to do or say what was necessary to work with her. Thorne highly doubted it would be as simple as them developing a plan and executing it. It would be naive to think that questions wouldn't be asked and answers wouldn't be demanded. For that very reason, Thorne considered running, punching the guard in the throat and darting out of the building.

Perhaps this was her punishment for past sins. Perhaps this was a form of retribution for every past mistake committed. Damien pushed the button that would take them to Elora. She wanted to say that she continued her journey to the daughter she had disowned because it was necessary, because it was the right thing to do. But it was also pride, a refusal to let that prick Richard be proved right once more. If this didn't work, she wouldn't be able to return to the council.

The doors opened and Thorne took a step back as the familiarity of the decor hit her. This wasn't where Killian's, and now Elora's, office would be. Instead, this is where her bedroom had been, where she curled up next to Killian and ran her hand down his chest before he disappeared in the middle of the night. It was where she had tucked Elora into bed and sang to her, stringing up tiny lights above her bed so they would look like stars when the light was shut off. It's where she had found her daughter hiding in the closet and where she had confronted Killian only to be fed lies and false promises.

"Your room, Iris." Damien extended his hand towards the door to the left of the elevator and her feet became stone, too heavy to move. The guard pushed her forward, his massive hand covering most of her back, and she almost tripped.

"I thought I was here to speak to her. Not rehash old memories." Thorne planted her feet in the hallway, glaring at the guard beside her, almost begging him to touch her again. This was a fucking joke, a taunt and punishment all at once. Elora was still angry, then. However, whether it was about Damien or everything else, Thorne wasn't sure. And it probably didn't matter at the end of the day. She had a feeling her daughter's rage would be fearsome to behold, would consume Thorne if Elora wanted it to.

"She's busy at the moment and wants to make sure you're comfortable while you wait." That smirk was back as his eyes gleamed with something dangerous.

"Now, are you going to go in there willingly or is he going to throw you over his shoulder?" Thorne refused to look at him as she marched forward and gripped the handle, desperately trying to force down every memory that came with something as benign as a door handle. Faces flashed before her eyes, scenes of Elora's smiling face as she ran in the gardens at Silas's manor, her giggling as they played hide-and-go-seek in the ballroom on the top floor of the Tower. She shook her head before twisting the handle and throwing it open, the sight tearing the air from her lungs.

"Go on. She'll be up soon." Damien's voice was almost a purr as he gave her a slight nudge and she stepped over the threshold. "Just as a friendly heads up. Be ready. Elizabeth won't be the only topic of conversation." Before she could ask why he would warn her, the door slammed shut behind her and her eyes squeezed closed at the sound of the lock clicking into place.

The room was largely the same as before with a few additions that made bile rise in her throat. Elora's drawings still filled the bookshelves that lined the wall, framed in expensive silver and gold. Each one was as dark as Thorne remembered and she ran her finger along one of the frames, taking in what was the earliest of her work. Thorne could remember when Elora raced to her, showing her the drawing with the biggest smile on her face, mouth stretched so far that it looked painful. It was meant to be a bunny in grass with flowers, like she had seen at Corvin manor the weekend before. If it hadn't been for the ears, Thorne wouldn't have known what it was.

Thorne moved on, touching each frame as she traced the decline of her daughter's happiness and innocence. Bunnies gave way to dark landscapes and bleeding roses, each one progressively harsher in the lines and shading.

The couch and the chair were the same, but the small dining table was new and Thorne assumed it was brought in while Elora was kept locked in here. But it was the bed that made her heart stop in her chest, made her blood run cold. Chains were attached to each of the four posts, hanging off the mattress and onto the floor. Silk sheets and pillowcases were the only bedding. Killian had always preferred it, claimed it was the sign of luxury and comfort. After she left, Thorne had never touched silk again.

"She was kept in here when she was brought back." Thorne jumped at the sound of her brother's voice. She hadn't heard the door unlock or open. Before turning around, she took a deep breath and exhaled slowly, trying to force away the guilt and shame fighting their way to the surface.

"I'm sorry to hear that. Killian was a monster." Silas glared at her as he stood in front of the door, hands clasped behind his back. He had cleaned up since the disaster at the Resistance headquarters. Not a single hair was out of place and his suit was perfectly tailored. But beneath the black jacket he wore, the burgundy shirt was wrinkled, as if someone had gripped it tightly in their fists.

"I suppose you would know that best. Or second best at least."

"I heard she killed him. Is that true?"

"It is. I have footage. If you wish to see her handiwork for yourself. It could prove educational." Thorne shook her head.

"Killian was always paranoid about you. He figured you had eyes and ears in the Tower but was never able to actually prove it." Silas chuckled softly before taking a seat near the door.

"When you were here, I did have some spies. But the intel was limited. I didn't really know what was going on until you showed up asking for help. When I found out she had been brought back, I managed to get cameras in his office. Luckily, your daughter inspires loyalty, which made my job a bit easier."

"Trust me, I know all about the loyalty she inspires. I lost two key members to it." Thorne's tone was full of bitterness that she didn't actually feel. At least, it wasn't about losing Denise and Viktor to her. It was that they had known her, spent time with her and gained her affection when Thorne had to force away any and all love she harbored for her only child. It was bitterness for the time that was lost, for the relationship that would never exist. They fell into a tense silence before Silas spoke again.

"Head of the Resistance? That's what you did with your time after faking your death? I'm curious if they know who you actually are." His voice was just as easy and smooth as the last time she heard it, when he agreed to help her with Elora. Thorne shrugged before looking over the room and dropping into one of the chairs at the small table.

"You always knew my feelings about humans and feeding from them without their knowledge. We deserve to know why we're controlled. It's all about information, Silas. They aren't cattle to be groomed and fed in order to make them more palatable." She sighed deeply. This had always been a spot of contention between the two of them. Silas had never seen anything wrong with how humans were treated and had simply cited the Accords as reason enough for how things worked. Thorne, however, had fought this fight many times before refusing to turn despite it being the only goal their parents had for them. Luckily, they had Silas to fall back on.

"And no, they don't know who I am. If this is a hint that you're going to blackmail me, don't bother. I'm not very popular right now."

"I imagine willingly working with two different vampires hasn't been a good look for the head of the human Resistance. Do they know you're here?" She nodded at the question. Yes, they did, but not a single one of them had truly supported it. The only way this didn't destroy her credibility was if it worked and Elizabeth was dealt with.

"Yes, they do. All we want is for this issue to be taken care of. We can worry about the rest later."

"What exactly is 'the rest,' Iris? Is it using your daughter as a weapon? Draining her dry to make a cure? It's hard to believe you would save her from Killian only to turn around and sacrifice her like a prized animal." Thorne ran her hand through her graying hair, tilting her head forward as she tried to ignore how beautiful her old name sounded coming from her brother. She had missed him despite everything. At night she would replay each conversation they had and each time they had teased each other without mercy. And then it had all fallen apart when she confessed she wasn't going to turn but live with Killian. Underneath the rage on her brother's face had been pain stemming from what he saw as a betrayal.

Thorne decided not to answer any of those questions but squeezed her hand into a fist to keep herself grounded.

"Why did she put me in here? Is this meant to be some type of psychological torture? An effort to hurt me?" Thorne stared at the floor as she spoke, noting the dark stains that were probably from blood.

"That would imply you cared enough about what happened in this room. And we both know that's not the case." Elora's voice filled the space, coating everything in ice and Thorne's head snapped up to find her standing right inside the doorway with Damien directly behind her. Bright red hair fell over her shoulders, settling on the dress she wore. The scars on her neck were clearly displayed, as if she wanted Thorne to see them, wanted them to serve as a reminder of their shared past. Her eyes moved from Elora heart-shaped face and bright green eyes to her feet, which were covered by socks. Taken as a whole, Elora didn't look dangerous. She looked like Thorne—a mirror image. There was so little of Killian in her that Thorne found it hard to believe that he had been involved in her creation.

"Not the best way to start off a potential partnership," Thorne mused even as her muscles tensed. The woman in front of her was dangerous. It radiated from her, flooding the room and Thorne knew a threat when she saw one. It was difficult to reconcile this version of her with the one who held Viktor as he died, who demanded he be buried with his love. She was a dichotomy, a lesson in contradictions.

"Neither is pretending to be dead and then working to sacrifice your daughter, but we work with what we have." Elora shrugged as if this was of no consequence, but Thorne caught the way her eyes flashed with something violent.

"Should we just discuss that? Get everything out in the open? Or will all of our conversation moving forward be filled with barbs and insults?"

"Whatever would make you comfortable," Elora sneered at her before turning from the room and moving across the hallway. Silas shook his head and stood, gesturing for Thorne to follow.

"This is going to be a fucking disaster," Damien muttered softly and Silas only chuckled as all three of them stepped into Elora's room where she was already seated on the couch, a glass of blood in her hand and death in her eyes.

Chapter 27

Damien

Each of them took a seat, spread out in front of Elora like her council. Damien positioned himself beside her, sinking into the chair to her right while Silas took the one to her left. Thorne was forced to sit directly across from her daughter, watching as she sipped the blood in her glass. It was a power move that made him want to take her into the bedroom and put that dominance to use in a much different way. A tense silence settled around them resting on their shoulders, pressing their bodies into the chairs and keeping their words in their throats.

"You've changed things," Thorne commented, breaking the silence like a pane of glass, all the pieces falling haphazardly around them. The corner of Elora's lips quirked slightly.

"I kept some things around." Her eyes went to the painting on the wall depicting the gardens at Corvin Manor, the exact spot Damien had found her after their initial conversation with Silas. Thorne followed Elora's gaze and her eyes widened slightly as if surprised that her art was here or still existed at all.

"How sentimental of you. Though I am surprised Killian didn't destroy them himself." Another beat of silence as they all stared at each other. Damien wasn't sure how this was meant to start. So much history was festering beneath the facade of calm. He knew he had his own questions for Thorne about how she could plan on using her daughter and draining every drop of her blood. The response, he guessed, would be something about the greater good and how the life of one vampire wasn't worth more than an entire species. Which was complete bullshit. Elora's life was worth every human in the city and he would see every single one of them dead at her feet before sacrificing her.

"Let's start easy. How were you planning on using my blood? What have your scientists discovered about it?

"I see my suspicions that Viktor was compromised were correct," Thorne mused. "Every person I sent for you ended up under your thumb. Curious, isn't it?"

"Stop sending your people after me. It seems like an easy enough solution. I do wonder at the intelligence of your group. It seems to me that there were many missed opportunities and missions that were handled horribly. Embarrassing for you, really." Damien suppressed his smirk as he watched Elora play with Thorne, goading her as she tried to get under the human's skin. It was working from what Damien could tell as Thorne grew tense, her lips thinning into a line as her hand twitched.

"By all means, educate me." Each word was forced from the human's mouth and Elora grinned so wide, revealing her dulled canines that only came out when she was about to feed directly from a human. A perfect disguise, and he wondered if Killian had planned that as well or if it had been a happy accident.

"The most glaring is not coming for me yourself. I would have followed you without a single question, but I suppose you had an identity to protect. You couldn't have them all knowing you were my mother, after all. Or that Killian was your lover. What was your cover story? No, don't answer. Let me guess. Your family was murdered by vampires, leading to your radicalization." Thorne's face grew more and more pinched, irritation becoming clearer by the second as Elora only continued to grin. She was like a cat with a mouse, playing with it after catching it. The question was what the end would be, if she would kill her prey or let her go.

"Any others?" Thorne's fingers were tightened into a fist at her side as she watched her daughter.

"Sending Elizabeth with Viktor. Because of you and your choices, a human is probably dead and another was turned." Something shifted as Elora continued to speak and Damien fought the urge to stand, to move to her side. Connie and Wyatt. As much as she blamed herself, Elora obviously placed some of it at Thorne's feet.

"Your insight is impeccable. It's always illuminating when your mistakes are right in front of you." Fury and hurt appeared in Elora's eyes, there one second before disappearing. But Thorne had seen it. It was vicious and Damien wondered who would be the one to kill Thorne when the time came. He would gladly take care of it for her and potentially craft her another souvenir. His eyes traveled to Elora's chest where his gift sat among her scars. She never took it off, not even when she showered. Only she knew exactly what it did to him to see it around her neck.

"We're getting off track. Answer her question, Iris." Silas, ever the voice of reason, interrupted the standoff. She flinched at the sound of her old name in a room that probably held so many memories. Within these walls, Thorne had probably told Killian she was pregnant, had celebrated the miracle that it was. They had more than likely discussed names while Killian laid his hands on her ever expanding stomach, feeling the life within.

The life that he would then try to destroy. Had Killian ever seen Elora as a daughter? How long had it been until Thorne had found out what he had been doing late at night? Damien ran a hand through his hair, pushing away the questions and focusing on the two opposing forces of nature clashing in front of him.

"For the sake of this going smoothly, I will. Your blood could be used to create a cure for vampirism. We never made it very far in our research, to be perfectly honest. It was why getting control of you was vital. It was all theories for the most part."

"You were going to drain my blood, potentially killing me in the process, because it was a possibility it could create a cure." Elora shook her head, not bothering to hide the disgust and revulsion aimed at the woman who had given her life.

"We were going to do what needed to be done. Killing you was never part of it. We planned on keeping you alive, harvesting your blood as needed."

"I can see why Killian married you. Same plan. Different goals." Elora shrugged as she finished her statement, as if the truth wasn't eating away at her, deteriorating her core as the meeting progressed. But Damien saw the hurt in her eyes, the realization that neither of the individuals who would be called her parents cared for her beyond what she could offer. He doubted Thorne had ever loved her, or perhaps it had disappeared over time as she came to understand what Killian had done. The question was on the tip of his tongue before he met Silas's gaze. The vampire shook his head slowly, as if warning him that now was not the time for those questions.

"What exactly did your people figure out? Anything of value?" Both Elora and Thorne turned their attention to Silas, whose question had filled the tense silence.

"No. We tried using Elizabeth blood for the small time we had her, but it didn't yield the results we were hoping for. Our people believe that something is altered when they are turned that makes them lesser. Anyone who was turned doesn't have the same characteristics as the original. We tried with a few bottles of her blood Viktor brought, but there had been no results."

"Denise told me that he was never able to replicate it. Whatever he did to me, that is," Elora added as she seemed to absorb the fact she was truly was the only one like her. There was a cruelty to it. Not only had she been painstakingly crafted gene by gene, but there would never be another. She would never find someone who she could talk to about the changes, about what it meant to be a unique species that was so similar to vampires yet vastly different. He could only imagine how alone she must feel.

"She's correct, as far as I know," Thorne leaned back on the couch once more, eyes moving over the three of them. "Now it's your turn to share. I'm assuming you have more information than I do."

"I do, but I need certain assurances before I start sharing."

"Such as?"

"My safety along with the vampires under mine and Silas's care, obviously. I won't share with you how to potentially use my blood to wipe out my people."

"I thought this would be a slight hiccup in us working together. I'm prepared to make certain promises and negotiate."

"You tell me yours and I'll tell you mine." Damien leaned forward, resting his arms on his thighs at Elora's words.

"Making vampires public knowledge. No more hiding. Turning would be tracked as would the population of both vampires and humans. If you are going to feed from us and use our donated blood, we should know about it." That was easy enough. Elora shared similar sentiments. The respect she held for humans was immense, especially considering she believed she was one for years. This would be a simple concession to make if Silas agreed. Chloe's vote wouldn't matter.

"Anything else?"

"I would still like to try and engineer a cure, if possible. For those who were turned against their will and want to be human again. I also want to make the medication you took available for the public, especially if it turns out there isn't a cure to be crafted." Again, all simple requests.

"We would need to vote, wouldn't we?" Elora turned to Silas, who nodded. He was watching Thorne with that same lingering expression of guilt. It was the same look he had given Elora for so long.

"You know how we operate, Iris. We would need to bring Chloe in and give her a chance to vote on it. However, based on both mine and Elora's opinions about humans, I feel it's safe to say that we can give you what you want." Elora stood and began moving through the room, her hands in her pockets to keep herself from picking at her sleeves or her fingers. She was agitated. Her mouth moved as she seemed to choose her words, preparing for whatever she was about to say.

"I spent about a decade of my life living as a human. I didn't feed. I didn't feel any urge to for a long time and then never felt the urge again after my one mistake. When Killian told me what I was, I was disgusted with myself even though a part of me had known already. And when I started to feed again, I was repulsed by it. I always wondered about who the blood had been taken from and if they knew what it was for, if they had given permission or if they had felt forced into it. This is one area, Thorne, that you and I are perfectly aligned. Yes, we need a vote and will have to bring that bitch Chloe here to do so. But with or without her vote, I promise you that I will work towards exactly that."

Pride filled him with each word she said. Silas had been correct when he called her a force of nature. Here she stood in the room where she had killed her father reshaping reality. He was honored to witness it and from the expression on Silas's face, he felt the same.

"Does that mean you're ready to share?" Thorne didn't comment on Elora's speech or her promise, but respect was clearly etched across her face. With a subtle jerk of Elora's head, Silas stood and grabbed the rather large file off of the desk along with one of the journals. Tiny tabs stuck out from the side of it, color coordinated and organized as if Elora had prepared for this moment. Perhaps she had. Damien wouldn't doubt that everything had happened according to her will since the moment he was taken. Her deal with Viktor and her invitation to Thorne had all led to this.

"That is the information we have. Some is from the scientist Killian employed, a Dr. Hartley who has been keenly interested in the project and me. Some are from Killian's journals. All the red tabs are about you while purple are about me and what they did." Silas handed the file to Thorne as Elora explained. She opened it instantly without a moment of hesitation as Thorne began to devour the information in there. Elora wandered the room once more, her fingers picking her cuticles as she came to Damien's side, leaning against the chair. He glanced up at her, studying her expression for a hint at how she was handling this. There would be a conversation when this was over. Once Thorne had been sent back to the room she was staying in and Silas had gone back to his condo, he would ask his questions.

"So, Killian succeeded in making you a beacon for humans. It explains Viktor."

"Actually, if you keep reading, you'll find out it doesn't. The medication suppressed all of that. Viktor cared for me on his own. It's only every human after him that you can lay at my feet." Thorne was lucky she was useful, that she was Elora's mother and Silas's sister. If it wasn't for those key facts, he would snap her neck.

"I stand corrected," she responded, sparing her daughter one glance before turning back to the file. "It appears that there is a possibility for a cure."

"A weapon. Not a cure. It would be a death penalty."

"I see no difference between the two." Elora huffed even as her hands clenched into fists and Damien stood, prepared to step in. Thorne was pushing her. He wasn't sure if it was deliberate, but the results could be disastrous.

"Of course you would see no problem with killing every person who was turned simply because they fell under Elizabeth's spell. A person who's willing to sacrifice their child probably wouldn't bat an eye at committing mass murder." Fuck. This was getting worse, quickly spiraling as mother and daughter faced off and a lifetime of resentment and anger bubbled to the surface. A part of Damien wanted to grab Silas and leave them to their own devices. But he had a feeling only one of them would be left standing.

"Okay. Let's address this since it keeps getting brought up. Even as a child you never let things go very well." Elora stopped her pacing and stared at her mother with the strangest expression. Anticipation. Answers were waiting for her and if Thorne didn't start offering them up to Elora on a silver platter there was a chance she would die by her daughter's hand.

"I'm waiting to hear your fantastic rationale for why you let him hurt me. Your reasoning for never coming to get me once you escaped Killian. Your reasoning for wanting to use me." Damien flinched with each demand that came from Elora's mouth. The amount of pain lingering under each word was agony to hear and he hoped it hurt Thorne just as much.

Thorne set the file down the table in front of her and leaned back, studying her daughter as if searching for something before she nodded slightly.

"There's no easy answer to any of that, no matter what you may think or want. I never came and got you from that foster family because you were a reminder of the life I needed to leave behind. I was carving out a new existence and having you with me would only draw attention. It's true that I could have easily asked Silas where you were, but then he would have known I was alive. I had to bend and break in order to survive. As for my reasoning for using you, it's simple. I could never justify protecting the only real chance humans have for freedom."

"And my other question? Why did you let him hurt me? For years, you allowed it to continue." Damien watched as Thorne shrugged and shook her head.

"I believed him when he said he would never do it again even when I saw the proof on your body. I was afraid and too proud to admit I needed help protecting you. Not until I went to Silas. But it was all too late by then." Elora stared at her for a moment, absorbing the words Damien knew were settling into her core, seeping into her thoughts and skin. Finally, she spoke with a voice so empty Damien was afraid of what was to come after all of this.

"You're staying in my old room. Feel free to take the chains off the bed. We will meet with Dr. Hartley in the morning for an update." She turned from her mother and went into the bedroom, closing the door behind her and leaving Damien to escort Thorne to her room.

Chapter 28

Elora

Dr. Hartley looked as if she had seen a ghost when Elora appeared with Thorne at her side. Blood drained from her face, and she almost dropped the file in her hand as she stared at Thorne with something akin to fear. An entire history passed between the two of them before Hartley recovered and nodded to each of them before gesturing towards the back of the lab. Behind them were Damien and Silas as they all marched into a meeting room in lieu of Hartley's office. It wouldn't house them all for this. Not comfortably.

Damien took his place beside Elora, sinking into the chair and folding his hands on the table as if to keep himself from reaching for her. She almost wished he would, but his silent presence was enough for now. They hadn't talked last night after Thorne had been taken back to Elora's old bedroom and Silas had gone back to his condo. She had wanted to, the words had been on the tip of her tongue, but she couldn't. They had lodged in her throat, taking root until not even the strongest of hands were able to yank them out. Damien had understood, as he always did, and had held her instead, gently kissing her cheek and brushing away the tears. No questions. No demands. He simply kept her from retreating, from disappearing in the wake of her mother's explanation.

"I was told you were dead, Iris. I see that Killian was mistaken." Hartley's face had regained some color as she began arranging files on the table in front of her.

"Killian was wrong about a lot of things," Thorne drawled, refusing to look at the scientist across from her.

"Not about you. Not about her. I was meant to get your body, you know. He wanted me to harvest everything possible from it. He believed not having you was the reason all his subsequent attempts to recreate Elora failed."

"I can't say I'm sorry about that. It sounds like I did everyone a favor by disappearing." Elora watched the interaction for a moment, listening to the shared history being hinted at.

"As much as I'm enjoying your reunion, can we get to the point?" All eyes went to Elora as she reclined back in the chair and wrapped her hands in the fabric of her dress. She had no interest in hearing the two women trade barbs and petty remarks. There was obviously something there—an undercurrent to each word they said. Elora wasn't interested in learning it or gaining any type of insight. Iris was dead as far as she was concerned. Sitting at the table was Thorne, the woman who wanted to kill her and harvest her blood. Not a mother. An enemy and ally for now.

"There are developments." Elora raised a brow at Dr. Hartley's hesitant words as she began picking at her fingernail once more, unease moving through her. A silence fell as they all waited for Hartley to continue speaking.

"Which are?" Thorne demanded, impatience lining each word. With a deep sigh, Hartley opened the file and began looking over it, as if reminding herself of its contents.

"There's no cure. Not in a traditional sense. There's nothing that will render them human again. All of our efforts have failed so far and there doesn't seem to be much of a chance of that changing."

"In that case, there's no real development. It's exactly the same as the last time I came up here."

"No, not necessarily. We can't make a cure, but we can make a weapon. From your blood, we have made something that would kill them. If we think of your bite as a virus that spreads, this is like an anti-viral." Hartley explained quickly, hands moving wildly as she spoke. Elora felt her heart drop into her feet as her body grew warmer by the second.

"Your solution is to kill them. Every single one. Even the children," Elora responded in disbelief, her brows arching high. That couldn't be the solution. Based on the hotel, there were at least a hundred of them and there could be more now that Elizabeth had continued recruiting, for lack of a better word.

"If we want to use your blood, then yes. That's the only real option without doing more experimenting. Given more time, we may find a different solution, but I have no real idea of how long that could take." And the fact that the city didn't have time went unsaid. Months at the most, before the entire human population was turned.

"We don't have time for you to keep playing around with her blood and hoping for a better outcome," Thorne stated bluntly, not looking away from Hartley, who nodded in response.

"Which is why I brought you all up to discuss this. This may be our best option."

"What about mass doses of the medication that was used on me? Could we potentially make it more potent so that it lasts in the system? It worked well enough for me."

"Until you didn't take it anymore and you attacked your sister, which started this whole fucking mess," Thorne spat out and Elora stared at her with an empty expression.

"Let's not talk about where the blame lies, mother. I'm not sure you'll like the outcome." Her voice was low, dangerous and Thorne seemed to shift as if moving away. Everyone went silent, tension filling the spaces between them. Elora stared daggers at Thorne, begging her to say one more thing, push her just a bit further. All she wanted was an excuse to hold her mother's throat in her hands again, squeeze and see the fear in her eyes. Before seeing Thorne in the flesh, Elora had felt only sympathy and regret for not remembering her, for only having snippets of pain associated with her. Now, Elora had to wonder if it was better she didn't remember her. It meant she didn't need to reconcile who she was now with the mother she had been.

"The medication could be made more potent, but it would be a short-term solution. We would have to keep them taking it continuously for the rest of their potentially exceedingly long lives. The fact is we would then need to keep track of them, force them to take the medication, and have consequences should they stop," Hartley explained, ignoring the obvious anger in the room. Elora knew what she wanted, which option she would pick.

"I don't think it's worth the risk when we have the entire population of humans to worry about. This is a situation where the loss of a few is worth saving the masses. Yes, even children."

"It isn't really a surprise that you're willing to sacrifice children," Elora sneered at Thorne, enjoying the way she seemed to flinch.

"This is something that needs to be discussed," Silas interjected as Thorne opened her mouth to respond. "We need to decide what comes next. I'm afraid that I agree with Dr. Hartley. I'm not sure the medication is a viable option."

Elora's focus shot to her uncle, whose face was impassive as he spoke. Two potential votes for the murder of a group of vampires who had done nothing truly wrong other than feed and fall under Elizabeth's control.

"Do we need Chloe before we continue this conversation?" Elora asked in hopes of postponing this. If she could stall, maybe she could come up with some alternative. Maybe she could devise a way to save them. Her heart raced in her chest as she picked more aggressively at her cuticles before moving to her wrists, toying with the scars there. She could feel Damien beside her, his own hands twitching as if to reach for her.

"I'm not sure Chloe is necessary since this has nothing to do with vampires," Silas explained, keeping his tone even. Elora knew he was trying to keep the peace, to try to help everyone maintain a level head as they discussed mass murder.

"I disagree. Vampires are also impacted by this since they could also become a food source should this all fail." She was desperate and she only hoped that it didn't show in her voice. From the expression on Silas's face, she hadn't been successful.

"You're trying to buy time, Elora. Perhaps you don't want us to deal with Elizabeth."

"I don't want to kill children!" she shouted at her mother. "Their only crime was listening to Elizabeth or their parents." Her breathing had gone harsh as she tried to force herself to calm down. All she saw in her mind was a child covered in scars from being turned, a child who wasn't given a choice in what happened to them. Why was this so difficult for them to understand? How could they be so callous? If this is what it took to run a vampire family, then she didn't want the position.

"What is your suggestion? Let them continue to turn humans while we try to find an alternative? Turn even more children?" Thorne seemed barely restrained as she spoke, her hands moving wildly with each word and question. The fight seemed to leave Elora's body as she tried to think of something.

"I don't know. I just know this can't be the only option we have." Tears threatened to stream down her face as her uncle stood, pulling at his sleeves to adjust them.

"I think we need to take a break. Sleep on this. We can come back tomorrow morning and discuss this again. I can also have

Chloe here for it, since I do agree with Elora on her being present. Vampires are impacted just as much as humans." Elora nodded vigorously, instantly standing and meeting Silas's eyes. It was for her that he was doing this. She could see it in the way he watched her, tracked her features.

"Fine. But my vote here won't change," Thorne declared and stood, marching from the room.

"Elora, if you could stay behind. I need to discuss something with you." Hartley glanced down at one of the files. "Alone, if possible."

Damien shook his head instantly, no doubt remembering the consequences of the last time Elora had spoken privately with the scientist. But she had a feeling that she knew what this was about and if she was correct, Damien couldn't be present. She didn't need to deal with whatever Hartley had to say as well as his reaction to it.

Elora nodded and gestured to Damien to leave. "Wait for me outside. It shouldn't take long." He hesitated for a moment as he took in what was technically an order. His lips thinned into a line as his jaw clenched and he spun around, leaving only his anger in his wake. Silas inclined his head, the only sign he was unhappy about this was the narrowing of his eyes and the stiffness of his shoulders. Otherwise, he was perfectly at ease as he followed Damien and Thorne from the room.

Elora sank back into her chair and played with her sleeves for a moment as she waited for Hartley to begin.

"There's something we need to address. I've been looking into what you asked me to. I can't find any real scientific reason for it, but there does seem to be connection between you and everyone who can be traced back to you. The way I see it, the bite itself acts like a virus and passes on each time. When they come near their source, they can feel it and so can you."

Elora listened, her attention only on the scientist and each word she said. It settled in her mind as she absorbed it, but wasn't entirely sure it was making sense. There was more to this than explaining what the connection was and how it worked.

"Here's the point I'm making. There's a real possibility that killing them can kill you. I don't exactly how connected you are to them and I'm not sure I can experiment to find out since any test we do with actual subjects could cause your death." Elora waited for the panic to set in as it always did. She waited patiently for the dread and the fear of her potential death to come. But nothing did. Only cold acceptance. It wasn't like when she planned on dying in order to kill her father. That had been defeat and desperation to end her pain and the abuse. It was the only way out of her torment that she could devise.

This came from knowing her death would mean something. It would mean no more humans were turned into her children, as Elizabeth called them. It would mean no more children would be bitten and fed from only to turn into a vampire without knowing what it meant.

"Do not tell anyone else about this. Hide the information and the file. I don't want this factoring into anyone's decision tomorrow." Hartley opened her mouth as if to argue, but closed it quickly and nodded instead. Quickly she closed the file and pushed it across the table.

"You have places to put this. I would rather not be responsible for this information." Elora's fingers touched the file and dragged it to her, already preparing where it should go.

"Thank you, Dr. Hartley. For telling me and respecting what I want." She hesitated for a moment, chewing on her lip in thought.

"Do you truly think this weapon you described is the best option? Do you really think the medication isn't viable?" The desperation was clear, and Elora couldn't make herself care that she sounded weak. Hartley stood and paced the room, hands shoved into the pockets of her black slacks.

"I understand your reluctance. I've seen children turned simply because their parents wanted them to or because a vampire wanted a pet. You're right that it isn't their fault, and they'll be killed despite that fact. But the risk they pose is vast. I don't think the medication is a long term option, or even a short term option. Not in its current form. There are too many variables. They could outgrow it, as happens quite often with medications. They could refuse to take it, and we end up exactly where we are now." Hartley froze and turned towards her, her face laced with so much pain that it felt like Hartley saw Elora as more than an experiment, a creature she helped create but something more like a child.

"And I say this knowing what it could cost you, Elora. And what it could cost them." She jerked her head towards the two vampires waiting outside the door, watching the entire exchange closely. "The weapon is the best chance we have of saving this city."

Hartley didn't say another word. She just gathered her remaining files and left. In the distance, Elora heard an office door close while she once again left Damien and Silas behind.

Chapter 29

Elora

"Elora." He said her name with such sincerity and love that it made her breathing hitch every time. It always felt like a dream, like she would wake up and find him gone no matter how many sweet promises he made. She turned to him, surprised that he had found her. Before twenty minutes ago, Elora hadn't realized there was a balcony off of the ballroom that wrapped around two sides of the Tower. An assortment of chairs and couches along with tables filled the area, but it appeared unused, as if even Killian had forgotten it existed.

Her hands gripped the cold metal of the railing as she stared out at the city. The wind forced itself past the fabric of her dress, causing goosebumps to rise. Lights twinkled as far as she could see, with some areas brighter than others. In the distance, she could hear music echoing throughout the night, a calling card to every person who wanted to lose themselves in dancing or drinking. Somewhere out there was Elizabeth and the strange cult she had crafted. Killing them all may be their best option, but it ripped something apart inside of her. Darian and Killian deserved what happened to them. The two vampires who attacked her had earned their pain. The vampires they were discussing murdering in mass numbers had done nothing.

"You said you wouldn't do this again." She sighed and hung her head, taking in deep breaths before she turned around to lean against the railing.

"I know. I needed to gather my thoughts and found this. I didn't realize the Tower had a balcony," she explained as he moved closer. His shirt shifted with each step, pulling tight across his chest in a way that begged for her to touch him, to run her finger over his skin. He smirked, that arrogant little slant of his lips that she had once found immensely annoying. Now she wondered if it bothered her so much because it had made him so hard to look away from.

"Are they gathered?" He asked as he finally made it to her and touched her arms, rubbing his hands up and down her biceps as he studied her.

"I don't know. Probably as much as they possibly can be." She lifted her shoulder in a shrug and smiled. "There's just so much, Damien. I don't know what to think or do. Every decision feels like the wrong one, and when she's around, it's even worse."

"Thorne?" He asked, and she nodded.

"I can't stand seeing her. I can't stand hearing her voice. I want her gone so I can go back to her being dead. It was better that way." The words spilled out as he pulled her closer to him.

"She called me a mistake to be fixed. Said that I was a sacrifice for humans and that my life didn't matter when held up against them. And a part of me understands and even agrees, but another part is so fucking angry. She's so detached while I'm over here barely keeping it together." She exhaled and closed her eyes, tipping her face towards the sky in hopes the cold air would help center her.

"You aren't a mistake. There's nothing to fix, and I would rather see the city full of vampires turned by your sister than sacrifice you to save them. You're worth more to me than every life walking this earth." Her heart twisted in her chest at his vow, at his declaration. It was what she was afraid of despite how much she loved him for it.

"What do you think I should do?" She asked, unable to keep the question from pouring out. Thorne and Hartley both had a point, but Elora wasn't sure it justified killing so many. Perhaps it was easier for Thorne because she had spent the last decade trying to eradicate them. This was simply another step in that direction.

"I don't know, love. I agree with both of you," he hesitated, watching her closely as he held onto her waist. "I also think that you're emotionally involved, and that may impact your opinion. A part of you is hoping Elizabeth can be reasoned with and that those lives can be saved. But the reality is that they might already be lost."

Elora tore herself from his hands and pushed past him, wrapping her arms over her chest. That was exactly what she thought he would say, and she hated it. She wasn't completely rational when it came to Elizabeth or Wyatt. The guilt and shame she felt whenever their names were brought up was wrapped into her very core, twisting and twisting until it was impossible to separate the various threads.

"If you were in my position, what would you do?" She dropped onto one of the couches and stared at her hands, picking at the skin once more. His steps were light on the balcony, as they always were when she was struggling. At times, Damien still acted as if she were fragile, as if she would explode into tiny pieces if he moved too quickly or harshly. As much as she appreciated the consideration, it was irritating, reminding her that he first met her when she was at her lowest.

"I would vote for Thorne and Hartley's idea, but I would also want a more concrete plan. Saying they want to use this weapon is nothing. Just words." Elora bit her lip as he sat beside her. She allowed him to pull her into his arms, placing her legs so they lay across his own. Her cheek fell against his chest as she listened to his heartbeat and absorbed the warmth from his body.

"I don't think I can order their deaths, Damien. I can't vote for something that kills children."

"Thorne will accuse you of working with Elizabeth. So will Chloe."

"I don't give a fuck what those two have to say about this," she spat as her heart began to race in her chest, blood rushing to her ears.

"I know, love. But it doesn't make it less true," he sighed and rested his cheek on her head as his fingers trailed up and down her arm. "Silas is right. We all need to sleep on this."

Elora wasn't sure she would be able to sleep. A part of her knew nightmares would make a return, and she would wake crying and shaking. Visions of children would merge with her own demons to create a personal hell. No, sleep wasn't an option, no matter how desperately she needed it.

She curled up closer to Damien and closed her eyes, letting her body relax against him. This was safety and contentment. Her breathing became easy as she lay there with his heartbeat as the only sound beyond the car horns in the background. Each muscle relaxed as she melted into him.

"What did Hartley want to talk to you about?" Elora stiffened and moved away from him, pulling her legs under her.

"More of the research she was doing. I had asked her to double check my blood's effect on vampires. I wanted to be sure." The lies fell from her lips easily.

"Why have her look into it? Do you feel like she got something wrong?" She shook her head.

"No. Nothing like that. I needed to be sure that drinking my blood didn't do something." It wasn't a complete lie. She had been afraid drinking her blood had been to blame for Damien's feelings, but they had been put to rest already. Elora had believed and trusted the scientist the first time, but this seemed like a decent enough lie. It was rooted in reality, in a fear that she knew he shared on some level.

"What did she say?" He laid his arm along the back of the couch and reclined slightly in a way that made conjuring coherent thoughts incredibly difficult. Elora forced her attention to something behind him, studying the city skyline in the distance.

"That my fears are unfounded, to quote her," Again, the lie fell easily. "There's no excuse for your obsession." She smirked even as his eyes darkened in a way that promised something made her squirm in anticipation.

"I never tried to make excuses for it. As soon as you kicked my ass in that hospital, I was yours."

"I thought it was when I stabbed you with the fork," she said, chuckling softly as his hand reached up towards the three scars where his neck met his shoulders.

"After that, I was consumed by you. You could have told me to jump off the Tower, and I would have done it without question." He extended his arm and gestured for her to come closer, which she did eagerly. Instead of curling into his side, she threw one leg over his lap and straddled him, playing with the neckline of his t-shirt.

"It was the sweater. The one you gave me when I went to see Killian the first time. It was yours. It smelled like you. I didn't know what to do with the act of kindness considering you kidnapped me." Damien gave her a sad smile as he held onto her hips as if he thought she would fly away, ascend into the sky, and disappear.

"Like I said, completely and totally yours even then." Elora leaned down and kissed his cheek, first one and then the other, before pressing against his lips. Fingers ran up her spine before moving into her hair, gripping it gently.

"Damien, I want to give you a new title." His brows knitted together at the change of topic, but this was something that had occupied her thoughts. Every time they walked into a room and he had to force himself not to touch her to keep up appearances. Every time he had to follow behind her like a shadow, a part of her screamed in protest.

"Elora, I don't—" She put a single finger to his lips and smirked.

"I want you to run this with me. I don't want you to be my second-in-command or a consort or some other stupid bullshit. You as a leader of this family at my side, as my equal. Co-head, I guess." Damien shook his head at her explanation even as something warm washed over his features, softening every single one.

"That isn't how it works, love."

"It does for the Corvin family. I don't see why it can't be applied here. Is there some rule written down somewhere? Perhaps the others have never taken a partner because they were too insecure to share power. I'm not, Damien. I'll announce it as soon as this whole mess is taken care of. Along with the new name for the family." There was something glistening in his eyes as he stared at her as if she were a deity.

"A force of nature, love. You're a fucking force of nature. Do I need to thank you for the new title? Prove that I deserve it?" She shrugged as if a fire hadn't been lit deep in her stomach, and her body grew warm. A lopsided grin appeared on her face as she ground her hips against him.

"How would you do that?" she purred as his fingers dug into her hips, pulling her down onto him so she felt everything. A moan filled the night air as her back arched from the contact.

"I have a few ideas," he replied, voice deep and husky as he stood, taking Elora with him. She squealed and giggled as he gripped her thighs, keeping her in place. Her ankles locked around his waist as he began leading them back to their bedroom, no doubt planning on demonstrating each one of the ideas.

Chapter 30

Damien

The room smelled wrong as he pushed the door open with his foot. He wasn't putting her down for a moment, not even to get inside. She giggled in his ear in between the tiny bites on his neck she knew drove him insane. The sound of her laughter was everything, and he would tear the sun from the sky if it meant hearing it for the rest of his life.

"What is that?" He muttered as she made a small noise in response before resuming her work. They had always been careful not to leave marks where they were visible. Their relationship was a badly held secret, but that didn't mean they flaunted it when she was still so new to her role. The last thing he had wanted was to deal with a vampire who used their connection to hurt her. Now, with the announcement of his new role on the horizon, all bets were off. He had a feeling she would leave behind a declaration to everyone who saw him that he belonged to her.

"I don't know. Blood?" Her bites and kisses ended instantly, and he felt her pull back. Her fingers dug into his shoulders.

"Something's wrong," she observed, wiggling out of his grip and dropping to the floor. Damien groaned before he adjusted himself, cursing whatever had happened in there that was drawing her attention. His fingers raked through his hair, pushing it back away from his face as she wandered the room. She was a vampire on a mission as she seemed to follow the scent until she stopped at her desk. Her shoulders tightened, and he watched her hands open and close.

"What is it?" He called out before making his way to her and following her gaze to the source of the smell. Elora's breathing had gone harsh, sharp intakes of breath that she held before letting them out slowly as they both stared at the letter on her desk. A pink envelope with Elora's name on it in elegant and elaborate cursive. Mingling with the blood was the smell of perfume, as if the goal was to cover up the evidence soaked into the thick paper.

Her fingers reached out, touching the envelope and underlining her name.

"It's her," she whispered, almost to herself instead of Damien. His first thought was about where it came from and how it managed to get inside their room. Had a vampire delivered it? Had Elizabeth's people managed to get inside?

After a moment of tense silence, Damien voiced those exact questions as she seemed to study it.

"Ask the people in the lobby. See if anyone came in or if anyone dropped it off," she ordered and Damien turned to leave. While he tracked down any leads, she would have a chance to deal with the letter in private. He could see every emotion flickering across her face as she touched it as if there was some remnant of Elizabeth there. A part of Elora wanted to believe her sister could be reasoned with. Even now, despite all the evidence to the contrary, she saw hints of good in Elizabeth. Damien wasn't sure it was still there. Only figments of the human she once was.

The door burst open in a flurry of a harsh breaths and stomping feet as Silas rushed in. His eyes were wide, a crazed and terrified expression shining in a way that was almost unnatural.

"Do you have a TV in here?" Elora spun around at the sound of Silas's question, her brows knitting together.

"Yes, in there," she responded, gesturing towards the cabinet in the bookshelf. Silas marched forward, not bothering to explain as he did so. Elora followed behind him, chewing at her finger as Damien sent a series of messages to inquire about the pink envelope.

The television turned on, the sound of a news anchor filling the room. As he sent the last message and shoved the phone in his back pocket, Damien finally glanced at the screen that had Elora and Silas both fixated. He approached her and placed his hand on her lower back before moving to her hip, pulling her against him. Every muscle was tightened. Every limb was stiff. He peeked at her, noting the way she bit her lip and how her eyes seemed to lack any semblance of light. She was afraid, as if she had some hint as to what it was.

"Here is the footage received. We would like to caution our viewers as it is graphic." A feminine voice poured from the television speakers before the scene shifted away. The composed news anchor in a blazer and flawlessly curled hair disappeared for a moment before a church filled the screen. At least Damien thought it was. His focus was on the figure standing at the pulpit in a long black gown, similar to the one she wore outside the hotel.

Elora took in a sharp breath, and his fingers flexed against her skin, tightening as he felt her start to tremble slightly. Together they watched Elizabeth smile into the camera, her bright red lips stretched wide enough to reveal her sharpened canines. She didn't seem to have the same ability to retract them as Elora did, and they were on full display for every human and vampire watching.

Damien's heart hammered in his chest as he fought to keep his attention on the screen. Behind Elizabeth stood Wyatt, hands behind his back, stretching the white button-up shirt across his chest. His focus was directly ahead. Not at the cameras or Elizabeth, but something beyond it. Candles lined the space around them, but it seemed to be more for the effect due to the lighting on the walls. The entirety of the scene was stone, as if it were an old church. The stained-glass window was broken, with several panels completely missing and others cracked.

"Tonight, we have invited you into our home to introduce ourselves. We are her children. Elora Ashcroft. My sister. My creator." A small whimper sounded from Elora at the sound of her name from her sister's lips, spoken out to every television and screen in the city currently turned to this channel. But it was more than the sound of her name, but the titles given to her. Elizabeth's tone was frantic, frenzied, like a religious zealot preaching to the masses in hopes of converting them.

"She has created a new creature in her image, and we are tasked with bringing you all to her embrace. And so, we will reveal to you our secrets and demonstrate just how glorious it is to be remade." Damien didn't disagree that Elora deserved to be worshipped, but this wasn't what she wanted. It was clear in the way she kept fidgeting, picking at her fingers until he grabbed her hand and held it. The scent of her blood filled the room, and Silas peeked at her from his spot directly in front of the screen. His lips thinned into a line as his jaw worked, the muscles there feathering as if he were considering saying something but decided to keep it to himself. That was probably for the best.

Together, Damien and Silas both returned their attention to the screen to find the camera moving and shifting so that the crowd in the church was shown. Row after row of pews were filled with all manner of people, from the elderly to older teenagers. Damien knew children had been turned, but there didn't seem to be any present. It probably didn't fit the image Elizabeth was attempting to project.

Light radiated from each vampire's eyes as if they were lit from the inside. A trait they all shared, it seemed. The camera moved back as whoever was holding it stepped onto the dais and provided a broader view of the audience. Along the front row of the pews was a line of people, all with faces of contentment as they stared forward into the camera. Behind them stood a row of vampires, one for each human kneeling in apparent supplication at Elizabeth's feet. Unease swirled in Damien's gut as he realized what was about to occur. Elora took a step forward and then another, moving out of his grip as she wrapped her arms around herself.

"Now, we welcome our new members and give them the gift Elora so graciously gave me." Elizabeth's voice rang out from the screen as the line of vampires approached the humans, their hands resting on their shoulders as they knelt behind them. It almost looked gentle, like the intimate touch that occurred between lovers. With each word from her mouth, Elizabeth was laying the blame and guilt for what was coming with Elora, announcing to everyone watching that each body rested at her feet. Elora would internalize this, take it all into her core, and let it fester and rot. Elizabeth had to know that this was how it would impact her. They were sisters and had been inseparable until the night Elora bit her and they were torn apart.

"Begin." The single word brought forward snarls that were audible even through the television as each vampire immediately leaned into the crook of the human's neck and opened wide. A brief flash of teeth before they sank their canines into their throat. Moans filled the church and Elora's sitting room as the vampires fed, drinking greedily until Damien wasn't sure they would survive. A choked sob sounded from Elora, and Damien tore his focus from the screen to her. Tears rushed down her cheeks, spilling onto her dress. Her arms were wrapped so tightly around herself, as if she thought it would keep her from falling apart. In the background, the sound of feeding continued until it went silent.

Damien returned his attention to the screen in time to see the humans gently laid down on the stone floor of the church, carefully positioned to ensure they were not harmed. Each vampire stood and stepped back, hands clasped behind their backs as every pair of eyes locked onto the unconscious bodies.

At first, they were still. Horrifically and terrifyingly still. Not a single breath or movement of their body. Then, a twitch. A rise of their chest. A hand lifting to touch their face, their mouth, their lips. One by one, each figure pushed themselves to a sitting position and twisted their head one way and then the other as if testing its flexibility. Fingers gingerly touched the wound that Damien knew intimately, and without realizing it, his own rose to his mark. The two puncture scars hidden in the wings of the moth tattoo, a gift from Killian.

In an unsettling show of unison, each new vampire rose to their feet and straightened their posture. Shoulders back. Spines straight. Chins raised as they stared directly into the camera as if they could see Elora on the other side of the screen. A smile stretched across their faces, revealing the new fangs as their eyes seemed to glow.

The transformation was completed. They were turned. As a group, every vampire that filled the screen bowed at the waist, holding the position for a heartbeat before the camera turned back around to Elizabeth and Wyatt standing side by side at the pulpit. Elizabeth's expression was one of pride and satisfaction as she stared out at the vampires she had created in Elora's name. Wyatt's eyes still held nothing. No hint or clue about what he thought or felt about this ceremony.

"Open the letter, dear sister. Come home." With those final words, the scene went black before returning to the news anchor, who wasn't bothering to hide the fear on her face or the way she was gripping the pen like it was a weapon that could protect her. Silas said nothing as he switched it off and stared at the dark screen before closing the cabinet doors that hid it.

Elora's sobs echoed in the silence as she sank to her knees, one hand covering her mouth while the other was wrapped around her stomach. Her entire body shook from the force of the sobs that tore from her, ripping her apart right there on the rug. For a long moment, not a single word was said as they each seemed to fade into their own thoughts. The fact that Elizabeth had to be dealt with was all Damien could think of. It wasn't necessarily that she was turning humans in some fucked-up ritual, but the fact that she was putting it all on Elora, leaving her to shoulder the blame and guilt. Furious vampires would be coming for her, demanding something be done about Elizabeth going rogue. Terrified humans would appear at the foot of the Tower, demanding Elora's head, potentially reigniting a war between humans and vampires.

"What letter?" Silas broke the silence as he turned to his niece, something unreadable on his face. Damien thought it was anger or perhaps fear. Or both since the line between the two emotions could be so very thin when self-preservation was involved. Elora didn't say a word, only continued to sob, weakly gesturing to the table where the pink envelope lay.

"What does it say?" A shake of her head in response to Silas's question.

"We didn't get a chance to read it yet. We found it right before you came in." Damien explained before he kneeled next to her, placing an arm around her shoulders. At the contact, she winced, almost jerking away from him as if she believed she didn't deserve an act of comfort or kindness.

He was going to rip Elizabeth's head off. That was all he could think as Silas marched to the desk and lifted the letter, holding it in his hands like it was covered in something foul. He tossed the envelope and Damien watched it fall in front of her.

"Read it. Now." Damien stood and faced Silas, prepared to hit him if necessary.

"What the fuck is your problem?" He demanded, his voice shaking with fury as Silas met his eyes with a rage that matched his own.

"My problem is that psycho is undoing centuries of work to establish peace. She is single-handedly eradicating our food source, and my niece is too concerned about a few children to do something about it. My problem is that I need her to grow up and deal with the monster she created." Damien didn't think as his fist shot out and hit the vampire in the jaw, sending Silas sprawling back against the desk. Papers flew as he found himself on his back, blood trickling from his lip.

"Stop," Elora demanded, now on her feet with the envelope in her hand. Her tears had been wiped away, but her eyes were red and puffy even as she glared at both of them. The disguise she had worn when she killed Darian and Killian had emerged. The dark part of her that radiated chaos and danger, violence and wrath had taken control.

"Leave. Both of you. I want to be alone. I need to think." Damien tried to rein in the hurt he felt at being dismissed, pushed aside when she was in such pain. Silas didn't seem to share his hesitation as he marched from the room, not bothering to spare his niece a single glance. Her eyes were focused on the pink envelope in her hand as she sank into one of the chairs, pulling her knees underneath her.

"I'm going to find out how the letter got here. If someone delivered it or if we have a security problem." His explanation was met with a slight nod of her head as she flipped the envelope over and started opening it with trembling hands.

He didn't want to leave her like this. But he understood the need to be alone, to consider every angle before speaking. She was once more gathering her thoughts, gathering every thread necessary to make what might be the hardest decisions of her life. Damien let out a breath as he approached and kneeled in front of her. She glanced up for only a minute, but it was long enough to see the fear in her eyes. The shame. The guilt. They were knives thrust into her body, and her uncle and foster sister had just taken turns twisting and pushing them deeper.

Damien really should have hit Silas much harder. He stood and pressed a kiss to the top of her head, breathing in the scent of lavender and blood from her ripped cuticles. As Elora finally opened the envelope and pulled out the letter, Damien left to find out how it had gotten there in the first place.

Chapter 31

Elora

Chloe glared at every person in Elora's office. It didn't seem to matter if they were human or vampire. Instead, every person in there had earned her anger, and she wasn't afraid to show it. Elora had snatched away power over two families, and Silas had helped. Thorne working with Chloe was not a secret, but it ended on bad terms, as far as Elora could tell. The only person Elora didn't understand Chloe's anger for was Damien, but she was sure there was a good reason. After all, a vampire couldn't work for Killian and not make enemies, especially when his job was to gain information from unwilling sources.

Elora leaned against her desk, arms crossed over her chest, as they all seemed to study one another. Eyes moved from figure to figure, lingering long enough to try and read their expressions. Everyone in the room was well trained at this and revealed nothing. Not a twitch of their brows or quirk of their lips as they waited for this to begin.

"We need to deal with Elizabeth," Elora began, drawing all the focus to herself. "And I suppose we need to address what was broadcast on television." She paused, giving them a moment to chime in if they wanted to. Chloe appeared ready to explode if she didn't speak, but Elora only gave her a smirk. Either the vampire knew that her words wouldn't be well received, or she was waiting for the perfect moment. It was probably both based on what Chloe thought of her. The word she used to describe Elora was never too far away from her thoughts— abomination. Even now, Elora didn't dispute the label. It felt accurate enough.

"Just before the video was shown to the entire city, I received a letter. I'm still looking into how it got into my rooms," Elora explained as she picked up the pink letter on the desk beside her. For a moment, she simply held it, feeling the smooth grain of the paper and inhaling the scent of blood and perfume. It was the same one Elizabeth had worn during high school. Vanilla. Pure and sweet and simple. She opened it, scanning the contents one more time as if to remind herself of what it said. It wasn't necessary. Every word was etched into her mind, carved into her skin. No matter how long she lived, Elora would never forget them.

Her hand stretched out, and Damien grabbed the letter, taking it to Silas, who promptly began reading. She forced herself not to watch him, not trace the way his body moved underneath the tight fit of his t-shirt. There was no place for distractions right now and Damien was immensely distracting.

"As it gets passed around, I'll give you the synopsis. It's an invitation. She wants me to come take my place with her cult and do some type of ceremony. As you can see, the details on that are fairly vague, but my assumption is something to do with my blood."

"Why is that?" Thorne asked, her knee bouncing in apparent agitation. Her eyes kept darting to the letter in Silas's hand, as if waiting for it was too much to ask for.

"It's always my blood," Elora drawled, giving her mother a sardonic grin. The letter hadn't outlined what the goal was, only that they wished to partake in her blessing. Silas finally passed it over to Thorne, who devoured it greedily as if the secrets to the universe were hidden in the lines of swirling cursive.

"Her plan is to create a city of vampires that are all connected to me. There's quite a bit of insane rambling in there, but it all comes down to the basic fact that she wants me to run the city and every vampire in it as some type of deity. Dr. Montgomery was right to lock her up. My sister has lost her mind." Guilt swirled in Elora's gut as she spoke, the tiny voice that whispered it was her fault, that if she had been able to control her hunger, then Elizabeth would still be human.

"You're going to take her offer," Chloe declared, leveling Elora with the accusation. Elora shook her head and chuckled softly. The vampire was a problem but was still the head of a family and deserved a seat at this meeting. There was no doubt Chloe would make this more difficult than it needed to be.

"That's exactly what I'm thinking." Four pairs of eyes shot to Elora. She hadn't shared this part of her plan. When Damien held her last night and asked her about their next moves, she hadn't said a single word about this. She knew how he would react. At least this time, he would be involved in everything.

"Let's talk this through first, Elora. We need to think through all the options before we rush into anything."

"For fuck's sake, Silas! Stop protecting her. If it wasn't for her, we wouldn't be in this mess to begin with." The venom in Chloe's voice was enough to kill someone as she stood and pointed her finger at Elora. Her normally stoic face was twisted and contorted in rage and frustration, and her entire body shook from it. Something like compassion stirred in Elora's chest. This was a vampire who saw the end of her species coming at an alarming rate and was reacting to that threat.

"The blame lies with Killian. But since he isn't here to take ownership of it, I suppose I will." Damien opened his mouth to contradict Elora's statement, but she held up her hand and silenced him. Chloe was scared and arguing over who was at fault wasn't going to move things along any faster.

"It doesn't matter who is to blame. It doesn't change the fact Elizabeth has proven to be intelligent despite any madness. We still need to consider all angles, Chloe," Silas argued in a placating tone, soft and gentle as if to tame an angry animal. Chloe glared at him, eyes blazing with a rage that could burn the Tower to the ground.

"Here. Sit down and read this," Thorne interrupted, thrusting the paper at Chloe. She held her standoff with Silas for a moment longer before ripping the letter from Thorne's grasp and dropping into her chair. This was a vampire who was at least seventy years old who was acting like a petulant child, and Elora had a feeling it would continue until her blood was spilled.

"Here's what we know," Elora began, gripping the edge of the desk beneath her. "Elizabeth has a base somewhere in the city, and for some reason, no one has been able to find it. My guess is that anyone who gets close or finds it ends up turned. Anyone disagree?" No one said a word, only shook their heads.

"Fantastic. We know that she doesn't plan on stopping. The letter outlines that she wants a city of just my children, as she calls them. Since I obviously need to say this, I do not want this." Elora stared pointedly at Chloe as she enunciated each word of the last part of her statement.

"The way I see it we have two options. One is that we continue trying to find them. I can try to use the connection I have to them in order to discover where they're hiding, and then we can move forward with eliminating them." She choked slightly as she finished. Despite seeing the ceremony on television, Elora couldn't come to terms with the fact they would need to die. It ripped and dug at her soul, and she wondered if there would be anything left of her when this was done. If she survived it, anyway.

"So, you would drive around the city until you feel your connection? That is ridiculous and could take weeks," Thorne responded.

"Plus, they can feel you as well. They would know you were getting close and hadn't taken the invitation. It could cause them to move or retaliate," Silas added, giving Thorne a harsh look at her assessment of what that plan would look like in action. But she wasn't wrong. In practice, that option required her moving around the city in hopes she would feel them and they wouldn't react to her presence. It was a risk. A massive risk, if she was honest. And not one Elora was sure she could take.

"The connection goes both ways?" Thorne asked, watching her daughter closely as if she thought a lie was coming.

"Yes," she responded instantly. "We feel each other and are connected. They belong to me, as Dr. Hartley put it. It's why Elizabeth ended the letter the way she did. It's their motto or creed. I'm not sure."

"Explain." Elora shared a glance with Damien and Silas at the sound of Chloe's demand. Both of them knew this already and understood what it meant to her, how much it had shattered her to discover. But Chloe deserved to know if they were all going to work together.

Elora pushed her fingers through her hair, forcing it back as she prepared to repeat Hartley's findings. She ran her hand over her face and let out a harsh breath.

"Hartley did a side experiment. I didn't sanction it or ask her to do it, but I'm glad she did. She was able to find out a bit more about what Killian did." Thorne sat up straighter at Elora's hesitant words while Chloe stopped reading the letter and looked up. Her face was blank. The fury was gone and replaced by morbid curiosity.

"Killian failed at making my blood addicting to vampires. All of that was his own darkness, and I refuse to say another word about it. But he did succeed at—" Elora froze, the words caught in her throat, digging their claws into her esophagus. Her mouth moved, but nothing would come out. Not a single sound. Silas gave her a sad look before standing and moving to her, gripping her hand in his. He pressed his lips to her forehead, the warmth almost searing before he turned around to face Thorne and Chloe.

"He made her a beacon, as Hartley called it. She draws humans to her, like a gravitational pull. Once she touches them, they feel connected to her. Like an addiction, in a way. It would make it easier to turn more humans and increase the number of new vampires Killian could sell and harvest from," Silas outlined in a smooth voice, as if it would ease the torment of them. In Elora's mind, all she could see was Wyatt's shy smile as he gave her the sketchbook, as he admitted he had never taken his aunt's bait before. Elora's hands came together as her thumb rubbed circles in the palm of her hand. She could practically feel his touch, the effortless kindness he had shown as he carefully pulled her out of a panic attack.

"Fucking Killian," Chloe muttered before tossing the letter onto the coffee table. "Never underestimate the ambition of men. Disgusting."

For once, Elora didn't think Chloe was talking about her. Thorne narrowed her eyes at her daughter. It was clear on her face that threads were connecting, a tapestry that would only depict Elora's death taking shape. She knew what her mother was thinking because she had considered it herself.

"What I'm hearing is that you will always be a problem. You're a constant threat to humans." Thorne declared, and Elora flinched visibly and violently. Everyone saw it and Damien pushed himself to his feet, prepared to deal with Thorne if necessary. Silas only gave her another sad smile while Chloe sneered. Each reacted exactly how Elora knew they would.

"Down boy," Thorne drawled, smirking at the murderous glare Damien was giving her. "We can deal with that after all of this. Priorities. The sister is the bigger problem right now."

"I agree," Elora interjected, preparing to step in if Damien didn't retreat slightly.

"Then the question becomes: What are we going to do? We already established that the first option won't work. What was the second option?" Chloe sounded almost bored, like she was done dealing with all of them.

"The other option is I accept the invitation. We use it to our advantage."

Chapter 32

Damien

"No." Damien's refusal was instant, and Elora's eyes closed as if trying to gather her patience. She had to have known this would be his reaction. Her last plan involved her putting herself at risk in order to deal with Darian. He wasn't about to let her do that again.

Damien met her eyes only to find her glaring at him, but no amount of anger could hide the softness that radiated when she looked at him. He didn't bother to even glance at everyone else in the room. They didn't matter. Thorne and Chloe would support this plan without a doubt. Both would hope it would solve their problems—Elizabeth's cult and Elora's alleged threat to humans once everything was dealt with. He was sure both of them were hoping Elora would die in the course of this plan. And Silas would support Elora. It didn't matter that it was dangerous, that they were sending her into a group that were unhinged and insane.

Fuck. He was outnumbered and outvoted, but it didn't mean he had to agree to this without complaint.

"What a surprise," Chloe commented with a mocking tone, and he had to put his hands in his pocket, debating if it was worth it to get rid of her. All Elora had to do was give him the signal, the slightest hint that she wanted Chloe dealt with and he would destroy her.

"I'm not sure there's another choice," Elora began as her hand flexed by her side. He knew she wanted to comfort him, pull him close to promise him that everything would be okay. Her breath would be warm against his skin as she whispered to him, asking for him to trust her. It wasn't that he didn't trust or believe her capable. No, it was the idea that he could lose her, and he would have to burn the city to ashes as a result.

"We should find out how the letter got here. Take that vampire and torture them until we find out where she is. Then, we attack with a force of vampires to prevent any others turning. Kill all of them and Elizabeth." He was making up this plan as he spoke, pulling it from thin air and they knew that. Silas only watched him with pity while Thorne was impassive, practically stone as they discussed her daughter's possible death. Chloe, of course, looked positively gleeful.

"That would take time. And what if the letter was just dropped off at the front desk? There would be no way to trace who delivered it." Thorne let the words linger for a moment. Her tone was soft, as if she cared that Elora was being sent into as a possible sacrifice.

"And let's say we find who dropped it off. There is no guarantee that they know where Elizabeth is. They could be some random human or vampire they paid to deliver it. There are too many variables in that plan. It would take too much time."

"The fact that you would get rid of your daughter doesn't have anything to do with it?" Damien accused, only to sense Elora shift somewhere behind him. He let out a harsh breath and ran his hand through his hair, desperately trying to force his emotions under control.

"Damien." The sound of his name on her tongue was the answer to every question, the cure for every pain and injury, the beginning and end of his reality. It was soft, a whispering plea that he felt under his skin and in every nerve ending in his body.

He met her gaze, nearly melting at the barest hints of a smile on her lips as the corner curled.

"If it wasn't me being sent, you know you would agree this is the best option." Damien refused to admit that Elora was right, that if it was Silas or Thorne being sent then there wouldn't be a single second of hesitation.

But it wasn't them.

It was her.

She gave him a look that screamed for him to agree with her, to stop fighting and arguing and accept reality. He wouldn't ever say that he accepted this plan or that he supported it. Instead, he sank back down into his seat and leaned forward, resting his arms on his knees as his head hung in defeat.

"Now that the dramatics are done, how exactly does this work? She says you are invited and that it's time to come home in three days." Thorne swiftly brought the meeting back to order as Damien stewed in his anger and fear, listening and absorbing every word. If they were going to do this, then the plan would need to be flawless.

"Yes, and this is where Hartley comes into play. She was able to create a weapon from my blood. I think that the plan is fairly simple. I accept the invitation and live with them until I can administer it. I'm thinking that I'll try to do it at this ceremony she mentions. You all can come in and clean up the mess and anyone left standing." Damien watched her as she outlined the plan, shrugging as if her words weren't sentencing hundreds of vampires to death.

"Will it be ready by the time you need to leave?" Silas asked.

"Not sure. I was going to go talk to her next."

"Wait," Chloe interjected quickly. "There's something to discuss." All attention turned to her as something vicious appeared on her face, somehow making her blue eyes brighter. It wasn't just cruelty there, but excitement, and it put Damien on edge.

"Who's in charge while you're gone? And, additionally, who takes over if you're unsuccessful in your goals?" Of course that would be Chloe's focus. Her ambition, her desire to see Elora fall in retaliation for taking over both vampire families. In Chloe's mind, Elora and Silas had tricked her, used her as a pawn and she was furious about it.

Elora met Damien's eyes and he nodded. Apparently, they would be announcing this earlier than anticipated.

"Damien will be in charge while I'm gone and will take over should something happen to me. I had made him my partner. A co-head of the family." The response to Elora's announcement was pure silence. It seemed as if no one was even breathing as that mischievous smirk played on Elora's lips. She was waiting for them to deny her, to argue that she couldn't do that.

"I see no problem with that," Silas remarked with a grin. "After all, the Corvin family has always had two heads. Until now, of course." Thorne glared at him but said nothing. She was human and had no say in the affairs of vampires. The excitement on Chloe's face evaporated instantly as something thoughtful settled onto her features, as if she had never considered doing this. Damien knew Chloe had struggled in the past, never doing more than taking lovers because of the retaliation from Killian and Darian. It had been a control tactic, in Damien's opinion. A way to keep Chloe in what they saw as her place. He had to wonder if perhaps a new world was opening up for her, if her reality was reorganizing to make room for this newest development.

"I agree," Chloe announced, and Damien stared at her in shock. He had expected her to vote against it, to argue that there had never been two heads of Ashcroft or Ravenwell families. For a heartbeat, he studied her expression, searching for any hint that there was some type of ulterior motive. But there was no malice or calculation behind her eyes. If nothing else,

Chloe would be supportive of Damien taking over should Elora—

No. He wasn't even going to think about it. It wasn't a possibility.

"Returning to the task at hand, if it's ready, then I'll take it with me when I leave. If it isn't, we'll need some other way to get it to me." Everyone nodded as she spoke. "Are we all in agreement?"

Damien instantly wanted to say no but knew he would be outvoted anyway. All he could do was support her by not causing a scene in the days before she left them.

"Fantastic," she announced. "Chloe, you're welcome to stay here for all of this."

"As much as I appreciate the redesign, this isn't really up to my standards. Just contact me when it's time to deal with your sister." She stood and smoothed out her tight black dress. The vampire was always polished, everything perfectly in place. Her heels clicked as she glanced down at Silas.

"Escort me out?" Damien caught the curl of her lips, the hint of something hungry in her expression. All the anger that had been there when she first walked in was gone. He had a distinct feeling Silas was about to be propositioned, and he fought back a grin. It was a well-kept secret that Silas had different preferences and Chloe's efforts would be in vain. A part of him wished he could be there when it happened, when Silas gently turned her down.

Silas nodded as he followed her, closing the door behind them. Elora pulled herself onto the desk, letting her legs hang off the edge as she took a deep breath, exhaling slowly.

"She's always such fun," Thorne commented, leaning her head back against the couch as Damien made his way to Elora.

"I'm surprised she didn't have more to say to you," Damien responded as he gathered Elora's hands in his. He couldn't see Thorne's face but heard her scoff.

"We already had that conversation. It wasn't pretty." He heard Thorne stand as she spoke, no doubt sensing that this meeting was over and her presence was no longer welcomed. The door behind them opened and closed once more, leaving them alone. He lowered his forehead to hers, breathing in her scent as he struggled to find words. He wanted to tell her he didn't support this, that there had to be a different option that didn't require her to offer herself up once again.

"She won't hurt me, Damien," she whispered even as he felt a tear fall from her cheek to her hand and leaned back. With a single finger, he lifted her chin so he could see her expression. There was no fear in her eyes. Only hesitation and pain.

"I wish there was another way, love." She nodded in response even as tears began pouring down her face.

"Maybe I can convince them to stop. Explain the danger that comes from them feeding so much and turning everyone they come into contact with. If they knew I didn't support this, maybe they would stop." Her voice broke as she desperately tried to develop a different plan. He could see connections being made behind her tears, which did not bode well for any of them. In the pit of his stomach, he knew there was a chance she would deviate from what they had just established. The question was exactly how much she would change and if she would tell anyone.

"I want to give them a chance, Damien. Give them a chance to denounce her and follow me. They could join us here, and rules could be put in place." It was agony hearing her try to find a way around this. He nodded as he pulled her into his arms, trying to still the shaking of her shoulders as she wept. Her fingers dug into his back where she gripped him, as if she were afraid he was going to leave.

"If you think you can do that without getting yourself killed, then I don't see a problem with it," he admitted. "I don't care as long as you come back to me."

Her fingers flexed before moving under his shirt, roaming along the muscles of his back as she nuzzled into the crook of his neck. The shaking and tears had stopped. He waited for her to promise she would return as she moved away from him and cupped both his cheeks in her hands, bringing his lips to hers.

Even as she pulled away and dragged him to the bedroom, Damien waited for her to promise she would come back.

Even as she nipped and kissed every inch of him, he waited.

But it never came.

Instead, it felt like she was saying goodbye.

Chapter 33

Thorne

When Thorne opened the door to the room she hadn't been able to sleep in since the first night, it wasn't Elora's face she expected to see. She wasn't entirely sure who she expected. Silas, perhaps. He was the only one who had anything to say to her that was beyond barbed or petty comments. Not that she hadn't earned them.

Thorne wrapped the robe around her body tighter and stepped aside to let Elora into the room. Her face took on a faraway expression, like she was reliving a moment in this room, and Thorne had to stop herself from reaching out towards her. It was there for a second and then gone as she shook her head. Each part of her body seemed stiff as she stood in the center of the room, eyes locked on the bed. Thorne wondered if she was searching for the chains. Those had been the first things she removed, earning herself some bruises in the process. After, she had spent the majority of her time studying the drawings, welcoming the memories that came with them. It had been years since she had allowed herself to drown in them, to relive holding Elora in her arms, hanging the tiny lights above her bed.

"Come to make sure your psychological torture is working?" Elora seemed to jump at the sound of Thorne's voice, and she ran her fingers through her hair. It was always a brighter version of Thorne's own—crimson instead of dark auburn.

"You removed the chains. It seems to me it was working," she responded, but the words held no bite. Thorne dropped into the chair in the corner just as Elora turned around. Her body flinched and a spasm of pain raced through her before she took the seat opposite her.

"That's where he sat, you know. When he let others come in and feed from me. He watched from that chair and gave them permission. He drugged me most of the time, but sometimes I was awake for it." Elora seemed to watch Thorne for a reaction before she pulled her legs underneath her.

"But there's no point in telling you. You would have to care for it to matter." Elora finally looked away, giving Thorne the chance to breathe. The air had been caught in her chest as her daughter referred to the abuse, as if she were holding it hostage while she spoke.

"I doubt you came in here to remind me of my failings." Thorne bit out, unable to school her voice into disinterest. When she was with the Resistance without seeing Elora in person, it had been easy to keep the emotions and memories at bay. Locking them in a vault so Thorne could work to use Elora to save humans had been crucial to her survival. There had been little resistance when she herded them inside and threw away the key.

"You're right. But, if I'm going to die in the next couple of weeks, then I want to know I made this as uncomfortable as possible for you," Elora confessed, giving Thorne a lopsided smile.

"I doubt you're going to die. Your sister won't hurt you." Thorne waved her hand dismissively as she spoke. Elora seemed to tense ,her body becoming rigid in the chair as she glanced down at her healed fingers. Picking at them was a habit she had picked up after the first time Killian hurt her. Denise had said it was a way to dissociate through pain, or something like that.

"It isn't Elizabeth I'm worried about." She seemed to play with the edges of her long sleeves, pulling them over her hands.

Thorne took a deep breath, forcing away the memory of discovering what Killian was doing. She had found the wounds on her daughter's body and asked her what happened. Elora had only descended into tears and muttered a single word—father. All the blood had drained from Thorne's body, her muscles losing any strength they had as she tried to keep herself from collapsing to the floor. Her hands had tightened into fists as she held the rage inside, tucking Elora into bed. Then she had confronted Killian and fell for yet another of his lies.

"Then what are you worried about?" Thorne crossed her legs, watching her daughter pick at her fingers.

"Hartley talked about the connection between me and my children," Elora began, choking on the end of her sentence like the words didn't form correctly. "I can feel them, and they can feel me. But there could be a possible consequence." Thorne saw exactly where this was going. She had wondered about it when it was mentioned earlier, but it hadn't felt like the right time to bring it up. If Elora wanted the rest of them to know, then she would have mentioned it. If anyone was an expert on keeping secrets, it was Thorne.

"That day, Hartley said there's a possibility killing them could kill me in the process." There it was. Thorne had known it was coming, but it still created a pit in her stomach, filling her with a sense of dread. For years, she had worked towards using Elora, knowing it would potentially kill her in the process. Yet, now that it was a true possibility, it sat wrong with her.

"Is it a guarantee or just a hunch?" Thorne spat out the reference to Hartley, not hiding the venom in her voice. Their history was volatile at best. Elora gave her a curious look, like she wanted to pursue that line inquiry.

"A hunch, but a good enough one that she felt the need to warn me away from Damien and Silas."

"And why are you telling me? To make me an accomplice?" If Elora died from this and Damien found out, Thorne had no doubt her head would be up for grabs. His rage would be earth-shattering, consuming everything in his path. For the sake of every living person in the Tower and the city, Thorne hoped this connection wouldn't result in her death as well.

"I didn't understand how you could be willing to sacrifice me. I couldn't wrap my head around it until last night. When I watched her turn so many humans, I understood, Thorne. I knew why you were willing to drain me to save humans." Thorne waited as Elora seemed to gather her thoughts.

"Silas and Damien won't be willing to let me go through with this if they knew. You understand the necessity of it. And won't have any issues with what might happen." Elora held Thorne's attention as if to ensure the words sunk in. Something uncomfortable dropped through Thorne's body, forcing her to shift in her seat. She wanted to tell Elora she was right, that her assessment was perfect and there would be no tears shed over her body. But they wouldn't form in her throat, wouldn't come forward, and so she bit her cheek instead.

"I need you to promise that if they find out this weapon could kill me, you won't let them try to stop me." Thorne swallowed thickly, suddenly wishing for wine or something stronger. It would drown out the guilt rising to the surface. She let her head rest against the back of the chair and closed her eyes, collecting the rogue thoughts that had resurfaced since Elora appeared at the Resistance headquarters.

"I—" Thorne started.

"Don't get motherly on me now, Thorne. It's a little late for that. It was too late the moment you brought me back after he hurt me the first time."

"He was so convincing, Elora."

"How the fuck did he convince you to stay after what he did?" There was such rage in her voice and every bit of it was warranted. This conversation had to happen eventually, and if Elora could potentially die in the pursuit of saving humans, then she had earned the truth. Even if it ripped Thorne apart in the process.

"He claimed he had let himself get too hungry. That he had gone too long without blood. He said that it was a mistake and that it would never happen again. I believed him. After that, it was fear that kept me there. I have no excuse, and I don't expect any type of forgiveness. I should have seen the truth, but I didn't want to." Thorne couldn't make herself meet her daughter's eyes as she spoke. The shame was pouring off of her, coating each word and confession that came from her. Silence settled in the room, coating the framed drawings and the furniture left over from Killian's design.

"And pride," Elora spat out. "I know you fought with Silas about even being with Killian. You didn't want to admit you fucked up."

Thorne shrugged. Her daughter wasn't wrong, no matter how devastating it was to admit it.

"I have one question," Elora started. "Did you know what he was doing? That he was playing with my genetics?"

"No. There were plenty of doctor appointments, or what I thought were doctor appointments. It was Hartley. They just told me it was going to be difficult to get pregnant, and we needed some help. I didn't question it. I wanted a child so much that I accepted what he said and did what Hartley asked." Looking back, it was obvious what Killian had been doing. Maybe not the specifics, but there was enough that should have made her question him.

"Is that why you hate Hartley and look like you want to kill her every time you see her?" Thorne chuckled at Elora's question.

"I suppose so. I didn't realize it was that obvious." Their laughter filled the space between them, and for a brief moment, the animosity and pain were gone. It truly could have been a mother and daughter enjoying a basic conversation, bonding and joking. As it quieted, Elora stood, stretching her back. Thorne's eyes stayed on the scars lining her neck, peeking out from the collar of the nightgown she wore. Cotton, or linen. Not silk. Never silk, Thorne guessed.

"If I survive this, I would like to keep talking. I don't remember very much, to be honest. Only bits and pieces. I was hoping you would help fill in the gaps. The positive stuff, anyway. The rest can stay forgotten." Elora didn't give Thorne a chance to respond, which was probably for the best. After that, Thorne wasn't sure she could hold on to letting Elora sacrifice herself. As she locked the door and turned towards the bed, Thorne forced away exactly how tempting Elora's offer was.

Chapter 34

Elora

She forced Damien to stay behind at the Tower, allowing only Silas to escort her to her family home. Other than the boarded up windows and overgrown lawn, it appeared the same. Elora's breath caught in her throat as her uncle pulled up along the sidewalk, peeking through her window to assess the house. There were no other cars or signs of life, but she had no doubt one of Elizabeth's followers was watching, waiting until Elora got out of the car and Silas left.

"I don't like this plan, Elora," Silas confessed as his hand reached out to grab hers. She tilted her head and gave him a small smile that she hoped was comforting.

"They won't hurt me, Silas. I'm their goddess." She meant it as a joke, an attempt at levity but it fell flat. There was too much truth in it for it to be funny.

"That's exactly why I don't like this. They're bordering on fanatical and insane. That can be a deadly combination if they think for one second you're not completely on board with their goals," he explained, voice a tad bit tight. Elora could only nod. He was absolutely correct. The thought that she might not meet their expectations had crept in more than once in the last three days as they prepared.

"Remember to keep track of my location. Bring the weapon as soon as possible. I have no idea when I might get a chance to use it, but I don't want an opportunity to pass by because Hartley didn't have it ready in time." The scientist's face was full of defeat when she explained to Elora and the rest of them that the weapon wasn't ready, that it still needed to be finalized before it could be used. Plans had been adapted due to this small snag. A tracker had been placed in Elora's clothing, hidden in the hem of her shirt. This was clearly not where Elizabeth was hiding and gathering her followers and they needed to know where Elora ended up.

"I'm sorry. For my anger and what I said. Damien was right to hit me," Silas admitted quietly. Elora shook her head. There was no need for apologies. Not between them.

He pressed a kiss to the back of her hand and let it go. After a sharp nod of her head, Elora pushed the door open and exited, allowing herself to watch as her uncle drove away. An ache ripped through her chest as he turned a corner and disappeared, leaving her with the only home she had any memories of.

She inhaled deeply, closing her eyes as she took in the scent of earth and flowers. Every other lawn was well kept with lines of flowers or bushes. The houses were perfectly painted and the windows gleamed in the sun. She had always felt fortunate to live in this area where they were surrounded by order. It had felt like a shield against the chaos of her thoughts, of the world that surrounded them. Now, it was a reminder of her failure, of the one mistake that had led to this.

Her eyes moved over the area, searching for any sign of someone watching before she headed across the lawn towards the house. The front window was boarded completely and there was a bright pink X painted over the front door. Elora shook her head and started moving around the house, noting the way the paint had peeled in some areas. It had fallen into disrepair in the years since her foster parents had committed suicide and Elizabeth had left.

A pink heart on the back door was like a beacon, calling for her to follow. Her pulse quickened as she wondered if following Elizabeth's directions was the best plan. This could be a trap. A dozen vampires could be waiting right inside the door to tackle her to the ground and tie her up. Her hand clenched as she straightened her spine and grabbed the handle, twisting to find it was unlocked. It creaked as she pushed it open and peeked into the dark space. Beams of light filtered in through the gaps in the boarded windows, revealing just how neglected the area was.

Dust covered everything from the floor to the forgotten furniture. Broken chairs littered the floor along with discarded knickknacks that tugged at Elora's memories, drawing forward the sound of laughter and gossip as she and Elizabeth had lounged in front of the television, watching the most horrific reality shows. Her sister had always enjoyed the romance ones where people searched for their other half and spouted poetry in order to court each other. Elora had preferred the cooking and baking competitions. Every night had been an exercise in negotiation as they decided what to lose themselves in.

"Come in, Elora. It's your childhood home, after all." Her heart stilled at the sound of Wyatt's voice. Sending him to collect her was brilliant. Elizabeth knew Elora wouldn't be able to deny him anything. There would be no fighting or arguing. Her eyes fluttered shut as she breathed in deeply. Under the smell of dust and dirt was cinnamon.

"Only for a few years. I wouldn't call it a childhood home," she responded before stepping inside, feeling the wall for a light switch. At one point, being with Wyatt in the dark would have been stimulating, but now it put her on edge.

"It's the only one you remember," he retorted smoothly. She could practically hear the smile on his face.

"Elizabeth has been spilling my secrets to you. That's quite rude." He chuckled at the accusation, the sound deep and rich as she found the switch, flicking it up and down. No electricity.

"I'll give you a flashlight if you give me a tour," he offered. Elora felt him move closer, heard his steps on the wood floor and her breathing hitched as he stepped into a beam of light. Nothing about him had changed since the night at the Rose Hotel. A button-up shirt that was fitted across his broad chest paired with jeans. The brown hair she had once gripped in her hand as she almost fed from him fell against his face, highlighting the sharpness of his cheekbones and jaw. Then there were his eyes—bright and almost luminescent. All of the vampires connected to her had this trait, as if the idea of her being a beacon had been taken literally.

She held out her hand and felt him place the flashlight in her grip. Without wasting a second, Elora turned it on and studied the room more carefully. It was the dining room. Behind where Wyatt stood in front of her would be the living room and the hallway that led to the two bedrooms and bathroom.

"Is this meant to be an informative tour?" She asked, pointing the light at his face only to wish she hadn't. His expression was one of reverence and worship. If she asked him to kill himself, there was a chance he would do so without hesitation and the realization was terrifying. The mania that Elizabeth had nursed and supported was so deeply ingrained Elora wasn't sure she would be able to convince anyone to turn away from her sister's teachings. Would the word of the being they seemed to worship be enough? When she had told Damien about this slight change to the plan, Elora had believed she would be able to save at least some of them. Wyatt's expression threatened to destroy that hope.

Wyatt shrugged. "Just a tour. If you want to share, then you can. I told you before that I wouldn't make you tell me anything.

I meant that." Her mind dragged forward the image of him sitting beside her on the couch in that tiny apartment, the gift he had brought her completely forgotten as she offered him tiny pieces of her past and savored the feeling of his hands on hers.

She gestured towards the room they stood in. "A dining room," she announced before pointing to the counters and appliances on the other side, where the open kitchen was.

"And the kitchen." He smirked and nodded despite his eyes never leaving hers, leaving her with the distinct impression this was a test.

"All the good stuff is through there," she said and pointed the flashlight at the area behind him. He twisted his body to the side and dramatically gestured for her to enter first.

"How do I know there isn't someone in there waiting for me?" She asked, hesitating a few steps before the framed doorway. Silence followed the question and Elora peeked up at him. A stricken expression was painted across his features, as if she had injured him by implying he would harm her. For a second, she almost apologized. Wyatt had been welcoming, offering her warmth and affection without question.

Not that he had a choice, the tiny voice in her head reminded her and she almost flinched. Instead, she took a deep breath and pushed past him, entering the living room. Couches were covered in tears where the stuffing was spilling out. The carpet was torn, with whole pieces missing to reveal the padding. End tables were on their sides, lamps broken on the floor with glass from the broken light bulbs imbedded in the fibers of the carpet.

"Living room, obviously," she announced, ignoring the way she was starting to feel like someone giving a tour in a museum. A shrine to her downfall.

"Did you love reality shows even then?" He asked as he came up behind her, standing so close she could feel his body heat through the t-shirt she wore.

"Always. Elizabeth and I fought over what type to watch. She loved romance competitions, but I preferred ones with cooking or creating."

"I'm sure it had nothing to do with your views on love and romance," he quipped and Elora couldn't stop the grin that appeared on her lips.

"My opinion on that has changed," she admitted before moving the flashlight to the wall, revealing peeling wallpaper.

"The roommate," he stated without a hint of jealousy or anger and she laughed softly.

"Yes, the roommate. Or the brute, as your aunt called him." Wyatt flinched, and she studied him for a moment, not sure she wanted to ask why mentioning Connie would cause that. Elora swallowed back the question and started moving down the hallway, pausing at her foster parents' bedroom. It was largely untouched, as if Elizabeth had someone protected this space from the elements. The only items missing were the framed photos.

"My foster parents were amazing. Silas—my uncle—knew them, I guess. They took me in as a favor to him."

"Elizabeth said they were forced, that he compelled them," Wyatt said. His words were soft, as if he wanted to make sure Elora wouldn't be hurt by them.

"That's what I always thought. I found out otherwise." She moved on, briefly shining the light into the bathroom where the sink had been ripped from the wall and the curtain rod was lying in the bathtub.

Her footsteps stopped at the entrance to the room she had shared with Elizabeth. The room had been utterly destroyed, as if a storm had ripped through there, displaying and tearing apart everything inside. The mattress to the bed they had shared was across the room from where the frame was. Springs stuck out from where it had been torn or cut open with a knife. Clothes lay scattered across the carpet that was burned in some areas, mostly round ash areas where it looked like someone had lit a fire. Elora hesitantly approached and knelt beside the largest one in the center of the room. Burnt paper was mixed in with the ashes, and it took her a moment before she realized it was the missing family photos. Pieces of the frame and broken glass filled the rest of the pile.

Wyatt's steps were gentle as he came up behind her, but she barely noticed him. Her fingers flicked through the ash, desperately trying to find anything with faces. She had taken no photos the night she was dragged to the hospital. This was all there was. The remnants of the only part of her life she remembered with any type of clarity.

Her eyes burned as she picked up one photo that had four smiling faces. The bottom left corner of it was gone, cutting off the majority of Elizabeth's body along with her foster mother's. Elora stood beside her foster father with Elizabeth beside her. The house stood in the background, and they all had their arms wrapped around one another. Elora thought the photo had been taken roughly a year into her stay with them. Her nightmares had decreased a little to only a few times a week instead of every night. They had found a rhythm in their life and were happy even if they did struggle to afford non-essentials, like the chocolate Elizabeth desired so much.

Elora stood and folded the photo carefully before putting it in her pocket.

"She burned them all," Elora whispered, wiping away a tear that had come free. Wyatt's hand settled on her shoulder and squeezed, a gesture she was strangely grateful for. If she didn't think about it, Elora could believe that Wyatt was still the same as he was in the apartment.

"Why would she do that?" Her question filled the empty room, covering all the spaces that had held life. Over the years, this space had held all their laughter and tears, all their horrible singing and ranting about school projects. Now it was a testament to Elizabeth's rage as hunger consumed her.

"Perhaps you should ask her yourself," Wyatt answered, mirroring her whisper as if the room demanded silence. "It's time to go join her." She felt him move away and then the sound of him rummaging through something.

"You need to change all your clothes. You aren't to bring anything with you. And I need to search you." In his hand was a bundle of fabric, and her eyes widened just a bit. Her refusal was waiting right behind her teeth, but she doubted she had much choice if she wanted to get to Elizabeth. Maybe she could get the tracker out of her shirt and hide it somewhere else. She nodded and grabbed the fabric, holding it out in front of her. A laugh bubbled up in her throat until she let out a slight giggle at what she was expected to wear.

"Is she serious?" Elora asked and Wyatt only nodded. "Fine. Are you going to watch me change?"

He gave her an apologetic smile and nodded once more. Of course he was. Elora handed him the phone from her back pocket before pulling off her shirt. The dress Elizabeth wanted her to wear was silver and made entirely of silk, and she moved to slip it over her head. The fabric settled against her skin as Elora removed the rest of her clothing until there was nothing between her and the dress.

"The necklace." Her hand darted to the pendant lying against her sternum, gripping it tightly in her grasp.

"No. It stays, or I don't go." He studied her for a moment, perhaps determining if it was worth it to fight her on this. After a heartbeat, Wyatt's eyes moved over her body before he nodded approvingly. He extended his hand, and she gripped it like it was the only thing keeping her on the ground. It was time for a family reunion.

Chapter 35

Damien

"What do you mean the tracker didn't work?" His shouts echoed in Elora's office. Or his office now, he guessed even if he didn't want to think about it that way. She would be back, and this would be hers again. Silas flinched and took a step back, as if he were afraid of what Damien would do.

"I waited for over two hours and watched the tracker. When it hadn't moved, I went back to the house. This was all I found. It was in her old bedroom," Silas explained, gesturing to the pile of clothes Damien hadn't noticed at first. For a moment, it didn't register what they were. Her shirt and jeans. Even her shoes and socks were there, along with her underwear and bra. His hand tightened into a fist at the thought of someone demanding she undress and seeing her in such a vulnerable state. Silas picked up the shirt and studied the hem until he found the tracker they had put in it.

"Elizabeth is smarter than we've given her credit for," he observed before tossing the shirt back down. Damien wanted to grab it and inhale her scent, or what was left of it. Instead, he watched as Silas grabbed the jeans and searched the pockets, pulling something out of the back pocket. He carefully unfolded it as the scent of ash filled the room. It had been burned.

No, not a paper. A photo.

"There was a pile near where her clothes were. Someone burned everything. I bet this came from there," Silas explained as he studied it, brows knotted together in pain. It took every ounce of restraint to not rip the photo from his hand.

"Recent?" Silas shook his head in response before begrudgingly handing over the item.

"The fire? No. Years perhaps. It could have been when Elizabeth was turned. She burned everything that was a reminder. Only this one survived." Damien took the photo and could only stare. It was a much younger Elora with her foster family. All four of them stood in front of what Damien assumed was their home, arms wrapped around one another with bright smiles on their faces. Elora had to be maybe sixteen.

"You knew the family, right?" He asked as he traced the long red hair that framed Elora's face and the high-neck sweater she wore, hiding any hints of the scars beneath.

"Yes. They were in the same foster home system Iris and I were part of. When I realized I needed somewhere for Elora to go, I went to them, and they agreed without any hesitation. All they really knew was that she was a young woman who needed to be protected." As Silas explained, Damien studied the two humans who flanked the sisters. Welcoming smiles practically radiated from the photo, and he could see their protective nature in the way their arms wrapped around Elora and Elizabeth, holding them close as if they knew threats were on the horizon.

"We can frame it for her. It'll be here when she gets back," Damien announced. He refused to even consider a reality where she didn't return, where she didn't survive this horrifically stupid plan. Silas gave him a sad smile that revealed he wasn't sure his niece was going to emerge from wherever Elizabeth was keeping her.

Damien sighed deeply and wandered over to the desk, opening the bottom drawer where Elora kept only the most important items. There weren't many from what he could see—one of Kilian's journals whose pages were covered in sticky tabs, a sketch of Silas as a child, and a folder marked with Hartley's name and "Results" written across the top. As he set the picture down on the desk gently, Damien's mind battled with part of him screaming at him to respect Elora's privacy, saying that if she wanted him to see it, then she would have shown him. The other part, however, reminded him that she kept secrets if it meant keeping others safe. Her self-sacrificing nature was one of her traits he simultaneously adored and despised.

His movements were hesitant as he pulled the file out and set it on the desk beside the photo. Damien forced his hands into his pockets while he simply stared at it, reading the words written in black marker over and over again. He felt Silas approach, stopping opposite him on the other side of the desk before tracing his line of sight to the file.

"What is it?" Damien shrugged at the question as he chewed the inside of his cheek.

"I don't know. It was in the drawer. Did she show you this?" Damien glanced up at the vampire, who only shook his head. His face was pinched, lips pressed into a hard line across his face. There was no hint of a lie in his expression, only concern and something like fear. Damien was sure Silas was thinking the same thing as himself—that Elora had once again kept something from them. The last time she had made plans, Silas had been included and functioned as a key player as she attempted to rearrange the world to her liking. This time, both Silas and Damien had been left out. There was a strange sense of satisfaction that came with knowing Damien wasn't the only one in the dark.

"Open it," Silas ordered. His tone was sharp, each word a razor. At first, Damien hesitated, and his mouth opened to contradict the vampire. He wanted to argue that Elora had her reasons and that they needed to trust her. But the churning in his chest and the overwhelming sense of dread forced his hand to move and flip open the file, revealing the notes inside. Damien read through them, deciphering each word and technical term as the pit in his stomach grew, threatening to consume him. His hunch had been correct.

"Damn it," Silas muttered softly as he turned the file around to get a better angle. The air in the room seemed to evaporate, leaving behind a void in which Damien couldn't seem to breathe. His steps were harsh as he moved around the desk and began pacing.

"It could kill her." The words seemed to ricochet throughout the room, bouncing off every book and knickknack Elora had collected since taking over. Damien's heart pounded in his chest as he ran his fingers through his hair, desperately trying to keep himself from exploding. No wonder she had kept this from them. From him. There was no way he would have let her go, even if it meant she hated him for it. Even if it meant she stabbed him again. This was a sacrifice he wasn't willing to make, and he was pissed off that she had walked head first into it.

Damien's jaw worked as he tried to think of something to say while Silas flipped through the pages. With each one, Silas's grip seemed to get tighter as the pages crumbled slightly.

"The connection between them," Silas read. It was a whisper, but it pierced Damien's ears as Silas continued. "I can't believe she didn't tell me. Or you."

"Of course she didn't!" Damien shouted, his hands flexing at his sides. "You're just surprised to be on this side of her secrets."

"Why wouldn't she—"

"Because we would stop her," Damien interrupted. He couldn't stand to hear Silas voice a question when the answer was obvious. If he knew even the tiniest piece of his niece, Silas wouldn't need to ask. Or perhaps it was because he needed to hear the answer out loud, hear the words to cement their new reality.

"Do you think she told anyone? Last time she did something like this, she told you." He studied Silas even as he started working through who she would have confided in. Hartley didn't count in this scenario. Silas shrugged and set the file down beside him before running his hands over his face, pressing into his eyes like it would change everything they had just learned.

"That was because she needed my help, Damien. There isn't anyone whose help she would need this time. This is a solo mission for her." He hated the truth in Silas's explanation, and he turned from him, unable to see the devastation that was painted across his features. Silas was behaving as if Elora was already dead, as if it were guaranteed.

Damien's mind snagged on the barest hints of a memory, of Elora sneaking out of the bedroom. He had barely been awake when he felt her stand up, followed by the door opening and closing. His feet were suddenly moving as if they had their own mind, and he threw the door open, not bothering to care that it bounced off the wall behind it. Silas hurried along behind him even as Damien entered the elevator and pressed the button for the next floor. There was only one person Elora would tell in order to make sure her plan worked and no one would interfere.

He didn't bother to knock before he pushed the door open to find Thorne reclining in one of the chairs. The blanket Damien had given Elora was spread across her legs as she glanced up at the two of them, taking in their expressions.

"Did she tell you?" Damien demanded, and Thorne's face paled for only the briefest of moments before she set the book she had been reading down.

"I'm going to need more than that," she responded as she pushed herself back into the chair like she was trying to widen the gap between them. Whatever Thorne saw in Damien's expression had scared her, but he couldn't find it in himself to care.

"Don't fuck with me, Iris. She told you about what could happen," Damien accused as Silas let his hand rest on his shoulder. If the vampire was trying to temper Damien's anger, he was failing. Thorne took a deep breath as if in preparation.

"Yes. She did."

"Why? Why tell the one person who never cared about her?" Thorne flinched at Damien's questions before standing, straightening her spine and widening her stance. She expected a fight and he couldn't deny he wanted one.

"For exactly that reason. She wanted me to know because I am the only one who will make sure her plan happens. You two wouldn't have allowed her to leave if you knew. It was my job to deal with you two if you found out and wanted to stop her." His body grew hot with each word she said.

He wanted to punish Thorne for being the person Elora confided in.

He wanted to find Elora and drag her away, hiding her somewhere no one could find her.

He wanted to hold her, to know that she was alive and breathing.

"There's a chance that nothing will happen to her," Thorne said, interrupting his spiraling thoughts. "Hartley said it was possible, but not a guarantee. You need to hold onto that piece of hope and trust Elora to know what she's doing."

Something like regret flashed through Thorne's eyes, and Damien couldn't decide what exactly the human felt regret for. Was it because they had found out, or was it for letting Elora leave? He couldn't imagine Thorne feeling even the slightest bit

of remorse about sacrificing her daughter or for keeping her secret as she marched to the sacrificial altar.

Damien glared at her, unable to think beyond the single vow
that left his lips before he left Silas and Thorne in that room.

"If she dies, so do you."

To her credit, Thorne only nodded as if giving him permission
for what he might have to do.

Chapter 36

Elora

The tall stone walls of the church and the iron fence surrounding it reminded her of every horror movie she had watched with Elizabeth. Side by side, they would curl up underneath a blanket with every possible light turned off to fully immerse themselves in the experience. It never lasted long. About a third of the way into every movie, they had scared themselves and descended into cackling laughter that rendered the moment gone.

"Home sweet home," Wyatt announced brightly as he pulled up to the gate and waited. Movement from just inside the iron revealed a few vampires approaching and dragging the two sides open until it was wide enough for them to drive through. Elora couldn't really make them out or identify any features before they bowed their heads deeply, causing unease to bloom in her gut. Perhaps this had been the wrong approach. Maybe Damien had been right when he said this was a bad idea.

It was too late now. The gates closed behind them as Wyatt pulled up to the end of the small driveway and parked in front of the entrance to the church. Fractured and cracked stone walls held only holes where glass had been at one point. It looked even more rundown than it had in the video. How had Elizabeth picked this place out of every possibility in the city? There were empty apartment buildings and homes. That wasn't even considering all the abandoned warehouses and some schools.

"Are you ready to meet your children?" Wyatt's question caused her muscles to constrict, her breathing to catch in her throat. Elora wasn't sure how to play this role. What would Elizabeth expect? What would she find most believable? There hadn't been time to strategize and plan this in detail before she left. Elora bit her cheek as she considered it. Hesitant. Elizabeth would expect her to be hesitant to a certain extent, but curious in a way.

"Yes," she answered finally, proud of the way her voice sounded strong and confident. Not a hint of the terror currently coursing through her. Wyatt exited the car and came around to her, opening the door for her. She gave him a small smile before taking his outstretched hand and stepping out, taking a deep breath to settle her nerves. Flowers and dirt dominated, but underneath it was the smell of blood. Faint, like a memory that had faded.

"I'm supposed to take you to your room. You'll be able to freshen up and prepare yourself. Then, the ones here are all waiting for you."

Elora could only nod as the pit in her stomach grew, opening wider and wider until it was a void threatening to consume her. She knew she would have to face them eventually, that the entire plan hinged on her meeting them and building some type of relationship. Gaining their trust was the key to convincing them to follow her and not Elizabeth, the key to making them understand she did not want whatever Elizabeth had put in motion.

"They aren't all here?" she asked as Wyatt offered her his arm as he had when he took her to the cafe. She smiled softly at the memory and nestled her hand in the crook of his elbow. He let his hand rest on hers as they began moving around the side of the church towards the building in the back. A dormitory, of sorts. A nunnery, perhaps. It was massive with three levels, but not all of it seemed usable. There were collapsed parts of the roof and windows without any glass. Parts of the wall seemed like they were one strong wind away from crumbling, revealing whoever was living on the other side.

"No," he answered as they moved down the path. Elora glanced at the overgrown weeds and flowers covering the stone grave markers. Her focus moved further into the depth until they found a single headstone with sunflowers purposefully placed in a glass jar.

"About half of the family still work to bring in money for supplies. Clothing, beds, and things like that." Wyatt explained as they approached the two massive wooden double doors that served as an entrance. She opened her mouth to ask how they decided who works and who doesn't, but she never got a chance to actually say the words.

One of the doors swung open and Elizabeth glided forward with that easy grace Elora had always envied. Even as a vampire, Elora wasn't able to reach her level of sophistication. Her breath caught in her throat as Elora was transported back in time to before her teeth sank into Elizabeth's neck, changing everything. Her sister was dressed more casually than the last time she had seen her. A basic grey sweater and a long black skirt with her hair falling in waves over her shoulders, even longer than the last time Elora had seen it. It had to be difficult to manage was the only thought that came forward. Hers was below her shoulders now, and it annoyed her to no end at times, ending up in a messy bun at the nape of her neck unless she needed to look like the head of a vampire family.

Elizabeth seemed to watch Elora as she approached with Wyatt at her side. Her face twitched for just a moment, her lips quirking and brows narrowing before Elizabeth sprung forward and into a run. Arms wrapped around Elora's chest, ripping her away from Wyatt's grip. Her sister's face buried itself in her neck as Elora froze at the unexpected contact, at the embrace that threatened to cut off her supply of oxygen.

"I knew you would come," Elizabeth muttered into Elora's hair before inhaling deeply as if she were trying to absorb every bit of her scent and essence.

"You were very persuasive," Elora responded, trying to force warmth into her voice. It was immensely difficult when all she could see in her mind was the footage of humans being lined up and turned in her name.

"I would like to think it was because you missed me." Elizabeth pulled back and released her sister, staring at the dress Elora had been given to wear. She nodded her head approvingly before twisting to the side and gesturing towards the door.

"Let's show you where you'll be staying. Then, I'll give you a full tour," Elizabeth explained and Elora could only nod in response. There was nothing else to say. Once Elora stepped through that door, there would be no escaping or turning back.

Wyatt offered his arm again as Elizabeth strolled gracefully back into the building. His face was impassive, nothing like how he was at the house or even the moments leading to Elizabeth's arrival. Elora settled her hand in the crook of his elbow and tried to smile up at him, but he wouldn't even look at her now.

The scent of blood hit her first as she entered the dormitory with Wyatt. Thick and unrelenting, Elora put her hand to her nose in hopes of escaping it. How long had it been since she fed? Before she left the Tower. Hours at this point. As she took in the cracked stone walls and staircase lined with rotting fabric, she wondered briefly if she would be expected to feed directly from a human. Unease bloomed once more in her stomach as she realized exactly how horrible this could be. Elizabeth could force her to drink and turn humans during her stay—humans she would then kill in only a matter of days.

"All of your vampires live here in the dormitory together," Elizabeth commented, her voice trailing down staircase. "To your right is the feeding rooms. We don't always feed from humans. Only during turning ceremonies. To your left is a type of living room. And up here and the next floor are all the bedrooms."

"How many of us are there?" Elora chose her wording carefully, ensuring that she sounded supportive of whatever this was.

"One hundred and twenty-six, so far. Things haven't been perfect, as Wyatt here can attest to. We've had some hiccups and things that weren't planned, such as a few children who were turned. Twelve children between the ages of seven and fourteen. But we have made strides to make sure it doesn't happen again." Elizabeth recalled this all as if it was no concern, as if it wasn't the greatest crime to turn a child who would now age so slowly they would be in the same form for decades, if not more. She swallowed and nodded, keeping her focus on her sister as she began to ascend the stairs.

"And how many more do we plan on turning?" Elizabeth smiled widely at the question, but shook her head, causing her pale hair to shift slightly.

"That's a later conversation. For now, you only need to know that we're planning a celebration in honor of your return. At the full moon, which is a week from tomorrow."

"And what will this celebration include?"

The smile grew wider, revealing her fangs. Only Elora seemed to have the ability to hide hers, resulting in them appearing when she was about to feed. A choice by Killian, no doubt. A way to hide the predator she was meant to be. This must have been what Hartley meant by the traits not transferring to those who were turned by her.

Those glowing blue eyes tracked Elora as she approached her sister, stopping on the landing with Wyatt at her side.

"A speech by you, of course. Your children have been waiting to see you, to hear you speak to them. Then, there will be an official celebration where we reestablish our connection through blood." Elora stared at her sister, trying to comprehend exactly what she was saying. Blood? Whose blood? In her mind, all she could see was a larger version of the footage. Hundreds of vampires with humans waiting to be sacrificed and turned would fill the church along with the screams.

"We'll begin collecting your blood tonight." For some reason, relief washed over Elora. It wouldn't be someone else who would be placed on the altar for public consumption. And this could potentially work for the plan they had put into place. If she could get the weapon into the distributed blood, then it would be easier. It would be dangerous and she could only imagine Damien's reaction to this development, his words of concern and demands that he knew she would never listen to.

Elizabeth began down the long hallway lined with door after door. The building was silent, only the faintest sounds of distant cars and nature filtering in from outside. Their steps echoed as they went further and further, passing door after door. Faces peeked out from where they had cracked them open, watching Elora with a level of fascination and reverence that made her want to turn and run, escape from whatever this nightmare was.

Wyatt let his other hand rest on hers, his thumb sweeping over her knuckles in a way that was so familiar that her eyes stung. All over again, she wanted to apologize, wanted to beg for his forgiveness. But she had a feeling he would only give her that sad smile again and repeat the line that had begun to echo in her head: I am you and you are me. It made her want to scream in rage and agony and self-hatred. No matter what Damien said or promised, she couldn't escape the fact all of this fell at her feet.

The three of them finally stopped at the end of the hallway and Elizabeth spun around, instantly noticing the way Wyatt was covering Elora's hand. Her brows arched slightly before she grinned and gestured towards the door.

"This one is yours," She explained, pointing to the door. "Now, please wash up. There are clothes in there along with blood. It's in a collection bottle. Not as nice as the ones you have at the Tower, but I knew you wouldn't want to feed directly from anyone."

A soft breath forced itself from Elora's lips as Elizabeth turned the handle and pushed open the door, revealing a modest room with a bed and dresser. The window opened towards the graveyard and there was another door along the side wall. The bathroom, Elora assumed.

Wyatt released her hand and she entered the room, giving the two vampires one more glance before shutting the door and locking it. Only then did she let the tears come.

Chapter 37

Damien

"We have footage of someone entering her rooms before the letter appeared," the vampire announced. Damien hadn't bothered to learn her name, but he knew she was left over from Killian's reign. She had been a teenager when she was turned, giving her the appearance of being fourteen or so. Killian had raged when he found out and her maker had been dealt with by Damien. He had savored each moment of killing that poor excuse for a vampire.

Damien rubbed his temples as he leaned back in the leather chair that still smelled of Elora.

"Care to explain why I'm only learning about this now?" He tried to conjure up her name. Lily, perhaps? That sounded right.

"They tried to delete the footage, sir. We were able to recover it," she answered instantly. He was pretty sure it was Lily. He finally looked up at her, hiding the instant reaction he always had when he had seen her in the past. Her chocolate brown hair fell in curls around her face, cascading down over her shoulders while her dark eyes revealed exactly how old she was. Plus, there was her stance, like a soldier awaiting orders. Spine straight. Shoulders back. It was how he looked when he reported to Killian. Damien swallowed, not wanting the reminder of what working for him had included.

He gestured towards the desk, and she rushed forward, putting down the laptop she had been holding in her hands. Her hands seemed to shake, as if she were nervous and the laptop dropped with a loud thud. She muttered a curse and opened it, typing in something before turning the screen towards him.

The footage was clearer than he expected. He had imagined something grainy where it would be impossible to tell who the person actually was. But the view of their bedroom door was perfectly clear as a vampire approached from beyond the camera. At first, all Damien could see was the back of their head with hair cut short to the scalp. He couldn't see the person's face as they entered the room. The screen emptied for a long moment as Damien tracked the time at the bottom of the screen.

One minute. Two minutes. Three minutes. Four. Five.

After ten, the figure emerged from the room and glanced up and down the hallway. Damien leaned forward in his seat just as the figure made the mistake of tilting their face towards the camera to reveal a young male vampire.

"Do we know who this is?" Damien asked as his focus locked onto the strange glow to the vampire's eyes, shining dimly in the video footage. He knew what that meant, had seen that brightness in bottomless green that he got lost in at every possible moment.

A knock at the office door kept Lily from answering his question. It opened before Damien could say anything, and Silas entered with Thorne in tow. He hadn't seen either of them since discovering the file in Elora's desk drawer, and the sight of Thorne still caused a rush of rage.

"We have a lead," Damien announced as the two approached him with wary expressions, as if they thought he would lash out right then. They had every right to be concerned. Silas had voted for Elora to join her sister in order to use the weapon.

Even if he hadn't known what it meant for Elora's own life, he had still been willing to risk her. And Thorne was the first person Damien would destroy if Elora died for this cause. And he would make it as slow as he possibly could.

Silas rounded the desk and stared down at the screen while Thorne simply sank into one of the chairs, seeming to study the young vampire standing at attention. Lily's focus was on the laptop as she chewed on her cheek, a motion that made her appear even younger. Disgust flooded Damien's body at the sight. He had never gotten used to seeing someone so young as a vampire. There were times when he wondered exactly how the change had happened for her, if it had been as violent and painful as his own. He shook his head and studied the screen once more, trying desperately to place who this was.

The problem was he didn't know every vampire who lived in the Tower. Not even Killian had. There were records. Files in the drawers behind the desk. He was sure of that. But it would mean searching through hundreds of them to find this one singular vampire. That was also assuming they were part of the Ashcrofts. Damien had a feeling that they were. It was difficult for anyone to make it past the lobby without being vetted by security and the receptionists.

"Lily, do we know who this is yet?" The vampire seemed startled by the sound of her name, as if she didn't think Damien would know it. She nodded her head excitedly.

"Yes. Once I saw the footage, I asked around a bit. Just vague descriptions of a male vampire with really short hair. There were a few options, since there are so many of us," Lily explained. Her hands moved wildly as she spoke while her focus was on the desk in front of her. Damien tried his best to remain patient, but his hands gripped the arm of the chair as his irritation rose.

"A worker in the feeding rooms seems like the most likely. The people I talked to asked if the person I needed had strange eyes." Damien leaped to his feet and began pacing once more. It had been almost nonstop since Elora left, giving him only a small kiss on his cheek that had faded much too quickly.

A plan began forming. They could grab this vampire and question him. He would know where Elizabeth was, which meant he would find out where Elora was taken.

"Wait." Silas broke him out of his scheming and he froze. Damien leveled the vampire with a glare. There was no reason to hesitate or delay.

"If you go straight in there, then you'll scare him off and we won't get any answers."

"Then what do you suggest, Silas?" Damien bit out. The words were gravelly as he struggled to stay in the room.

"First, we find out where this vampire is now. Is this his shift? Does he live in the Tower? Once we have more information, we can find him. We don't even have a name right now." Silas was making sense, which only pissed Damien off more. His own plan had been to storm down the collection rooms and find him. He hadn't considered the possibility that the target wouldn't be there.

"Again, what the fuck do you suggest?" He didn't understand how Silas could be so calm when his niece's location was so close to being discovered. A little questioning along with a little pain and they would know where Elora was.

"We look at the files pertaining to the workers in the collection area. In the meantime, we send this young lady down there to pick up a bottle and look for him without raising the alarm. If he's there, we request him bring up a bottle and corner him here." Silas's plan was intelligent and would give them the best chance. In the past, it was exactly what Damien would have come up with before going on Killian's missions. He would have investigated every possible angle, gathered every shred of information, and considered every possible way it could go wrong.

But those missions had never been about Elora or her safety. They had never been assigned after he discovered he could lose her in a matter of days or weeks. Any ability to think rationally was gone, had disappeared along with her.

Damien gestured to Lily, who nodded curtly and left to complete her part in this. He sighed and ran his palm down his face before he stood and walked to the drawers along the wall near the shelves. Killian had always been paranoid and kept his own files, dividing them up by who they were and what role they played within the Tower.

His pulse raced slightly as he pulled open the first drawer and looked through it quickly before slamming it shut. Only high-ranking vampires and those who worked in the labs. The next one proved more useful, containing the files for those who worked in the collection rooms. With a grunt, Damien pulled out a stack of folders and hauled them to the desk, cursing Killian's paranoia with each step. Once more, he returned and grabbed the rest, placing them along with the others.

He glanced at Silas and Thorne, who hadn't said a word.

"You take some. I'll take some. Thorne can take what's left," Damien ordered and dropped back into the chair, grabbing the first file off the stack. He wasn't happy he had the human leader of the Resistance reading their files, but if it meant they would find the vampire quicker he was willing to risk it.

The silence was somehow comfortable as they worked through them, simply glancing at the photos. With each one that Damien tossed aside, he grew more and more impatient, the files hitting the floor with more and more force.

"Got him." Thorne's announcement dragged Damien from the chair as he rounded the desk and stared down at the photo over her shoulder. Sure enough, there was the vampire from the surveillance footage. Angular features stared at Damien as blue eyes stared out, seeming to glow even in the photo.

Derek Mora was written at the top of the page along with his age and role within the Tower. Thirty-seven years old when he was turned roughly fifteen years ago. A bottler, someone who was in charge of transferring the collected blood into the containers, placing them in the refrigerator afterwards. The vampire was a nobody within the family, someone who went unnoticed and filled a space. Easily replaceable as well, so it didn't matter if he died during questioning.

Lily didn't knock before she opened the door and shot the trio a small smirk. Once inside, she shifted to the side as another figure entered. The vampire. She had brought him back up here with her, rendering the second part of Silas's plan pointless.

Derek wandered into the room and marched to the table. Tall glasses clinked together as he set the tray with two collection bottles down. He was perfectly at ease. His hands didn't tremble and there was no sign that he knew what was about to happen.

The door to the office closed with a soft noise followed by the clicking of the lock. Damien straightened and sauntered over to the vampire, who had finally realized something was wrong.

"Derek. Correct?" The vampire nodded before swallowing. His eyes held the same glow, though it was dimmer than Elora's.

"Yes," he began before hesitating. "I was asked to bring this up."

"And I thank you for it. Questioning people can make a vampire thirsty." Derek finally spun around, dashing towards the door where Lily stood with her arms crossed over her chest. She shook her head before Derek yanked her by her shoulders, tossing her to the floor. His fingers fiddled with the lock, trying desperately to manage anything.

A dark chuckle fell from Damien as he made his way over to him and grabbed him by the nape of his neck. His fingers dug into Derek's skin until a choked sound filled the room. For the first time, Damien felt a sense of calm as he dragged the vampire back towards the desk and tossed him into one of the chairs. His focus darted to Lily, who had stood and was rubbing her shoulder. Before he could ask, she nodded curtly as if to tell him she wasn't badly hurt.

Damien jerked his head and she left the room. She knew what he needed, what she had been ordered to bring back.

"There's no need for that. We're only going to talk," Damien explained before leaning against the desk, watching Derek as his focus moved frantically over the room.

"I don't understand. I just brought the blood." There was a high pitch to Derek's voice that made Damien smirk. Fear. It had a unique effect on a person, altering how they sounded as they spoke. But it could also lead to stupid and rash decisions, demonstrations of defiance and rage. Or the vampire could crumble, spill each and every secret he held.

"Listen, Derek. I don't do anything without a purpose and I also don't like being lied to. You know why you're here and why I'm not letting you leave." Damien watched each twitch of his features, searching for any signal of which way this vampire would go. Derek's brows knitted together, his eyes narrowing into slits as his jaw sharpened and he tilted his chin.

Defiance. Of course it would be.

Damien sighed and shook his head before running his hand through his hair. The vampire was brave now, but he doubted he would be when the questions truly started coming. The door opened once more and Lily entered, handcuffs dangling from her grip.

"I'm going to tie you up. To that chair over there. Then, I'm going to gather some supplies and prepare the room. Tarps and plastic for the floor. I wouldn't want to make a mess. While I do that, I need you to think about how much pain you're willing to take for Elizabeth. I need you to decide how many fingers or limbs you're ready to lose for your misplaced loyalty."

"It's not for her. It's for our mother. I can take anything for her." Damien stepped forward and knelt in front of Derek, noting the brightness in his eyes and the set nature of his face. He truly did believe that Elora supported him and everything that was being done. Elizabeth was brilliant and persuasive. If they all felt the way Derek did, then it was possible Elora's plan to try and save some of them would fail. And it would destroy her.

"Lily, tie him up. I don't want him to be comfortable." The order was barely out of his mouth before she moved into action, securing each limb. He would give Derek a few hours, let him consider his choices. But once Damien came back through that door, the vampire's time would be up. He would answer every question he was asked no matter how much blood was spilled in the process.

Chapter 38

Thorne

An hour later, Damien was armed with a small yet impressive collection of tools as well as information. Derek, the vampire currently strapped to the chair in the center of the room, was freshly turned and had only worked in the Tower for a few months. There was also no record of who turned the vampire, which was fairly unheard of. Even when the turning was unsanctioned, there were always names. This was all counter to his file, which meant Killian had been lacking his last few years.

Thorne stared down at Derek, who was handcuffed to a chair in the center of the office. His face was arranged into an expression of calm defiance. Thorne wondered briefly how long it would remain once Damien began his questioning. Her guess was not very long based on the stories she had heard about his handiwork.

The most important factor was whether Damien would be able to keep his emotions in check. That was the one part that could render all of this pointless. If he killed the vampire before they got any real answers, then they would be in the same place they had been to begin with. No information. No clues as to where Elora or Elizabeth was.

The reminder was waiting on Thorne's lips as Damien took a moment to rearrange the plastic lining the floor and adjust the items on the metal tray waiting on the desk. It was all a show

and one that was working no matter how much Derek was trying to hide it. His eyes flashed before searching the room as if
trying to find an escape route. He yanked his arms, hissing as
the metal of the handcuffs bit into his skin. It seemed like Derek
had just realized where he was and what was about to happen.

"Are you staying for this?" Damien asked, glancing between
Thorne and Silas, who was reclining on the sofa with a glass of
blood in his hand. He appeared very much at home within this
scene, as if witnessing torture and interrogation was a normal
afternoon. And perhaps it was. Thorne had no idea what her
brother had been doing since she left. She had to imagine that
he hadn't held onto power without shedding some blood or removing threats.

Silas nodded curtly but didn't move. It seemed like he was
there to observe, to gather the details for them to comb through
later. Both his and Damien's focus switched to her, and she followed her brother's lead, mirroring his movement. She doubted
she wouldn't be only observing, though she couldn't explain
why she knew that. It was something in the way Damien
watched her with an expectant expression, like he knew Thorne
would want to play her part in this.

Damien reclined against the desk with his hands hanging at
his sides in a display of ease. Beside him was the tray of instru-
ments-- scalpel, hammer, pliers, along with some that seemed
more like household tools than anything else. Thorne wasn't going to question his choices. Only he knew how many times he
had done this or something similar. Well, he and Killian, but
only one was still around.

"This can go fairly easily if you answer my questions,"
Damien began as Derek seemed to be trying to prepare himself.
He wasn't going to answer anything unless forced.

"I only have one question. One question, and if you answer
it honestly, I'll let you go." There was such patience in Damien's

tone. Perhaps her concern about him controlling his emotions was misplaced. He seemed perfectly composed. It was the same cocky attitude he had when Thorne had attempted to torture him. The only person who had been in pain during their inter-action was Thorne as he taunted her with memories and com-ments about Elora. Damien had been unbreakable, even after the beatings administered by her guards. He had only smiled and spat the blood at their feet, daring them to keep going. Even then he had known Elora would come for him and that Thorne would pay the price.

Derek said nothing in response but stared at something be-hind Damien's head. He was trying to block out the agony that was no doubt coming. It was pointless. It was only a matter of time before Damien broke him.

"Where's Elizabeth and the rest of her followers?" Derek shook his head at the sound of the question.

"What does Elizabeth want with Elora?" Another shake of his head, but Derek's eyes brightened and his hand twitched at the sound of Elora's name. Chloe had a fair point about the threat Elora posed. Once Elizabeth was taken care of and her followers eradicated, Elora still held the power to create a new army. All it would take is one more mistake, one more time when she went without blood for too long. Letting Elora live required a level of trust that she could control and contain herself.

"I'm not a fan of repeating myself, but I'm going to. I'm going to give you one more chance to answer my questions before I start carving them out of your flesh." Damien was quiet for a moment, as if to let his word sink in for Derek. The promise of violence settled heavily in the room, resulting in a sense of an-ticipation that was similar to waiting for thunder to crack or a storm to break.

"What is the location of Elizabeth's base? Where is she?" There it was. The edge to Damien's voice as his patience began to wear thin. His love and dedication to Elora was immense. Killian had never loved her like that. He had never been willing to rip the stars from the heavens to lay at her feet, wasn't willing to eradicate her enemies to save her from the effort. No, Killian never cared for her. Not like what Damien felt for Elora. No matter how their love had blossomed, it was clear Damien would destroy the world for her.

"What does your group want with Elora?" Again, Derek perked up at the sound of her name. He sat up straighter and glanced around the room as if hoping she would materialize. Damien gave him a few minutes, waiting to see if he would speak at all.

Nothing. Not a word.

Damien chuckled softly and pushed himself away from the desk, twisting to study the instruments on the table. His hand wandered over each one, touching them with only the very tip of his fingers. He lingered on the one item Thorne hadn't noticed—a syringe that looked incredibly familiar. Damien lifted it and turned back to Derek, holding the item up so everyone in the room could see it.

"Do you know what this is?" Derek didn't move, but his eyes narrowed on the syringe. It seemed Damien was taking inspiration from Thorne's own process when questioning him, and a smirk appeared on her lips.

"I know what you're thinking. He'll cut me or break my fingers or something like that. But then I'll heal, because that's one of the perks of being turned. The damage won't last, so I'll be able to handle it. Is that roughly what your thought process is?" Derek twitched slightly, giving away the answer without speaking.

"That's what I thought," Damien drawled before striding towards Derek and plunging the needle into his neck, pushing the plunger until there was nothing left. Thorne knew it would take about five minutes for it to fully work.

"You see, that was a dose of a medication that nullified your healing. Your body won't react the way it normally does. Each cut I make will continue to bleed. Each bone I break won't mend. Do you understand?" For the first time, there was a hint of fear in Derek's expression, and Damien's lips curled into a grin at the sight.

"Unfortunately, we have to wait a few more minutes until it fully kicks in. So, take that time to consider if you really want to keep Elizabeth's secrets. Or if--"

"It's not for Elizabeth. She's simply the voice of Elora." Thorne watched as Damien rolled his eyes at Derek's interruption and his hand tightened into a fist around the syringe. After a long moment, he turned and set the needle down only to pick up a thin blade that reminded Thorne of a razer. The blade was loose in his grip as he approached and twisted Derek's hand until his palm was face up. He hissed as the handcuff cut into his wrist, but he didn't try to jerk away or beg.

"We're just checking," Damien assured him before the blade sunk into the meat of his palm, dragging across the space. Blood came forward, dripping down onto the tarp. Damien crouched beside the vampire and waited, watching the cut for a change.

One second.

Thirty seconds.

One minute. Then two.

The cut didn't close even as the bleeding decreased, a sign the medication had kicked in enough to begin. Damien gave Thorne a feral grin and jerked his head, gesturing for her to join him.

"Do you want to ask the question or give out the punishment?" He asked and she considered it for a moment. On the one hand, she wasn't excited about torturing Derek. She hadn't even wanted to torture Damien, but it had served a purpose. But on the other hand, she wasn't sure Damien could be trusted with the blade if Derek decided to fight them every step of the way.

"Punishment. We can't have you killing him too quickly," Thorne responded, and he chuckled softly before handing her the blade.

"If he refuses to answer, cut him. If he gives an unsatisfactory answer, hurt him. Anything other than plainly stating where Elizabeth is, make him hurt." Damien gave his command quickly and then leaned against the desk, crossing his arms over his chest as if to keep himself contained.

"Where's Elizabeth?" Derek shook his head at Damien's question and Thorne began. She pressed the razor against his forearm and began a long slice, resulting in blood rushing forward. It wasn't enough to kill him or cause him to bleed out, but enough to do its job. His body jerked as he tried to escape, whimpers and soft grunts filling the room. Thorne watched the wound, waiting for any sign it would heal. But there was nothing, only a steady stream of blood.

"What do they want with Elora?" A whimper followed by a sob before Thorne repeated the process on his other arm. Again, she waited, studying the cut.

"Break his fingers if he doesn't answer," Damien ordered and she nodded, standing to grab the hammer beside him on the table.

"Where is Elizabeth?" His tone was growing more strained by the moment. With each question he was forced to repeat, his self-control was slipping. There was a danger lurking beneath his calm exterior that was terrifying to behold.

Silence and Damien nodded. The hammer came down quick and heavy, smashing into the right index finger. A scream filled the air as Derek threw his head back and howled in agony, tears pouring down his cheeks. Thorne wanted to tell him to just answer the question, that Elizabeth wasn't worth this.

Damien repeated the question again and Derek's head fell against his chest as sobs forced his body to shake.

Another nod. Another finger. Another scream. The middle finger this time. Damien laughed darkly at the sound, almost as if he were savoring it.

"Eight more fingers to go. Then we can move on to your hand. And then your wrist. Maybe then your toes. Systematically work our way through your body." Another sob punctuated Damien's explanation.

"Where is Elizabeth?" Silence for a moment and another finger. Two of them. The hammer hit both the ring finger and the pinky at the same time. The scream this time seemed to last forever, reverberating off the walls. Silas stood, setting his glass of blood on the end table before taking his place beside Damien. Both vampires stared at the writhing figure as if they could somehow sense the end of this was near, that he was going to break.

"A church. Please, no more. They're at a church." Damien tutted and shook his head in disappointment.

"We know that already, Derek. Which church? Where is it located? Details, or we move to the next hand."

"Edge of the city. North or so. I don't know the name. It was already abandoned." His words were broken as he struggled to speak through the pain. Thorne stood and took a step back, glancing at Damien, who seemed ready to leave the Tower and find her. Blood soaked through her jeans, drying on her hands and she kept her eyes from it, unable to bear the sight.

"What about Elora? What do they want with my niece?" Silas demanded, and Derek began to shake his head, groaning slightly. The blood had stopped pouring from the wounds on his arm, but the flesh was still open. Beneath him was a massive puddle of dark liquid along with footprints from where Thorne had stepped into it. Sweat was beading and trailing down his brow as he mumbled something incoherent.

"Another finger?"

"No! No, please. We just want her back. She's the mother of us all. We're all connected to her. We'll drink from her." Stilted words fell from his lips, each one forced and difficult. Thorne studied the vampire and noted the way his color had gone pale along with how he seemed to be fighting to stay conscious. He didn't have much left.

"What are you going to do with her?" Silas once more. Her brother's tone was different than she had ever heard it. He always had a sense of stoic power about him. It was what they had been taught and trained to be. Silas had always radiated the type of authority Killian had only dreamed of, but now there was murder lingering in his voice. It was like a monster hiding under the surface of a perfectly still lake.

"Worship her. Put her on a pedestal." Derek's voice had gone quiet, each word barely audible. "She is us and we are her."

Damien darted forward and wrapped his fingers around Derek's throat, forcing his head up to meet his gaze. For a long moment, Damien simply stared at the vampire, tracking the way Derek's eyes were fluttering shut and his body kept slumping further down in the chair. Thorne's breath was caught in her throat as she waited, trying to figure out if the vampire would survive. From the expression on Damien's face, Derek's chances were slim. Damien leaned forward until his mouth was beside Derek's ear, mumbling something Thorne could only vaguely make out.

"She's mine. Not yours." With those final words, Damien stood and walked away, leaving behind Derek's dead body for someone else to deal with.

Chapter 39

Elora

They were all waiting for her in the common room of the dormitory. It reminded Elora of the cafeteria at her high school—linoleum floors and banquet-style tables with attached benches. Nearly half the room was full as they crowded as close as possible to the front as if they were desperate to be near her.

Wyatt held out his hand for Elizabeth as she stepped onto the table and smiled benevolently out at her congregation. The crowd quieted instantly, the side conversations ending once Elizabeth took her position. Elora only watched from her place beside the table, waiting for her sister to introduce her. Eyes kept darting to her, lingering on her face with a sense of adoration or reverence. They all knew who Elora was, understood the role she played in their creation.

"I promised you that our creator would come to us and I have fulfilled that promise. Elora is here with us and wants to speak to you all. She wants to meet and learn about you. Welcome her. Worship her as we're meant to." Elizabeth bowed her head and took Wyatt's hand, stepping off the table before pulling Elora beside her. Her hands rested on Elora's shoulders, squeezing tightly before pushing her forward towards the vampires she had inadvertently created.

Tension settled over the group as each person stared at Elora, waiting for her to speak. But she wasn't sure what to say to the vampires who gazed at her with such adoration and reverence. Words were stuck in her throat, full sentences refusing to form in her mind. She felt her hands begin to sweat as her heart raced wildly in her chest. This was torture. She would rather face Jonas again. Or Darian. At least then there was hatred that rendered her actions so easy. Now, there was only pity and guilt, both of which ate away at her like a poison.

Wyatt's hand settled on her shoulder, and she glanced up at him. Whatever he saw on her face made him give her a small but reassuring smile before nodding. Elora turned back to the crowd and inclined her head as if in a bow.

"I wish to speak with you all. To learn about you and hear your stories." Her voice rang out over the crowd, loud and firm but welcoming. It took every ounce of her strength to force in some semblance of warmth.

There was nothing else she could say, no other thoughts that sprang forward. Elora knew she should probably say something about them being her children, about how she loves them or welcomes their worship, but she couldn't voice that. Bowed heads were the only response before a few of them stepped forward, arranging themselves at the table beside Elora.

She studied each face, noting the glow to their eyes and the sharp point of their canines as they smiled at her. Two men and two women, all roughly the same age. Late twenties or early thirties at the most. They all bore their scars on their neck proudly, with the two women arranging their hair on top of their heads. The sight only made her think of Damien, of the moth tattoo that covered his puncture wounds from where Killian had turned him. There had never been this type of pride in Damien, or any other vampires that she knew. It was in an effort to let themselves blend in more, hide their identity from humans. It seemed these vampires didn't feel that need.

"I was one of the first to be turned," the woman on the edge began. Her hands were clasped on the table in front of her as she leaned forward as if trying to get closer to Elora who sat across from the four of them. Behind her, Wyatt stayed in place with his hand on her shoulder in a strange show of comfort or solidarity.

"What is your name?" The woman grinned and shifted slightly, adjusting herself in her seat.

"Amber. I knew your sister before. I was her nurse at the hospital. When she offered to turn me, I was afraid at first. But then she told me about you and I knew I needed to be connected to you. And so, I accepted her offer and then returned to my family." Nausea swirled in Elora's stomach and the blood she had drank before coming down threatened to spill out onto the table itself. The woman had willingly been turned because Elizabeth spouted some lies about who Elora was. It was a sickening realization, a heavy burden that crashed down on her shoulders.

"It's hard to imagine what my sister could have said to you to convince you of that. I wasn't exactly known for drawing people to me. That was always Elizabeth." Elora chuckled softly as she spoke in hopes of making her words sound humorous, not like the damnation that it was.

"The things your sister said about you were intoxicating and so beautiful. You were indeed a goddess to her and she made you one for me. For all of us." There was such a frenzied nature to Amber's explanation and Elora felt Wyatt squeeze her shoulder a bit tighter.

"I just hope I'm not a disappointment now that I'm here." Amber shook her head fervently as her hands reached towards Elora and grabbed them. Her grip was punishing, forcing Elora's fingers to press into one another until she almost cried out.

"Never. You're everything that I knew you would be. Everything that she promised you would be." Again, bile rushed forward as Elora forced herself to give Amber a soft smile accompanied by a small tilt of her head, hoping it made her seem like she was welcoming the praise, accepting her role.

The woman beside Amber shared her story, explained she had been given the choice by her wife and had accepted it without question. When Elizabeth explained who Elora was, she had known this was where she was meant to be. The same was true for the two men, each recalling how they wished for this existence, how they wanted it.

Elora stood, letting Wyatt hold her arm as she did so. There was only so much of this she could listen to, only so much praise and worship. Already it settled on her skin like a toxin, seeping into her pores and running through her veins. Her heart began to beat rapidly, her pulse racing beneath the surface. Her focus moved from the four in front of her to those hanging along the back wall, watching her with something like apprehension. For a few of them, it was more like hatred.

Those were the ones she wanted to speak to. They were the ones who needed to hear her truth, not whatever Elizabeth had told them.

"Do you need to drink something?" Wyatt's words were in her ear as he bent down and Elora nodded. Her hands trembled slightly as she began to work her way through the tables and bodies, all conversing about mundane things. Elora wasn't sure why she thought that they would be discussing their next victim or who they planned to turn next. At the very least, she thought she would hear gossip about how life was inside the dormitory, about animosity or petty disputes. But no. It was about who would be in charge of washing the bedsheets or the money they had gotten from selling all their possessions.

"Who are they?" She asked and Wyatt followed her line of sight before scoffing.

"They keep themselves separate. You need to know that not everyone was accepting of being turned, especially in the beginning. Mistakes were made and there were some who were turned without their permission."

"Can I talk with them?" Wyatt's brows knitted together before he glazed down at her.

"You're welcome to talk to everyone. We all belong to you." Elora flinched as he spoke. They didn't belong to her, and she would not claim them.

"Wait," she called out and the group of vampires stopped, twisting to watch her approach. "I just want to talk with you." Their eyes moved to Wyatt, who stood beside her as a silent guard. He seemed less at ease, stiffer as if he thought they would attack her. If that was the case, this group was exactly who she needed to speak with.

"Wyatt, if you could get me a drink, I would be grateful." He seemed to hesitate for a moment before nodding and leaving through a side door where Elora assumed blood as stored. But she wasted no time before turning to the five vampires in front of her.

"You didn't want to be turned." There was no point in trying to ease into the conversation or tiptoe around what Elora knew to be true. Indeed, the group only nodded and gestured to a table in the back of the room, safely away from the others.

"No, we did not. We weren't given a choice. For me, my brother dragged me here and turned me. She was turned by her teenage son who returned home after a ceremony." The vampire who spoke was an older woman. She had probably been in her sixties when she was bitten. The other one was younger, maybe in her early thirties. The other four kept silent, seemingly content to let the older woman speak for them.

"And they did it for you. Because they bought into whatever Elizabeth is selling." The woman's tone was so bitter that Elora was surprised it didn't cause her physical harm. The words landed like blows against her stomach and face. Yes, the blame belonged to Elora and she didn't deny that.

"I didn't ask them to. Did she explain anything? About how this started?" The woman shook her head at Elora's questions.

"No. Only that she had been the first chosen and her mission was to spread word of a life without aging or disease. Many of the vampires you see here bought into it without bothering to ask what the cost was. My brother was one of them. He had been given six months to live. Most of those who were turned early were terminally ill. She offered them hope on a silver platter without telling them the consequences. Then she set them loose. She let them go home to their families." Elora suppressed a shudder at the woman's explanation.

"No one was chosen. My hunger had been suppressed for years through medication. When I was unable to take it anymore, my hunger returned. Elizabeth was nearby when I lost control." A spark of hope appeared in the woman's eyes and Elora glanced at each one of them in turn. All of them held the same shred of optimism as the request for the medication rested on their tongues. Elora could see it, could feel the way they were holding themselves back from begging.

"Does that mean you don't condone this?" Elora peeked over her shoulder where Elizabeth stood surrounded by vampires, all smiling and laughing at whatever was being said.

"I don't. And I want to stop it. I want to give people a way out." The words were dangerous. If any of them decided to tell Elizabeth, it could mean the end of Elora. Her sister's wrath would be legendary, and Elora doubted she would be the only recipient of it.

"We don't feed directly from anyone," the young man at the end muttered softly, and Elora snapped her attention to him. "We know that's all it takes to turn someone. Each of us feeds, but from bottles. We just want to live our lives, whatever that means now."

Elora's heart cracked in her chest as the young man spoke. It was the exact words she had said so many times. No matter who she was or what purpose she was meant to fulfill, all Elora had ever wanted was to exist. Maybe, if she was lucky, one day she would be able to be happy and content with Damien and Silas at her side. Perhaps even Thorne would someday play a role in her life. It was such a glorious thought, a fantasy ending to whatever this hell was.

"When the time comes, do not follow her orders," Elora said as she leaned forward, whispering softly to them. She wasn't sure exactly what the plan would be. The one she currently had was even less detailed than the one that involved killing Darian. But if she could get the weapon from Hartley, then she could dose the blood. That was another complication to figure out. Another hurdle to leap over if she was going to stop this.

Wyatt emerged from a side door with a large glass in his hand. His focus moved over each of them as he handed it to her. The expression on his face made Elora's heart skip a beat for a moment. It was too aware, as if he could read each of their thoughts. After a moment, he extended his hand towards her and grinned. Perhaps he had simply sensed the tension and didn't realize the beginnings of a coup had been set in motion.

Chapter 40

Elora

It felt like she had traveled into the past, tripped and fell into her darkest memories. It was all too similar. The feel of the alcohol pad on the crook of her arm. The needle pierced her skin. The latex gloves. The sensation of blood draining from her body, filling the container sitting on the end table beside her. The vampire in charge knelt before Elora, not meeting her eyes. Instead, once the needle had sunk into her vein, their eyes had closed as they inhaled the scent, causing their entire body to shudder.

It was too familiar and Elora felt herself falling into waking nightmares, the memories she worked so hard to keep at bay rushing forward with a vengeance. She could hear Killian's voice in her ear, whispering promises and apologies.

"How much do you need?" Elora asked as Elizabeth stepped inside the room and leaned against the dresser.

"Enough for the ceremony. Another few collections. It needs to be enough for everyone to partake. We are officially making ourselves a vampire house, just like the two you currently run," Elizabeth explained.

"Is that what you want? Your own recognized house and the respect that comes with it?" It seemed too simple that this was all to create her own family, her own collection of vampires who would answer to her.

"To a certain extent. I do want to create a family, but I don't want to be in charge. I want to follow your command along with every other vampire in this city. Think about it, Elora. Every vampire in this city being connected to you with you as our leader. It's perfect. Better than we ever thought possible growing up."

"What if that isn't what I want?" Elora hadn't voiced this since she arrived at the church, but she did now in a quiet whisper. For a second, Elizabeth didn't answer and Elora wondered if perhaps her sister hadn't heard her.

"It doesn't matter if you do. We're all connected to you no matter what. And so will every human we turn."

"And those who are already vampires? What's your plan for them?" This had been a nagging thought in the back of Elora's mind ever since they had figured out what Elizabeth seemed to want. Drinking her blood had no effect, as Damien and Hartley had so clearly demonstrated. But what about if Elora drank from them? Would her bite do something? Perhaps she should have asked Hartley before leaving. Elizabeth tilted her head as if she were considering the question.

"I would like to think we can live in the city together, especially considering you are the head of two different families. A city of vampires, either those connected to you or those under your care. Either way, you remain in your rightful place. On a pedestal for us to worship."

"It's easy to fall from that height. Don't set me up there. You know who I am. I'll never live up to what you want me to be."

"I'm getting the feeling you don't support this, Elora. That you don't love your children here. Do you understand what I have done for you? The plans I have put in place for you?"

Elora pushed herself up on the bed and glared at her sister. "I never asked you to. I never wanted this. You did this on your own. All because I made one mistake."

"It wasn't a mistake. I understand now what happened with the medication. But what you see as a failure I see as a blessing. We'll reshape the city." This conversation was horribly pointless, leaving Elora with an emptiness in her chest. Every time she thought that Elizabeth could be reasoned with, sentiments like this poured from her lips. It was like a splash of cold water that dragged Elora kicking and screaming back to reality.

"You'll come to see it eventually. I know this must be a lot for you. But at the ceremony, you'll understand." Elizabeth bowed her head as she did every time she was in Elora's presence and spun from the room.

"I'll understand what?" Elizabeth seemed so sure that Elora would change her mind once everything came together. For a brief moment, Elora felt a tinge of fear that perhaps her sister was right, that she would end up accepting whatever the big picture was. She could see the pieces of the puzzle and could put them together, but the picture they made was still blurry, as if she were seeing it through a fog. Or perhaps there wasn't anything greater. Perhaps there was nothing beyond simply turning every human and creating a world that Elora was in charge of. Somehow that was more horrifying.

"Do you miss them? Our parents, I mean." The question caught Elora off guard and her mouth opened as she struggled to understand exactly what her sister was asking.

"Of course, I do. I've missed them every minute since I left." Elizabeth nodded before studying her hands.

"Wyatt said your uncle knew them. How?" Of course Wyatt had told her everything they had discussed. He was her loyal servant and had probably knelt at her feet while he explained every detail.

"He never really said. They were friends from the group home they lived in from what I gathered. Silas was an orphan before being adopted by the Corvin family," she explained, shifting a bit to make herself more comfortable. It took more effort than she was expecting, and she groaned as she settled into her new position.

"I always thought they were forced to take you in. That your uncle compelled them." There was a sense of wonderment in Elizabeth's voice as she spoke. It was like she couldn't believe how fate seemed to work, that it wasn't realistic that Silas would give Elora over to someone else as compared to a complete stranger.

"Why would you think that? Did you somehow imagine Silas picking a random house and dropping me off? How did that make any sense?" Elizabeth shrugged away the harshness of the questions. There was an undeniable desire to defend Silas, a need to make sure Elizabeth didn't view him as some evil or manipulative vampire who forced his way inside her home. There was a shared history, an affection and loyalty that led to Elora's place in their family.

"My parents never talked about their past. I never even knew they were in the system, that they were orphans. All I knew was they didn't have any siblings, and no grandparents came over or showed up for holidays." Elora nodded as Elizabeth spoke. She had always thought it was that they didn't tell her, that Elizabeth would know everything since she was their biological child for fifteen years.

"I guess I never thought about how I ended up with your family. I suppose I was distracted by the nightmares and not remembering anything before waking up in your bed the morning I was dropped off," Elora drawled, causing her sister to chuckle lightly.

"True. I always knew something horrible had happened to you, but I never guessed vampires. You never gave the slightest hint. Only vague complaints about vampire movies not being realistic." Both of them chuckled at the shared memory, the sound echoing in the room. It was strange to Elora to hear it in a place like this while they were surrounded by the scent of blood and eerie silence despite the number of vampires in the building at any given time.

"I didn't know anything for sure either. Not really. Being taken back to the Tower reminded me of a lot, but I don't know that I'll ever remember everything. I don't think I want to. There's a lot of pain and fear," Elora explained as her fingers wrapped around the blanket on her lap, clutching them tightly in her fists. The nightmares had decreased to one or twice a week instead of every night. The sight and smell of roses no longer instantly destroyed her hold on reality, the feeling of silk no longer dragged her back to her memories. It was progress and this was threatening to undo all of her efforts.

"I'm curious about something," Elizabeth began and Elora couldn't help but be grateful for the change of topic no matter how abrupt it may be. Her sister had always been like that. For the longest time, it had driven Elora insane to have a conversation change without warning as something grabbed Elizabeth's attention and pulled her in like a fisherman with their catch. After a while, Elora had gotten used to it, became attuned to when the shift would happen.

Elora nodded as she waited.

"Viktor. What did you do with him?" Image after image rushed forward, all fighting to be the one that lingered—Korina taking him as a hostage to force her compliance. His face as she held him in her arms. The peace in his eyes as she pulled the blade from his flesh and watched as he faded.

"Dead," she responded curtly. Something that looked strangely like grief rushed across Elizabeth's face, shining just long enough for Elora to identify it. There was no reason why Elizabeth would feel anything other than pride that her gift had been accepted and had been used as intended.

"You? Or did you pawn Viktor off on someone else?" Underlining Elizabeth's questions was some version of anger. It was both cold and sharp with each word forced from her clenched jaw.

"You seem more upset by Viktor's fate than me. If you cared about him, then you shouldn't have handed him over," Elora snapped, trying desperately to force away the vision of his blank face as he laid on the floor in a pool of his blood. She watched as Elizabeth struggled to control her expression. Each muscle and feature were seemingly determined to give away whatever she was trying to hide. Regret. It was so clearly displayed that Elora wasn't entirely sure what to make of it.

"He was fun to play with. And his blood was exquisite, as you know." It was a deflection, a way to explain away whatever Elizabeth had come to feel for him.

"I didn't kill him. And neither did Damien. He died during a rescue mission." Elizabeth's eyes narrowed at Elora's confession. Her lips thinned into a line as she studied Elora's face, searching for signs of a lie. If anyone would be able to see them, it would be her. They had been inseparable for years and knew each other as well as they knew themselves.

"That's too bad. Why not turn him? Save him that way?" Elora shook her head, finally succumbing to the urge to pick at her cuticles. The blanket was wrinkled from where she had been gripping it so tightly in her hands in an effort to save her skin. As the conversation continued, the need had only grown, the urge to pick her flesh in an effort to center herself. Or punish herself, perhaps.

"He didn't want to be turned," Elora forced out as the scent of her blood filled the room and her sister inhaled deeply, as if savoring the smell.

"It's nice that he was given a choice, I suppose."

"Don't you fucking dare. I had no control over what I was doing. I went from believing I was completely human to being unable to stop myself. Neither of us had a choice." Elizabeth hummed softly in response to Elora's declaration.

"There has been so little choice in all this, don't you think? You didn't have one, and neither did I. Wyatt didn't either. Among the others here, some picked this life while others were dragged in. Bitten and turned without any voice in the matter."

"It should always be a choice, Lizzie," Elora said softly, reverting to her childhood nickname for her. Something in Elizabeth softened as her hands dangled at her sides and her lips turned downward.

"I'm sorry I didn't give you one. It's one of my greatest regrets." Instantly, Elizabeth transformed. Her features became stone, sharp and dangerous as she marched forward. The sound of Elizabeth's hand connecting with Elora's cheek was loud and crisp in the otherwise silent room. Her face snapped to the side from the force of the strike as the pain radiated throughout her cheek. A sharp gasp erupted from her as her hand reached up and gingerly touched the spot before meeting Elizabeth's eyes once more.

"How dare you? How dare you regret the most important gift I was ever granted. I wanted this life! I wanted to be special! You gave me that, and now you say you wish you hadn't."

She had fucked up, had misread the interaction and the emotions motivating the conversation. Elora had thought Elizabeth felt remorse for everything, that perhaps she wanted to hear an apology for ripping away her future. Wrong. Elora had been horribly wrong, and it may have cost her everything. She took a moment to gather her thoughts, desperately trying to identify a way to salvage this.

"All I meant was I regret taking away your choice. That's all. I don't regret the fact you were turned or anything that came from it. Only that you didn't knowingly walk into my arms and offer me your neck." The lie slipped easily past her lips, sounding so sincere that Elora wondered for a moment if perhaps she truly did feel that way.

Elizabeth softened once more, and her hand reached out, causing Elora to flinch. Guilt flashed in Elizabeth's eyes before she touched her cheek, letting her knuckle trail across the spot that was no doubt red from where she had been hit. The apology was wordless as Elora watched her sister turn away, letting in another vampire armed with a collection bottle and supplies.

Chapter 41

Thorne

It was clear that the scientist hadn't expected to find Thorne waiting in her office when she returned from whatever she had been doing. Hartley's arched brows rose and her lips pinched together as if to hide the surprise that flashed in her eyes. Back when Thorne was Iris, she had found such comfort and strength in Hartley's face and presence. With Killian at her side they had sat in this very office, in these exact seats and discussed how Iris could give her husband a child. She had wanted nothing more than to feel life growing inside her when so much of what surrounded her was violence and death. Iris would fantasize about experiencing every kick and milestone, of holding and nursing the child she brought into the world.

But Iris had been blind, had ignored the side glances between Killian and Hartley, the meetings and consultations she was never invited to. She had never asked questions, just gave them anything they asked for and laid back with her feet in the stirrups. No questions. No comments. Only desperation and compliance.

"To what do I owe the visit?" Hartley asked as she rounded the desk and dropped into her leather chair. Files were stacked high while a laptop was closed beside them. Pens and scrap paper littered any remaining space. Thorne considered how to answer, questioned the reason why she had found herself here.

She didn't want to admit that something in her feared the loss of Elora, feared losing her daughter all over again.

"After all, I doubt you're here to talk about the past." Thorne smirked before crossing her legs and leaning back in the chair.

"The past doesn't really interest me. I left it behind a long time ago."

"I always wondered how you got away. Killian said he had killed you, that your body was for me to harvest anything from. I think he wanted to try to recreate Elora," Hartley calmly explained, as if it was of no consequence that it was Thorne's dead body they were discussing.

"I clawed my way out. Inch by inch. I had another human who helped me once I managed to get out of Killian's office. They gave me a place to stay while I healed up. After that, I joined the Resistance under a different name," Thorne responded. It didn't matter if Hartley knew what happened after Killian tried to kill her. They both went quiet for a moment before Thorne shifted slightly and broke the tension.

"You were always more involved in Killian's plans than I was." There wasn't any bitterness in her words. It was a statement of fact, a simple observation.

"Not to be cruel, but you were meant to be the vessel. Not an active participant. An incubator, for the most part. And Killian handpicked you for that role." Hartley's tone was cold, almost clinical as she spoke, and Thorne only shrugged.

"It doesn't matter now. You're right. I didn't come to talk about our history. I want to ask about the possibility of Elora dying." This had plagued Thorne since Elora appeared in her room, confiding in her that she may not survive this. She didn't want to admit how much the thought of losing Elora bothered her. No one would believe her if she said it. Certainly not Damien and Silas would probably question her at the very least. After all, she had spent years searching for Elora in order to collect her blood to create a weapon, had been willing to sacrifice her without a second thought.

But would she have been able to do it? Even with Elora in her grasp, Thorne wasn't entirely sure she would have been able to do what was necessary.

"I told her that it wasn't a guarantee that she would die. But the tie between her and the others is unstudied. There was no way to study it beyond having her turn someone and testing the connection. It felt dangerous even within a controlled environment." Thorne nodded as the scientist explained. Despite understanding what Hartley was saying, it didn't ease the pit in her stomach or help her heart unclench.

"Is there any way to block the connection?" Perhaps if the tie between them went dead, Elora wouldn't be impacted by the weapon. Hartley stared at Thorne for a moment before she leaned back in her chair and let her eyes focus on the ceiling. It was a gesture Thorne recognized immediately. The scientist was deep in thought, considering every possible option. A small seed of hope took root in Thorne's core as she waited, desperately trying not to fidget. She needed an answer. Even if the answer was no, Thorne needed one. At least then she would know she tried to find a way around this.

"I've actually been looking into that. I'm not in favor of Elora sacrificing herself. The vampires need her. The same is true for the humans. Our city is on the brink of war again and she can be a connection between the two sides." Thorne had considered this as well. It was clear the city was growing more and more angry, the attacks and retaliations growing more common and violent. Bodies found drained and set on fire. Vampires found dismembered in public places to send a message, which Thorne knew intimately since she had ordered those attacks.

Elizabeth turning entire families and attacking randomly throughout the city hadn't helped. The only possible hope of preventing a fight was Elora and her cooperation with the Resistance, which she had already promised. Thorne had no reason to believe that she would turn on them, would break the agreement they had made.

"Unfortunately, based on the information I gathered from her, the medication didn't necessarily block the connection. She could feel Elizabeth when they were both at the hospital. It seemed like it wasn't very intense, so maybe it dampened it a bit. Elora explained she felt a tightness in her chest, but nothing like when Elizabeth showed up at the apartment," Hartley explained calmly, not truly bothering to hide the small glint of hope in her words. Perhaps they could dampen the connection just enough to keep her from dying.

"Do you think it's worth a try? Having her dose herself before giving out the concoction you're making?" If Hartley thought it was worth a shot, then it was a matter of getting the medication to her along with the weapon. The scientist shrugged slightly.

"It's my hypothesis despite being unable to test it. Either way, it can't hurt. We give her the vials of what I've created along with the medication. She can plan from there. It isn't as if we have had contact with her and know what is happening. Only Elora can decide how to use what we give her."

"We know where she is now. We have that at least." Knowing her location meant they could move forward and Hartley seemed to understand that because she stood and moved towards the door, gesturing for Thorne to follow. Her knees popped as she did, weaving her way through the various bodies and tables until they entered a back room filled with refrigerators with clear doors, revealing vials and equipment that Thorne didn't know the name of.

Hartley made a direct line for the vials in the fridge on the back wall while Thorne reclined against the tall workbench that filled the center of the room. She had never been able to get over the sterile scent that came with this floor, the underlying smell of disinfectant and latex. It always made her uncomfortable, as if life had been banished in all its various forms. Or perhaps she was so used to the undercurrent of blood that settled in the hallways and rooms.

One by one, Hartley set down three vials roughly the size of her index finger onto the bench before picking up the one at the end. She lifted it and held up to the light, studying the pale grey liquid inside.

"I'm not sure how well this will work. I wasn't able to test it before she left. That isn't even factoring in how many vampires will be there and if I'm even sending her enough." Hartley set the vial down and let out a harsh breath before letting her head hang. Never in the three decades Thorne had known the scientist had she seemed so concerned or hesitant. Each choice Hartley had ever made, every word she had spoken was always done with conviction and confidence, as if she knew everything she said held weight.

"You fucking care for her. This isn't just a scientific curiosity or investment. You truly care about her." Disbelief coated each word from Thorne's mouth. Hartley had never given off any clues that she was interested in anyone beyond what they could offer her. Vampires and humans were both separated into two distinct categories—interesting and not interesting. This wasn't a simple interest in Elora, but a desperation that kept her alive.

"I helped create her, Thorne. I didn't carry her in my womb or give birth to her, but I still labored day and night over her genetics. She's as close to bearing a child as I can get."

"How old were you when you turned?" Thorne had never thought to ask this question, never thought about Hartley beyond her role as the scientist tasked with helping her become pregnant with Killian's child. For the first time, Thorne wondered what had led the scientist to work for the previous vampire head, what had led to her being turned in the first place.

"Twenty-three. The child I carried at the time didn't survive the change." Hartley's voice wavered the tiniest amount, as if she were working to keep it from showing with each syllable.

"I'm sorry. I can't imagine." No other thoughts came to mind, no other responses to the revelation. Thorne had asked the question, but hadn't considered what she would say if Hartley answered.

"It was over half a century ago." She responded, waving her hand slightly like she was trying to brush away the conversation, eradicate it from the air between them. Hartley stood and turned around, grabbing another vial from the refrigerator. This one was clear, but the same size. Thorne recognized it instantly. She had used it on so many vampires over the years, rendered them human to encourage them to answer her questions. It had worked on every single one. Except fucking Damien. Admirable, really.

"This one, as I think you know, will render her human. I don't think she should drink it all."

"And why is that?"

"The others may notice the change. All it would take is one injury or them noticing a change in her scent and everything would fall apart. I would suggest half." Thorne nodded and gathered up the vials, already outlining a plan in her mind. Damien would take it to her. There would be no other option because if Elora did end up sacrificing herself, he deserved to see her one more time.

Chapter 42

Elora

It had taken days to gather the time and strength to venture out of the dormitory or even her bedroom. Four days of them taking bottle after bottle of blood had left her sleeping and feeding with only her dreams of Damien as comfort. Wyatt came a few times a day, sitting in a chair beside her bed, telling her stories of his childhood. His tone always brought her a semblance of ease, almost lulling her to sleep. Or that could have been the exhaustion brought on by losing so much blood. In the dark of the night, she would cry, holding a pillow to her chest as she lay on her side. Her only hope was that no one would hear her, that they wouldn't come to her aid.

Vampires wandered the grounds around her, moving with purpose between the church and the dormitory. It seemed some of them had returned from their jobs while others were attending to chores—laundry and blood collection. From what Elora had seen, they seemed to have taken control of at least two blood donor locations. She had seen them returning with coolers with biohazard signs on the side. Three or four a day. Elora imagined it required quite a bit of blood to feed an entire family this size, especially since any vampire connected to her needed blood once a day at the very least. She had found she needed it twice—once in the morning and again in the late afternoon or evening.

Elora could hear them talking, snippets of conversations that felt so banal that it was out of place. Work gossip along with who was attracted to whom. There were hints of a debate on what to do with the children who had been turned and home schooled since attending an actual school was dangerous. The children were struggling to control their hunger and urges to feed.

Ice rushed through her veins as the sound of laughter reached her and her eyes found the source. Four of them were playing in what used to be a garden. They were all of various ages, ranging from seven to twelve. All bright eyes and grinning faces. It was almost like innocence was permeating the air, mingling with the smell of lavender. Everything was fresh without the tinge of the city, the scent of car exhaust, and thousands of bodies all working towards the same goal—survival.

Elora tore her attention away from the children and to the grave in front of her. It was newer than the others. It lacked the decay and plant life growing up and around it until names and dates were obscured. Instead, the name on this one was carved recently. It wasn't as smooth as the others but looked like it was done by an amateur. Elora fell to her knees as she read the text, desperately trying to ignore the stinging in her eyes as she read the gravestone over and over again as if it would change what was written there.

Constance Emily Hadley
Beloved mother, aunt, and grandmother.

There were no dates listed. No year was listed for her birth or her death. But Elora knew her death hadn't been that long ago. The question was how she ended up in a wooden box under the ground at a random cemetery. Elora knelt in front of it, brushing the few leaves and vines away from the stone. The dirt dug into her knees as the sundress rested on her thighs, the pink fabric a perfect complement to how pale she had become from the lack of blood. Her fingers trailed over the lettering, tracing each word engraved there.

"She didn't have any burial plans. Not that I could find. Honestly, I don't think she thought she would ever die." The voice coming from behind her caused her body to stiffen, each muscle constricting until she nearly fell over into the dirt. Elora sat back on her heels and closed her eyes, letting out a soft breath. She had hoped no one would follow her out here, that she would be granted a single moment of fresh air and peace.

Elora felt Wyatt step beside her, and she peeked at his shoes, dirty and covered in wet earth as if he had been gardening. She grabbed a small flower and tore it from the ground, letting the loose earth fall from the dangling root. One by one, she touched each white petal before bringing it to her nose, inhaling the sweet scent.

"She's a force of nature. Shaping reality how she wanted it to be." Her gut twisted as she waited for his response.

"Yes, she was." Wyatt let his words hang heavy over her, the use of past tense causing her eyes to fill with tears once more. Elora knew that Connie was dead, but this was confirmation. A sense of relief fluttered through her even though guilt and shame ate away at her, ripping and tearing pieces of her for their consumption. With each bite, she faded away, diminishing into a hollow shell. All she had to do was not answer the door when Connie first knocked. Or she shouldn't have taken her panic attack into the hallway. If she hadn't done that—

"I went back to see her. After everything happened, I woke up in a warehouse, and I was starving. Elizabeth was there and gave me some blood. She explained what had happened to you. She told me that you bit her, which turned her, and then she did the same to me." Wyatt knelt beside her, letting his hands rest on his thighs. She turned to him, studying his profile as he stared at the words carved in stone. Regret was etched into each feature. What was once soft warmth was now hard ice. Only his eyes revealed the depth of his pain, becoming bottomless pits of despair and self-hatred. Elora had a feeling what was coming next in this story but gave Wyatt his moment, allowing him to piece together his thoughts and gather his strength to continue.

"She kept asking about what happened. The door to your apartment had been fixed, but she had seen them working on it when she woke up." He chuckled softly and shook his head. "Muffins. She said she had brought out a batch of muffins for the maintenance workers as they installed the new door. Blueberry, of course. It was always her favorite."

Another long moment of silence as Elora played with the flower in her hand. Her heart raced in her chest as she waited to hear the words that would render it real.

"We fought at first. I threw some things, and she got scared. She sat me down and asked if you were hurt. I didn't want to worry her, so I told her you were fine. She asked if it was the brute who was to blame. I defended him, said it was the group who was searching for you and I helped you escape, which is somewhat true. Elizabeth convinced her to come with us, and we went to the warehouse. But when we got there, I couldn't control my hunger. I guess it's common when a vampire is first turned. Then, everything gets hazy. I only remember bits of it. The feeling of her neck in my grip. Her blood on my tongue. Her pulse disappearing. I took too much. Elizabeth found me with her and took care of everything. Brought her here and buried her," Wyatt explained, his voice shaking with each word.

Elora reached over and grabbed his hand, clutching it tightly as if it would keep them both grounded, prevent them from falling into the guilt that threatened to consume them. Or perhaps it already had. Perhaps this was what it was like to wear guilt like an ill-fitting jacket. It was itchy and too thick, sitting awkwardly on their shoulders. Slowly, moment by moment, it became fused with their flesh, and Elora knew she would never be able to completely remove it. No matter how precise she was as she attempted to excise. It was simply part of her now.

"I'm sorry. I loved her. She was one of the few people who treated me with any type of kindness without expecting something in return. I never meant to drag either of you into this." Elora felt the stinging of tears as the apology spilled from her lips. She had already said she was sorry before, when Wyatt had handed over Viktor in front of the hotel. At that time, he had only smiled sadly and said there was nothing to apologize for, that they were now one. This time her words were met with a heavy silence. It wasn't that she wanted him to absolve her of her guilt. That was impossible. But something would be better than this. She would even take him screaming at her, releasing his wrath in front of Connie's grave.

"You didn't bite me, Elora. The blame isn't at your feet, but hers. I know you never wanted any of this," Wyatt confessed before his head twisted and turned as he searched the space around them. In the distance were the children playing, but the adults seemed to have dispersed now that the sun was beginning to set. Orange and red painted the sky, mingling with the wisps of clouds. The sound of crickets filled the air as Elora searched for the right thing to say, forcing down the sense of hope that had erupted in her chest.

"I don't. You're right about that. I would stop it if I could," she confessed as her heart hammered in her chest. A part of her expected Wyatt to run away to find Elizabeth and tell her about the lack of enthusiasm for whatever this madness was. But he didn't. Instead, he turned completely towards her and studied her face, eyes moving over her features. She knew he was searching for any sign this was a trap, that she was testing his faith and devotion.

"Could you stop it?" Elora raised a brow at the question before twisting towards him as well. They stared at each other, both suspicious that the other would betray them as soon as they left this place. Sometimes trust took a leap of faith. Hopefully, she wouldn't splatter on the rocks once she did.

"I think I can. It's why I came. There's no cure, Wyatt. Only a weapon that could kill every vampire here if everything goes according to plan," she admitted. It was done. She had jumped from the cliff, and now it was time to see if she would fly or plummet to her death. It was all in his hands now.

"All of them?" His jaw clenched slightly, and she shrugged.

"I want to give them an opportunity to leave her behind, to join me. There would be rules, with the main one being no feeding directly from humans." Wyatt nodded after she was done explaining.

"There are many who already do that. They don't want to turn anyone. They aren't happy about their new life. To be honest, I would say about half of the vampires here agree with your sister and follow her blindly. They are the ones who will present a problem."

"And the other half?" she asked, not bothering to keep the hope from her voice.

"Either want to die or just want as close to a normal life as possible." Thoughts raced through her head as he finished speaking. She could offer them a normal life, no matter what form they wanted it to take. If they wanted to be human, she could offer them the medication she had taken. And if they wanted normalcy as a vampire, she would take them and provide them with collected blood.

Already a plan was forming in her mind. Entire floors of the Tower could be dedicated to them, allowing her to house them and make sure nothing went wrong. Chloe would protest this, of course. And Silas as well, perhaps. But Thorne's ideas about a system to keep track of who was human or vampire, who was turned along with who did it could help ease anxieties about allowing Elora's children to live. There would be consequences for them if they did turn someone. Death, more than likely. There was no room for any of them to go rogue.

"I see your wheels turning, Elora. What're you thinking?" She smiled at him, bright and unrestrained.

"That I have hope for the first time since learning about what Elizabeth was doing." Wyatt returned her grin before she threw her arms around his neck, pulling him into a tight hug. She could sense his hands hovering over her body before she felt them on her back as his lips pressed into her hair.

Wyatt held her for a long moment as the sun continued to sink behind the trees and a chill settled. Only once it was dark did they disentangle themselves from each other and go their separate ways, with him promising to spread the word to those he knew supported her vision.

Chapter 43

Damien

Seeing her was like taking a deep gulp of air after being held underwater. It was like seeing the sun after being held in a dark cave for years. At the sight of her closing the door behind her, Damien was able to breathe again. As her scent enveloped him, he felt every muscle relax and his thoughts slow. He hadn't realized how desperate he had been to simply see her, and he took a moment to drink her in before she noticed him.

Her face was pale, and there were dark circles under her eyes. A pale pink sundress clung to her frame, but she seemed smaller, as if she had been starved. Her collarbones stuck out in a way that was almost garish, and he could see the sharp lines of her cheekbones. Something here was very wrong. He had believed she wouldn't be harmed here, that Elizabeth's obsession would keep her from hurting her in any way. Apparently, he had been wrong.

She pressed her hand onto the dresser as her eyes closed for a moment. Her knees buckled and just as she began to fall to the wood floor, Damien darted forward and wrapped his arms around her waist. A shocked cry filled the room before she finally met his gaze. Her eyes widened and her lips parted as she stared at him in total shock. He tried desperately to smirk down at her, to hide the concern that was probably clearly displayed on his face. She looked exhausted, like she hadn't slept or fed.

Neither of them said a word as her arms snaked around his neck and she dragged his mouth to hers, pressing a long and deep kiss to his lips. It was perfection, and he wanted to stay trapped in this moment even as he inhaled her scent.

Cinnamon. She smelled like cinnamon. Not lavender or even blood, but fucking cinnamon.

"Been cozy with Wyatt, I see." Amusement shone brightly in her eyes as the words left his mouth. He had never been jealous before in his entire life. He hadn't even felt it when Korina left him for Killian. But the idea of her touching Wyatt and letting him touch her was threatening to undo every rational thought he had. When Damien didn't say anything else or laugh to show he was teasing, hurt replaced the mirth in her expression.

"Really? You haven't seen me in over a week, and that's the first thing you say to me. Ridiculous. Fucking ridiculous." She pushed him away and slowly made her way to the bed. Each step was heavy, feet almost dragging across the floor. He followed her, prepared in case she fell again as he berated himself for his stupidity.

"I just recognized his scent. That's all."

"And what? You think I've been cuddling him? Fucking him? If that's what you think, then you can leave. I don't have the energy for this right now." She sank onto the bed, every ounce of fight gone as soon as she stopped scolding him. Is that what he had been afraid of? That she had sought comfort and companionship with Wyatt in his absence?

"You did get fairly close to that once, if I remember correctly." He could honestly punch himself right now. If he were smart, he would fall to his knees and beg her forgiveness. Something was wrong with her, and he was only making it worse. In the back of his mind was the whispering reminder that this could be the last time he saw her, that she could die once the vials he had brought her were administered.

"Fuck you. Leave whatever it is you obviously brought for me and get the fuck out." She sounded so tired, so defeated, and he dropped down in front of her, crouching so he commanded her field of vision.

"I'm sorry. It caught me by surprise." Damien waited for her to punch him, slap him, or even just push him away. But when she met his eyes, he realized she probably didn't have the strength to do any of that. Elora nodded and gestured to the space beside her, which he took eagerly. The bed frame groaned as he sat beside her, wrapped his arm around her shoulders to bring her in tight.

"They've been draining me. Two or three times a day sometimes. It's for the celebration." That explained it.

"Have you been feeding?"

"Not enough. I think she wants me weakened for right now," she admitted, and he cursed, mind racing. He had no collection bottles with him. Only a small cloth bag with four vials and a letter he had been forbidden from opening.

Damien scooted back on the bed and dragged her with him, maneuvering her until she was in his lap, sitting between his legs. He didn't think about what he was about to say, what he was about to offer her.

"Here. Take some of mine." Her eyes widened, and she shook her head. "Yes. Don't argue with me. I have plans for you before I leave, and I can't have you on death's door for them." He gave her a crooked smile.

"We don't know for sure what will happen," she protested as her hand pressed against his chest before gripping the fabric of the t-shirt he was wearing.

"Nothing. Nothing will happen. Hartley would have said something if it could be a problem, right?" She whimpered as her eyes settled on his neck, lingering where he knew his pulse was racing. His hand rested heavily on her hip as he gripped the soft flesh, focusing on how impossibly perfect it was to have her back even if only for a few hours at the most. Her eyes were pools of intrigue and hesitation. She was scared, but there was nothing to be afraid of. Any consequences that could come from this they would deal with.

"I've never—" she hesitated, swallowing thickly before continuing. "I've never fed directly from someone. Not that I remember anyway." He smirked, enjoying the strange sense of honor that he would be the first. She didn't remember biting Elizabeth, and he decided it didn't count. He would be her first.

Damien gently gripped the nape of her neck, and a shudder raced through her at the sensation, causing a self-satisfied smile to appear on his face. He brought her closer, bringing her lips to the place where his pulse was pounding.

"Are you sure?" Consent. She was asking for his permission, ensuring that this was what he wanted. Fuck, she was perfect.

"Take everything, love. As much as you need." A moment. A mere moment of hesitation before her fangs sank into his neck, and he felt the burning sensation give way to pleasure. His entire body reacted to each draw, each swallow she took. Heat rushed to his cheeks and skin as his cock strained against his jeans. Other than being turned, he had never been fed from, and even that had been a hazy blur of pain and exhaustion. This was ecstasy beyond anything words could ever describe. She adjusted herself, moving one of her legs to the other side of his thighs until she straddled him, sinking down onto his lap.

Another drink of his blood, and he felt every part of his body go rigid. He groaned as her hands wandered up his chest and over his neck until she held a handful of his hair in a tight grip.

Another drink, and she ground her hips against him, like this was just as pleasurable for her as it was for him.

One more deep pull, and she broke away, meeting his gaze. Her hand never left his hair while the other rested on his chest, gripping the fabric of his shirt as if it would keep her grounded. Glassy green eyes stared at him as blood trickled down her chin, dripping onto the swell of her breast in the sundress she was wearing. Vaguely, somewhere in the pleasure-induced haze, he questioned where it had come from.

"Thank you," she whispered before running her tongue over her lips in a way that threatened to undo him before anything even started. He nodded, unable to speak as he used his thumb to wipe away the rest of the blood from her chin. Her fingers wrapped around his wrist, and she brought his hand to her mouth before languidly licking it off.

All he could do was let out a groan before he grabbed her hips and spun them both around so she was flat on the mattress. The pink dress slid up her thighs as she opened her legs, grabbing his shirt and positioning him where she wanted.

Demanding. She was always demanding and feral. Never afraid to show what she wanted. Never afraid to reveal the darkness in her. And he wanted to experience it all. Every thought and desire, every word or sound that fell from her lips. He leaned over her, using his knees to widen her legs and she grinned, revealing the sharp canines that hadn't retracted quite yet.

"I thought you had plans," she purred softly, running her finger down his chest and to his jeans, where she played with the button.

"I do," Damien forced out, resting on his elbow that was beside her head. The other hand traveled over her stomach and hips to her ribs before he palmed her breast, squeezing until she arched her back and moaned.

"You're wasting time," she scolded, and he only chuckled before leaning down to nuzzle her neck.

"I think of it more as savoring. I don't want to rush this." He almost added that he wasn't sure when he would see her again, if she would survive whatever plan she had concocted. It was too much to say out loud. Her face turned solemn at his words, and she nodded.

"I don't think we have time for savoring." She granted him one sad smile, the corners of her lips barely curling at the edges.

"Yes, we do. I don't give a fuck if they walk in here. I'm going to kiss every part of you, worship you, and memorize every dip and curve of your body. I refuse to fucking rush this if I could lose you." His voice had gone harsh the longer he spoke, and the secret she had attempted to keep from him clawed its way to the surface. She nodded and undid the button on his pants.

"Then we won't rush. We can pretend we have all the time in the world."

Once more, Damien had the feeling she was saying goodbye. His hand cupped her cheek before he ran his thumb along her bottom lip before she pulled it into her mouth, biting gently. Even if this was goodbye, even if this was one of the last times he would see her alive, Damien would give her everything and anything she wanted from him.

Chapter 44

Elora

The afterglow didn't last long. It couldn't. Not when Elizabeth or one of her blood collectors could come through the door at any moment. Under her cheek, Damien's heartbeat was so steady it could lull her to sleep as he held her in his arms. His hand rested on her hip, holding her tightly to his body as if he thought she would melt into the sheets and mattress, collapse into a cloud of mist. He didn't want to leave her there. But dawn would come quickly and there was still too much to discuss.

Elora let her fingers trail over his chest, moving from his collarbones to the band of his pants. He groaned as her touch wandered, and his grip tightened. She tilted her face up to see him only to find his eyes closed with a soft smile on the lips that had touched every part of her.

"Damien," she whispered and watched as his brows narrowed.

"Shh, love. Not yet." His voice was gravelly as he begged to remain in their small bubble of pretend for just a little longer.

"We have to. They'll come to take my blood soon and you can't be here." It broke her heart to tell him he needed to leave her when she knew there was a chance she might not survive the ceremony. The full moon was tomorrow night, which meant she had little time left. He groaned and began to move, pushing himself up so he could lean against the headboard. Elora adjusted her position, sitting beside him with her legs crossed in front of her as she picked at her fingers.

"How are you feeling?" He asked, studying her. No doubt he was searching for the dark circles under her eyes, the paleness of her skin.

"Better," she responded, staring at her fingers. A part of her wanted to forget that she had drank from him. She didn't want to admit how euphoric it had been, how it had lit a fire in her that seemed to burn hotter and brighter with each pull of his blood into her system. That part of her was drowning in shame that she had been brought to the point.

"What about you? Any different?" Fear lined each word as she continued to stare at her hands, picking at the skin around her cuticle. She didn't want to look at him, didn't want to see if something was wrong or altered.

A single fingertip touched her chin, lifting her face to meet his gaze. There was that small smirk on his lips, that sheen of concern in his eyes.

"I feel no different. If it would make you feel better, I'll get checked out by Hartley when I get back," he offered and she nodded despite knowing she might not be around long enough to find out the results. Damien pulled her close, nestling her in the crook of his arm so her head would rest on his shoulder before he pressed his lips to the top of her head.

"She sent me with the vials and a letter," he announced, moving the conversation to where it needed to be. If they didn't press forward, then they would try to stay in this moment forever. All she wanted was to stay here with him, held tightly in his embrace. Here she didn't need to be strong or confident. She didn't need to threaten violence or become the darkest version of herself. In his arms, she could simply exist. He didn't demand anything from her—no performance or expectations of what she would give him.

"What does the letter say?" Her hands trailed across his chest again, outlining the lines of muscle under his scared and tattooed skin.

"If you keep doing that, there's no way I'm going anywhere," he forced out and she giggled softly before placing her hand flat on his stomach.

"So responsive," she muttered against his skin and pressed a kiss to his collarbone before meeting his gaze. His eyes were dark, revealing his hunger and she felt her core tighten at the sight. She pushed herself back up and leapt from the bed as he let out a low sound of protest.

"We both know this will go nowhere if we stay on that bed together," she scolded before finding his shirt and pulling it over her head. He raised a brow, no doubt realizing he would be sneaking out of there half-naked. Elora could hide the shirt from Elizabeth and her followers, keep it in a safe place where she could pull it out and lose herself in it. Was it worth the risk? Having Damien in this room this long was already enough of a risk. A single shirt wouldn't make anything worse.

His muscles flexed as he reached over to the nightstand and grabbed the small cloth bag. He studied it for a minute, holding it in the palm of his hand as if debating handing it over. Her heart sped up as she realized exactly what was in there and what she was meant to do with it. Before this moment, Elora had known what she had to do, understood in the way she understood she needed to feed twice a day or that she needed to shower. It was always there in her mind, but now it was real.

Damien tossed her the bag, and she barely caught it as she huffed out a laugh. The future of vampires and humans was in this tiny parcel that was being thrown around like a ball. She pulled it open where the drawstrings had tightened to keep it closed, peeking inside despite not being able to see anything. With her pulse racing faster and faster with each moment, she dumped the contents onto the mattress—four vials filled with a grey liquid and a paper folded up to the size of her palm. For a moment she ignored the vials and lifted the paper, reading the quick script on the front. Hartley's handwriting, from what she recalled. It was a rougher version of the observation and lab notes in the files on her desk.

Read after he leaves. Elora swallowed and put the paper in her pocket before lifting one of the vials. The color was slightly off in this one, a paler version of the other three. She held it between her fingers and lifted it to the light, studying its contents.

"You aren't reading the letter," he commented, and she glanced at him, tearing her eyes away from the vial for a heartbeat.

"Not yet." She didn't explain or add any other details. If she was meant to read this once he left, obviously the contents were sensitive. Elora guessed it had to do with her potential death.

Damien said nothing in response, just narrowed his eyes as she returned her attention to the vial and the tiny star on the top in black ink.

"Why didn't you tell me that this could kill you? That the connection between you and them could kill you along with them?" At the sound of his questions, her breath was caught in her throat and she almost choked on air. She dropped the vial onto the bed and turned away from him for a second, gathering her thoughts.

"Did Thorne tell you?" She asked as she twisted back around to him. Damien jumped from the bed and marched towards her, grabbing her hands before she could blink. She had expected to find anger in his eyes. Rage. Betrayal. But there were no hints of that. Only fear, cold and bottomless in those brown eyes. The flecks were gone, like the stars had ceased to shine and left behind a void.

"I found the file in your desk. I was putting away the photo in your jeans and found it."

"And you read it despite it saying 'confidential' in big letters?" He may not be upset, but she was. Not that he had seen the file or went into her desk drawer, but that he had found out at all. He was never supposed to. If she lived, then he never needed to know exactly how much was at risk. And if she died? Well, they knew that was a risk going into this and no one would necessarily be surprised.

"Yes! That's what happens when you hide things from people. You said you wouldn't hide anymore, love."

"I wasn't hiding it!" she shouted, tearing her hands from his grasp.

"What were you doing then? What would you call it?" Her mouth opened and closed as she searched for words. Instead, she shrugged and moved to walk away before his fingers wrapped around her wrist.

"Damn it, Elora! I could lose you in a matter of days and you still won't talk to me. What would it take? For you to be honest with me? To let me in completely?"

Tears stung her eyes as she crumpled under the weight of his questions because she didn't have an answer. She considered screaming back at him, telling him that she had been trying, but secrets were always better kept if it meant no one else was hurt. Except he was hurt, and the realization nearly ripped her in half. She shook her head before licking her lips, preparing her words.

"I knew you and Silas would try to stop me from coming and would be willing to sacrifice anything if it meant keeping me alive. And my life isn't more valuable or important than anyone else's in this city. I wasn't hiding from you. Not intentionally. If you want to know my innermost thoughts, I'll tell you. If you want to know my every emotion or nightmare or fantasy, I'll reveal everything. We just need to get through tomorrow night, and then I'm yours for as long as you still want me." She let out a breath after she was done and waited. Her eyes stayed focused on his face even as the sky began to lighten and bird calls rang out. His jaw unclenched and his lips softened. He pressed a kiss to her forehead, and her eyes closed at the sensation. She would never grow tired of his touch, of the feeling of his body against hers.

"I don't want you to leave upset with me. I don't want to go into that ceremony knowing we parted like this," she whispered into his bare chest as her arms wrapped around his waist.

"You're right, even if I don't like that you kept me in the dark. I would have done everything I could to keep you from coming. I would have let this entire city burn if it meant you lived. No one is more important to me. If I lose you, there's nothing left for me. My reality begins and ends with you. So, you're right. I would have stopped you even if you hated me for it. Even if you kicked me out of your life as a result. Because I could keep going as long as I knew you were alive."

His words were a mirror to the ones she had said to him not that long ago when she confessed he had fed from her after being shot. She smiled warmly at him, hoping with everything she had that he could feel her love radiating from her being, seeping from her touch into his skin. Love wasn't a strong enough word for what she felt for him. The emotions that flooded her at the very sight of him were all-consuming, enough to make her remember that the world did have beauty, that there was kindness in people no matter what she had been taught. It was enough to make colors brighter and sounds more musical.

From the expression on his beautiful face, Damien knew every thought rushing through her mind, every desire and urge to pull him close. As she pressed a kiss to his lips, standing on her tiptoes to reach him a bit better, Elora knew that both of them understood that as soon as he walked out that door and disappeared into the sunrise, this may be the last time he saw her alive.

"The vials are the weapon. We need to figure out how to use it," he said as he pulled back, staring down into her face.

"I have an idea. A plan. Just be ready outside the church tomorrow night. Bring whoever you can in case there are problems." She ordered gently. He nodded and pressed his lips to hers once more. Elora could tell that he was holding back, that he was struggling to be gentle with her. Her fingers lingered on the place where her teeth sank into his skin, the place where he had trusted her without question to only take what she needed. For him, she would try her best to survive, to not let this kill her. But they both knew it wasn't up to her or him.

Chapter 45

Damien

He returned to the Tower less than thirty minutes after he snuck out of her bedroom, clothed in only his jeans and his shoes. His shirt had been left behind, hugging her body as she seemed to melt into it. There had been no reality where he asked her for it back, that he wasn't willing to make his way back to the waiting car bristling and shivering in the cold. There was a sense of pride, of possession that filled him every time she wore his clothing, every time she inhaled his scent as if it would provide her with every bit of strength she needed for this mission.

Damien didn't bother with even looking around the lobby despite sensing every single body in there. The Ashcroft vampires had accepted his role as the partial head of the family easier than he had expected and he wondered if his reputation had something to do with it. They all respected Elora. That much was clear in their deference to her, in the way they referred to her when speaking and followed her restrictions when they came to rescue him

To his surprise, he found everyone waiting in their sitting room just outside the bedroom. Hartley was standing along the bookshelves, fingers trailing over what was left of Killian's journals. The majority of them were housed in their bedroom, waiting for Elora's return on the nightstand, tabbed and organized in a vaguely obsessive fashion. Hartley wouldn't gain much insight from the journals left there. Silas and Thorne both sat on the couch, looking more comfortable with each other than before. Perhaps something had finally shifted in their dynamic. Perhaps Silas had forgiven Thorne for faking her death and leaving him to pick up the pieces. Chloe was reclining in one of the chairs, eyes closed as her silver hair cascaded over the back of the headrest. It was the most relaxed Damien had ever seen her, seemingly perfectly at ease in this space. The sight caused unease to swirl in his stomach. It was as if she felt like she belonged there.

"I don't remember inviting you all here," Damien announced as he wandered through the space and into the closet, searching for a shirt. He had considered taking a shower once he returned, but that would require washing away her scent and the feeling of where she had touched him and he wasn't ready to part with any of that quite yet.

Damien grabbed a random shirt off the hanger and pulled it over his head before returning to the room where they were all waiting. Every bit of attention was focused on him, waiting patiently for him to tell them what happened. Thankfully, they seemed to be granting him a shred of space. They knew what it meant for him to visit her, for him to be the one who delivered the package and outlined some type of plan. He poured himself a glass of whatever alcohol was left in the bar and tossed it back, barely feeling the burning in his throat as he collected his thoughts. It was strange being on this side of the exchange, like he was wearing clothing that didn't fully fit. Normally, he would be standing before the desk with his hands in his pockets as he waited for Killian to ask questions that he would answer without thinking about the consequences. This was different. He was still giving out intel, but he was in charge. They would only know what Damien decided to tell them.

"Did you see her?" Silas asked, voice calm and even as if he were afraid of Damien's reaction.

"Yes," Damien responded before turning around to face them. All four of them were staring at him with varying degrees of empathy. To his immense surprise, Thorne's face displayed the most concern. It was almost like she cared about her daughter, about what her fate would be.

"And?" Thorne's tone was harsh, as if she was trying to disguise the fear.

"They're draining her. Two or three times a day. They're gearing up for whatever the ceremony is," he explained, trying desperately to keep his words even. Thinking about how weak she appeared when she walked through the bedroom door would be a mistake. The shadows under her eyes, the way she almost fell to the floor was dangerous. It woke up every violent part of him, the beast that slept deep inside that screamed for blood the moment she collapsed into his arms.

"And is she feeding to replace it?" Hartley's question this time and Damien could only shake his head because if he said anything else, he would feel her teeth in his neck again and everything that came with it. It was a stark reminder of the promise he had made to Elora to convince her to feed. It was lucky Hartley was already here.

"Not enough. She's weak, and I think it's on purpose. Elizabeth doesn't fully trust her and keeping her weak lessens the chance Elora could turn on her." The words were bitter on his tongue, but they were the truth no matter how much he hated it.

"But will she be able to do what's necessary?" Chloe's voice held too much hope for Damien's comfort. She wanted Elora to fail, wanted her to fall to Elizabeth because it would prove she had been right the entire time, that Elora hadn't been strong enough to fill her role. The ambition was practically radiating from her, filling the room until every bit of oxygen was replaced.

"Of course. And we need to be ready by tomorrow night. The ceremony takes place during the full moon," Damien explained, glaring at Chloe. It didn't matter if every drop of blood was taken from Elora, she would figure out a way to make sure Elizabeth was stopped. It might take her last breath, but Elora would end this.

"Ceremony?" Silas's question broke the tension and Damien nodded, finally tearing his eyes away from Chloe. He had a distinct feeling she would prove to be a problem. Chloe was a weed, one that needed to be ripped out by the roots to make sure she never posed another problem.

"I don't know anything about it. At least not details. Neither did Elora. It's her blood. I think they are planning on drinking it as some type of joining." Silas's eyes widened as he probably understood exactly how much they would have had to have taken from her in order to accomplish this, but Chloe only stared at him with suspicion as if she thought he was hiding something.

"They haven't told her anything? She's their deity or whatever, correct? And they aren't giving her every bit of information about this? I find that difficult to believe, if I'm honest," she drawled, leveling Damien with a hard expression. He only shrugged. It didn't matter what Chloe thought. She could believe whatever she wanted as long as she didn't interfere or become even more of a nuisance.

"Like I said, Elizabeth doesn't fully trust her," Damien replied smoothly. Silas stood and pushed his fingers through his hair, messing it up slightly. It was always a strange look on him considering he was always polished to perfection.

"In that case, we need to get ready. We don't have much time. I'm assuming the plan is to drug the blood that will be handed out." Damien only nodded at Silas's statement.

"We need to be there to handle any who refuse it. But you all should know something," Damien began before pausing. He wasn't looking forward to telling them this part, to revealing Elora's change to the plan they had all concocted in this very room.

"She wants to give them the chance to join her. To leave Elizabeth behind and come here. They wouldn't be allowed to drink directly from humans, and the punishment for doing so would be death. No questions asked."

"Of fucking course, she does. I told you she was weak," Chloe bit out. Damien straightened as he prepared to defend Elora, but to his surprise, it wasn't him who spoke first.

"The mass murder of a group who didn't chose to be turned isn't a decision to make lightly, Chloe. This proves she isn't the monster we all thought she was, that we all wanted her to be. She's giving them what she never got," Thorne interjected quickly.

"Which is?" Chloe sneered at Thorne, who only regarded her coolly.

"A choice," came Thorne's voice. Her tone made it clear she believed the answer should be obvious despite Chloe's lack of understanding. Indeed, it seemed to Damien that it was clear to everyone in the room exactly what the answer was, but Chloe only rolled her eyes.

"Not every vampire is given a choice. She isn't anything special." Damien took a step forward, only to be stopped by Silas, who shook his head softly.

"Only part of that sentence is correct. You're right that not every vampire was given a choice before turning, but there's no denying that she's unique. There are no others like her, and there never will be. There's no recreating what Killian did, and she can never have children. Even those turned by her are not perfect replicas, only pale imitations. She's the first and the last.

That sounds fairly special to me," Silas answered smoothly even as Damien was struck by his words. There was no way to imagine what it would be like to be the only one of his kind, to know that there was no one else like him anywhere in the entire world and there never would be. There was a type of torture in that realization, a type of loneliness that no one could ever cure.

"I'll gather up some of my own vampires. I have about twenty that are trained for fighting and will follow orders," Silas finally said, breaking the silence that had fallen in the wake of his words. Even Chloe had gone silent, as if she had never realized what it meant to be a singular creation.

"I have some humans who can be trusted," Thorne began before Damien shook his head.

"No humans. They're too easily turned. One bite and we add to their numbers." Thorne nodded without a word. He was right, and she knew it.

"I'm not offering any of mine. If this goes wrong, I'm not risking their lives for her." Chloe's words were expected and Damien only chuckled, shaking his head as he did.

"We don't need you or anyone you offered. I don't trust you. I would prefer for you to retreat back to your cave until this is done," Damien explained and she lifted a single shoulder in a shrug. His direct interactions with her were limited since not even Killian ever wanted to deal with her. Damien had always assumed it was pure paranoia on Killian's part, but perhaps it was this childishness. Despite being the oldest person in the room and the oldest vampires he currently knew, Chloe was like a teenager with an attitude or a child throwing a tantrum. How she managed to stay in power this long was baffling if he was honest.

"Either way, I'll be there. My food source is under attack, and I want to be there in case someone needs to step in as the voice of reason." No one responded to Chloe as she looked at each of them in turn.

"I'm going to gather my own people and bring them here, if that is alright with you," Silas announced as he began heading towards the door. His cellphone was already in his hand, his fingers hovering as if already preparing the message that would be sent out.

"There is a hallway of empty rooms on one of the lower floors. I'll make sure they're prepared for you," Damien responded, finally dropping into a chair. Now that there was a plan, or at least a hint of a plan, he felt lighter than when he walked in the room. Thorne stood and followed Silas, both of them exiting together as Chloe trailed behind them to return to wherever she was staying. Damien refused to offer her a room in the Tower, refused to allow her into this space where she could spew poison and try to destroy everything Elora had built so far.

"Hartley, I need you to do something." The scientist had stood, no doubt preparing to return to whatever she did outside of the lab. She halted, twisting slightly to stare at him where he sat on the couch. He leaned forward, his fingers touching the marks on his neck that had gone unnoticed during the meeting.

"Does this have something to do with her feeding from you?" By now, Damien knew he shouldn't be surprised that Hartley seemed to know things, seemed to notice every minute detail around her. He nodded and turned his head to the side, giving her a better view of the marks that had mostly healed by then. Elora had taken more than he expected, but it was worth it. When she had leaned back away from him, the circles under her eyes had been gone and there had been that delicious flush to her cheeks once more. And the glow to her eyes. That had returned as well, drawing him in exactly as Killian had intended.

"I'll test your blood, but I doubt it had any effect. He hadn't expected her to feed from vampires, so he never made any plans for that. Is this for your peace of mind or hers?" She raised a brow as she asked her question, and he let his arms rest on his thighs.

"Hers. It was the only way I could convince her to do it. She's concerned." Hartley turned towards the door and jerked her head towards it, gesturing for him to follow.

"Let's get a sample now. If there were any changes, they could dissipate the longer we wait. But Damien?" He stood and approached her, hands shoved deep in his pockets as he waited for her to finish.

"You need to consider something. If she did do something by feeding from you, are you going to tell her? Because I don't know if she can handle anything else." His mouth opened and closed as he went to answer, to declare that he would tell her no matter what the results were, that she deserved nothing less than total honesty.

But they refused to be voiced, refused to make themselves known as he realized he wasn't sure if he would be telling the truth. Hartley was right. Yet another way she was unique and a threat to everyone around her could be the last straw. Instead of lying, Damien closed his mouth and pushed past Hartley, heading to the lab where he would find out if he was going to be hiding the truth from her. After the speech he just gave her in the drab bedroom, it would make him a hypocrite of the worst kind. But, he could live with that guilt if it meant she didn't have to bear yet another burden.

Chapter 46

Elora

It seemed Connie's grave was their meeting place. After she had read the note that contained four lines of hurried script, Elora had gone straight to the showers and washed away any trace of Damien from her skin. With each pass of the floral soap against her skin, it had felt like removing something vital from herself. His shirt was inside the pillowcase on her bed, laid out smoothly to make sure it appeared as normal as possible. She wasn't sure how Elizabeth would take the news that he had been there, that he had discovered where she was and had infiltrated the church.

Elora hadn't asked how Damien had found her. It didn't matter. She figured he got the information through violent means. He hadn't become Killian's right-hand vampire without learning how to extract information. She knew his reputation and skill. She also knew there was nothing he wouldn't do to find her. The thought made her core tighten as she found comfort in the thought that their darknesses called to one another, intertwining in a way that left the two of them perfectly matched. She didn't balk from his violence just as he always welcomed hers.

Elizabeth had always believed love was about finding your opposite, the soul that would complement your own and provide balance. That wasn't the case for them. There was no light in either of them to counter the other's darkness. Instead, they were made of the same material, a tapestry that had been torn in half and was now being threaded back together with each smile and caress.

As she stepped outside the dormitory, wet hair plastered to the ridiculous dress that was too formal for everyday wear, Elora found Wyatt instantly. He stood in front of Connie's grave, with two mugs in his hand. The scent of blood reached her, an undercurrent running beneath the early morning air and the smell of flowers and damp earth. At least one of those mugs contained his morning ration of blood and she watched as he raised it to his lips, sipping it slowly as if savoring it. No. Not savoring it. Wyatt flinched slightly, the light sweater shifting across his strained muscles. There was no enjoyment to drinking, no desire or contentment that came from consuming blood. Guilt raced through her. The simple act of feeding had to be a reminder of Connie and what he had done to her in his newly turned state.

As she approached, the red dress trailing behind her on the ground, she inhaled deeply. She hadn't fed since Damien, which had been hours ago. At this point, Elora knew she should be feeling clear signs of hunger, but there was nothing. Not even the tiniest tinge of pain in her stomach. Perhaps feeding from vampires was more potent for her. Perhaps it would be the solution for her and the others who decided to follow her. There didn't seem to be any chance of them turning since Damien hadn't shown even the tiniest sign.

"Coffee?" Wyatt's voice rang out in the cold air, and she grinned as she came up beside him. Elora had been correct that one of the cups was blood, but the other had been poured for her as if Wyatt had anticipated her needs.

"How did you know?" She chuckled before taking the cup from him, wrapping her fingers around the warm porcelain and glancing up at his face before turning her attention to the grave marker in front of her.

"That you would want coffee? Or that you wouldn't need blood?" He raised a brow and waited while she swallowed thickly. Did he know Damien had been there last night? Did he know that she had fed from him? If so, there was a possibility she was fucked no matter how much Wyatt professed to be loyal to her and not Elizabeth.

"Both, I guess?" She answered, trying to quell the rising panic as her pulse raced as she gave him a small smile that he didn't return.

"She will know he was here. Underneath the floral soap, even I can smell him, Elora. It was a risk. A massive risk. I hope it was worth it." Wyatt took a deep drink from his mug, leaving behind a line of blood along his lips. It smelled fresh, as if it had been harvested recently. Elora pulled out the vial she had hidden in the pocket of her dress and held them up to the light, which shimmered through the grey liquid inside.

The fourth was currently nestled between her breasts along the underwire of her bra. After talking with Wyatt, the next step was to find somewhere to hide it, somewhere she could easily get it before the ceremony. The timing would need to be perfect. The liquid inside needed enough time to take effect, but not so much time that Elizabeth would figure out what Elora had done. The note had outlined the dosage, the amount she should drink to ensure her safety both before and during the ceremony. But it was all a hunch, a desperate move that Elora was surprised Hartley even offered. Perhaps it was guilt that caused the scientist to try and help her survive this. Or perhaps it was simply curiosity. If Elora was dead, Hartley couldn't keep studying her and whatever effects the experiment had caused.

"What is that?" Wyatt asked softly as his focus moved over the space around them, darting from the church to the dormitory to the gates that led into the city. No one else was outside yet. Either they weren't awake, or they were still inside feeding before going about their business. There was no reason for him to be paranoid.

"The weapon I told you about," she said, lowering her voice despite the fact no one else was out there. He nodded and took the vial in her hand, studying it closely.

"What's your plan?" Elora shook her head at his question. She wouldn't exactly call it a plan. It wasn't fully formed, but that tended to be how she worked. When she had concocted her scheme to deal with Darian, there had only been a vague outline that left room for adjustments based on how everything progressed. There was no place for that now. Everything would need to be executed perfectly.

"The blood, I think. She plans on handing it out like some horrific communion ceremony tomorrow night. I was thinking of drugging the supply of it."

"And those who want to follow you? This plan would eliminate them as well." Elora bit her lip as she considered this.

"Tell them not to drink? To not come to the ceremony? I could send them to the Tower now, I suppose. It would keep them out of harm's way when it all happens," she outlined. She was grasping at straws, trying desperately to find a rope to hold onto. Wyatt nodded along until she fell silent and met his gaze. There was a brightness to his amber eyes, a determination that fanned the small ember of hope in her chest.

"Let me take care of this for you. I can talk to the ones I know want to leave. I can get the weapon into the blood. She's going to be watching you, Elora. Closely. She's grown paranoid the closer we get to this. She sees enemies around every corner." Her fingers wrapped around the remaining vials in her hand as if to protect them. A part of her screamed that she couldn't trust him, that he was Elizabeth's pet. But he had known about her plans before and hadn't betrayed her. Her eyes narrowed as he watched her, waiting for her to make a decision.

"Why? Why volunteer for this? If she finds out, she'll kill you. We both know that." Elora had a feeling she knew exactly why he was doing this, why he would risk his life.

"Her," he answered, jerking his head towards Connie's grave. "It won't bring her back or fix anything. But if I can help stop this, then maybe my sins can be absolved." His eyes were locked onto the gravestone before them, where they glistened with unshed tears. Elora took his hand in hers, squeezing softly as she pulled him into a hug. Her arms wrapped around his waist as she felt him rest his cheek on her head.

"I understand," she whispered softly before moving away from him. A thread connected them, the desire to atone for their mistakes even if it had all been out of their control. Elora handed over the vials and he shoved them into the pocket of his jeans.

He grinned as he offered her his arm as he had before at the apartment.

"They'll want to collect blood soon. I'll take you back." Her body tightened as her hand went to her wrist, tracing the scars. Every muscle contracted and the scent of roses filled her nostrils. The memories were dragging back. Reality was fading, growing dimmer at the edges as she fell into her worst fears.

Something warm wrapped around her fingers and pulled them close. Wyatt settled her hand into the crook of his arm, running his thumb along the edge of it. Her chest filled with air as she inhaled deeply, holding the breath for a long moment before exhaling. Connie's grave came back into view as Elora was once again able to smell the damp earth and the flowers that had been left behind. Only the evergreen trees were still alive as winter came quickly.

"She should only collect it a couple more times. Twice today, more than likely. Maybe tomorrow as well. I know what it does to you. It's almost over," he said softly as we entered the dormitory, where others sat at the tables with cups of what was either blood or coffee. She could hear snippets of conversation as they passed. It seemed there was an undercurrent of excitement for the ceremony, gossip about what it would entail or what it would mean.

"What're you going to do, Wyatt? What's your plan?" Her voice was a whisper as she leaned towards him, pulling his arm to her body. His warmth bled through the dress she wore, another of Elizabeth's gifts.

"It's better if you don't know. You go to the ceremony and do what she wants. I'll talk to the ones who support you and take care of the weapon."

"No, I--"

"Stop. We don't have time to debate this. Listen." They both stopped as they reached the top of the stairs. The sound of chaos echoed down the hall, a collection of voices and items crashing. Elora took a deep breath, preparing herself for what she knew was coming. Step by step, they went down the hall until they were in front of her room. The door had been flung open, revealing Elizabeth standing in the center of the room with her back to them.

The chairs beside her bed were tossed to the side while the mattress had been thrown out of the frame. White sheets and bedding lay on the floor in a crumpled mess. Drawers were open or flung across the room. A vampire Elora didn't recognize stabbed a knife into the mattress, ripping it down the center so the springs and material cascaded out.

Elora let go of Wyatt's arm, stepping into the room to better survey the damage. Her eyes moved frantically across the space, searching for the pillows that had been on her bed. They were against the far wall in a tattered mess. Feathers were scattered across the floor along with strips of the pillowcase. But no signs of the shirt, which meant—

Elizabeth spun around, a dark bundle clutched in her hand. Damien's shirt. She held it up, staring at it for a moment before turning her focus to Elora. Her face was stone as her blue eyes blazed.

"Your room will be moved. If he comes back, I'll have him killed. I won't tolerate threats to what we're building here," Elizabeth hissed. Her voice was harsh, as if she hadn't drunk anything for days. Or like she had been crying. Elora studied her face, noting the pale redness around her eyes where they were still a bit puffy.

"And the shirt?" Elora knew she sounded weak, but she wanted that bit of fabric. Even from where she stood, Elora could pick up his scent. In any other circumstances, it would have been enough to ease her mind, stop her from picking at her cuticles until they bled. Elizabeth smiled cruelly, shaking her head slowly.

"Take her to the room between ours. Lock the door. She doesn't leave until tomorrow night." Wyatt nodded at the instructions and gripped Elora's biceps, dragging her away from Elizabeth. Tears stung Elora's eyes as she allowed him to drag her away, already mourning the loss of a stupid shirt.

"I'm sorry," he whispered and led her to her new prison cell.

Chapter 47

Elora

The young vampire gathered up her materials along with the two bottles of blood she had drained from Elora. In her brown eyes, Elora saw the hint of resentment before the vampire turned away and marched to the door, unlocking it with her free hand.

Elora took a breath, pulling the blanket up to her chest as she moved to snuggle back beneath the covers. She could hide, pretend that she was back in her room at the Tower and that Damien would be coming back. The sunlight disappeared as Elora pulled the blanket over her head, burrowing deeper into the fantasy she was creating. She would sleep, hoarding any energy she had left for the ceremony that night.

"Come on out, sister. We need to talk."

"Can't this wait?" She asked from under her blankets. Her entire body felt like jelly, like there were no bones or muscles left, leaving her a bundle of blood and skin. Elora listened as her sister seemed to move about the room, coming closer before sinking onto the mattress beside her.

"I have something you desperately need." Curiosity got the better of her and Elora threw the blankets back to find Elizabeth holding a bottle. Her heart raced at the sight, her mouth salivating at the promise of what that bottle contained. She sat up, leaning back against the headboard and closed her eyes in hopes that when she opened them, the room would no longer be spinning. It was difficult enough to hold her head up. Focusing on anything specific was too much and so she waited as Elizabeth did whatever she was doing. Elora imagined that it was opening the bottle and pouring some in a cup, a rationed amount to make sure she didn't gain too much strength. Just enough to stand up and give some speech about how this was everything she wanted and how she welcomed them all.

"Here. Drink this and then we can talk about your betrayal." Elora didn't bother to argue or defend herself as she grabbed the large plastic up and devoured every drop. Blood— sweet and thick— poured down her throat, resurrecting every nerve and limb she had. It was like being struck by lightning, every inch of her suddenly alive and demanding more. Elora thrust the cup to her sister, who refilled it and set the now empty bottle aside. Once more, Elora consumed the liquid in a few deep drinks and closed her eyes once more, letting the sensation wash over her. The throbbing in her head that hadn't fully gone away disappeared along with the pressure behind her eyes.

"To be honest, I probably shouldn't have collected your blood this time. It's been tainted, after all." Elizabeth leaned back on the bed, holding herself up with her palms as she reclined. It reminded Elora of the days they spent on their bed after school, gossiping and giggling over anything. Back then, it hadn't taken much to send them spiraling into a fit of laughter that only ended when their stomachs hurt and water filled their eyes.

"Tainted?" Elora asked. She knew what Elizabeth was referring to, but she would feign innocence as long as possible. Elizabeth's eyes flashed and darkened for a moment before she reverted back to her usual ease.

"With *his* blood. The one you fed from. If you were hungry, you only needed to say something. It was dangerous having him come here," Elizabeth explained with no shortness of irritation.

"No one—"

"Don't lie. I smelled him. I found his shirt bundled under your pillow. Pathetic, really. Are you that desperate for affection?" Elora straightened, leveling her sister with a glare.

"Are you upset that I found someone who cares for me? Who loves me? I'm not sure I'm the pathetic one," she retorted. Now that Elora had fed, every emotion that had been held at bay by weakness came rushing forward. A dam had broken, and every thought wanted to barrel out of her mouth. Elizabeth had always been the romantic, the one who devoured every book and movie with the slightest love story. She would hold a pillow to her chest with a blanket over her legs as she watched and read each one. It had bordered on an obsession.

"I have this entire community who answers to my every whim. They follow and love me," she responded, brushing a hair away from her face.

"Only because of your connection to me. They follow you because of me." Elora's response was harsh, bordering on cruelty, but she couldn't find it in herself to care even as Elizabeth seemed to jerk away like she had been struck. Once more, she recovered quickly, letting a small smile play on her lips to cover the pain in her eyes. If Elora hadn't spent every waking hour with her for years, she would have missed it, would have only seen the smirk. But at their core, despite everything that had happened, they were sisters, connected in a way that was impossible to fully describe. They had stood up for one another, beaten up other people, and kept secrets.

"Why did he come here? I doubt it was just to see you." Elizabeth studied her, no doubt searching for any sign of a lie.

"He wanted to make sure I hadn't been hurt and to ask about his role at the Tower. I'm the head of two families, but I'm here instead." The lie was easy, rolling off her tongue without any hesitation. Elizabeth's face gave away nothing, no hint of whether she believed the explanation.

"And that required him to leave behind his shirt?" Elizabeth drawled, causing Elora to chuckle softly.

"No, that isn't what required him to take off his shirt. Or anything else, for that matter."

"I wanted you to be with Wyatt, you know. I could have your little lover removed to make sure it happens." The threat landed heavily, settling on Elora's chest to the point she wasn't sure she could take in a breath. Elora couldn't decide if her sister was playing with her, toying with her fears in an effort to regain some semblance of control.

"Why? Why would you even say that?" Her voice shook, trembling with each word of her questions and Elizabeth grinned. Her eyes were bright, rendering the luminance they all had more intense. Elora's pulse raced beneath her wrist, in her neck as her heart rate sped up at the threat.

"Wyatt deserves you. He sacrificed so much for you." Blood rushed to her head, pounding in her ears as her palms grew sweaty. It felt like her body was shaking, vibrating with rage. Sacrifice? What happened to Wyatt wasn't a sacrifice, but a curse and assault.

"That word implies he did it willingly, that he volunteered for this. I don't remember him asking for you to bite him in that fucking apartment, Lizzie!" She cursed at the mistake, at the show of rage and reverting back to the childhood nickname. It was so easy to slip back into the past, into their arguments and disagreements they had about silly things. It seemed so long ago. An entire lifetime had passed since then.

Elizabeth shrugged as if it made no difference if Wyatt agreed.

"I never agreed either," she whispered as she stared out the window behind Elora's head. It was as if she was lost in thought or memories.

"Do you remember it?" Elora asked. She knew her own answer. Only snippets and fragments remained of that night. Elora assumed it was due to the blood haze she had found herself in, the feral instinct to consume until there was nothing left.

"Of course. Every second. Every sensation. The fear and ecstasy and exhaustion afterwards." A part of Elora hoped her sister wouldn't remember, that she would be spared that memory. With the way Elizabeth's voice became almost breathy as she spoke, it was as if it had been a spiritual experience.

"I'm disappointed you don't remember. But you don't remember much." Before dealing with Killian and Darian, Elora would have shrunk; she would have crumpled under the insult that it was. Her memories were gone, and she had come to terms with the fact the burned holes in her mind would never be mended, only replaced by new ones. Perhaps it was better they stayed forgotten. Perhaps her mind knew what it was doing by protecting her from them.

"I don't need those memories. Even the nightmares have decreased." A warm smile stretched across Elizabeth's face, and to Elora's immense shock, it felt genuine.

"They'll decrease with Wyatt, as well. I stand by what I said. If he comes back and we catch him, I'll have him killed in front of you." The air in the room seemed to grow thick and heavy as Elora glared at her sister, silently begging her to give her even the smallest reason to hit her.

"The last people who tried to hurt him were killed, Elizabeth. Remember that when you threaten him," Elora promised and closed her eyes, leaning her head against the headboard. The blood hadn't lasted long enough, barely enough to give her the energy to deal with Elizabeth. She needed to conserve her energy. The celebration would require everything she had.

"I'll send in another bottle along with your outfit for tonight. You need to look the part." Elora only waved her hand before snuggling back under the blanket, pulling it over her head in an effort to block out the light. Thankfully, Elizabeth took the hint, and Elora felt the tug in her chest as her sister stood and left the room, leaving only the minor ache that could spell her death behind.

Chapter 48

Damien

Across the street was the church with its tall steeple, broken stained glass windows, and iron gate. Through the overgrown weeds and flowers that weaved between the trees and gravestones, Damien could make out the figures of Silas's vampires positioning themselves. Among them were the dozen or so who came from the Tower, volunteers each and every one of them. When Damien had sent out the call for a team to help Elora, the response had been instant and required the office to accommodate them. Even in the large room, the space had been cramped as they listened to Damien explain everything. They already knew about Elizabeth, about the threat she posed. But it had been the knowledge the group was hurting Elora that had caused a rush of rage among them. In such a small time, Elora had earned the respect of each vampire under her.

Damien leaned back against the car behind him while Silas stood along the curb, arms crossed over his chest as he tracked each vampire as they settled into their hiding spots. The plan was poorly devised at best, but that seemed to be how they thrived. Damien's plan to get Elora away from Killian had been rushed and barely outlined. Her plan to deal with Darian had been the same. As far as Damien could tell, the only mission that had been thoroughly planned had been his own rescue and it hadn't exactly gone perfectly. If this was the best they had, then it would have to work.

"Did you talk to her about the fact she could die tonight?" Silas asked without twisting to meet Damien's eyes.

"Not exactly," he responded as he thought through the conversation. He let out a breath and explained they hadn't truly discussed it, that he had brought it up, but nothing had come from it. Silas nodded after Damien finished his explanation, leaving out certain details that her uncle had no need to hear.

"And what is going on with Hartley? Why have you been visiting her?" Suspicion coated both questions and Damien approached Silas, mimicking his stance as they stood side by side staring at the place that could become Elora's grave.

"She needed blood. They weren't giving her any." Damien let him fill in the blanks, not really wanting to go into any more of an explanation.

"Now, she's worried about the possible repercussions," Silas stated bluntly. It was her way, and they all knew that. It drove Damien mad, and he was fairly certain Silas felt the same. She had already given enough in her life, had already sacrificed enough. It felt like a cruel joke, a cosmic insult that she would die now.

Damien gave him a sardonic grin. "Of course she is. I had Hartley test my blood for anything strange." Silas raised a single brow as he seemed to wait for more detail.

"There were no results yet. This whole mission took the majority of her focus for right now." A lie, but Silas either couldn't tell or didn't call him on it. It wasn't that the tests showed anything devastating or problematic. But she deserved to hear it first, not after everyone else already had.

Over the top of the church's steeple, the sun sunk, leaving the area in twilight that was rapidly becoming darkness. There were no lights along the outside of the stone walls, only the bit flowing out from the windows.

"Let's get into position. Thorne is already in place." The human was meant to be hiding near the back entrance where she could enter easily if necessary. Damien had been plagued all night by nightmares, of finding Elora too late, of holding her lifeless body in his arms. His hand twitched at the memory as he started across the street, dodging the few cars making their way through the area. Silas kept a step or two behind him searching the street and churchyard for any sign of a problem.

There wasn't a single vampire around other than the ones Damien and Silas had stationed. It seemed everyone connected to Elizabeth was already inside. Both vampires squeezed through the iron gates, forcing their bodies between the ornate bars to prevent any unnecessary noise.

Damien was surprised at exactly how chaotic the grounds were. A single gravel path led to the massive double doors of the church before moving further into the grounds, where he assumed the parking area was. When he snuck in to visit Elora, he hadn't truly paid any attention to the front. Instead, he had snuck in through the back gate, moving through the gravestones until he was able to follow her scent to her room. Dozens of vampires had wandered the grounds, moving in and out of the church and dormitory, but none had seen him. Or perhaps they had and simply thought he was one of them.

They took their place on the far side of the church, kneeling along one of the broken windows. It would give them a clear view of the area they expected Elora to be and there would be little to block any sound. They needed to be able to hear what was said, be able to know when to storm in and deal with the problem.

Damien's knees creaked slightly as he pushed himself up to peek over the edge of the window ledge. His focus moved over the space, trying to count the vampires that were now mingling or finding their seats. All were dressed in what seemed to be their nicest clothing—long dresses, suits and button-up shirts, slacks, dress shoes, and heels. It was the same as it had been the night they came to the hotel.

"This isn't the spot to hide in. Elizabeth will scent you. She already did once." Damien spun around at the sound of the voice that made him want to punch something. Wyatt stood tall against the background of dwindling twilight and massive trees with gravestones hidden between the flowers and weeds. Damien had been so consumed with the scene inside the church he hadn't heard Wyatt approach. Silas had been as well and now they both waited, staring at the vampire who had almost stolen Elora's heart.

"What do you mean?" Silas asked gently, shoving his hands into the pockets of his leather jacket. It was a strange look for the vampire head who only ever seemed to wear slacks and button-up shirts that looked like they would pay someone's rent for a year.

Wyatt studied Silas for a long moment, probably wondering who he was or what role he played here. The urge to introduce them waited on the tip of Damien's tongue, but he clamped his mouth closed. He didn't know why Wyatt was here, if he was there to announce their presence or something else. Elora's voice whispering that he should trust him repeated in his ear and so he waited to hear the response.

"She knew Damien had visited her. Letting her keep your shirt was a mistake," Wyatt answered as he leveled Damien with an even stare. There was no jealousy there, no anger, which had been what Damien had expected based on their interactions. The question of whether Wyatt knew about the effect Elora had on humans came rushing forward. He could imagine Elora admitting everything, spilling out her pain and guilt like a buffet for Wyatt to feast at. She would cry, tears streaming down her face as she took whatever Wyatt gave her—screaming, hatred, insults, or even forgiveness.

"I didn't let her do anything. You know that as well as I do," Damien retorted and was rewarded with a small smirk on Wyatt's lips. They both knew that nothing would have stopped Elora from keeping that scrap of fabric no matter the consequences.

"Elizabeth is on edge now. Elora did a decent job trying to put her at ease, claimed you two needed to talk about what was happening at the Tower. But Elizabeth is already paranoid about everything, and it didn't help." Wyatt stepped closer, moving so that he could touch them if he wanted to. To Damien's right, Silas shifted slightly, no doubt reaching for the knife he had been forced to bring with him. It was only by telling him that Elora would never forgive herself if something happened to him that he relented in his refusal.

"What's going to happen in there?" Silas jerked his head towards the church window where voices were filtering out, giving them small snippets of conversation. The excitement mixed with grumbling about being forced to be there, about how this was all a ridiculous performance that did nothing of value. The laughter of children mingled with the adult voices, giving additional weight to what was about to happen.

"Elizabeth will give an opening speech. More than likely it will be about coming together to create a new type of vampire family and then she will turn it over to Elora, who will give her own speech before the blood is handed out."

"Elora's guess was correct then," Damien commented and Wyatt nodded in agreement.

"Elizabeth sees this going only one way despite her paranoia. Elora gives the speech telling them all how much she appreciates their efforts and how this is what she always wanted," Wyatt explained smoothly before grinning. His eyes were bright in the darkness, shining through from the shadows that lined his face.

"But we both know that isn't how this is going to happen," he added, looking from Damien to Silas before letting his attention focus on the window behind them.

"Do we?" Silas asked, staring at the vampire like he was a threat that needed to be removed. Wyatt only gave him a small grin before jerking his head towards the back door.

"That's where you should be. Take that door and you'll be inside just behind where Elora will be standing. It will give you a better spot when everything begins." Damien stood straight, not bothering to care that the light from inside rendered him visible now. The voices inside had begun to quiet down, the sound of moving feet and child laughter disappearing. It was almost time.

"How do we know there isn't a group of vampires waiting inside the door?" Wyatt pulled his hand out of his pocket and held up the empty vial that Damien recognized instantly. She had held it just like that the morning he had left her here.

"Because Elora trusts me. You should as well." He didn't wait for a response but spun on his heel as he forced his hands into his pockets once more and moved towards the front of the church. Damien had no doubt that Wyatt had his own role to play, his own performance to give. They were working together, leaving Damien to wonder why. When Elora survived this—because it was *when* and not *if*—he would ask exactly what brought Wyatt to her side when all evidence showed him to be a loyal lapdog to Elizabeth.

Silas and Damien watched as Wyatt disappeared into the darkness, listening as his footsteps on the gravel grew more and more faint. After a moment, the only sounds were the hushed conversations inside the church and the nightlife waking up all around them.

"Do we trust him?" Silas asked, finally turning back to Damien.

"Yes. If she does, then we do." Not too long ago, the words would have tasted bitter on his tongue, the jealousy and rage making his throat dry and hands tighten into fists. But she was his now without question. She had trusted him when it came to Korina. He would trust her when it came to Wyatt.

Damien went first, ducking down once more and moving slowly along the stone wall towards the door Wyatt had gestured to. He could hear Silas behind him, moving gracefully and almost silently through the bushes and weeds. His pulse was steady as it was on every mission he had completed for Killian despite the extra weight this one carried. Her life was on the line, which meant his life was as well because there was no world where he continued if she died.

They exchanged a glance as Damien wrapped his fingers around the handle, twisting gradually in case this had been stupid and there was a group waiting for them on the other side. Slowly, so painfully slowly, Damien pushed the door open, ignoring the slight creak of the hinges. The door finally opened enough to see inside and sense that there wasn't an ambush ready to strike. Damien nodded at Silas before moving into the room, taking in every corner and potential hidden place. Systematically, he searched behind the desk and inside the small armoire before nodding once more to himself as if confirming that the room was indeed empty except for the two of them.

"Now what?" Silas whispered, closing the door behind him. He kept his palm pressed to it as he inched it closed, ensuring that it made as little noise as possible. They both moved to the only other door in the room, the one that would lead directly into the church and behind the pulpit where Elora and Elizabeth were sure to be. Damien leaned against the door, ear pressed so hard he could feel each grain of the wood. Word by word,

Damien listened as the ceremony began, and Elizabeth's voice filled the room.

Chapter 49

Elora

As everyone settled into the lines of pews and crowded around the back and side walls, Elizabeth raised her hands in the air and waited for silence to settle. It took less than a heartbeat for them to go silent and every pair of eyes locked onto the pulpit where Elizabeth stood in her black silk gown that fell from her shoulders in waves. The sleeves fell over her hands as she brought her arms back down and let them hang by her thighs. To Elora, her sister looked like a priestess, a creature from the movies they had watched together. Her features were arranged into an expression of peace, of benevolence, as she stared out over the congregation waiting with bated breath for her first words.

"This is the beginning. Before tonight, we've been in limbo as we waited for our creator to join us here, to accept us and welcome us. I've done what I could to protect us, to keep us safe while we waited. Now, she's here, and we can move forward. After tonight, we'll establish ourselves among the other vampires and cement our place in the city. We'll break it down and rebuild it in her image." Elizabeth paused her speech to allow for the outbreak of polite applause that Elora couldn't decide whether it was real or expected.

There didn't seem to be much enthusiasm as Elora scanned the crowd, lingering on each face to search for any sign Wyatt had been telling the truth. She had heard with her own ears that some were unhappy, but that was different from them harboring the potential for outright rebellion. Most expressions were stoic, calm and shielded, which Elora took as a positive sign that her plan could work, that lives could be spared. She took a deep breath, steadying her trembling hands as she clasped them together in front of her.

"Our salvation is here with us. I'll now turn the floor to our creator, Elora." The applause this time was deafening, rising to the point that Elora was terrified the entire church would come crumbling down on their heads. She could have sworn she heard the remaining windows rattling in their frames as she stepped forward. With each step, Elora felt the disguise she wore when addressing others slip into place. The coldness settled, rendering each feature hard yet gentle as she stared out at the crowd. Children sat along the front row, fidgeting as they played with their sleeves or hems of their clothing to entertain themselves. Her heart stuttered, the rhythm of pumping blood interrupted by the sight of them.

Would they be allowed to leave?

Allowed to abstain from the tainted blood that would quickly be making its way to them?

Her mask faltered as she watched them, forcing back the stinging of tears at the sight. Movement along the wall caught Elora's attention and her eyes darted to the figure standing at the end of the pew. Wyatt was dressed impeccably in dark slacks and a black button-up. He had attempted to tame his hair by brushing it back, but rogue strands still fell against his forehead and cheekbones. His amber eyes met hers for a moment, just the briefest of seconds before he turned to the child seated at the edge of the pew and knelt beside them, whispering something that caused them to nod their head excitedly. One by one, they all stood and followed him outside, all of them holding hands like schoolkids on a field trip.

Elora's chest rose and fell as she let out the breath she had been holding since seeing the children. Oxygen rushed back into her lungs, and she turned her attention back to the rest of the waiting faces. They were all staring at her with an intensity that made her want to retreat to a dark cave where no one would find her.

"Thank you, sister," Elora began, nodding at Elizabeth. "When I turned Elizabeth when I was nineteen, I never expected this to be the outcome. I didn't know what I was at the time or what role I was meant to fulfill. Now, I have stepped into the position you all created for me, and I have to admit, it's an uncomfortable one." She smiled and was met with a soft wave of laughter, a polite chuckle at her poor attempt at a joke.

"However, my vision for this group differs from my sister. She imagines us living together while turning the rest of the city into creatures just like us. She knows that our hunger is more intense and frequent, that our bite is enough to turn a human. And after the humans are gone and we're living here with the other vampires, we would drain them dry as well. We would be left with nothing to consume and would destroy ourselves. This is our future unless we change course." Elora felt her sister shift, moving closer as if to stop her speech. There had been no rules outlined for this little moment, no list of points to focus on to stay on message. Elizabeth had been completely confident that Elora would follow suit, that this was what she also wanted, that she hadn't made any demands on what words would come from Elora's mouth. She twisted slightly, meeting Elizabeth's gaze long enough to see the rage and disappointment there.

"I'll be leaving here and returning to the Tower and the manor that I'm in charge of. If you want to follow the rules, I'm offering you a place among the vampires I lead. You would live in the

Tower under my protection. You wouldn't be allowed to feed directly from any human. I could offer you a medication that would render you all but human as long as you take it. I offer you a choice, something that some of you were never given."

The crowd before Elora shifted in their seats as their eyes darted to the vampires beside them. Elora took a step forward, standing at the end of the platform. She could hear Elizabeth's breathing go harsh as she seemed to struggle to take in a single breath. Elora didn't dare glance back at her, didn't dare take her eyes off the crowd before her that was full of shock and careful optimism. Face after face was bright, as if the options presented to them were a piece of candy being dangled before them and all they needed to do was reach out and grab it.

"If you choose to remain, that's your choice. I only ask that you complete the ceremony Elizabeth planned for us to take part in. I only ask that you consume my offering and obey my sister. She was my first and will act as your leader in my place. And should you ever change your mind about your place, my doors will always be open to my children." Each word sliced into her flesh with such ferocity Elora was sure she would be bleeding, that her lies and twisting of the truth would be on display and written in blood on the stone floor beneath her.

But heads only nodded in response as a silence fell on them, wrapping them in their embrace as they all seemed to hold their breath. Elora watched, waiting for someone to stand, for someone to make the first move that could save so many lives. The only comfort was that even if no one stood, the children were gone and hopefully tucked away with those who would protect them and spirit them away to the Tower.

Then, Elora let out a harsh sound that may have been the beginning of a sob as one vampire stood—a young man with blond hair cut close to his scalp. His piercing blue eyes met Elora's before he turned, marched to the door, and left without glancing back. Another heartbeat of silence as they all waited before one more stood and then another and another.

Six. Ten. Then twelve vampires all stood and made their way to the door.

"Wait!" Elizabeth's cry, broken and full of pain, echoed against the walls as she darted towards the standing crowd. Her movements were frantic as she pushed forward, trying to reach for them as if it would stop them. Elora spun towards her sister, pressing her hand flat against Elizabeth's chest just below her collarbones.

"Let them make the choice I denied you," Elora said softly, meeting the pale blue eyes that now only revealed pure devastation. It was as if the entire world was crashing down around them, as if reality had fragmented into a thousand pieces and there was no one to pick them back up.

Slowly, the sound of departing footsteps grew lower until all Elora heard was the door closing once more. Her heart raced in her chest and beneath her palm, she could feel Elizabeth's doing the same. Both vampires turned and looked out over the remaining crowd, about half the size of who was originally in there. The back five pews were empty, leaving only the front four full on both sides of the aisle. Elora nodded, quickly trying to calculate how many rooms would be needed. It would be Damien's job to figure it out. Not hers. She wouldn't be there to tell him her orders, to tell him her vision for the vampires tied to her if they survived. She may have given them a chance, but there was always the possibility that none of them survived this, that they all fell dead the moment she did. There was a chance that the Hail Mary that Hartley had sent wouldn't work.

Elora gave the remaining vampires a wide smile that she hoped read as warm and welcoming before she felt movement behind her. She twisted her head just enough to see Wyatt with a large container filled with her blood. Their eyes didn't meet as he moved into position, setting the offering down on the table set up in front of the pews with a line of ten cups. One by one, Wyatt poured the thick liquid into eight of them before setting the container back down.

"For those of you who have decided to remain, I wish you every happiness and joy. Wyatt, distribute the offering, please," Elora announced, projecting her voice despite it no longer being necessary. If Damien was waiting outside, then he needed to be able to hear her, to know what was happening. One person from each pew stood and came forward with faces bright from whatever religious fever was controlling them. It was the only explanation for why they didn't take the chance she gave them, the only reason why they decided to remain here.

It was also the reason this had to happen, why the threat they posed had to be removed. Following Elizabeth meant feeding indiscriminately, meant turning the city into their personal hunting grounds.

Each vampire took a glass and returned to stand at the end of the pew. In unison, they lifted the metal cup to their lips and took a deep drink before passing it to the next. In her chest, everything went silent as Elora waited. No heartbeat. No blood pounding in her ears.

Just as the last vampire in each row put the cup to their lips to consume the last bit, a shout rang out.

"No! Stop! Don't drink it!" Elora spun around and faced her sister. Her face was pale, drained of every drop of blood in her body. Realization rang out in her words. She had figured it out, had finally understood that this was all a performance where the finale was death.

Chapter 50

Elora

"How could you?" Elizabeth demanded as she rushed forward, stopping only inches away from her sister. Elora planted her feet and squared her shoulders, refusing to show Elizabeth even the tiniest hint of fear. She had entered this church ready to die, prepared for Elizabeth to understand that the vampires who followed her weren't going to survive.

"Plagues must be stopped," was all Elora said as she prepared for what would come next. But Elizabeth didn't move, didn't even twitch as she stared out at the congregation in horror.

"Elora." The sound of her name filled the room and she spun around to find its source. Wyatt stood between the two pews with a full glass held between his hands. A small smile played on the corners of his lips. Elora knew that the other vampires behind him were beginning to feel the effects based on the sounds erupting from their mouths, but she could tear her eyes away from him. She knew this moment would come, knew that Wyatt had no desire to remain alive and that he saw this moment as atoning for Connie's death. It didn't change the fact she didn't want to lose him, didn't want him to sacrifice any more than he already had.

Elora shook her head as her hand curled into a fist at her side.

"No. Stay with me," she begged. She didn't care that her voice was breaking, that each word was fractured by incoming tears.

All she wanted was for him to put the tainted blood down, to step away and leave with her once this was done. Behind him, stricken faces glared at her, the betrayal they felt almost physical in the way it filled the church.

"I'll make more. You've accomplished nothing." Elora had expected these words, had heard Elizabeth making the same declaration in her nightmares where she failed and they had all died for nothing. After. She would deal with Elizabeth after he had made his choice.

Wyatt nodded slightly before lifting the cup to his lips and drinking deeply. There was more blood in there than for the others and her heart fell further and further into her stomach with each swallow he consumed. He tilted his head back to take in the last of it before placing the cup on the table and smiling at the two of them, letting the thin line of red show. His eyes fluttered shut as if he could feel the blood course through his veins, as if he could feel the weapon work in his system. Elora had no idea how long it would take for it to work or if it would. For all she knew, this would all amount to nothing.

She felt the shift before there were any physical signs. At first, she didn't believe the sensation rushing through her, didn't believe the feeling of something being carved from her. Anything she felt should be subdued. It should be so minor that it was barely noticeable. At least, that was the case if she was meant to survive. Her focus moved from Wyatt to the vampires lining the pews behind him. Dull eyes stared at her as their mouths twisted and turned in a way that was almost comical if it wasn't for the reality of the situation.

A choking sound erupted, shattering the silence and causing Elora to jump. Frantically, she searched for the source, finding a vampire in the front row gripping the armrest as they pushed themselves up. Long brunette hair fell like a curtain around the vampire's face as they doubled over. Their knuckles were white from where they gripped the wood while they seemed to gasp for air.

Elora tracked each movement, each frantic attempt to survive as the vampire finally met her eyes, revealing the desperation in the pools of pale brown. There was a knowing there, mingling with the fear that was so palpable that vampire seemed to wear it like a jacket. They knew, without a shadow of a doubt, that this was it.

Death had entered the church and demanded they enter its embrace.

"Did you hear me?" Elizabeth screamed behind her. The screech of her voice was grating, forcing Elora away from the dying vampires before. "I will make more. They are replaceable!" Her shout forced goosebumps to erupt on Elora's skin, lining her arms underneath the gown. She turned away from the row of vampires before her, all grasping at the air in front of them as if the cure was hovering just before them.

"No, you won't. It's over, Elizabeth," she announced in an even voice, watching Elizabeth's hands tighten before releasing as if she was trying to calm herself. This was the end and nothing Elizabeth did would stop that. Both of them would die if necessary. Both would be sacrificed.

A loud cackle poured from Elizabeth's mouth as she tilted her head back, letting the sound flood out into the limited space between them. Elora took a step back and then another, desperate to get away from this version of her sister. She had seen her unhinged, seen her cruel and depressed and vengeful. But this was something else, something darker and more dangerous. Elora had seen this only one other time—the hospital room for the so-called confrontation therapy. It had spelled agony then and Elora could only guess what it would mean now.

"Did you think I didn't know? Did you think I bought your story about your fuck boy's visit? I'm insulted," Elizabeth scolded before hitting the podium to her right with her fist. The sound echoed in the room, the vibrations from the impact traveling through the wood and into the floor beneath their feet.

Behind Elizabeth a side door opened with a bang and eight bodies emerged from the darkness, each one dressed in what looked to be protective clothing. It was like witnessing modern warriors preparing for battle, lining up to meet the incoming threat. She could only hope that Damien was there, that he had brought his own backup.

"You let them all drink that. You had a hunch at best," Elora tossed back, glaring at her sister. Elizabeth shrugged lightly, as if it wasn't the life of dozens of vampires they were talking about. Did she not feel the hollowness? The empty cavity in her chest that seemed to grow wider and deeper with each vampire who succumbed?

"I knew that something could go wrong. I'll admit I never thought you would drug the blood. I never really thought you would kill them."

"I did what needed to be done," she forced out between gritted teeth. "I saved those who wanted a different life than whatever the fuck this is." It felt like an excuse. It felt like a lie that coated her mouth, making it difficult to speak.

"You're more heartless than I ever thought possible. You threw this gift back in my face. All I wanted was to give you the city. A thank you for everything you gave me." Elora shook her head. This was insanity. Every word from Elizabeth's mouth was pure madness that made no realistic sense in any version of reality.

"What would make you think this is what I would want? What did I do or say in our years together that made you think this is what I would want?" Her voice cracked as she spoke, as Elora forced out the questions that had plagued her since she found out her sister's plan. Over and over, she had run through every memory they shared, searching for the hidden clue that would make this all seem sensible. Or perhaps she was simply seeking evidence that would prove Elora was at fault. Perhaps she was searching for a reason to hate herself even more.

"You didn't need to say or do anything. I always knew what you wanted once we were connected. I can feel you."

"That isn't the same as knowing what I want. The only thing I have ever wanted was to be safe. To not fear the smell of roses or the feeling of silk. To not be afraid of a locked door or container of blood," Elora revealed. A surge of strength cascaded over her at the confession, at the sensation of voicing something held so deep inside her that she hadn't admitted to it before this moment. Not even with Damien had these words been spoken out loud. There was always the fear they would be used against her, that they would render her more trouble than she was worth and those she loved would walk away.

Elizabeth darted forward, taking Elora's hands in her own as her eyes widened in something like excitement.

"This would give you that. I would be able to give you all of that and more!" Her words were desperate, frantically spilling out over each other in a way that made it difficult to understand. It was no longer love that Elora saw in her sister's eyes, but an emotion akin to what Elora figured a penitent gave their god. It was toxic and terrifying and all-consuming.

"At what price?" Elora asked, taking her hands from Elizabeth and crossing her arms over her chest.

"It doesn't matter," she responded, her face falling as the light fled her eyes.

"Yes, it does. And I'll never let you do it. I'll kill you before that happens." The venom in Elora's vow was enough to make Elizabeth hesitate as a flash of hurt appeared and disappeared in less than a heartbeat. Behind her, Elora heard Wyatt fall to his knees, heard the table topple over and the glasses clatter onto the stone floor. The scent of blood filled the air as the contents of the container spilled out. That was it. No matter who stood at her sister's back, Elora had at least accomplished that much. No matter the void in her chest, no one else would be turned and the city would remain standing.

"I'm your sister. You could never hurt me, Elora."

"You haven't been my sister since the night I bit you." The strike came fast and swift, leaving Elora unprepared for the impact. She wasn't sure if it was a punch or a slap as she dropped to the ground, the stone hitting her knees and making her cry out. Fingers were in her hair, gripping it tightly until Elizabeth pulled and yanked like a schoolyard fight. Another hit. A foot to her to ribs and Elora screamed, the sound ripping from her throat as the pain rushed through her in wave after wave. There was no end as it settled into a continuous ache that left Elora wondering if her ribs were broken or fractured at the very least.

A copper taste field her mouth. Blood. She spat it out onto the ground just as Elizabeth released her hold, letting Elora catch her breath. She didn't stand, but stayed on her knees, trying desperately to catch her breath.

"You're not healing. The cut is still there." Elora raised her fingers to her face, gingerly touching her bottom lip before breaking into a wide grin that only tore at the wound more, causing a fresh trail of blood to trickle down her chin and drip onto her dress. The vial had worked.

"Nope. I also can't feel you fully. Or them. Or him. I'm human." Elora waited for another hit, another kick or even something much worse. But Elizabeth only stared at her as if she was something from another world, a creature that rendered truth pointless. With a small vial of the medication, Elora had upended Elizabeth's entire world, and it was a glorious feeling.

Then, the atmosphere shifted. The air grew fraught, as if waiting for an explosion to occur or a roar of thunder to crack. It began with Elizabeth's brows as they settled into an arch. Then, her eyes as they hardened and grew dark. Tiny lines appeared around them, aging her in a way that felt unnatural. Finally, her plump lips became a thin line as her jaw tightened, her teeth crashing together as she clamped her mouth shut. A shadow crossed over her face as goosebumps rose over every inch of Elora's flesh. Only a single word echoed in her mind—danger. Finally, her face cracked open and Elizabeth spoke, each word ominous and dripping in the promise of violence.

"I won't let you destroy the life I built."

Chapter 51

Damien

Her scream called to something dark in Damien as it filtered through the door, forcing itself through the cracks in the frame. The instant it filled the small closet, his fingers wrapped around the handle and ripped the door open. His heart raced in his chest, pounding against his ribs until he was sure he would fall down dead before he made it to her. Damien could feel Silas beside him as they took a brief moment to survey the space. More vampires than he thought had left when given the chance. Bodies were writhing on the floor and draped over the pews as small whimpers rushed forward. Wyatt knelt before the pulpit as he fell to the stone, fingers digging into the ground as he tried to crawl forward. His focus was on something in front of him, features contorted and twisted in rage and fear and something Damien couldn't quite identify. And he didn't have time to do that. Not now.

His eyes followed Wyatt's line of sight until he found them. Elora knelt on the floor while Elizabeth stood, towering over her as she stared down with nothing less than hatred. Behind her stood a line of vampires, each one with bright eyes as they watched the scene with hands behind their backs.

"Elora," Silas called out, drawing the attention of every single vampire in the room. All eyes turned to them as a type of stand-off settled, each group waiting for the other to make the first move. Damien cursed, wondering if Silas should have spoken at all, should have drawn attention to them before they had fully assessed the situation. But it was too late now.

"Of course, your little fuckboy has come to the rescue. And who are you?" Elizabeth nodded towards Silas, who stood up straighter and took a step towards his niece. His only focus seemed to be her safety and protection. Elizabeth didn't move or twitch as Silas bent down and gripped Elora's biceps, helping her to her feet. The scent of her blood was all-encompassing as Damien understood two things simultaneously. The first was that she was hurt, that someone had hit her. And the second was that she hadn't healed, that there was still blood coming from the wound on her lip. He barely stopped himself from darting forward. He needed to touch her, to pull her into his arms and hold her if only for a moment.

"Her uncle," Silas bit out as he glared at Elizabeth. There was no doubt that if Silas could, he would kill her where she stood.

"The one who left her on our front doorstep," she stated evenly. It wasn't an accusation, but it was clear there was an undercurrent of suspicion.

"Your parents agreed to take her in. We grew up together and wanted to help. I've heard what your paranoia has concocted." Silas brushed away the bit of blood from Elora's chin as Damien shoved his hands into his pocket, searching for the button there that would alert everyone to make their move. His fingers wrapped around the small remote as he pushed his thumb onto the only button there, pressing once and then twice and then three times before releasing it and dragging his hands back out. Mentally, he took note of the weapons he had. A knife in his boot, another up the sleeve of his jacket, and the one attached to his belt.

"They never mentioned you." Silas finally turned back to her, his eyes almost devoid of any life.

"Who do you think paid their wages? Who do you think owned the restaurant your mother worked at? Who do you think paid for their funerals? Or bought them that fucking house?" Each word became more unhinged, angrier than the last as whatever the history was rose to the surface. Damien could see the surprise on not only Elizabeth's face but also on Elora's. Neither of them had known how well Silas had known their family.

A beat passed as the three of them stared at each other, tension growing with each passing moment. Damien's body vibrated as he let his focus move over each body in front of him, lingering on Elora who was staring at her sister.

"Are you going to try and kill me, Elora?" Damien watched Elora's mouth open to answer, no doubt preparing to form a single word.

The front doors crashed open, both of them striking the walls behind them before vampire after vampire marched into the church, lining up just as Elizabeth's had done. Her eyes went to the group now ready and prepared to follow either his or Elora's orders. Damien could see the wheels turning, could see the vampire practically calculating her odds. He should have seen the moment Elizabeth shifted, when her eyes darkened and something feral took over.

A flash of silver went through the air between the two sisters, paired with a growl and cry of pain. Elora staggered back and out of Silas's arms, staring down at her bodice of the dress she wore. Red soaked through the fabric as her scent filled the room until there was nothing else left. Damien didn't think or hesitate but shot into action. He pulled the knife from his belt before wrapping his arm around Elora's waist, dragging her back away from the threat. Elizabeth had made her goal clear.

Elora jerked in his grasp, twisting and turning her body to break his hold but Damien held her tight. Warmth flowed over the hand that was flat on her stomach, the blood soaking through the fabric to his skin. Elizabeth would die. Elora may have wanted to prevent it, may have wanted to try and convince her sister that there were other options, but she had proved there was only one end to this. It was death.

The row of vampires behind Elizabeth darted forward, moving to defend their creator and Damien whistled loudly. The two groups met, clashing with a roar of growls and threats and curses. Weapons appeared, knives and guns as violence began to rain down on the church. The first gun shot rang out, echoing in the stone church and it took every bit of effort to keep Elora contained.

"Stop," he forced out, whispering in her ear in hopes it would ease whatever was going through her mind.

"Let me go. Now," she hissed back, bringing her elbow into his ribs. He grunted at the impact but kept his hold tight.

"If you don't let me go, I'll banish you from the Tower," she threatened, and he couldn't stop himself from chuckling. "I'll compel you. Don't make me do that."

His hold loosened at her words, at the threat that they were. Not just against him, but herself as well. Using that ability went against everything she believed. It would send her back down into the depth of her pain, lock her in with the monsters that haunted her nightmares. If she was willing to wield that ability, there was nothing she wasn't willing to do.

"Promise not to get yourself hurt? You aren't healing, love," he murmured against her neck and felt her tense in response before nodding curtly. He released his hold and stepped back before grabbing the knife hidden in his sleeve.

"Take this." She met his eyes for a moment. Her expression displayed every word she couldn't say right then, every thought they didn't have time to entertain. All around them was chaos and blood as the vampires fought for dominance. He wanted to drown in her, grab her again and run away from this. He didn't care what happened to the city or the vampires under their protection. She mattered. Her safety and peace were all that drove him. She would never find any hint of happiness if this was left unfinished. It would always be there in the corner of her mind, bubbling to the surface in the quiet moments of the day and dead of night.

Damien would never regret leaving them to their fate, but she would and so he did what was necessary. She pressed a kiss to his cheek before spinning around and finding Elizabeth waiting. The knife hung in her grip, dripping with Elora's blood.

"I don't want this. I want you to join me. We can remake the city, change how things are for humans," Elora begged her sister. Listening to her beg was worse that hearing her agree to marry Darian or admit she never planned on surviving entering Killian's office. Someone like her didn't beg and yet here she was doing exactly that to try and save lives.

Damien tore his attention from her to look over the room, noting the dead bodies in the pews and Wyatt's now still form at the foot of the platform. His brows furrowed as something unfamiliar settled in his chest. There was one death Damien would regret in this. The human hadn't deserved this end. His only crime had been comforting Elora during a panic attack and bringing her back to reality. That was something Wyatt should have been praised for and yet this had been his fate.

The sound of metal on metal drew Damien back to the scene beside him. Elora and Elizabeth fought, their knives striking like some ridiculous version of a sword fight. He stepped forward, prepared to intercede when one of Elizabeth's vampires rushed him, tackling him so they both fell to the ground in a flurry of weapons and sprawled limbs.

"Fuck!" Damien growled as he swung at the attacker, hitting him in the jaw. He was bigger than Damien by at least four inches and had a wealth of muscle, but it made the vampire slower, less agile.

"Get the fuck off of me!" He shouted, pushing the giant body off of him and grabbing the blade in his boot, suddenly grateful he had decided to bring one more. Damien twisted, preparing to use one hand to push himself up while holding the weapon. His heart was surprising calm as he kept track of his attacker. Every moment of training from Killian or the streets as he grew up settled within him. It had forged him into a weapon just as it had for Elora. They were blades sharpened on the darkest and cruelest things life could throw at a person, vampire or otherwise.

Her cry rang out once more and his head snapped towards the sound to find her bleeding once more. All he could think was he should have trained her, should have taught her to fight. But there had been too much to deal with and not enough time. Dealing with Darian or the two vampires at the Ravenwell manor had been easy for her. There had been no emotional attachment, no shared history of laughter and trust. Elora knew how to fight her enemies, but Elizabeth wasn't one.

Damien turned back just in time for his attacker to rush him again, causing their bodies to collide. He felt it as it happened, as the blade sank into the vampire's chest right below his sternum. It took a moment for the attacker to understand what happened as his green eyes widened in understanding. Damien said nothing but kept his face blank. No emotions or thoughts as he pressed his palm to the vampire's chest and pushed with every bit of strength he had. Slowly, the attacker slid off the blade and fell to his knees with surprise still lacing his features. It was as if the vampire never believed it was a possibility that he could die during this, which made Damien wonder exactly what Elizabeth had promised them, exactly what lies she had spewed to buy their loyalty.

His hand didn't shake as Damien pressed the blade to the vampire's throat and dragged it along his neck. Blood poured from the gaping wound as the attacker fell to the ground in a lifeless heap and Damien searched for her, finding her crawling away from Elizabeth. Crimson ran freely down Elora face from a cut he could see along her forehead. Her nose was bleeding, but it was her eyes that broke something in him.

Fear. She was terrified. Elora's eyes moved wildly through the church, finally finding him. She grimaced and swallowed, her clawed fingers reaching out towards him as Elizabeth's own hand wrapped itself in her hair and threw her. Damien jerked forward, prepared to dart to her side but firm hands gripped both arms before kicking the back of his knee, causing him to fall to the ground.

He called her name. Screamed for her. Searched for Silas, who was being held the same position. They exchanged a look. This wasn't supposed to happen. This was not the outcome they had expected. They would show up, deal with the lingering vampires, kill Elizabeth, and go home. That was the plan. Elora dying at her sister's hands was never part of the equation, never a possibility.

Together, Damien and Silas shared a look that revealed only defeat and loss before they turned their attention back to the only person in the world who mattered to either one of them.

Chapter 52

Thorne

She didn't expect to intercede. If Elora died, she told herself, then it was for the greater good. Chloe was right that Elora would also pose a threat, that a single moment could put them in the exact same position all over again. Yet, seeing her daughter bleed out on the stone floor of the church destroyed each and every thought she had held.

Thorne darted through the side door where the nuns would have come and gone outside of service. Quickly, she scanned the scene, noting where each player was located. About eight vampires fought near the front door, stepping on the bodies piled in the pews. Damien and Silas were both being held down by another group while Elora laid on the floor, bleeding freely from the numerous wounds on her body. There were so many. Her face, chest, and arms were covered and Thorne had a flash of the moment she found Elora for the first time after Killian visited. The wound had been on her neck, just above where her collarbone was. A small cut that would leave behind a scar. The first of many.

Suddenly the bleeding vampire on the floor wasn't a full-grown woman who had survived what would have killed others. It was her daughter—eleven years old and trying to stop the bleeding as she hid in her closet. Elizabeth was on the verge of killing her sister, was on the verge of destroying the one person who created her.

Thorne darted forward, hands out in front of her as if to placate the obviously insane vampire. Elizabeth gave her a brief glance before returning her attention to Elora on the ground in front of her. She sprawled on her back, resting on her elbow and forearms. The bleeding on her face had slowed down, almost completely stopped as the wounds formed scabs. But the ones on her chest and arm were still flowing, the crimson liquid spilling out onto the floor.

"Wait. Let's not do anything we'll regret." Thorne took another step forward as she spoke, tracking the other vampires in her peripheral. Damien and Silas were both still held down, knives now pressed to their throats to make sure they behaved.

"Trust me. There's nothing about this I will regret," Elizabeth snarled, adjusting her grip on the knife. Her pale blonde hair was tinged red from the blood splattered while more dusted her face, giving her the appearance of having freckles.

"You would regret killing your sister. Trust me." Elizabeth shot a look at Thorne at the sound of her words. A question was lingering in her eyes, one that Thorne was prepared to answer if only to buy time.

"I was willing to sacrifice her. You know that. I'm sure Viktor explained it all. But she's my daughter and I know now I would have never been able to live with myself if I had. I would have regretted it every single moment of the rest of my life. The same is true for you, Elizabeth. You will regret it." The confession felt like a weight was gone. It was the secret she had kept for a decade, from the moment she decided to use Elora to fix the vampire problem. Thorne had built up wall after wall to try to force the truth away. If she didn't have to face it, Thorne could pretend that Elora was someone else's child, that she was simply a weapon to be used and disposed of.

"She killed them all," Elizabeth choked out, gesturing towards the dead bodies on the church floor. Thorne nodded and swallowed, desperately searching for words.

"She also gave them the chance to live. Those who left are now at the Tower, being settled into rooms and getting adjusted to life there. They are being given the choice to suppress their hunger or continue feeding. Elora offered you all a choice and that's the one they picked." Thorne's tone was even as she kept her focus on Elizabeth. She couldn't look at her daughter, couldn't risk meeting her gaze and losing all semblance of control over the situation. This was a powder keg, and a single spark would cause it to explode, taking all of them with it.

"That bitch betrayed me!" The scream was harsh and broken, cracking with each syllable. Thorne felt it deep in her core, felt the reverberation of its strength. She had dealt with this before, had felt this sense of betrayal when Killian hurt Elora for the first time, when he beat her and left her for dead. There was no reasoning with it or placating it into submission. There was only coming to terms with the pain, working through it. For Thorne, it had been through her efforts to undermine everything Killian had built.

"Maybe. I can see why—" Thorne wasn't able to finish her statement, wasn't able to say the words that could have prevented another attack. Elizabeth cried out, a shout that filled the room as she darted forward just as Thorne did the same.

Damien and Silas both cried out at the same time, mingling with the renewed sound of fighting. Skin hit skin and gunshots rang out as Thorne only moved. She didn't think. She didn't question. Instinct—pure and maternal—drove every muscle in her body.

"Iris!" Silas cried out her name before she realized the reason why. She hadn't felt the blade enter her chest, just below her ribcage, nor had she felt her own knife be swallowed up by Elizabeth's throat. Both of them fell back onto the ground. The stone crashed into her bones, causing Thorne to cry out in pain.

"No!" Elora's this time as Thorne stared into the lifeless eyes of the vampire across from her. Regret flooded Thorne's body even as her blood seeped out around the blade. There were so many things she had wanted to say to Elizabeth, things that could only be said once everything had settled or at least calmed down. Thorne had wanted to thank her for befriending Elora, for taking care of her through school, for defending her from those who ridiculed her scars. Elizabeth had done more than that any family member Elora ever had and that deserved to be recognized, to be voiced.

"Thank you," Thorne whispered towards Elizabeth. The knife was lodged in her throat, protruding from her windpipe. She wrapped her fingers around it, pulling it as gently as possible from where it was stuck. Elizabeth's body jerked and moved from the effort until the blade finally came free, leaving the vampire lying there in a growing puddle of blood. But at least the vulgar weapon was gone. At least she had that dignity at this moment.

The sounds of fighting behind her stopped. Bodies hit the floor while footsteps rushed towards what Thorne assumed were the exits. Some had escaped then. They would need to be hunted down and taken care of. She rolled over onto her back and stared at the ceiling, at the fading tiles of the mosaic that depicted an angel helping a beggar.

"I'm sorry. I'm so sorry. I can fix it. Turn you. Please." The begging voice came from her right while another figure knelt to her left. An arm forced itself under her back and dragged her to them, letting her rest in their lap and against their chest that was still damp.

"No, Elora. I never wanted that." Words were difficult for Thorne as she gazed into her daughter's bright eyes, falling beneath the waves of green.

"I'm not losing someone else like this. I fucking refuse. I'm not done with you. There are things I need to say. Things we need to do."

A hand, cut and bloodstained, appeared on Elora's shoulder, squeezing gently. Thorne let her eyes travel from the pale and crying face of her only child to Damien, who was watching her with a strange expression in his dark eyes. It could have been devastation, or perhaps it was unease about what this would do to the one person they both loved more than life itself.

"Take care of her. She deserves it." The words were breathy, difficult to force out, but they needed to be said. What Thorne needed more than anything at that moment was to hear Damien say he would protect her, that he would remain with her for no other reason than to make her happy.

"Don't you dare say that. Don't promise her that. Don't you fucking dare." Elora's eyes moved wildly between her mother and Damien, her head twisting one way and then to the other to level them both with equally intense glares.

"I will, Iris. So will Silas. We'll take care of your daughter." There was a solemness to Damien's tone that said he understood that there was no other end to this. Thorne nodded weakly before twisting to see her brother's face one more time. It was like staring at a photograph of him as a young man, of him at twenty-eight and not the almost fifty-year-old that he was. But his eyes. They revealed every year he had spent alive, every decision he had made that he regretted. Their fight was one of them. Thorne knew that. They hadn't fixed their relationship in the time they had spent together since she came to the Tower, but it had been a start. If it wasn't for the unfortunate knife in her chest, they could have created something new. Not the dynamic they had growing up, but something formed from betrayal and reconciliation, from forgiveness and acceptance.

"I'm sorry. I should have protected you better," Silas murmured, leaning down to press a kiss to her forehead. It felt like being a child again, like when she wept in his arms because of a nightmare or because the bunny in the garden wouldn't let her pet it.

"Stop! Both of you!" Elora's scream rose above the sound of people flooding into the church. Reinforcements, Thorne assumed. Footsteps stopped, no doubt watching the scene. Thorne met Damien's eyes over Elora's head.

"Chloe will come for her."

"I know. I'll deal with her when the time comes." Thorne nodded at Damien's promise, finally feeling the coldness she felt when she had been bleeding out on Killian's carpet. This was all familiar in a way. Dying was an old friend, someone she was being reunited with.

Her mouth opened, prepared to tell her daughter how sorry she was, how much she regretted not protecting her better. But words faded as her thoughts did. The room grew dark as a smile stretched across Thorne's face. The last sound she heard as her life ended was her daughter's sobs and the title she had never earned fall from Elora's lips.

Chapter 53

Elora

This wasn't happening. It was a dream or nightmare brought on by blood loss. It was the only explanation for why the universe had decided to punish her even more. In a single night, she had lost her mother, her sister, and Wyatt. It was too much.

Sobs fell from her in violent waves as she held her mother's body to her chest. Because underneath all the bullshit, that was what Thorne was. She was Iris, the woman who gave birth to her and tried her best to protect and raise her. They should have had more time. More to talk and grieve and rage and come to some type of peace and acceptance. It was all Elora had wanted. Now that had been ripped from her grasp and she felt the loss like something vital had been excised from her.

"Elora." Damien said her name as he knelt beside her, hand still squeezing her shoulder. But she couldn't turn from the woman in her arms. Her face had gone so peaceful, as if every weight had been lifted from her. Once sharp and harsh features were smoothed out, whittled away to reveal the woman underneath. Not even as a child could Elora remember seeing her like this. In the few memories and pictures she had of her mother, Thorne had always had a sort of sternness to her, a hardness that spoke to what she had already dealt with. In this way, they were the same. Elora's childhood pictures painted the same picture—a child who had grown up too quickly.

Elora sniffed and used her free hand to wipe away the tears, causing it to come away tinged red from the blood.

"I'm going to address everyone. We need to deal with the bodies," Damien said gently, as if he thought she would break if he was any louder. Irritation rushed through her. Did he think she was fragile once more? That because she couldn't defend herself against her sister, she was weak? Of course he did. She would think the same if she were in his place.

Disgust replaced the anger as she gently pulled her arm out from underneath Thorne's body and laid her on the stone floor. For a long moment, she only stared at her mother, taking in and memorizing each part of her face, from the wrinkles around her eyes and lips, to the scars on her cheek, to the small collection of freckles that only appeared on the bridge of her nose. No detail was too small, too insignificant.

Elora pushed herself up, using Damien as a crutch as she did. Her eyes moved over the church, searching for every lost life. Her heart skipped a beat when they landed on Wyatt and she moved slowly towards him. He was laid out as if he was reaching for something or someone just before the platform where the pulpit was. His face was turned to the side, his stubbled cheek flat on the stone floor in a small puddle of blood. She stopped beside him, kneeling down to brush away a strand of hair. His eyes were closed, his expression calm and peaceful.

"Thank you," she whispered as she kissed the tips of her fingers and pressed them to the side of his mouth. Elora stood, turning away from Wyatt's body.

"Bury him outside. His aunt's grave is out there. Connie. I can show you where, but I want him buried next to her." Her voice rang out in a command, no hint of the grief or rage simmering below her surface.

"Right away." She had no idea where the reply came from, but she knew it wasn't Silas or Damien.

"And the others?" Another voice she didn't recognize and a sense of panic rose. There were too many pieces to take care of, too many problems to fix when all she wanted to do was curl up in a ball and weep.

"We will bury them in the cemetery behind the dormitory. Call for backup from the Tower and tell them to bring shovels and tarps. We can at least try to give them a decent burial," Damien answered, taking control of the situation as if he knew how close she was to breaking down. She turned to survey the room, searching for anything else that required her attention.

"I'll take her to the manor, Elora. We can bury her in the garden she loved so much," Silas explained through broken words and tears. He was holding Thorne, had sunk to the ground and pulled her into his embrace. Elora could only nod in response because words were too difficult to even consider.

"Is there anything else?" she asked, spinning around to see if anyone spoke up. Heads shook as they worked. Vampires gathered the bodies while others wandered out the door to gather materials to perform their tasks. A hand settled heavily on her lower back before the owner came into view. Damien stared down at her, looking between her eyes as if searching for something. His brows knitted together before he took in a sharp breath and dragged her close, holding her body to his as his arms wrapped around her. He squeezed, drawing her closer and closer as if they could become a single person, as if he could take all the pain from her.

His lips found her hair as he pressed kiss after kiss into it before she tilted her head up, offering him her mouth. The infuriating smirk made a brief appearance before he kissed her softly at first. It was almost tentatively, like the first kiss between inexperienced youths. He pulled back, searching her face once more. She scoffed and rolled her eyes before sinking her hands into his hair at the nape of his neck and gripped it tightly, drawing his face to hers.

Before this moment, they hadn't been sure she would survive, that this would ever happen again. Her lips parted, granting his tongue access as it swept into her mouth and explored in a way that always set her on fire. Right now, she simply wanted to feel something. Love or passion or lust, it didn't matter. Anything to drive away the grief. Anything to remind her that she was alive.

A soft cry fell from her lips and she felt Damien chuckle softly as she pulled away. Desperately, Elora tried to suck in a breath, tried to understand the sensation that was washing over her.

"I did. You all saw it. I am now the head of not one or two, but three vampire houses." Chloe's announcement rang out behind her. Elora reached around, trying to find the item she could feel lodged between her shoulder blades. Chloe's hand found it first, tearing the blade from her body with a triumphant cry. It was as if she had won a battle, had defeated some great enemy and was reveling in her success.

"You stabbed her in the back. And she isn't dead." Silas explained evenly from where he had stood, leaving Thorne's body on the floor.

Elora could feel the skin on her back piecing back together. Not that quickly, but enough that the wound wouldn't be fatal. She had moments to make her point, to make it clear to Chloe she had done nothing but make an enemy. She spun around and faced the vampire, who was dressed in something that felt completely out of place among the death and blood. A short white dress with long sleeves that were tight at the wrist. Blood droplets stained the front of it, defacing what Elora was sure was an expensive piece of clothing.

"I can appreciate the attempt, but I'm afraid you failed this time." Her tone was even, almost mischievous as she spoke to the vampire head. Her silver hair was pulled back in her normal low bun and her face was perfectly painted—red lips and dark eyeliner. She looked every bit the part she had anticipated playing right now. If her timing had been better, if she had struck just a little earlier, then Chloe would be celebrating.

Damien darted forward, grabbing the vampire head by the neck. He squeezed tighter and tighter until Chloe's eyes widened in fear. Elora only watched him, enjoying the way he protected her, the way he would kill for her. Her fingers went for the pendant settled between her breasts and she ran her finger along one crescent moon and then the other. She loved him like this—violent and unhinged and it was all for her. There was something intoxicating about the way his hand flexed around her throat, the way his teeth were bared as he threatened her life without a single word.

"Let her go. Your point was made," Silas broke through, but Damien only glanced at Elora, seeking her permission.

"Let her leave. If she tries again, she knows what awaits her," Elora drawled. She didn't care if Chloe lived or died, but she had no desire to deal with it right then. She was exhausted, emotionally and physically, and the blood loss wasn't helping. She needed to feed, consume copious amounts of blood and then cry herself to sleep in Damien's arms. He released her neck and returned to Elora's side, wrapping an arm around her waist until his hand settled on her hip.

"In a few days, I'm inviting the Resistance to the Tower to establish a new Accords. I'll then announce to the city that we exist along with how things will work from now on. I would love for you to be involved, Chloe. But if you're going to be a problem, I would prefer for you to stay away." Elora smiled sweetly at her before Chloe turned and fled. Her heels sounded on the stone floor as she pushed past the vampires who were still work-ing to remove the bodies.

As soon as her silver hair faded beyond the doorway, Elora collapsed, cursing loudly as her knees hit the ground. Arms wrapped around her back and under her legs before they pulled her to their chest. Damien smiled down at her, but it couldn't hide the concern in his eyes.

"Let's get you back to the Tower," he muttered to her, leaning down to speak softly before pressing a kiss to her forehead. Her eyes closed at the contact and to her surprise, they didn't open again. Instead, she fell asleep in the safety of his embrace.

Chapter 54

Damien

It had been two fucking days. Forty-eight whole hours since they returned to the Tower and their rooms. Damien had washed her carefully. He had cut away the ridiculous gown Elizabeth had put her in and then gathered the water and clothes before meticulously washing away every drop of blood, both hers and Elizabeth's. It had been a long process. Every so often, Elora would whimper or make small noises, and he would hesitate, not sure if he was hurting her or if she was having a nightmare. He had dressed her in one of his shirts and a pair of her underwear before tucking her into bed, tightening the blankets around her. Only then had he showered and ordered blood to be delivered.

Now, he sat to her right and Silas sat to her left. Iris had been buried and so had Wyatt and Elizabeth along with the rest of the vampires in the church. Damien had no doubt she would want to have a ceremony or funeral once she woke and came back to reality. He had already called multiple florists and ordered a few vampires in the Tower to start organizing a memorial. Then, he had made sure the vampires who came with her were settled. To his surprise, most had requested the drug Elora had been given and Hartley had been working non-stop to manufacture it in high enough quantities. Silas had been instrumental in this, but Damien would be lying if he said he wasn't cautious about exactly how much Elora relied on her uncle. Perhaps it was the part of him that Killian had crafted, the hours spent listening to him rant about Silas and his reach. The sheer number of cameras in the Tower had only made that paranoia worse for Damien, but he kept his mouth shut out of respect for the only vampire who mattered to him.

A soft whimper broke the silence. Silas put the book he had been reading down on the bed and twisted towards her, leaning forward to reach her. Damien did the same, gripping her hand in his so that the first thing she felt was him.

"I passed out, didn't I?" She asked groggily, each word heavy and clumsy with sleep. Damien chuckled softly.

"Only for a day or two," he responded, and her eyes squeezed tighter.

"Embarrassing. Not exactly a sign of a great vampire head."

"You were cut in four different places and stabbed twice. You also lost quite a lot of blood and didn't heal. I think you did just fine, love." Her eyes opened and she found him instantly as she smiled gently. Silas stood, patted her hand and then left, retiring to the room outside. Damien could hear him making a phone call, something about a few bottles of blood. Silently, Damien thanked Silas for taking the initiative. She had to be starving based on how long she slept and how much she had lost during the fight.

Damien shifted from the chair to the bed, settling beside her and leaning against the headboard. She followed his lead, pushing herself up with shaky arms and letting her head rest against his chest. He listened as she inhaled deeply and gripped his shirt, bundling the fabric in her fist as if making sure he couldn't go anywhere.

"How are you?" he asked, pressing a kiss to the top of her head. She sighed heavily and nestled down deeper in the crook of his arm, wrapping her arm around his stomach. He was sure she could feel his heartbeat, how it always ticked up when she was close.

"Exhausted. Starving. Other than that, I don't know yet. I don't think it's sunk in exactly how many were lost. I thought more would leave. Even when Wyatt told me—" Her voice broke and she sucked in a breath before holding it. He ran his fingers through her hair, marveling at how fast it had grown.

Elora shivered slightly as she let out the breath and he gave her the moment he knew she needed to gather her thoughts, to prepare what she had to say. That was how it was with her unless she was pushed too far. Every thought was fully formed before she articulated it, every issue completely thought through before proposing a solution or approach. In her natural state, she wasn't impulsive or calculating. She was careful. Only he saw when she came undone, when she lost control and turned into the violent and feral monster he somehow fell in love with.

"He told me only half of them would follow me. He warned me that many of them believed everything Elizabeth had said. I still hoped more would walk out that door." He nodded despite the fact she couldn't see him, but he pulled her closer.

"You saved some of them. Including the children. No one else even wanted to give them that option. Not even Silas. Remember that before you start blaming yourself for the ones who stayed behind." She nodded, but he doubted she believed him. It was the one thing he had vowed to work on for the rest of his time with her. If it took every single day, he would remove every negative thought she had about herself, remove every ounce of blame she held for things that were outside of her control. He would spend every hour reassuring her that he loved her, that he would be there when she woke up even if they had an argument. Killian and everything else had left their mark on her and she thought it rendered her somehow unworthy of love or loyalty when the truth was the exact opposite.

"And now they are downstairs, settled into their rooms. Most of them are taking the medication to suppress their hunger while others are content feeding from collection bottles. They're grateful, love."

"You've talked with them?" She asked, words full of amused shock.

"Some. Just enough to make sure everyone was okay. I figured you would want to know when you woke up." Her fingers tightened around his waist, digging into his skin as she seemed to hold him closer.

"You know me so well," Elora laughed as a soft knock sounded at the bedroom door.

"Come in," she called out, pulling away from him in a way that left him feeling incomplete. Silas always had impeccable timing. Damien watched each move she made as she stood from the bed, letting the shirt hang down around her thighs. She winced slightly as she stretched, arching her back and twisting as if to warm up the muscles. The stab wound on her back must still be sensitive, but a couple glasses of blood would help.

"How about you come out here in a few minutes?" Damien shook his head at Silas's request. No doubt he had no desire to see his niece in anything less than fully clothed.

"Okay," she called out before heading into the closet. Damien followed suit, standing and adjusting his clothing before joining Silas, who was pouring a rather large glass of blood. Two smaller ones sat beside it, filled halfway as if to make sure Elora didn't feel self-conscious about feeding. Silas nodded at him before handing him one of the cups and sinking into his usual spot, the corner of the couch near the end table. Damien sank into the other couch directly across from it and sipped from the cup. He wasn't necessarily hungry, but it felt wrong to let it go to waste.

Elora strolled into the room somewhat awkwardly. Her steps were stilted and jerky no matter how graceful she tried to be.

The pain was obvious in the way she moved and the expression on her face. Damien resisted the urge to stand, to carry her to her chair and hand her the cup of blood. She wouldn't appreciate it, not in this context at least.

"Thank you," she said to Silas before she picked up the glass. Silas and Damien watched as she finished it in three long swallows and used the back of her hand to wipe away any remaining blood on her lips. He doubted there was any given how hungry she had to be. Her eyes closed and she exhaled, letting her shoulder drop and her jaw loosen.

"Update me, please. I've been unconscious and would like to know what happened after I passed out." Elora was trying to make her statement sound nonchalant, like it didn't bother her that she blacked out from blood loss but there was an undercurrent of bitterness that Damien knew came from her fear of weakness. Or, most specifically, being perceived as such.

"We buried Wyatt beside his aunt and added a gravestone, and Elizabeth was buried with her parents. As for Iris, I took her back to the manor and buried her in the garden," Silas explained smoothly, moving through the dead with efficiency.

"By the roses?" Elora asked, tone sharp and biting. There was only one clear answer that would be acceptable.

"No. Sunflowers. Those were her actual favorites. Killian assumed roses because she enjoyed painting them." Elora smiled and nodded at Silas's answer.

"I didn't know that. Thank you." She went quiet for a moment, staring at her empty cup and swirling the last remnants in there. "What was her maiden name? Or I guess your name before being adopted by the Corvins."

"Hawthorne," Silas answered, smiling bitterly. "I should have known who she was when I learned the name of who was leading the Resistance."

Elora only nodded once more, biting her lip as she eyed the second collection container that hadn't been opened yet. Damien stood, cursing the fact she was refusing to pour more and grabbed the bottle, holding it up with his brows raised at her. It was silent as he opened and filled her cup once more. Gratitude was clear on her face as she took another drink, sipping slowly at first before she devoured it with two swallows.

"It's understandable, you know. You were unconscious for two days and you lost a lot of blood. Drink your fill, love. You get very cranky when you're hungry." She gave him a faux hurt look before setting the glass down and standing.

"Okay. First thing is to contact the Resistance members and ask them to meet here in two days. That should give me time to prepare---"

"Us. Give us time to prepare," Damien interrupted, and she rolled her eyes in response.

"It will give us time to get everything set up. And we need to invite Chloe."

"She literally stabbed you in the back. I'm not sure I want her here." Damien couldn't be sure he wouldn't eviscerate the vampire as soon as she stepped foot in the Tower. Her smirking face as she ripped the knife from Elora's back was lodged in his mind like a splinter, constantly festering as it seeped toxins into his bloodstream.

"We extend the invitation. I doubt she shows, but I don't want to give her a reason to fight me on the changes I'll be making." There was the tone, the one that made him want to take her back into the bedroom. Commanding and resolute in a way that made his blood boil in a completely different way. He smirked at her to tell her exactly what she had done.

"You plan on making changes to the Accords." Silas's statement was met with a glare, an expression that begged him to argue with her, to deny her the option of doing this.

"Isn't that the deal I made with my mother? Isn't that what I said I wanted from the very beginning?" Elora spat the questions at her uncle's feet and watched him flinch before sitting up straighter as if in preparation.

"I assumed that—"

"That since she died, I would go back on my word. You assumed I was a liar. That I had no loyalty or honor. Let me be clear. The way humans are farmed like cattle is wrong. They should have a choice, Silas." Once more he flinched, visibly and violently.

"That isn't how I would articulate it, but yes."

Elora towered over him. "If you do not support me, Silas, then leave. With or without you, I will meet with the Resistance and do what neither you nor my father would do."

"Which is what, exactly?" Silas was trying to keep his tone even, trying desperately to not let his anger show but he was failing.

"Peace, uncle. Peace between humans and vampires."

Chapter 55

Elora

She was honestly shocked to find not only the three humans sitting around the conference table, but Chloe as well. Silver hair was back in a low bun as always and she was dressed impeccably in a white pant suit. Elora gave her a wide smile as she walked in and took her place at the head of the table with Damien to her right and Silas to her left.

"Introductions are necessary, I assume." Elora began, looking at each individual at the table. Heads nodded, but it did nothing to ease the suspicion lining their features. All three humans looked as if they had made a terrible mistake, like the mouse walking right into the trap that would kill them.

"Elora Ashcroft," she began, placing her hand on her chest. Damien introduced himself next and then Chloe, who was sitting beside him with a chair to separate them. It was for the best. Elora knew he wanted nothing more than to get revenge for the knife that had ended up in her back.

The balding man with salt and pepper hair and wrinkles was called Richard while the woman with sharp features and dark brown hair was Sarah. The final person was Daniel, who reminded Elora a little too much of Wyatt if he had lived to reach his fifties. Finally, Silas introduced himself.

"Did you kill Thorne?" Richard demanded with barely restrained hatred. He didn't want to be here, that much was clear to everyone who only looked at him. Elora's guess was he had been outvoted by the other two.

"No. Elizabeth attacked me, and she stepped between us. They killed each other," Elora explained calmly. She wouldn't let this man rattle her or draw any reaction that she didn't want to give. He was nothing but a means to an end.

"She was your mother, correct?" The one named Daniel spoke up, leaning forward on the table and interlacing his fingers. "The resemblance is uncanny to be honest."

Elora could only nod because words were threatening to bring tears along with them. Two shocked intakes of breath happened—Sarah and Richard, which meant they hadn't been aware of Thorne's history.

"Yes, Iris was my mother. Thorne was her Resistance name, the one she adopted after my father tried to kill her.

"Well, that explains a lot." Elora's eyes snapped to Richard, who sneered at everyone at the table.

"What exactly does it explain?" Each word Elora said was perfectly articulated in hopes the human would rethink whatever foolishness was about to come out of his mouth.

"Her willingness to work with you and the others. She already fucked one and had a kid, working with another wasn't much of a reach." Silas moved before Elora could. His fingers wrapped around the human's neck, squeezing harder and harder until his pale face turned red from the lack of air.

"Thorne is the only reason I'm entertaining your stupidity right now. My mother is the only reason why there's any chance of peace between vampires and humans. I suggest having a little respect if you want to leave this room alive. My mother and I may not have been close, but I won't tolerate a man who never got his hands dirty disrespecting her." Elora nodded and Silas let go of Richard's throat before leaning back in his chair. He pulled a handkerchief from his pocket and began wiping his hands, as if he would rid himself of the human. Elora wasn't lying. She would kill the human without a second thought. Or allow Silas to do it. He seemed too interested in seeing Richard's blood flood the conference table.

"Now that the unpleasantness is done, it's time to talk. Before she died, Thorne and I outlined what we wanted to see happen in the city and I'm prepared to follow through despite her death. The first thing we discussed was making vampires public. It'll obviously take time, but I'm preparing to make a televised announcement. There will obviously be those who don't believe me and will say it's a hoax. Over time, that will stop being an issue." Elora leaned forward, reading each face to see the reaction. Richard was clearly uncomfortable, shifting from side to side. Daniel on the other hand was intrigued.

"Another was she wanted vampire and human numbers to be tracked and for there to be a system to do that. It would also count how many were being turned. This would be part of the new Accords, which would make consequences for those who turn humans without their consent."

"And what would those punishments be? A slap on the wrist?" Richard asked, breaking in. Elora swallowed down the irritation at being interrupted and turned to him, leveling him with a glare.

"Death. The same punishment that will be in place for anyone who hunts and kills vampires. This is not something I'm prepared to play around with."

"Fair. Please continue." Daniel seemed to be the human voice of reason, just as Silas always was for Elora. He smiled encouragingly and inclined his head.

"The last one was that we produce and offer the medication I used before. It would be available for those who were turned without their consent and want to suppress their vampire urges. All of these I readily agreed to and am prepared to fulfil." Elora leaned back in her chair and moved her hands into her lap, playing with the hem of her shirt. It was better than picking at her cuticles.

"We want humans to be included in vampire affairs. If this is to work, we need to have a council of both vampires and humans making decisions. It would allow for both viewpoints to be present," Sarah added, and Elora nodded.

"Agreed. How shall they be selected? For vampires, it depends on who is in charge of the families, which means it is me, Damien, Silas, and Chloe. Are you three going to be the voice for humans?"

"For now. Later, I would like to have elections, but that's for later down the line," Sarah responded quickly, as if she had anticipated this question. It made sense. At this moment, they needed to focus on moving everything into place and making the vampire presence known. There would be those who panicked or lashed out in fear, but that could be easily dealt with.

"Any objections?" Elora asked and waited as she met everyone's gaze. She tugged and pulled at the hem, twisting the grey fabric around her fingers until she knew the shirt would never be the same. At least it was hers this time and not one of Damien's. At this point, she had ruined enough of his clothing.

"And what about you? What about your children who are currently living downstairs?" Chloe finally spoke and Elora felt Damien shift beside her. The sound of her voice brought back the feeling of the knife in her back. It had hurt, but not in the way she had always thought it would. It was more of a breathlessness as all the oxygen was forced from her lungs.

"What about me? Honestly, your obsession with me is getting a little concerning." Chloe seemed to snarl at Elora's barb, but it passed quickly as an amused expression settled on her face.

"All it takes is one more mess up. One more accidental bite from a loss of control. The same for those downstairs. We could end up right back here."

Elora let go of the hem of her shirt and leaned forwards again, resting her hands on the cold table.

"Do you know exactly how that loss of control happened, Chloe?" She shook her head and Elora continued. "I had been taking the medication for years. My hunger was gone without any hint of it. Not a single hint. Then, my family couldn't afford it, so I stopped taking it. I didn't know what I was and was unprepared for the hunger. I didn't know the signs or what to expect. That won't happen now. I'm not going to suppress my needs but will only consume collected blood." Chloe opened her mouth to speak, but Elora lifted a single finger, silencing her.

"As for my children, as you call them, they're aware of the parameters and the consequences should they feed directly from anyone. None of them wanted to be turned. They didn't ask for it. What they asked for was the medication I took. Hartley is going to create a stronger version that will be administered as a shot. It would last months potentially. And we'll continue to research in hopes of making it more potent." Elora leveled a glare at Chloe, begging her to open her mouth again.

"Is that acceptable to everyone at this table?" She asked, not taking her eyes away from Chloe. A collection of voices all agreed at once. Even the human Richard voiced his agreement. Elora had thought he would be the other problem, but he seemed on board with everything as of right now.

"Now, who wants to be on TV with me? Who wants to help me reveal that vampires exist?" Only Daniel raised his hand like a child at school eager to answer a question. Elora nodded and moved to the seat beside him, pulling out the papers she had prepared earlier. A speech of sorts. Reading it now, she realized it was just as ridiculous as it had sounded earlier.

One by one, everyone else left as the human helped the vampire draft their announcement. They could only hope it didn't spark retaliation and fear.

Chapter 56

Epilogue

The ballroom was stunningly beautiful. Sunflowers and lavender were paired with ferns and baby's breath to create an arrangement that had Elora gasping and rushing to touch each one. Her fingers gently held the petals, touching the leaves as she leaned down to smell each one. Her eyes fluttered closed as she grinned before moving on to the next one.

Damien followed behind her, chuckling as he held her shoes. She would put them on before everyone appeared, trailing in through the massive elevator. Faint orchestra music played in the background. Light and almost whimsical, like a melody used to lure humans to their graves, Elora had read about such creatures as a child, wicked elves who tempted people away from the path by song and feast. These evil beings would whisk the poor victim to a magical land and force them to remain. When she first read about them, she hadn't considered it to be a horrible fate. There was nothing worse she could come up with back then. She had already known so many monsters, lived through cruelty and pain that made living with those elves had seem like an improvement. It became a fascination, resulting in her searching for fairy rings in the forest behind Silas's manor.

Damien touched her shoulder before extending his hand. She took a second to drink him in. He was devastating when he wore an old shirt and jeans with his hair an absolute disaster. Even in sleep, shirtless with his hair a mess, he was undeniably gorgeous. But in his black suit that was tailored perfectly to his frame and hair brushed away from his face, he seemed like a painting made real, like a statue made flesh. And he was hers. There was always something in her rendered feral at the reminder.

"Stop looking at me like that. Dance with me," he said, breaking through her increasingly inappropriate thoughts. They were meant to be preparing for a solemn ceremony, a memorial for the lives lost. It was also a welcoming ceremony where she would announce the family's new name.

"I'll have you know I can do both at the same time." Elora took his hand as he let the other rest on her hip.

"Then do it for my sake," he asked as they began to move. Elora let him lead for once. She had never learned to dance like this, and she wondered exactly when he had. Was it part of his training under Killian? Was it left over from his life before her father?

"Only if you explain why." Her voice was sickly sweet, a complete show of faux innocence that made his lips curl in the corners.

"Because if you don't, neither of us will be here for the ceremony. Who would give your speech?" Heat coiled in her stomach. There was a dark promise gleaming in his eyes. He knew what that grin on his face did to her, knew exactly what those words would do. They fell quiet and her eyes fell on his neck, where her teeth had been. The coiling in her stomach turned, shifting into something more like fear than anything else.

"Damien, did you talk with Hartley? About me feeding from you?" A part of her didn't want to ask this, didn't want to hear the answer if she had done some irrevocable damage to him. Not something that would heal, like stabbing him, but something that would linger forever. He gave her a sad smile that only caused the unease in her gut to grow.

"Nothing happened. I had her test my blood twice. You didn't do anything bad to me. I officially volunteer as your personal blood bag." Her laughter filled the ballroom, nestling in every corner and in each bouquet. She threw her head back, letting the sound erupt from her in a way that sounded strange and for a moment Elora couldn't understand why it felt so foreign. When she met his eyes again, all she found was bewilderment.

"Fuck, you're gorgeous. Words truly can't do you justice. I've thought that since the hospital, but when you laugh like that it's indescribable." Her brows narrowed at the surprise in his voice.

"You've seen me laugh before," she retorted even as she re- alized he hadn't. He had heard her chuckle or cackle. He had even heard her giggle before, but never something as boisterous as what just came from her.

"Not like that, love. I'm going to spend every waking moment trying to hear it again. I hope you know that." Her feet stopped moving, leaving them standing in the center of the ballroom. She took her hand from his and wrapped both arms around his neck. His own arms enclosed her waist, drawing her impossibly close as she played with his hair. Her fingers trailed down his neck, lingering on the place where she had stabbed him. Three puncture marks were stark on his skin. From their hatred for each other had grown something more precious than anything she had experienced.

"Don't make promises you can't keep." She whispered as she stared at the scar she had left behind, wondering how long it would be until she became too much and he left. As if he heard her thoughts, he pressed a kiss to her forehead.

"I never do, love. Now, put your shoes back on. They should be coming any moment." On cue, the elevator chimed and the doors slid open. She took a deep breath, letting it out slowly as she shifted into this version of herself. The vampire head. The woman who killed everyone who had hurt her. The one who should be feared and respected in equal measures.

Damien knelt and lifted the skirt of her gown just enough to slip her shoes onto her feet like a prince from a fairy tale. She giggled as he stood and adjusted his own clothing. With the heels on, she was almost at eye level. She tilted her head before pressing her lips to his in what was meant to be a soft kiss but had the potential to turn into something more.

Damien leaned back and shook his head. "Not yet. Now, get on that stage."

"So assertive. I like this side of you." His eyes darkened instantly.

"You're going to kill me, you know that?" Again, a giggle before she spun around and took her place on the stage. A microphone had been set up to ensure she was heard by every living soul in the room. Her heart raced in her chest, pounding against her ribs in a way that was concerning. At least if they did crack, they would heal instantly.

In groups of two and three, vampires filtered into the ballroom, gathering before the stage in silence. Only once the space was filled to complete capacity did Elora step up to the microphone and begin.

"Welcome to a new era. One in which vampires and humans live side by side and no one is forced to hide, where there are consequences for feeding without consent or turning a human against their will. And anyone who seeks to destroy what we have built will be dealt with." Cheers erupted and Elora allowed them for a moment before holding her hands up to quiet them. Damien stood to her right, directly beside her. They would remain co-heads of the family. He would never stand behind her again, never be anything less than her equal.

"We are now the Hawthorne family, and we will honor our dead, both human and vampire. We'll build this city into something they would be proud of."

Tears stung her eyes as she watched the crowd applaud and press their fist to their hearts, swearing their allegiance to the family named after her mother. Elora's eyes found Silas, settled in the corner of the ballroom and dressed in a crisp black suit. He inclined his head, hiding the tears running down his cheeks.

"Now, we celebrate the living and the dead. We celebrate the hope the future brings." Music began to play as servers appeared from the sides with trays of glasses and vampires coupled off to dance. Damien stepped close, leaning down slightly.

"I'm not sure we're needed anymore." She smirked as she watched her vampires dance, swirling and gliding in a way that was graceful and elegant. It was a symphony made physical as they moved with the music.

"Did you have other plans?" She purred as he pressed closer. His body was flush with hers, and she pushed back against his chest.

"A few. All of which require us to leave." Without another word, Elora marched forward with Damien falling in step. The crowd parted as she made her way through the ballroom and approached the elevator. Every part of her burned, every nerve ending was on fire as anticipation made her move faster. As the door slid shut to take them to their rooms, arms wrapped around her, lifting her off the ground. Her legs wrapped around his waist, causing her dress to pool around her hips, the fabric falling down over her thighs.

As they shut the door to their rooms, locking it behind them, it was easy to ignore the world and lose themselves in each other. It was easy to reap the rewards of their labor. Every moment of darkness and cruelty and pain was worth it because it brought them there.

He was her reward, her paradise made flesh.
And she was his.

Acknowledgments

I started this journey because the idea for this series took root in my brain and refused to go away. I would be teaching or grading or waiting to pick up my child from school and scenes would play out in my head, lines of dialogue whispered in my ear. After years of graduate school, I never thought I would write for pure enjoyment again. But Elora's story needed to be told and I found myself healing along with her.

There are so many people to thank—my partner for his unwavering support, my daughter for her encouragement. My mom and grandma who have my books displayed in their home along with my family members who used them for their book club. Thank you to my readers who have been with me since book 1.

I am somewhat sad to say goodbye to Elora and Damien, but excited to finish their story. I only hope I did them justice.

About the Author

Misty Thomas (she/her) lives in the desert and lives off coffee and snacks. She is a parent, partner, educator, and cat mom. When she isn't teaching composition or writing, she spends her time with her family, playing video games, and reading an unholy number of books in an effort to escape reality. Her debut book, Tower of Blood, is the first in the Blood and Silk Trilogy.

Other Works

Blood And Silk Trilogy

Tower of Blood

Streets of Hunger

City of Death

Fractured Onyx Trilogy

The Bound Prisoner

www.ingramcontent.com/pod-product-compliance
Lightning Source LLC
Chambersburg PA
CBHW030332120726
47901CB00007B/1762